For the first time in longer than he could remember, he felt actual fear…

Buzzer could hear his rapid breathing, his heart pounded in his chest and for the first time in longer than he could remember, he felt actual fear. He dove to his stomach and belly-crawled to the edge of the doorway, retrieving both blasters along the way. Peeking around the edge, he caught a faint glimpse of movement, the form of a man moving across the street from the woods.

In a heartbeat, he was up and running after the man, leveling his half-charger and firing blast after blast into the night. Pure adrenaline drove him on, making him forget about the intense pain in his side and, more importantly, making him forget his fear.

The man rounded a corner and disappeared. Buzzer ran ever harder, jumping over debris and the bodies of more dead U.E.N. soldiers. Pulling one of his blasters from its holster, he stopped near the edge of the building on the corner and whipped the weapon around with his left hand.

An arm lashed out and struck the blaster free. Before he could react, his left arm was clasped tightly and twisted backwards and behind him. Buzzer was caught unawares, something that genuinely surprised him, and he allowed himself to be tossed backwards to the ground. As he rolled he could see the man trying to take aim on him with a small weapon, most likely a mini-blaster stolen off of one of the dead soldiers he had passed.

Buzzer came to an abrupt stop, lying flat on the cold street, and snapped off a blast with his half-charger. His adversary dove to the side to avoid the blast, his own shot veering wildly into the woods.

Up and running toward the man, Buzzer covered the short distance in less than two seconds. He crashed into the smaller man with everything he had just as the other was gaining his footing. Buzzer heard a loud grunt escape from his opponent and the sound of a weapon clattering to asphalt. They both hit the street hard and bounced away from each other.

Buzzer was up first and began to bring his half-charger to bear but the man dove at his knees, sending him sprawling to the street once more. The Guarder

1

saw the glint of what seemed to be a blade rising above him and hit the man hard in the abdomen with the butt of his half-charger.

The man's breath exploded out of him and he rolled frantically away. Buzzer rose to one knee and, leaving the larger weapon slung from his shoulder, grabbed his second blaster and fired at the rolling figure. A large chunk of asphalt popped out of the street inches from the man's face but missed the target entirely. Buzzer fired again but heard nothing but a click. The blaster was fully drained…

What Reviewers are saying about THE GUARDER FACTOR...

If you like Robert Heinlein, enjoyed the film of Starship Troopers...then this book is well worth consideration.

~Steve Mazey, **The Eternal Night**

What Reviewers are saying about GUARDER LORE...

Fans of military science fiction are going to love GUARDER LORE, an action packed story line that starts out at warp speed and accelerates from there.

~**Midwest Book Review**

The tales of GUARDER LORE are rife with blood, guts, blaster fire...and high-action adventures.

~**The Outer Rim**

An awesomely creative horrific sf story by an extremely talented author.

~**Brutal Dreamer**

This is an action-packed book, kids, so the squeamish and the laid back need not apply. But even if you aren't a devotee of space-opera-shoot-em-ups...the guy can write. His characters are real, their dialogue tough yet fresh, and they take on a semblance of reality that goes a long way towards suspending that darn old disbelief. If I were writing or directing an action movie, I'd ask Shawn's opinion, and that's more praise than I should be allowed to give anyone.

~Bob Yosco, **Shadowkeep**

There is a history here, with wars, treaties and exoduses to the stars that I'd like to explore with the characters. In short I want more! Thankfully there are sequels and other works planned—get writing, Shawn!

~Steve & Lesley Mazey, **The Eternal Night**

THE GUARDER FACTOR

by

Shawn P. Madison

Writer's Sanctum Publishing LTD

Copyright © 2003 by Shawn P. Madison

I0685333

Writer's Sanctum Publishing LTD publishes books online and in trade paperback. For more information, check our website: www.writerssanctumpublishing.co.uk or email writerssanctumpublishing@gmail.com.

Edited by: Kat Thompson

ISBN: 978-1-9998786-7-2

Dedication

Dedicated to my Dad, Edward P. Madison, who passed on to me his love of reading and who encouraged me to keep on writing. Although he may no longer be here with us, he will always be with me

Acknowledgements

I would like to thank my editor, Kat Thompson, for all of her hard work and assistance with this project. I am extremely grateful to have had the opportunity to work together on THE GUARDER FACTOR with such a talented individual. Her editorial expertise was much appreciated.

PROLOGUE

"Watch out!" Taylor shouted as another volley of missiles rammed into the enormous ship just below the small bridge, causing several consoles to explode inside the already smoky room and sending various members of his crew skidding across the floor. The massive ship trembled and creaked all around them as the beating continued to get worse.

"I can't hold it, Manny," Jim Forbes shouted back. "She won't let me do anything!"

"Do whatever you can!" Taylor answered and fought to launch whatever defensive weapons they had left against the swarm of attacking ships. They were everywhere, swooping in from all directions, throwing everything they had at his super cargo-liner...and they were winning.

Manny Taylor looked around the dark room, lit only by red emergency lights, and saw three dead among his crew. The fires were still crackling at many of the consoles and the smoke was growing thicker. He coughed several times at the stinging in his throat.

What can I do? What can I do? Taylor pounded his fist into the side of the console before him in frustration. These people, his crew, were depending on him to pull them out of this Godforsaken mess but the attacking horde was no longer interested in negotiations. Their last few hails had been met by nothing but static.

No, he thought, *not by static but by death...*

These...pirates, or whatever the hell you wanted to call them, had appeared out of nowhere on the long-range scanners moving quickly and purposefully toward his ship. Their first message had asked for surrender and a demand to come aboard. Both had been denied as per the well- known and long-standing unwritten code of the cargo-liner captain and crew. That had turned out to be a mistake...

Now his ship was in trouble, bad trouble, and if he didn't make it into orbit around that snowball of a planet directly ahead, Manny Taylor was afraid that his ship would punch through the thin atmosphere and lay waste to whatever lay in its path on the surface.

More explosions and more trembling under his feet. The deck plates felt as if they were alive, cringing with fear at the inevitable outcome that they all feared.

"Missiles!" Sara Kelly yelled, and Taylor braced for impact. The ship seemed to buck as the full force of the explosions ripped through the hull, shredding his precious cargo and peeling back the hull plates on a major section of the fuselage.

Three small ships approached now, swooping in from the side, trying to stay out of the bridge's line of fire. Taylor could see the tips of their weapons systems glowing and he knew that they meant to deliver a deathblow to him and his crew.

"Not so fast, you sons of bitches," Taylor growled as he managed to wrestle partial control back from one of his weapons batteries and commenced firing toward the approaching attackers.

One of the ships disintegrated almost immediately and Taylor could hear Freddy Simon whoop from his position at the bridge's auxiliary engine controls. The super cargo-liner's captain was struggling to bring his weapons to bear on the next ship in line when a huge explosion lit up space directly in front of the bridge, tearing his ship apart. The ear-splitting squeal of tortured plexisteel and ruptured bulkheads seemed to permeate the entire bridge, and half the consoles in the small space exploded simultaneously.

Taylor scraped himself up off the deck plates and gasped in horror at the dead look in the eyes of Freddy Simon's disembodied head. He quickly looked around the darkened bridge and could see only Sara Kelly still moving. By the amount of blood pumping out of Jim Forbes' neck, Taylor could tell that his navigator would soon be moving on to the next place, too.

"Goddammit!" Taylor screamed and struggled to lift his battered body into the captain's chair. For some reason the explosions had stopped and he couldn't see any of the attacking ships on the main forward viewscreen. *Well that's good news*, he thought, *but will it hold?*

"Sara," he called to his young apprentice engineer. She raised her head to look at him with glazed eyes. Her pretty face was covered with soot and her blonde hair was matted to her scalp with thick, dark blood. The vision of the young woman was made all the more horrifying by the dark red light inside the bridge. Taylor could only wonder if he looked just as bad if not worse. "I need your help with the steering, kiddo."

"Okay..." she muttered and began to move toward Jim Forbes' former station. "What can I do?"

"Try to gain whatever control of the steering that you can," he said. "We need to get into position to establish some kind of orbit around that planet."

"What about the..."

"Don't worry, they've stopped," Taylor said. "For whatever reason, they've stopped their attack."

"But..."

"Just concentrate, Sara," Taylor said. "Just concentrate." He made his way over to the auxiliary engine console, taking care to step over what was left of Freddy Simon. One look at the console was all he needed to know that it was non-operational. He stumbled his way across the bridge and slumped into the seat next to Sara. The youngster was sweating and trembling but she was handling the damaged controls like a pro and he smiled in spite of their dire situation.

"You're doing great, Sara," he said and tried to gain some directional control from the helm console.

"It's not working, Captain," she squeezed out through gritted teeth. He reached over to put his hands over hers. Together, they were able to loosen a stuck lever and push it all the way up where it belonged. As a result, the ship began to level out slightly. The bright white planet was growing larger in their viewscreen. How they would ever be able to avoid smashing into it was beyond his means to contemplate at the moment. Taylor noticed that all was silent other than the sound of his and Sara's breathing. He knew that the rest of the crew were dead. Their enemies had delivered a surgical strike that no one could have survived. Engineering was gone, the life- support module was off-line...all that was left were the two of them.

9

"We're stabilizing," Sara said, and he felt the first glimmer of hope return to his doomed spirit.

"Keep going, Sara," he said. "We're almost in orbit now. I don't know how long we'll be able to hold it once we establish ourselves around this planet but someone down there may have the means of getting us out of here before our orbit deteriorates."

"Are we gonna make it?" She asked and Taylor saw the tears in her eyes. He nodded once but knew that it was not convincing enough. As more tears streamed down Sara's face, Taylor leaned over and kissed her bloodstained cheek and then turned back to his console. *We're almost there...*

The next explosion was a small one but he knew where they had hit. *You bastards!* He raged and felt the ship buck underneath him again. Several other small explosions trembled along the enormous ship's hull and Sara felt the controls go slack beneath her hands.

"They hit the directionals," Taylor said and switched the helm station over to emergency manual control.

"I have no more response!" Sara screamed.

"I know," Taylor said and punched in several commands on the helm's computer module. The readings came back instantly: planet Shining, collision course with main population center, CharterCity.

"Shit," Taylor rasped and looked at the young woman beside him. "Sara, listen to me. We are going down, no question, but you have to help me try to avoid hitting that population center directly ahead of us."

Sara Kelly was rocking back and forth in her chair now. She didn't seem to be listening to him and was withdrawing further into herself with each passing moment.

"Sara!" Taylor shouted to break her from the trance, and she glanced toward him. "Grab your controls. I've slaved them to my console so you might have some better results. We have to thrust ourselves downward at a steeper angle. We have to hit that barren plain instead of smashing into the capital city of this planet. Do you understand?"

"No, no, no, no, no..." Kelly stammered. "Do you understand?" Taylor barked.

Kelly did not answer but her hands reached out and grabbed the failing controls. She began to manipulate everything she could think of to try and get some kind of response. The ship began to vibrate violently as they smashed through the thin atmosphere of Shining. The glare was intense and the temperature inside the bridge began to grow swiftly hotter. Taylor could feel his lungs burning from the smoke flowing off of several still-burning fires and the intense heat building up inside the bridge.

The viewscreen suddenly snapped off, thrusting the small space into almost total darkness, and Sara Kelly screamed. "Hold on, Sara," Taylor muttered. "Just hold on to the controls..."

Manny Taylor said a silent prayer and a goodbye to his wife and two children back home on Corinthia. *I love you*...he thought just as the intense heat of their uncontrolled reentry into Shining's atmosphere stole his breath away and plunged everything into black...

~*~

In the chambers of the United Earthian Nations Judiciary Board, all was quiet as the group of men and women watched the horrific spectacle playing out on the wall screen before them. A spectacular wall-sized view of the blackness of space had replaced the windows just moments ago, and a raging battle had exploded into view, casting stark shadows on many of the faces in the room. No sound was available on this recording. The device used to record the battle had apparently been mounted on the outer hull of an unbelievably large super cargo-liner, positioned over what looked like one of the outer cargo holds. Ships of all shapes and designs were swooping by, releasing energy weapons and missiles at the enormous ship, causing massive destruction throughout the outer hull. Several intensely bright explosions rocked the view momentarily before the image disappeared and was replaced, once again, by the bright morning sun of Aegis filtering in through the windows.

Transportation Secretary Mecham Bali stood abruptly from his chair and shuffled several sheets of scribbled notes. Honorary Judiciary Board Chairman Mozart Livingston noticed again how the tall and wiry Bali always seemed extremely nervous whenever he was addressing the Board. *Have to keep a watch on that one,* he thought as he continued to scan the other faces in the room.

"Fellow BoardMembers," Bali began and cleared his throat before continuing. "The FlightForce HQ based here on Aegis has recorded several hundred individual cases of pirating in the SouthWestern Corporate Grid-Sector over the past four e-years. Although these cases have ranged from simple piracy of pleasure cruisers to the hijacking of supply transports involving murdered crew-members, we have never before seen such a case as was reported just hours ago."

Bali hesitated momentarily, expecting a question or two from his fellow BoardMembers but none were forthcoming. He continued, "What we have all just observed were the last moments of a super cargo-liner as it was attacked by unknown assailants, presumably pirates. That ship was more than five kilometers in length. It was traveling along the Berking Line that intersects the Sarkennon System in the SouthWestern Corporate Grid-Sector. It was completely and utterly destroyed. This particular ship was hauling sixteen standard-issue containers of advanced military weapons prototypes in addition to its usual manifest of supplies."

"What were the circumstances of the attack?" First Secretary A.J. Clifford asked. "Simple piracy, it seems," Bali answered. "Initial data indicate that the invading party demanded immediate permission to board and the complete surrender of the crew. Both requests were denied as is standard policy on most cargo-liners and then...well, we just saw what happened next."

"Were these attackers somehow aware of the military portion of the cargo on board that vessel?" Secretary of Defense Billings asked.

"We do not know at this time," Livingston answered, and he saw Billings' right eyebrow rise with caution. "But we have confirmed that the entire shipment of prototypes was destroyed beyond any capacity to recover."

"How does this affect all of the involved parties economically?" The Secretary of Finance asked.

"The total loss is incalculable at this point," Bali said. "But those military prototypes were valued at several trillion InterGridactic dollars alone. The ship itself was worth considerably more than that. It is indeed a truly tragic event."

"The local governments involved have been requesting help with their piracy problems for quite some time. Needless to say, now they are fairly demanding it," Livingston said. He looked sternly at each of the faces before him. "Fellow BoardMembers, I now wish to grant that help and grant it swiftly."

"We could send a FlightForce Fleet into the general sector," Defense Secretary Billings voiced. "They could be there rather quickly."

"Not so fast," Livingston countered. "The presence of the military would only deter these people temporarily while our ships were in position. Once gone, I fear it would be as if nothing had changed. We must have a complete and thorough investigation into this piracy situation before the FlightForce is called in."

"What do you propose, Mr. Chairman?" A.J. Clifford asked, knowing his boss well enough to realize a hidden agenda was present.

"I suggest that we utilize the Guarder Squadron for this investigation," Livingston offered tentatively, knowing the BoardMembers' aversion to using the mysterious soldiers of the Guarder Squadron in assignments directly related to the Board itself.

"Mr. Chairman," Billings responded. "With all due respect to Sergeant Harrison Jekel and his covert team of Guarders, I hardly find it necessary to involve that elite group when there are multiple military units currently at our disposal."

"I understand your concern, Secretary Billings," Livingston said. "But a military team does not have the same power of, shall we say, creative opportunity that the members of the Guarder Squadron possess. Fewer men would be risked during the initial phase of the investigation, less equipment needed as well, and we would be secure in the knowledge that the best possible personnel were handling this particular problem if we decide here today to utilize the Guarder Squadron at the outset. If, during the course of their investigation, they feel it necessary to involve the other branches of the U.E.N. Military, I will allow them to make that decision."

"Is it possible, Mr. Chairman," Secretary of Commerce John Percy interrupted, "that pressure from certain SouthWestern Corporate Grid-Sector organizational governments are influencing your proposal?"

"It's not only possible, John, it's true," Livingston barked. "And with good reason! Simple piracy is one thing but when several hundred planetary economies are severely strained by one major incident like the destruction of that super cargo-liner it becomes a problem to be dealt with and eradicated. Do I make myself clear?"

"Yes, Mr. Chairman," Percy answered.

"And by the way, John," Livingston added. "The pressure is coming from all four Corporate Grid-Sectors, not just SouthWestern."

"I understand, Mr. Chairman."

"Good...then, let us put it to a vote," Livingston said.

"All in favor of utilizing the Guarder Squadron for the initial phase of this investigation, please raise their hands," Clifford said. Every hand in the room went up. *This isn't surprising*, Clifford thought, *especially since the Honorary Chairman's speech made his desired outcome quite clear.*

"All BoardMembers are in favor, Mr. Chairman," Clifford said. "The vote is unanimous." "Very good, First Secretary," Livingston said, shuffling some of his papers on the table in

front of him. *A.J. did a fine job in preparing the other BoardMembers for this meeting*, he thought to himself as he realized that his proposal had been approved just a bit too easily. The politics of gaining such a quick approval would, no doubt, soon start to become apparent as the other members of the Board began making seemingly innocent requests for additional funding and improved services for their respective departments. "Contact Sergeant Jekel at Guarder HQ, First Secretary," Livingston ordered. "Tell him that his presence is required in Judiciary Board Chambers immediately."

"Yes, Mr. Chairman," Clifford replied and briskly left the room.

"Everyone, let us take a few brief moments for recess until Sergeant Jekel arrives," Livingston said and eased back in his chair. The inevitable political bickering and maneuvering that would ultimately follow this meeting was hardly in his thoughts at the moment, although he was sure it was high among those of many of the BoardMembers in attendance today. No, it was the big picture and the ramifications of this latest pirate attack that held his thoughts. He could only hope that the men and women of the Guarder Squadron would be able to settle things out there in the SouthWestern Corporate Grid-Sector as soon as possible and bring the local economies and trade industries back into balance. If not, he hated to think of how bad things could really get out there before they began to get better...

United Earthian Nations
SouthWestern Corporate Grid-Sector
Sarkennon System

Shining Mission—Day One

During the early evening hours of May 5, 2008, a small group of European terrorists detonated a large yield nuclear warhead in the heart of Mexico City, Mexico, vaporizing more than two million residents and tourists instantly. Fallout from the blast resulted in the deaths of three million more from radiation poisoning in the ensuing months. Until that day, modern terrorism had reached its pinnacle with a mere total of several thousand dead during an attack in 2001 known, at the time, simply as "9/11." The Mexico City Event immediately took over the Number-One spot from that fateful day in September and proved to the people of the Earth the insanity of nuclear weapons stockpiles. This prompted the Nuclear Arms Abolition Negotiations between the newly re-formed Soviet Union and what was then known as the United States of America. Unfortunately, despite this unprecedented effort by the world's two Super Powers to finally attain global harmony, that time of peace was all too short-lived...

(Excerpt:*A History of Modern Earth and Beyond—the People, the Politics and the Insanity of Our Past* by Joseph Mullens)

CHAPTER ONE

The snow crunched hard under his boots as he ran through the wreckage of what was left of the huge super cargo-liner that had been heading for the Copernicus System several days ago before it had been attacked. Another shot rang out, the blaster bolt clanging against a piece of wreckage to his left in a shower of sparks. The debris had been strewn over an area that encompassed some one hundred square kilometers of Shining's surface when the monster ship had come crashing down from space.

His partner was close on his heels. From what they had seen so far, there were only two of them left. Three others had already been taken out, one by Razor and two by his own blasters.

"On two..." he whispered to the younger man as they reached the cover of a particularly large piece of debris. He received a nod in response. "Ready...one...two."

Razor popped up from his position and poured covering fire into the debris across the field as Buzzer rolled out from behind an enormous jagged block of battered cargo container with weapons blazing. He unleashed three precise bolts toward the untrained amateurs who had ambushed them just minutes ago within the crash-zone and knew that his aim had been true.

Before Buzzer could regain his footing, both men had gone down in a bloody spray of bones and organs, the detritus staining the virgin white snow where their corpses fell.

Suddenly all was quiet in the huge debris field. Buzzer's two blasters remained steady, held at arms length and shoulder height, as he quickly surveyed the scene.

"Do you think that's all of them?" Razor asked.

"Right here, yeah," Buzzer replied and felt the tension wash away. "Nice little greeting, wouldn't you say?" Razor smirked.

Buzzer turned a serious gaze on his young partner as he holstered his weapons and said, "Get used to it. That's usually how it plays out these days."

Razor stopped smirking and fell into step beside Buzzer as he walked over to the nearest of their dead assailants and stripped him of his weapons. Buzzer had to admit, despite what he had just told the younger Guarder, he had been somewhat surprised at the sneak attack by the five gunmen. So far, this one wasn't carrying any type of identification on his body. He was pretty sure the other four would turn up empty also. All five had been very heavily armed, carrying at least two weapons each. Just not very well trained.

Buzzer turned back toward the wreckage. The debris field seemed to span as far out as the eye could see. *What a way to start a mission,* he thought.

What had caused the enormous super cargo-liner to fall out of the standard cargo-lanes of the Berking Line and smash through the small planet's atmosphere to its doom on the rocky, snow- covered terrain was no mystery. The ship's optical security systems had caught most of the attack as it happened. It was the unknown identity of the attacking party that had been haunting the Judiciary Board's top scientific and research teams for the past few days.

Nevertheless, this was just another chapter in a recent series of mysterious planet falls and disappearances being reported all over the SouthWestern Corporate Grid-Sector. This latest had evoked an unprecedented outcry for assistance with the ongoing piracy problem from the hundreds of planetary systems directly affected by the super cargo-liner's loss spread throughout the Known Grid-Levels of Space. This in turn had prompted the Judiciary Board to take action and order a full investigation by the Guarder Squadron.

Of course, Buzzer thought to himself, *Jekel hands this one to me.* This first assignment after his brief vacation was supposed to be 'routine', a simple Phase-One only investigation. Instead, after a few short days of rest and relaxation, he found himself roaming all over a quarter of known space and getting shot at in the process. The danger didn't really bother him, though. The travel and the fireworks were just another part of the job. Being a Guarder was all that Frank Buzzito had ever wanted to be while growing up, the roots of the job itself flowed steadily within the blood coursing through his veins. His father and grandfather before him had also been Guarders. Buzzer just considered it a part of the family business.

"Jesus Christ, what a mess," the young man muttered at his side, a blaster still gripped firmly in his right hand.

Buzzer had accepted Sergeant Jekel's choice of Razor as his partner on this mission for a very simple reason—he liked the kid, recognized his potential and thought that he could use the experience. Some simple investigative duties, Buzzer had thought at the time, would be a good way to introduce the rookie Guarder to some of the more boring tasks that Guarders were often assigned.

"This thing had to break up long before it hit the ground," Razor said.

"Yeah, the pilots didn't stand a chance of landing this ship," Buzzer agreed. "Even if it had been intact when it broke through the atmosphere there was no way this cargo-liner was going to make landfall safely. The pilots wouldn't have been able to jump ship at that point either."

"Why not?"

Buzzer reached out and patted a massive piece of twisted metal, and an eerily empty echo answered back. "Because these things are fitted with emergency escape shuttles that are designed solely for travel through space, linking the best paths between main cargo-lanes and a possible rescue intercept. The propulsion systems of both the cargo-liners and their shuttles aren't made for traveling through any medium other than vacuum. Like air for instance."

Razor nodded and once again scanned the seemingly endless sea of debris. "What about these guys?" He asked, pointing down at the nearest dead body.

"Who knows," Buzzer said. "Probably a group of local criminals out to salvage what they could from a brand new crash site. I guess they just weren't willing to share the goods with newcomers."

"Wouldn't they have tried to chase us off first if that were the case?" Razor asked.

"Not necessarily, Razor," Buzzer answered and faced his partner. "You have to understand that things out here in the Grids aren't always as cut and dry as they appear back home on Aegis. People do some crazy things on these backwater planets. Believe me, I've just about seen it all."

"I've heard," Razor said with a grin and squinted against the biting wind sweeping across the snow covered plain. "So much, all to waste. What a damn mess."

Frank Buzzer remained silent but inwardly he had to agree with the younger man. With thirteen e-years in the ranks of the Guarder Squadron he was pretty sure that he had just about seen all there was to see, good and bad, and when a five-kilometer long InterGridactic super cargo-liner falls apart and crash lands on an unsuspecting planet, a damn mess was usually the result.

"You see where most of the snow is melted around those large chunks of iridium?" Buzzer asked, pointing to some debris about twenty meters away. "Those are pieces of the engines and fuel compartments. If they were hot enough to melt that much snow when they hit the ground, I'm sure that the main drive engines were still on maximum output when whoever was responsible for this first hit them. We'll probably find a lot more of this kind of debris in shallow orbits around the other planets and moons of this system. Pieces of this thing will be burning up in Shining's atmosphere for years."

"At least it hit in an abandoned area of the planet's surface," Razor said.

"Thanks to the skill of the pilots," Buzzer replied. "The initial telemetry we've received shows that the original crash-zone tracked for this monster lay smack in the middle of CharterCity, about one hundred fifty kilometers to the north. My guess is that the pilots who survived the initial attack did everything they could to steer this ship as far away from the capital city as possible, knowing full well that they stood no chance of surviving the crash."

"So, they used their last moments to help save lives," Razor considered. "Very noble." "I agree. The ship was probably still intact enough after the initial attack for the pilots to attempt an approach this close to Shining," Buzzer said. "The captain would have been thinking that he could stabilize the situation if he could just settle into a standard orbit. What he didn't count on was being hit again, even harder than the first time."

"It sure looks like the attackers knew what they were doing," Razor said.

"Absolutely," Buzzer said. "Whoever attacked this ship knew exactly where to inflict the most damage. They probably waited until the ship was too close to Shining's gravitational pull before launching their second attack. Then they just blew away the forward and aft directionals and retros. That's all it would have taken."

Razor studied the large man before him for several seconds and realized that, other than the legends surrounding him, there wasn't much that he actually knew about his partner. "You sound like you were trained to work on one of these, Buzzer."

"No, but I've spent enough time on ships like these to know how they work, how well they fly and how hard they fall," Buzzer said.

"Don't tell me you've seen another one of these things fall out of the sky?" Razor asked.

After several moments of silence, Buzzer whispered, "I was on one. Hitching a ride undercover in a customized cargo-crate equipped with a self-contained life support system. It usually works when you don't want anyone to find you. Even the most sensitive deep-space sensors can't penetrate the interference created by the massive engines of a super cargo-liner. When the trouble started I sprung the crate's hatch and worked my way to the cockpit. The pilot was very good, the best I'd ever seen. He kept his cool all the way down, right up until the moment of impact. These things aren't designed to glide through air, they usually drop like so much dead weight, but he somehow got it to glide right in over Sabarro's western marshlands. All fourteen of us would have been dead if it wasn't for the skills of that pilot. He still flies these things for the Berkings. He gets a little surprise every year on the anniversary of that crash, anonymously of course."

Razor just shook his head and decided that most of the legends he'd heard about his partner might just be true. "Unbelievable," was all that he could think of to say.

"That's what I thought, too," Buzzer said and walked towards the three dead men lying amidst the debris on the frozen ground some fifty meters away.

"What do you think our chances are of catching the people who did this, Buzzer?" Razor asked as he struggled to keep up with Buzzer's brisk pace.

"I've got a solid idea where to start so I like the odds," Buzzer replied. "I had some trouble in this system some time ago with an upstart group of paramilitary types who weren't acting very nicely toward the local officials. Although I handled them pretty quickly, I could never shake the feeling that the group I eliminated was just a small part of something much larger. I'm beginning to think that my hunch was right."

"You think the recent rash of hijackings and sneak attacks in this sector are related somehow to those same people?" Razor asked.

"Yeah, and not just in this sector," Buzzer said as he reached one of the bodies and searched it for weapons and ID. "There are constant reports from the Tiwanese of altercations with illegal bands of drifters throughout their system. The news is always full of strange disappearances and mysterious marauders who leave no trace of their presence, especially in the Masternine System, which isn't very far from here. I think it all boils down to one answer."

"A well organized and unusually large band of...pirates, for lack of a better term?" Razor offered.

"I guess you could call them pirates," Buzzer agreed. "But there's more to it than that. I was thinking more along the lines of an intricate networking of small pirate-type bands operating together throughout the SouthWestern Corporate Grid-Sector. It was inevitable that all the smaller groups of marauders who every so often raid the big ships for food and money would join together into a larger force."

"Sounds like a solid place to start, partner," Razor said as he finished checking over the last of the corpses. "Where would you like me to begin?"

"Once we get back into CharterCity I'm going to be awhile with the Statesman in charge," Buzzer replied. "I want you to get a message to HQ about what we've found so far and then start sniffing out some leads on the local criminal element. See if you can set up a meeting. Use the offer of drugs or black market items as a lure. I want to get the ball rolling on this. I'm starting to get a bad feeling..."

"Oh, great," Razor muttered to himself. "I've heard about those, too."

~*~

Sergeant Harrison Jekel stepped through the doors of the Guarder Squadron Control Center and made his way over to the communications console. Cougar watched him as he approached and quickly punched up a Hi-D Scrappy of the message that was coming through. Jekel grabbed the printout and started to scan through the message.

"Just came through from Shining, Sarge," Cougar said as he tried to read the Scrappy's contents from behind one massive shoulder:

```
...CRASH SITE INVESTIGATED...FOLLOWING
LEADS...OBVIOUS SIGNS OF POWER WEAPONS USE ON CARGO-
LINER...DELIBERATE ATTACK CONFIRMED...NO APPARENT
SURVIVORS...SERIES OF SIMILAR EVENTS THROUGHOUT THIS
GRID-SECTOR...100 SQUARE KILOMETER DEBRIS FIELD IN
SHINING BARRENS...WILL BE IN CONFERENCE WITH LOCAL
AUTHORITIES SOON...COVERT MEET WITH SHINING UNDERWORLD
PARTIES PLANNED...B HAS INKLING OR TWO...WILL REPORT
SOON...R...
```

"Well, I'm glad Razor's finally getting a chance to gain some valuable experience," Jekel muttered then looked at Cougar. "I was worried that Buzzer wouldn't like the idea of teaming up with a rookie on this assignment."

"Buzzer was a rookie once himself, Sarge," Cougar said.

"Yeah, but that was a long time ago, Cougar," Jekel replied. "A long time ago."
"Not for Buzzer, sir, he takes it day by day out there."

Jekel considered that for a moment and then nodded his agreement. "I just hope that Razor can keep pace with him. Buzzer works real fast when the situation warrants it."

"What's the matter, Sarge?" Cougar began. "Don't you trust your own judgment anymore?"

Jekel fixed him with a steely glare and walked away from the console. Cougar could hear him mumbling under his breath as he crossed the room and left the Control Center.

~*~

"Excuse me, Statesman Humechy," Buzzer said from across the ornate desktop in the Shining Statesman's plush office. "But the U.E.N. Judiciary Board has dispatched me here for that very reason. I am a member of the Guarder Squadron, one of the leaders of that organization, and my mission on Shining is to perform a full investigation into the recent crash of the InterGridactic super cargo-liner whose debris field lies across a hundred kilometers of the barrens not too far from this very spot."

"I realize that, Guarder, but..." Humechy started.

"Allow me to finish, Statesman," Buzzer interrupted. "My interests here in the SouthWestern Corporate Grid-Sector do not center on this planet alone, although I am greatly aware of the recent troubles you have been experiencing with piracy in the nearby space lanes."

"Not just mere troubles, as you say, Guarder," the elder Statesman said, sitting up a little straighter in his high-backed chair. "These merciless undesirables have disrupted Shining's trade patterns for more time than I care to recall and the first response to my frequent requests for assistance comes only when a major catastrophe occurs on my planet and that pitiful response is in the form of only one man!"

"I am not alone in this matter, Statesman," Buzzer said. "I have been conducting my own investigations for some time, choosing to come to you now to seek out only that information which you can provide."

"That being?" Humechy prompted.

Buzzer paused for several seconds while he glared down at the older man. If the Statesman wanted to play these petty games of power with a Guarder then he obviously did not know who or what he was up against. "I require complete access to the records of any and all instances of unprovoked attacks on all vessels occurring on the surface or in orbit around Shining within the past four e-years. This includes all case files and the dossiers of each of the victims, both alive and dead."

"And when shall you be requiring all of this material, Guarder?" Humechy asked. "Immediately, Statesman," Buzzer replied. "Make no mistake, I plan on a very thorough

investigation into your current situation and I hope to end your troubles as well."

"Immediately, you say," Humechy said and scratched his chin while leaning back in his chair. "I am sorry to deny your requests, Guarder, but you must understand my position. I will have to go through channels to provide you the type of access you are seeking. This could take days, maybe weeks—you can never be certain in matters such as these."

"I will have the access I require immediately, Statesman Humechy," Buzzer stated in a smooth, flat tone. "I hold the position of Honorary Official to U.E.N. Judiciary Board Affairs.

The parameters within which I operate override your powers of authority within the Sector- Council. If you need an official seal of approval on my actions all you need do is contact the nearest U.E.N. Outpost. Until then, you may direct me to the logistics lab that houses Shining's historical archives. I will need to start on this as soon as possible." Buzzer laid his Guarder ID on the desktop in front of Humechy. The great golden seal of the Judiciary Board was centered in the middle of a giant falcon, the symbol of the Guarder Squadron. It was signed by Mozart Livingston, the Honorary Chairman of the Judiciary Board. "As a Guarder I have the powers of court and judge at my disposal. My decisions are law, Mr. Statesman. I expect your complete and unbiased cooperation during my stay here. If you do not comply with my requests, you and your career as the Ruling Statesman on Shining will suffer the consequences."

"Is that a threat, Guarder?" Humechy sneered.

"If that is the way you would like to interpret it, by all means, do," Buzzer said and watched as his words simmered around inside Humechy's newly worried mind. The man deserved to be put in his place for his not so subtle attempt at a power play but, from what he could make of the elder man's expression, Humechy had grown somewhat more than just worried. It seemed that Shining's Ruling Statesman now felt very threatened by Buzzer's presence in his office and Buzzer hated to play the tyrant. Especially since this man had at least shown enough consideration toward the welfare of his people to actually submit a request for some type of official aid to help deal with his planet's current criminal problems.

Buzzer approached the desk and planted his arms squarely across the desktop so that he could face Humechy directly. "Statesman Humechy," he said. "I am sorry if my tone seems threatening but I intend to follow through with my investigation, an investigation that you officially asked for, and I will require the access I have requested in order to do so. Please understand my position regarding the state of things on Shining. Believe me, your planet is not the only one in the surrounding systems experiencing a recent wave of hijackings and raids. The Masternine System is having a worse time of it than you. The Judiciary Board has been trying to provide assistance to all of you. The SouthWestern Corporate Grid-Sector seems to have been subject to an onslaught of attacks on anything from innocent merchant ships to luxury liners in the neighboring traffic lanes. We have been working diligently in this area for quite some time and, as I have said before, have only now been able to directly answer your request for official aid."

Humechy's face softened a bit and he let out a long sigh. "I thank you for your honesty, Guarder," he said and sagged somewhat in his chair. "I gather I was just being a foolish old man. I can tell you that I am more than a little angered by the sheer amount of time that has elapsed since I put in my request. But, of course, I understand that the U.E.N. has not been neglecting its duty to the worlds it provides for."

"We try, sir."

"I'm sure you do," Humechy smiled and reached a hand out in a friendly gesture.

Buzzer shook hands with the elder diplomat and was pleased to see that his hand was met with a firm grip. "Now, down to business."

"Of course, I will summon someone to lead you to our Archival Hall," Humechy said as he stood very slowly and made his way around the desk. "I trust you will be needing suitable accommodations during your stay here in CharterCity?"

"No, that's perfectly all right, Statesman," Buzzer replied. "I prefer that my presence here continues on in a seemingly unofficial capacity. Because of the people we'll be dealing with, of course."

"Of course," Humechy said with a somewhat puzzled look on his face. A visiting official from the U.E.N. itself turning down lodging in the Shining Statesman's ManorHouse in preference to life in the streets had been unheard of until now. This man was very strange, very strange indeed. But, for some reason, the Guarder seemed like the right kind of man to get this ugly job done.

~*~

The bartender handed him a small scrap of paper and nodded back toward the dark side of the smoky bar. Scrawled on the dirty piece of paper in a sticky red ink was a short sentence: NOON / TOMORROW / BACKWATER TROPICS / THIRD TABLE ON LEFT.

"Thanks for the help, barkeep."

"No thanks necessary, just the payoff, stranger," the short and filthy man behind the bar grimaced, revealing more grit in his teeth to go along with the grit covering his stinking body.

Digging in his pockets, Razor produced a fifty-mint coin, one of the newer Felking Issues, and the bartender's eyes widened in surprise. "Keep the change."

"I had every intention of doing just that," the man rasped and grinned, showing some missing teeth to go along with the grit. The subdued lighting and haze of smoke inside the filthy bar made it next to impossible to get a clear view of Razor's dark face. He was so tall that his ebony skin and black hair blended in very well with the dark ceiling panels less than a meter overhead. Despite that, the grimy bartender continued to squint at Razor's face as he tried to get a better look at the man in front of the bar, obviously intending to provide some kind of a description of him to anyone who was likely to pay for it.

Razor made sure to watch his back as he made his way across the bar and out the door into the snow covered streets. Underneath his baggy clothes and olive drab outer coat he was dying for a nice hot shower.

~*~

Buzzer stared at the information scrolling down the screen before him and began to realize just how serious the situation was here on Shining. The downing of the super cargo-liner, while a major event, was not the most troubling thing to have happened here over the past several e- years.

As he read the small screen, it became more and more evident that there had been a major lapse in communications between the Sarkennon System and the U.E.N. Governmental Complex on Aegis. Thousands upon thousands of attacks had been recorded in this system and many of the surrounding colonized systems in the local sector. The damage done and financial losses to the affected parties were astronomical to say the least.

Buzzer noticed how eerily quiet it had become in Shining's Archival Hall, located deep within the lower levels of CharterHouse. It seemed that the few people who had been present in the massive library upon his arrival thought it best to clear out while their dark visitor was at work.

Marveling at the dozens of requests put forth by Shining Statesman Dabner Humechy to the U.E.N. for assistance with the planet's ongoing and ever growing criminal problems, Buzzer's concern over the situation continued to mount. To his knowledge, and from what he had learned during his preliminary research of this assignment, only three of those pleas for help had ever been officially received and logged by the U.E.N. Sector Council. That in itself was very suspicious.

Someone, somewhere in the upper levels of Shining's political establishment, was interfering with the planet's off-world communications; of that there could be no doubt. Buzzer was sure that the U.E.N. Sector Council would have reacted long before now if they had received only half of Humechy's requests for assistance.

After several minutes of deep thought, Buzzer decided that the safety of the citizens in the Sarkennon System and those surrounding it would best be protected at this very moment by the presence of the U.E.N. Military. A large and powerful military presence should serve to slow down the alarming level of attack activity Buzzer had learned about in just a short time of researching Shining's criminal archives. Although newsworthy and unprecedented, the presence of the U.E.N. FlightForce in an orbit around Shining shouldn't do much to interfere with his present investigation.

Buzzer began to program his sequencer for a Priority-One broadcast to the nearest U.E.N. warship and wondered how Razor's end of this assignment was playing out.

~*~

Shining Statesman Dabner Humechy thought better of contacting the CharterCity Chief of Police personally about the presence of official U.E.N. personnel on Shining, not wanting to get caught up in one of Chief Parker's droll and meaningless conversations.

Instead, he contacted the Chief's office at the CharterCity Police HQ Building and asked the young officer who answered to take a message to Parker as soon as she was able.

The message was short and to the point, but full of smug satisfaction at finally getting an official response to his consistent requests for assistance to the U.E.N. *Chief Parker will be impressed,* Humechy thought as he closed the com-link, *I do hope that Guarder can follow through on his claims to bring this senseless crime-wave to an end.*

Just as quickly as the thoughts were swimming around within Humechy's mind, a new set of economic growth charts on his desktop monitor took over his immediate attention. He frowned at the lack of growth predicted for the next quarter. The recent rash of attacks in the surrounding shipping lanes had caused a serious drop in consumer confidence. He vowed to himself that if the U.E.N. didn't allocate acceptable resources toward solving the problem in the Sarkennon System, he would have to seriously consider secession from the union.

~*~

"All systems check, sir," the young Flight Corpsman called from his station. "We will be entering the Sarkennon System in approximately twelve minutes."

"Very good, Lieutenant, inform me when we enter orbit around Shining."

"Yes, sir."

Harold Turner sat back in the command chair and relaxed. He and his crew had just completed a fifth circuit of the SouthWestern Corporate Grid-Sector searching for any signs of unidentified hostile forces operating within the area and had thus far found nothing. Of course, the presence of a FlightForce Carrier in any system usually tended to chase those with bad intentions far away.

A sudden Priority-One beacon had ordered them to the planet Shining in the Sarkennon System just hours ago. Now, the U.E.N. Ruffian was mere minutes away from the snowy planet and the purpose of the mysterious command had yet to present itself.

Who in the Known Grid-Levels of Space could have enough pull on such an insignificant little world, he wondered. Pull enough to call a FlightForce Carrier off its designated course and to override the orders of the U.E.N. Military Command Post in this sector.

He couldn't figure it out just yet but whoever that person turned out to be, Captain Harold T. Turner was not in the mood to deal with whatever plans he or she had made for the Ruffian.

"Sir, we are within hailing distance of Shining Starport," the ComTech said from his console.

"Should I try to raise them, sir?"

"Yes, Hansen," Turner decided. "See if you can get through to the joker who interrupted our mission."

"Yes, sir."

"Try a Mission Sequence Order, that should get their attention," Turner said smugly. "Maybe let them know that I'm a little bit pissed off at all this."

"Sending a Mission Sequence Order, Captain," Hansen replied.

"Should I put in some supply req's while we're here, sir?" A voice called from across the expansive bridge.

Turner laughed at that and nodded his head in agreement. "Good idea, Commander Malone.

Why not deplete their stores and supplies since they called us off course. Get right on it..." "Sir! I have at least ten small vessels approaching on my sensors," an excited voice called from the Ops Console. "Two larger ones are laying back at three thousand kilometers. I've run an identity check and none of the ships match up."

"Unidentifieds?" Turner asked.

"Yes, sir, and four more have just entered sensor range," came the response. "Six of them are showing weapons systems armed status."

"Full alert! All decks! Battle stations!" Captain Turner stood and leaned over the sensor screens. "Arm main and forward guns, put all Flight Squads on full battle-ready alert, cut engines' forward power. Hold position until they come within five-hundred kilometers, then I want you to ram this ship down the throat of their formation at full acceleration."

"Should I try to resume this position at the end of that maneuver, Captain?" Lieutenant Miller called from the helm.

"Hell, no!" Turner barked. "Take us out of this system as soon as they open fire. I want this ship clear and stabilized before we turn around and come back for seconds."

"Yes, sir."

"Captain, I have the Starport on com-link," Hansen said. "Should I inform them of our situation?"

"No, just patch it through to my command chair." "Patching."

"Shining Starport, here," the voice sounded strong and steady, not like the dozens of other voices he had encountered while on this patrol. "Report your position, Captain Turner."

"We are currently being stalked by more than a dozen unidentifieds, some of them armed, just outside of your orbit," Turner replied. "I demand to know exactly why the Ruffian was called here and for what purpose other than sailing us directly into a trap."

"Captain Turner, I am mobilizing Shining's small unit of space-capable forces to assist you at this very moment," the voice sounded through the com-link. "Please fall back and fire only when fired upon."

"I will fire at will as soon as these hostiles close to within five-hundred kilometers, Mr.

Statesman!" Turner said. "Please try to restrain yourself from issuing orders to..."

"This is not the Statesman of Shining, Captain Turner."

Turner took several seconds to scan the forward viewscreen and locate the approaching targets. "Well, then just who in the hell are you?"

"I am a U.E.N. Guarder, Captain," Buzzer said. "And despite the fact that you are the commanding officer of the Ruffian, it is my duty to remind you that I currently hold rank in this situation and you will follow my orders. I am not interested in causing harm to you, your crew or your vessel, sir, but I do want one or two of your attackers to be taken into custody."

Several silence-filled seconds followed while Turner tried to think of the proper comeback but nothing came to mind.

"Now," Buzzer continued. "If you would just fall back and fire only when fired upon we may be able to accomplish this."

"We, Guarder?" Turner scoffed. "I don't see you up here risking your life."

"I am reasonably certain at this time, Captain Turner, that your ship has at least one gun locked on to every approaching target, as any CO worth his salt would," Buzzer said. "Those guns will most certainly possess the capability of destroying their targets without the slightest drain on your resources, as per the strict adherence to modern military FlightForce Carrier designs under which the Ruffian was constructed. Taking all of this into consideration, I am assuming that your life is as much at risk right now as mine is down here on the surface. Am I correct?"

"Absolutely correct," Harold Turner said, slumping down into his command chair in amazement. He had heard all of the tall tales of the Guarder Squadron and had seen them mentioned in various mission reports and newscasts throughout his career but he had never really believed the legends. Now, in searching his memory, he did seem to remember the regulations stating that Guarders held top authority on any mission they were involved in, an authority over even that held by top U.E.N. Military brass.

"The Ruffian is falling back and awaits further orders," Turner grumbled, and the helmsman complied. The roar of the Ruffian's reversing engines was a steady hum on the bridge and Turner watched as the approaching hostile ships maintained their pace. Subconsciously, he went through the motions of checking all the systems on the ship from his console. All of the Ruffian's gun emplacements were armed, fully staffed and ready to fire. All twenty-five of his ship's Flight Squads were on standby alert and could be deployed within two minutes. The evasive retros and directionals were all in the green and each compartment had been air-sealed in case of a hull breach. His crew was at the ready and he was intensely concerned about the combat credentials of the man on the surface of Shining who called himself aGuarder.

"I have ten of Shining's Defense Unit on an intercept course with the approaching ships, Captain," Commander Malone called from his position looking over the OpsTech's shoulder. "And another five converging on the positions of the two ships that are holding back."

"Very good, Commander," Turner said and turned back to his com-link, "Guarder, can I count on these forces helping to defend the Ruffian if things get touchy up here?"

"Have faith, Captain," Buzzer replied. "These hostiles have most likely never come up against a military target. Once they actually get a close enough look at the Ruffian's size and armaments, I expect that most of them will attempt to flee the area..."

"Sir! We have ten missiles homing in on our position!" the OpsTech called. "Evasive action, Helm!" Turner roared. "Main guns, take out those missiles!" "Main guns firing, sir!"

"Shining's forces have engaged the enemy ships, Captain," Malone said as he continued to monitor the scanners at Ops.

"Well it's about damn time," Turner swore under his breath.

"All incoming missiles have been destroyed, Captain," Malone stated. "As well as nine of the attacking vessels. Two others have been disabled, the rest are fleeing."

"Lock our long-range weapons on to those targets and fire at will," Turner ordered. "They are out of range, Captain," the WeaponsTech reported.

"Orders to pursue, sir?" from the Helmsman.

"Dammit," Turner mumbled and visibly relaxed in his chair. "No pursuit, let them go." "Captain Turner," Buzzer's voice once again sounded through the com-link. "Please tow one

of the disabled vessels into spacedock with you over Shining Starport." "Whatever you say, Guarder," Turner sneered.

"Thank you, Captain."

"The com-link has been disconnected, sir," Hansen said.

"Bring us on course for Shining Spacedock, helm," Turner ordered. "Ops, attach a tractor beam to one of the two disabled ships and, Weapons, please make haste in destroying the other."

"Yes, sir."

Harold Turner leaned forward in his chair and watched the Ruffian's main viewscreen as a tiny flash of light signified one of the two disabled ships being caught in a tractor beam. Two seconds later another brighter flash signified the other ship's destruction.

CHAPTER TWO

Razor slipped through the door of the shabby room and closed it tight behind him. He was sure of at least two men on his tail, possibly a third staying just ahead. Within seconds, the outer coat and filthy garments making up his disguise were discarded and a blaster filled his right hand.

Where in the hell was Buzzer? The small rented room was void of life and sound and looked like it had been for quite some time. A glance out the window proved that two of his unwanted companions were still lingering around. His cover as a newly grounded member of a distant- system band of malcontents had been hastily put together and, at some points during some of his recent meetings, he had felt a bit poorly informed. Evidently, his feelings were solid. The locals wouldn't have thought it necessary to put a tail on him if his story hadn't aroused a little suspicion. Now he would have to find out if their intentions were strictly observational or leaning more toward taking him out.

He felt a sudden sensation within his wrist sequencer and saw a message from Buzzer coming through. Quickly keying in the command for internal communications, he said, "Razor here."

"Razor, be careful with your contacts," Buzzer's voice came clearly through the micro receptor implanted behind his right ear. "The U.E.N. Ruffian was attacked just minutes ago upon entering this system and all local hostiles will be on heightened alert."

"Understood, Buzzer," Razor replied and crouched lower in the room as a shadow passed outside the window.

"Avoid further contact with anyone until I return with additional information," Buzzer said. "I'm leaving the Starport now and heading back to CharterHouse. Meet with you soon."

"Very good," Razor said as he primed his blaster and readied himself for action. "I've got a little unwanted company outside, partner."

"Be careful and report afterwards, Buzzer out."

"I'm already past careful, my friend," Razor muttered to himself now that the com-link had been disconnected.

A sound came fuzzily through the neighboring room, a room that should have been empty since the two Guarders had paid for that one as well. He stole another quick glance out of the small circular window toward the front of the room and found only one man out front now. "Damn," he swore and made his way over to a spot just on the other side of the outside door, where he could still see out the window.

The man seemed to be fidgeting with something in his right ear. A glint of sun off metal proved it to be some sort of communications device, probably a very old model. The next thing the sun glinted off of was the metal casing of the blaster in the man's right hand, and Razor prepared himself to react.

A tingling in his spine screamed danger to him from behind and Razor dove to the floor as a large blast leveled the back wall and sent him flying against the sofa. In one quick move, Razor rolled with the impact, set his sights on the front door and pressed off two shots. The man standing behind the door took one bolt full in the face, a red mist filling the doorway where he had been standing.

Razor continued his roll as another major blast blew the sofa to bits, sending a cloud of dust and cushioning materials into the air throughout the room. The small cloud served to outline the man standing in the hole where the back wall had been. Razor smiled, took aim and was about to eliminate the target when some of Buzzer's past advice appeared in his mind, *make any potential target a prisoner, information is more valuable than a decrease in enemy numbers unless those numbers could serve to overwhelm your position imminently...*

He loosed off a shot and watched it tear into the man's shoulder, sending him shrieking to the floor in a spray of blood and muscle tissue. Razor covered the short distance to his prey and kicked the man's weapon out of reach. A quick scan of what was left of the room and the area outside proved that nothing hostile remained in the vicinity.

The approaching sirens grew closer and two police cruisers came into view down the short block, sliding to a stop just outside his demolished room. One look at Razor's Guarder ID was all the officers needed to allow the Guarder to bypass the usual paperwork and official statements and be on his way.

"Be sure to see that this man lives to undergo interrogation, Officer. The other can be scraped off the front steps and used as fertilizer, for all I care," he said to one of the policemen and motioned toward his cruiser. "Catch a ride back in that other vehicle, I'll need this one for awhile."

A grunt of confusion and acknowledgment was all the reply he received as he gunned the powerful engines of the small police cruiser and roared away toward the center of CharterCity. Now all he had to do was make it to CharterHouse and inform Buzzer that his cover had been blown. It seemed to have happened way too soon.

~*~

Frazier Sampson paced slowly around the small circle of battered men and women, a look of sheer disgust on his face. One of the men glanced up at him, pure fear crowding his features, and Sampson promptly spat in the man's eye.

"I can't believe the fools you are!" He shrieked at them, most flinching at the anger in his voice. "Couldn't you idiots see what you were dealing with? Did you not recognize a FlightForce Carrier? Couldn't you see the small armada of Shining's back-up forces waiting for you and your lousy Sleeksters?" The group answered him with silence. "I am weary of your stupid little games of greed! This is my outfit! I run it the way I want it run! Do I make myself clear?"

Grunts of agreement came from several of them but most were too scared for words. "To even dare to come back here after suffering such a miserable defeat...the only reason I let what is left of your original group land here was so I could find out exactly what kind of fools I've been dealing with. Now I know, more than ever. Twenty ships, twenty! And only nine come back.

What a pitiful group you are. Do you realize what they've done? They allowed you people to live. The ultimate insult! To be considered unworthy of killing by the enemy! Well, I tell you this—I am having serious feelings about your fate. Obviously someone on Shining called that carrier here off of its regular mission-course. But who on that dismal little planet could have such clout? Certainly not Humechy, he has called time and again for help but never has any arrived to aid him."

"They weren't battle-ready when we first read them on our sensors, Frazier," the smallest figure among those in the circle offered. Sampson answered him with a glare.

"It was an United Earthian Nations Military warship, Ernest," Sampson said. "They do not have to be battle-ready to enter a combat situation. They are ready for just such a contingency at every given moment of every single day. Otherwise, how do you think they can get their job done? Don't you realize that a ship that big could be brought down as easily as a freighter if that weren't the case, you imbecile!"

Sampson stood very still just outside the circle for several seconds, trying to calm his already shattered nerves. Just watching the sad looking crew of misfits in front of him made that next to impossible. "So, out of stupidity and reckless greed, you have lost me eleven ships, Sleeksters no less! The fastest in my fleet of which I formally had over fifty and now have maybe forty. Three of those are most probably beyond repair, hapless piles of scrap metal. And what do you have to show for it? To offer as compensation to me for the loss of these vessels? Nothing. Nothing more than a never-ending sob story not fit to be a children's tale let alone an excuse for a blunder of this magnitude!"

The volume of his voice took the group by surprise. The look on Sampson's face meant only one thing, they all knew it. Blood would be spilled by Frazier Sampson's hand before long. If not all of them, surely some in their group would pay.

"Now, the question at hand seems to be, what do I do with the sorry lot of you?" The question hung in the air thick and ominous. Sampson's head hung low for a moment before he lifted it to look once more at the horror-filled expressions on the circle of faces. "Well, as for your ships, what repairs they require will be performed. Have no doubt, they will once again ride with my fleet."

Sampson paused then and a complete and utter silence encompassed the enormous room. The thousands of spectators and the battered ones in the circle in front of him dared not breathe in fear of incurring their leader's wrath.

A feeble voice split the silence, coming from the same man who had spoken earlier. "What...what is to be-be-become of us, Frazier?"

Sampson glared down at the bruised and bloodied man as he approached the frail figure cowering on his knees. The patch on Ernest's right arm that indicated the wing-group and ship he was assigned to stood out brightly against the drab gray jumpsuit he wore. Sampson bared his teeth in a vicious snarl, grabbed the man up to a standing position and sliced the patch from his sleeve in a single movement. His blade glistened with Ernest's blood where the sharp edge had sliced through flesh while freeing the patch from the coarse fabric. Ernest grimaced in pain and looked with horror into Frazier Sampson's intense eyes. "I sentence you and this entire group to death!" Sampson screamed and brought his blaster up to the small man's face. Ernest's gasp was cut short by the blaster bolt that destroyed his head.

The next few minutes were a confusion of charger blasts and muffled explosions mixed with a terrible cacophony of human screams and shrieks of pain as Frazier Sampson's Utility Guardsmen opened fire on the small group of men and women. When it was all over, smoke and the smell of spent charger casings and charred flesh was overpowering in the assembly hall.

Where there had been a circle of living, breathing people just moments ago was now a pile of things hardly recognizable as once having been alive. Thick puddles of dark red blood were forming in some spots on the uneven ground. Thousands of frightened faces peered at the organic mound of dead flesh, whatever emotions they were feeling hidden by masks of terror.

Frazier Sampson walked over to one section of the heap of body parts and climbed carefully to the top. Blood oozed out of the places where his boots took grip. Slowly, Sampson turned to take in the sight of over seven thousand of his followers. He soaked up the fear he could feel emanating in waves from these people, people who were living and breathing only because he willed them to be. People who would be just as dead as those beneath his feet if he commanded it.

Taking a deep breath to fill his lungs with the exhilarating smell of death and fear, he allowed his voice to boom across the great hall, "My fellows, this is what happens when greed overpowers common sense! When the wants and desires of the few take precedence over those of the whole! I command this unit for the benefit of all, not for those who choose to defy me and end up in defeat! What did this little venture cost them besides their lives? It cost the whole of us eleven of our fastest ships. No small loss to a force our size. One thousand ships strong, we have controlled the SouthWestern Corporate Grid-Sector with an iron fist. No one soars through this space without having some fear of us and when we may strike! And soon we will invade even further into space, but not if we have more fools like these among our numbers! I will tolerate no future mistakes! Do you hear me?"

The room reverberated with the sound of thousands of voices expressing their compliance. The enormous building had never sounded quite this rapturous to Sampson's ears before. Over the past decade he had built his empire here on Sarsat-15, a small moon of Sarkennon-8, deep in the outer limits of the Sarkennon System. Sarsat-15 was so small and cold and devoid of even the smallest of living organisms that it had never been considered worthy of a charter by the U.E.N. Department of Space Exploration. When Frazier Sampson had been a U.E.N. Marine, in one of the first units to keep the peace in the frequently unsettled Masternine System, he had been exposed to all of the fruits and riches that the illegal outfits operating in the Masternine had to offer. Once his initial tour had been completed, and while his already established contacts in the local underworld were still operating in conjunction with his former Sergeant, he took up a position as liaison with the Masternine Syndicate. Within two e-years he had broken away from the complicated political machinations of the Syndicate and recruited his own small unit of raiding ships and sleek cruisers.

At first he had operated strictly within the boundaries of the Masternine Syndicate and Sergeant Sheffield, but once his team had grown enough to operate on its own, Sampson had torn into the action with a vengeance. Destroying every Syndicate ship they could trap in the quadrant, Sampson's unit had blazed a name for itself throughout the SouthWestern Corporate Grid-Sector. Now, e-years later, he had enough of a following to spread it out and keep the tails and leads to himself and his base of operations on Sarsat-15 to a minimum. Thus far it had worked. Sarsat-15 was so far out of the way of the cargo-lanes, travel routes and civilization in general that a working colony was unthinkable. At least to the U.E.N.Government.

That is why the small moon worked so well as a headquarters for his various units. Until now, nothing had ever gone this wrong. He had sent those twenty ships out to Shining near-space just to take a simple look around, more of an observational mission, with permission to raid if the opportunity came up. He never thought in his wildest dreams that those ships would be stupid enough to attack a U.E.N. Military warship, let alone a FlightForce Carrier. Stupidity and senseless greed were not what he wanted among his people. The wealth they brought in was always evenly distributed among his followers. Of course, his percentage was larger overall, but the men and women had always been well compensated for their work in his unit and quite content with their lives. Especially with the freedom he allowed them. They didn't have to spend all their time on this dreadful dead hulk of a moon like he did most of the time. In fact, he encouraged frequent trips to local spaceports by his men and women. Mostly because such things kept them happy, but also because it provided him with a wide variety of intelligence and secondary information, which continuously passed through the InterGridactic grapevine. Those trips were an essential element to his business and the black market was a wonderfully plentiful business.

Sampson shook his head, bringing himself back to the moment. A sea of faces stared back at him seemingly from all sides. The silence must have been lingering for several minutes, exactly how long he did not know, but for the first time in his life he felt spooked. Clearing his throat loudly, he steeled himself and looked slowly over his followers.

"Today," he began, "we have acquired a new and immensely powerful enemy. It seems that we have the proud honor of being considered a threat to the U.E.N. FlightForce in this sector. The poor fools who now lie in pieces underneath my boots were idiotic enough to think that twenty Sleeksters could bring down a cruising FlightForce Carrier. They somehow got it into their moronic heads to attack the first real military presence to invade this system since this organization began. And why? Why did they try something so impossible? So inevitably disastrous? Because they didn't follow their mission plan. Because they thought it wise to go off on their own and disobey my orders! As a result, I finished the job that the U.E.N. Military Forces failed to do—eliminate the enemy! And hear me now, any fool who attempts to go against what is good for all of us only to fulfill their own desires will be considered my enemy and the enemy to us all!"

The roar of applause and cheers echoed off the walls of the assembly room complex and Frazier Sampson climbed down off the pile of human debris and over to his second in command. "Once this place is empty gather up this mess, take it outside and burn it. I don't ever want to see this trash again, Gilfred."

"Yes, of course, Frazier."

"Thanks, Gil," Sampson said and began heading for the hallway leading to his personal chambers. "And keep the security beefed up in the scanner room. I want to know the very instant we pick up any sign of an approaching ship."

"I'll get right on it, Frazier."

"Good...I'll be in my chambers if you need me."

"Get some rest, Frazier," Gilfred Thornberg said as Sampson passed by.

Sampson stopped, glanced back at Thornberg and then at the still oozing pile of now rank smelling death. Although a rapturous feeling of overwhelming power had gripped him tightly during the events of just moments ago, the reality of his actions were now hitting home and Sampson felt as if ghosts were walking with him. "I'll try, Gil..."

Thornberg gripped Sampson's shoulder lightly and nodded his understanding. He watched the distraught figure of his leader disappear down the hallway and knew that what had happened tonight would wear heavily on the man for quite some time.

~*~

"I understand your distress, Captain Turner, but I did not override your orders and bring you to Shining in order to test out a hypothesis on whether the raiders operating in this sector had enough destructive capability to take out a

FlightForce Carrier," Buzzer said sternly and the military man backed down. "I disrupted your mission plan because I felt that the presence of a FlightForce Carrier, a true symbol of the U.E.N.'s power, in the Sarkennon System would show these people that the U.E.N. will not stand for any more of these unprovoked attacks in their nearby shipping lanes."

"Right, Guarder, but all it served to do was get my ship fired upon and put my people in danger!" Turner blurted.

"If your ship was in any form of danger from a fleet of a mere twenty Sleeksters then it doesn't say much for the state of the U.E.N. FlightForce!" Buzzer countered.

"Gentlemen, please!" Statesman Humechy stood and glowered at Buzzer. "We are not here to argue, let me remind you, but to try and put a stop to the frequent attacks in Shining's neighboring shipping lanes."

"All I want to know is when I can prep my ship for departing Shining orbit and get on with my mission," Turner growled and once again took his seat.

"Captain Turner," Humechy said. "Once this Guarder gave his orders turning your ship around, this situation became your new mission. Guarder orders override your military orders. This you should have been aware of."

Turner grunted and Buzzer turned toward Humechy. "Thank you, Mr. Statesman," he said and walked to the head of the conference table.

Just then Razor entered the room and stopped in his tracks. "Good afternoon, gentlemen," Razor said and looked to Buzzer for a proper introduction.

"My colleague and fellow Guarder, gentlemen," Buzzer said and took Razor off to the side. Looking over his partner's torn and bloodied clothing, he whispered, "What happened, John?"

"Well, there's not much left of our room or one of the guys who tried to kill me," Razor whispered back. "But I did get us a prisoner out of the deal."

"Damn, our cover is blown already," Buzzer said.

"Yeah, I set up a meet between the local drug-pusher for a large buy tomorrow," Razor said. "I was figuring on getting a small fish to fry to start out with. I guess that's blown now."

"That's all right," Buzzer said. "At least we have someone to question."

"Excuse me, Guarders," Turner said. "But can we get on with this briefing or whatever it is you are choosing to call it? My time and the time of my crew is being wasted here..."

Buzzer whirled around, covered the distance to the Captain almost instantaneously and grabbed the man by his collar. "You listen to me, *Captain*," he snarled. "I am your superior officer at this time. If you have any problems with me you will keep them to yourself and do whatever the hell I tell you to. With no questions asked! Do I make myself as Goddamn clear as I possibly can?"

Turner's eyes were wide with surprise at the sudden outburst but he managed to nod. "Now," Buzzer continued. "If I get any more trouble out of you or any more backtalk I'm going to bust your ass all the way down to FlightCorpsman and throw a court-martial into the mix as well. Do you hear me, Captain Turner?"

Turner's face turned red, both from embarrassment at being treated in such a way in front of his Flight Commander and First Officer, and from anger at the big man who was now calling the shots. "Yes, sir, Guarder," Turner managed through gritted teeth. "Perfectly clear, sir."

Buzzer released him and let the man slump back down into his chair. Razor took his hand off the butt of his blaster, glad that the other two members of the Ruffian's crew had not wanted any trouble from Buzzer.

"Please be seated," Buzzer said to Razor, motioning for an empty seat at the conference table. "Gentlemen, the man who just entered goes by the name Razor and he is a colleague of mine.

The two of us make up the team that the U.E.N. Judiciary Board has assigned to the problem that this system has been experiencing with raiders and hijackers."

"There are only two of you working this investigation?" Humechy questioned.

"Yes, Statesman," Buzzer said. "On the home front. There are other teams operating throughout the SouthWestern Corporate Grid-Sector at this very moment in addition to others operating on Aegis. Do not worry, we are well staffed in this matter." Buzzer cast a quick glance toward Razor, who returned the look with a questioning expression of his own.

"Now that you have seen that these...pirates, or whatever you want to call them, have no qualms about firing on a FlightForce Carrier," Avril Garcia, the Ruffian's Flight Commander, started, "what do you propose to use the Ruffian for? You can't expect our fighters to go up against a fleet of these suicidal bastards, Guarder."

"No, you are absolutely correct, Commander," Buzzer said and began to pace the room. "I do not expect the Ruffian to be attacked again, at least not any time soon."

"But they've shown no fear..." Turner interrupted and Buzzer shot him a glare.

"When they turned tail and ran for the outer reaches of this system I think they had little else than fear on their minds, Captain," Buzzer offered. "I think it's obvious that for once these people came up against a force that they were not prepared for. Not once has a U.E.N. Military warship been attacked by these marauders. Not once have they even come within scanner range of a FlightForce Carrier's sensors before today. Am I correct?"

Turner nodded and Buzzer continued. "In my opinion, what happened today was an accidental encounter between two forces of far from equal strength. The one exception was that the Ruffian knew what to expect and they did not. What they saw was a cruising FlightForce Carrier, seemingly non-battle ready and flying with minimum systems operational. In their eyes, your ship was a treasure for the taking, a trophy to bring back to their superiors in order to gain a greater position within their particular group. A quick surprise attack by twenty fast maneuverable ships against one big hulking monster whose weapons weren't even armed must have been an opportunity just too sweet to pass up. They probably had no idea that your ship was fully capable of warding off an attack force ten times their size with hardly an effort. As soon as your first salvo slammed into them they hightailed it back to hiding with eleven fewer ships and at least three more that we know of that sustained severe damage."

"As for the ship we towed in, the pilot and copilot were already dead when we cleared them into our cargo hold," Turner said.

"What happened?" Razor asked.

"The shots from our forward guns which disabled the ship also punched a hole through the outer hull," Turner explained. "The hole was too large for their auto-repair unit to patch."

"Exposure to vacuum," Razor offered.

"And a nasty case of suffocation," Turner added. "What about the ship itself?" Buzzer asked.

"Nothing special, a cruiser type, the sporty Sleekster model," Turner explained. "It was outfitted for heavy weapons, just like the others that got away."

"Speaking of which," Commander Malone, the Ruffian's First Officer, said, "the ships that did manage to slip away left us a very easy trail to follow. We now know exactly where they landed."

Dabner Humechy sat up straighter in his high-backed chair at the head of the conference table and nodded in satisfaction. "Now we are getting somewhere," he said. "Where did they land?"

"From the sensor readings aboard the Ruffian we charted them to the far side of Sarkennon- 8," Captain Turner said and saw Humechy's eyes widen in surprise. "Further scans of that planet revealed no surface activity, it seems to be made out of mostly ice and useless rocks, and no activity on sixteen of its seventeen moons. But the fifteenth moon showed some signs of life on its dark side. Nothing more than a small settlement, mind you, but something human in nature where no settlements have been officially logged with the U.E.N. Department of Space Exploration."

"So, Sarkennon-8..." Humechy said in wonder. "I would have never guessed they'd be so close."

"Don't worry, Statesman," Buzzer said. "Things like this happen more often than you realize.

They are right here in your backyard and now we know it."

"Excuse me, Guarder," Garcia said. "But you still haven't answered my question. What further use do you have for the Ruffian?"

Buzzer stared at the large man, looking sharp and crisp in his dress whites. *Obviously a good commander,* thought. *Turner seems like a man who won't settle for anything less than the best.*

How best to answer this question was Buzzer's immediate concern. He was unsure of his plans for the Ruffian at this point. What he really wanted to do was clear in his mind—send the big warship out to Sarkennon-8 and have the FlightCorps handle the problem for once and for all. But five hundred fighters against however many ships these raiders had in their fleet might be more than the Ruffian's forces could handle. Buzzer wrestled with the thought that a decision of that nature could quite possibly doom more than half of the Ruffian's FlightCorpsmen to death. However, it could also turn out to be a one-sided battle, over in mere minutes, with most or all of the pirate ships destroyed.

In all honesty, with the minimum amount of information he had available at the moment, Buzzer couldn't really formulate a decent answer to Garcia's question. "To tell you the truth, Commander," Buzzer said. "I need the Ruffian to continue to orbit Shining until the necessary information can be obtained concerning the size and strength of the pirate forces. Then, if the statistics gathered indicate a high success rate on the part of a Ruffian-based attack against them, I will want your fighters to attack the base our opponent has established on Sarkennon-8's fifteenth moon..."

"Sarsat-15," Humechy offered and Buzzer nodded.

"Other than that, I wouldn't mind it, Captain Turner," Buzzer continued, "if the Ruffian maintained a routine planetary patrol heading for the time being. The very presence of your warship around this planet should serve to more than deter any additional attacks at this time."

"Would it be all right, Guarder, if I made some calls to Aegis and informed my chain of command of the Ruffian's new orders?" Turner asked, seemingly uncomfortable in the heavily cushioned chair usually intended for diplomatic meetings and conferences.

"Feel free to contact whomever you feel should be informed, Captain," Buzzer said and met the man's gaze in a show of support. "Try to remember that we are all in this together. I may be giving the orders at this time but you are the leader of your crew. I need your cooperation on this more than anybody else. Do you understand?"

Turner nodded, a look of satisfaction finally creeping on to his face.

"Good," Buzzer said and then turned to face the rest of the men in the room. "I'll be open to whatever constructive criticism you may have, gentlemen. Believe me, I am fully versed in the strategies of warfare and have a great amount of combat experience, but a FlightCorps battle is something I personally have a minimum of experience in. I need input from all of you on this one. Please bear with me and make sure to bring any concerns or ideas you may have to my attention."

Looking around the conference room, most of the faces stared back at him expressionlessly, in the standard military way. In some of the faces before him, Buzzer could detect the slight hint of anticipation that hit every soldier from lowly grunt to four-star general, whenever a potential combat situation was just around the corner. Of course, Humechy just stared ahead in wonder at the situation his planet had been thrust into. And Razor, Buzzer noticed, had a somewhat confused expression on his face...the kid just didn't possess enough experience to realize the severity of their situation and what would be necessary to see it through.

~*~

"That was some show in there, Frank," Razor said as they stepped out of the lift-car and into the lobby of CharterHouse. "I think Captain Turner finally realized that all of this is more important than his overblown ego."

"I was surprised at how he was carrying on in there," Buzzer said and took in his surroundings. At least fifty men and women were milling around the large room and the police officer manning the information desk was being swamped with questions. "I realize that he thought for a couple of seconds during that skirmish that his ship and crew were in danger up there but after he saw how meager the force opposing his ship actually was, I thought the man's military sense of superiority would kick in and his brain would turn tactical."

"Well, maybe Captain Turner hasn't seen much in the way of combat and he just got spooked," Razor said.

"I don't know, Razor," Buzzer replied. He noticed something out of the corner of his eye. It wasn't much but it was just enough to trigger a tingling in the back of his mind. Two men, near the side entrance, they looked just like everybody else in the lobby. Their clothes were average but the faces seemed out of place. And the dark glasses while indoors only served to make Buzzer more aware of their presence. With a subtle nod of his head, he warned Razor of the potential for danger in their present situation. A return nod was all the answer that Buzzer needed.

But instead of an attack response, Buzzer opted for luring the two strangers to a quieter and less crowded location, away from any innocent bystanders who might get caught in crossfire. Then they could get down to business.

The two Guarders exited the building and continued their hurried walk, talking all the while, playing the role of oblivious officials to a tee. After several blocks, and a series of additional body language signals between the two of them, both Guarders had relayed all that their casual backward glancing could glean from the pair of unwanted followers some thirty meters behind.

All in all, both men were armed, at least one blaster was tucked under each suit jacket. They could also expect various knives and several smaller, more physical weapons designed for up- close combat to be scattered throughout the clothing of both men.

"Some heavy artillery for a couple of guys just out for a stroll," Buzzer whispered and Razor nodded slightly as they casually turned a sharp right down a small alley. Razor had remembered the place from his earlier drive over to CharterHouse and knew that it was well out of the way of the usual crowds in case things went badly.

Once out of the sight of their pursuit, Buzzer and Razor burst into action. Two of Buzzer's three concealed weapons filled his right and left hands as he climbed cat-like up the small metal ladder lining one of the walls in the alley, probably attached to a warehouse of some sort. Razor quickly buried himself behind three large garbage barrels and the chute leading to them from the second floor of another building across the alley, his blaster primed and ready. Buzzer was nicely hidden behind a sharp angle in the wall. Holding on tightly to the rusted ladder while also keeping a firm grip on both of his blasters was proving to be quite a task. But the annoying pain in his fingertips, wrists and forearms disappeared as the two men rushed into the alley with guns drawn.

Both men stopped and looked around the alley in confusion; neither had yet noticed Buzzer on his perch about one story up.

"Shit..." Razor heard the one nearest him mutter as the man stamped his foot down on the trash-covered ground of the alley in frustration.

"I know they didn't just vanish, Karl," the other man said. "Where in the hell did they get to?

Maybe in through that door over there?"

"Damned if I know, Rooney," the first man said and holstered his weapon.

Good, Buzzer thought to himself, *that's one down...*

"Jesus Christ, they were such an easy tail until this damn alley!" The one named Karl snarled and kicked a piece of trash against a nearby wall.

"No, it wasn't this door," Rooney grunted as he pulled and twisted on a rusty old cargo door. "Maybe that one," he said, indicating another door across the alley.

"Just shut up and put away your blaster, Rooney," Karl said. "Anyone sees you with that thing out and they'll raise an alarm for sure."

"Calm down, Karl," Rooney muttered and slipped his weapon underneath his jacket. From the side of the wall Buzzer took aim on the more dangerous looking of the two, the one named Karl, but hesitated as the man whirled to face his partner.

"Dammit, you can calm down if you want to, asshole," Karl spat. "But in case you haven't figured it out yet we're going to get shit-canned because of this! Jacob Dukes doesn't take kindly to screw-ups," Karl lashed out at a nearby trash container with a well-placed kick and sent it flying across the alley. The metal container banged against the far wall and Razor suddenly found himself exposed. Buzzer saw the eyes of both men go wide in surprise. Then all hell broke loose.

Buzzer leapt from his perch and caught Rooney on the shoulders with a vicious kick, the impact knocking him into Karl, and both men went down hard to the alley floor. Karl tried to pull his blaster free but Razor was up and running, hitting the man in full stride and knocking him into the wall behind. Razor used his momentum to hit the man again hard with his shoulder. The impact knocked the air out of Karl's lungs and sent him flying further along the alley.

Buzzer was on top of Rooney within barely two seconds of the thug's hitting the filthy ground. He delivered a few quick jabs to the man's ribs, a vicious kick to his abdomen and a strong chop to the neck, rendering him unconscious. Razor, on the other hand, wasn't out of trouble yet with his man

Karl, short on breath and looking rather beaten, now stood about four meters from both Guarders. He reached into his jacket and pulled out what looked like several small marbles. Buzzer looked up from the unmoving Rooney and recognized the mini-grenades in Karl's right hand. His finely tuned survival instinct took over. Grabbing hold of the large Rooney, he forced the unconscious form to a semi-standing position and covered the distance between himself and Razor in two huge strides. Razor sent two blaster bolts flying into Karl's stocky chest. As blood and gore splashed against the walls of the alley, Karl's hands went limp and sent the now armed explosives scattering to the ground.

Buzzer slammed into Razor and they landed heavily in the trash heap left over from Karl's initial kick, the dead weight of Rooney landing hard on their backs. As Buzzer covered his ears and opened his mouth to lessen the concussion of the coming blast he looked up to see Razor do the same. Across the alley, on his knees and barely alive, Karl's face contorted with fear and anger as he realized he would live just long enough to be blown apart by the small grenades scattered on the ground around him.

Knowing that at least four seconds had passed since Karl had armed the marbles, Buzzer lowered his face deep into the trash and hoped that they were far enough away to survive the impending fireball the alley would soon become.

The explosion ripped through the small space, tearing both rusty doors to the buildings on either side off their hinges and flinging them against their opposite walls. One of the trash cans hit Buzzer flush in the lower ribs; the pain lanced white behind his closed eyelids but he kept his face buried. He could feel the skin on his exposed arms and hands start to burn as the short burst of flame washed over them. His hair smelled of singeing and for a brief moment he worried that his clothes had caught on fire. Once the silence came and the intense heat had passed he immediately opened his eyes to look for signs of fire. Luckily, their clothes were not burning but there were several small patches of flame on the tattered remnants of Rooney's suit jacket. The big man was still breathing but his back had been badly burned.

Karl was a different story. The man had been nearly cut in half by the explosion, his upper- torso burned to a crisp in the burst of flame that had followed. All four of his appendages had been ripped from his body and a bloody stream of cooked entrails was scattered around what was left of his corpse. Hopefully, for Karl's sake, he had been dead before the blast had ripped into him. Otherwise...Buzzer shuddered to think about meeting that particular demise.

A blackened hand peeking out of torn cloth still smoldered on the ground at the front of the alley. Buzzer coughed twice as he stood and helped Razor to his shaky feet. The sirens he had been hearing since the explosions finally arrived as two police cruisers turned the corner and came to a screeching halt at the alley's entrance. Buzzer flashed his Guarder ID at the two shocked officers and made his way over to one of the cars.

"You all right, sir?" one of the officers asked. Buzzer just waved him away.

Razor appeared beside him as the two policemen quickly covered Karl's corpse with a white blanket. Rooney stirred on the ground and groaned in pain as his newly wakened senses took stock of his injuries and noticed the burning in his back and hands.

"Get a medic for that one and take him to the infirmary at CharterHouse immediately," Buzzer barked, and an officer ran to the other cruiser to call in a request for a medical response. "Cordon off this area," Buzzer said to the other officer. "I don't want anyone but those under my direct authorization to investigate this alleyway, understood?"

"Yes, sir," the policeman said from the other cruiser as he grabbed a handful of crime-scene tape from a compartment in the vehicle's side.

Buzzer looked up at Razor and rubbed the grit and dirt from his eyes. "How do you feel, partner?"

"Like hell," Razor rasped. "How about you?"

"Same," Buzzer laughed and spat several times on to the asphalt of the street. "My mouth tastes like I swallowed garbage back there."

"I think I actually did," Razor said and wiped his hands across the front of his shirt. "Officers," Buzzer called, and one of the men looked up. "I need to get the information regarding this attack to Statesman Humechy at CharterHouse as soon as possible. I will need to borrow this cruiser in order to accomplish that." The officer was about to protest when he realized that it was Guarders he was dealing with. Instead, with a fearful look on his face, he nodded his understanding and passed a worried glance to his partner.

Buzzer turned to look at Razor. "Get in. I think we need some medical attention ourselves."

Razor nodded and slumped into the passenger compartment of the police cruiser. Buzzer tested the accelerator and maneuvered the vehicle into the street.

"Wake me when we get there, Buzz," Razor said and closed his eyes.

"Don't get all sleepy on me just yet, Razor," Buzzer snapped. "I have the feeling that the fun is just beginning."

United Earthian Nations
SouthWestern Corporate Grid-Sector
Sarkennon System

Shining Mission—Day Two

When the Kingdom of Saudi Arabia fiercely resisted the swarming hardline Communist-controlled troops of the Red Union in 2026, the horrific offshoot of the former Soviet Union responded by bombarding the region with several nuclear missiles. The resulting Holocaust left millions dead throughout the Middle East and laid waste to most of Saudi Arabia, Egypt, Ethiopia, Jordan and The Sudan. This single act of unbridled terror sent shockwaves flowing around the world. The United Nations was up in arms at what it termed "the greatest crime against humanity the world has ever seen" and moved quickly to condemn the outrageous actions of the Red Union as proof of the insanity of Communism. As the United States and its allies prepared their massive military forces for an attack on Moscow, the very heart of the Communist regime, the Red Union continued its push for worldwide domination with an invasion of the African Continent. Never before in the history of mankind had global warfare seemed so imminent. Of course, that would change in time...

*(Excerpt:A History of Modern Earth and Beyond—the People, the Politics andthe Insanity of Our Past*by Joseph Mullens)

CHAPTER THREE

A sharp knock on the door snapped Sampson out of his thoughts and he slowly sat up on the small bed. "Frazier?" He heard from the other side of the door. "May I come in?"

"Yes, Gil," Sampson sighed, relieved that it wasn't one of his annoying Outer-Wing Commanders come back to brief him on their latest raid. Thornberg silently let himself into Sampson's chambers as the leader of the pirate band slumped back down on to the bed.

"Get up, Frazier, it's a new day," Thornberg laughed and sat down hard on the edge of the bed. "It's not like you to sleep in this late, old boy."

"Lay off, Gilfred," Sampson groaned. "I'm much too shaken up over last night for your tedious remarks."

"Sorry, Frazier," Thornberg said and let the seriousness of the last day's events flood back into his mind. "I know how hard it was for you to do what had to be done last night. They were fools, the entire lot of them, of that there is no doubt. But the fact that they cost this fleet so many important vessels, the fastest ships we have… I stood behind your decision if that makes you feel better."

"It does not," Sampson answered sharply. "Thank you for the attempt at lightening my mood, Gilfred, but I've been trying to justify what I did last night to myself ever since it happened. I know that an example had to be set before something like this ever happened again, believe me. That little stunt of theirs could have led that carrier right to this dust rock and that would have been disastrous to us all. But, did my actions have to be so final? I looked Ernest right in the eyes as I blew him away. I don't really think I was aware of what was happening in reality until I saw the little fellow die. I mean, you were there, Gil, you saw it...the whole thing was so terrible. I know I've killed before but that was the worst thing I've ever done. Some of them I've known for a very long time, some have stuck by me since I started this outfit. Now they are gone,

Gilfred, forever. And by my hand. Even though it had to be done for the good of the entire group, I just don't know if I can deal with what I did yesterday."

Thornberg leaned over and looked his friend in the eye long and hard for several moments while both men maintained the silence. "Frazier Sampson," he began. "A man responsible for the deaths of thousands of men and women throughout this quadrant. A man who I have known to be ruthless at times, cunning and even savage when warranted. But, my good man, I do believe you are getting somewhat soft in your old age."

Sampson was taken aback by the cold seriousness on his Second's face. What he had first taken for a joke was now apparently nothing of the sort. With a hot fury that threatened to boil over and explode from within he raised his finger towards Thornberg's face and screamed, "Who are you to be talking of softness, Gilfred Thornberg? If it weren't for me you would be the fossil of some long forgotten skeleton in a back alley of Cumuani, picked clean and dry by the scavengers who you couldn't compete with. Remember this, I preserved your dismal life once already and it is totally within my powers to reverse that decision at any given moment. Do you understand me?"

Thornberg raised an eyebrow at the sudden outburst and leaned back slightly. "Yes, I understand, Frazier," he said and grinned mischievously. "Now that's the Frazier Sampson who leads this group with an iron fist. I was just testing you for yourself. You've done far worse in your life than what was done yesterday and you're quite ready to do worse in the future to any and all who would stand in your way. Listen to me, Frazier, it may have been devout followers of yours, people who have stuck by you in the past, who were shot to bits last night but, in terms of expressing your power of leadership to this group of thousands, it was the best thing you could have done. No matter how horrible a thing it may be to say, Frazier, it was the largest morale booster this lowly band of miscreants has had since you began your organization. Maybe you should have small groups of your most devout followers killed more often, present company excluded, of course."

Frazier felt the rage within him subside as Thornberg was speaking. *A test*, he laughed to himself. Leave it to his Second to provide him with a test. "Are you quite finished with this?"

"Yes," Thornberg said. "As finished as I can be."

"Good," Sampson said and fixed Thornberg with a glare. "Then why you don't you tell me what you came here to tell me?"

"Right. Sorry, Frazier," Thornberg said and stood again. "Yesterday our top man on Shining, Dukes, put a tail on the two men who were responsible for the carrier being there."

"Which team did he assign?" Sampson asked. "Shining Team Twenty-Seven," Thornberg replied.

Sampson took several seconds to allow the faces to fall into place in his memory then nodded, "Big man named Rooney and that trigger-happy Karl something or other?"

"Yes, not one of his best teams but more than experienced enough to perform a simple tail," Thornberg said. "It seems that they were in the process of trailing the two so-called visiting officials when the trouble started. One was killed and the other captured by CharterCity Police. The captured one is awaiting an interrogation session later on this morning."

"Which one got captured?" Sampson asked.

"Rooney," Thornberg said and looked down at the message containing the information. "It's been reported that he suffered major injuries during the encounter and underwent immediate medical treatment prior to being transferred to the Police HQ."

"Do we have anyone close enough in the building to where he's being held who can silence this Rooney?"

Thornberg considered that for less than a moment before replying, "Yes, several. In fact, I have someone who can be briefed immediately and who is in position as we speak. Your confirmation will get it underway."

"Give him my go ahead," Sampson said, still lying flat on his back on the bed.

"Very well," Thornberg said. "And there's one other thing, Frazier. It seems that Dukes tried the same thing once before on one of the visiting officials earlier yesterday and the results were the same—one dead and one captured."

"Well, well, well, our man Dukes has been quite busy lately, hasn't he?" Sampson said, his eyes narrowing in anger at the two failed missions. "Send him a message immediately ordering him to stop these foolish tails at once. Obviously, he is choosing the wrong personnel for such tasks. Besides, I'd like to see what else these visitors have up their sleeves, especially if they are powerful enough to order a FlightForce Carrier off its regular mission schedule."

"Done, Frazier," Thornberg said. "Should both of our captured men be silenced or just Rooney?"

"Both," Sampson grunted and closed his eyes.

"Yes, Frazier," Thornberg said and silently let himself out of Sampson's chambers.

Once Sampson was certain that Thornberg was gone he got up from the bed and stretched his aching muscles. Faintly, he could hear the shower going in the other room, and memories of Francesca and the night before stirred within him. Smiling, he dropped his robe and headed for the shower.

~*~

"Did you say dead?" Buzzer said to the sergeant on duty at the front desk of the CharterCity Police Headquarters. "What do you mean, dead? How could this happen?"

"I'm not sure, sir," the young officer stammered. "I was told that early this morning both men had died of complications resulting from food poisoning."

"Food poisoning!" Buzzer growled. "Where is your supervisor?"

"Standing right here, smart mouth," came a reply from several meters away. "And just who in the hell do you think you are, Mister..."

Buzzer crossed the room in several brisk strides and lunged at the man before Razor had time to blink. One quick move had twisted the Police Chief's arm behind his back and brought him to his knees.

The entire room full of CharterCity police officers began going for their weapons. Razor couldn't believe what was happening. He quickly unholstered two of his blasters and saw Buzzer bring out one of his own. "We're U.E.N. Guarders, Goddammit!" Buzzer roared throughout the large room. "Hold your fire!" Buzzer released his hold on the Police Chief and he flashed his Guarder ID first to the crowd and then to the man still on his knees.

"It's all right, it's all right," the Chief of Police said as he struggled back to his feet. Razor had seen the older man's eyes go wide upon first catching sight of the Guarder ID. "Put your frigging guns away right now."

Slowly and with a room full of nervous murmurs, the thirty or so policemen began to holster their blasters and half-chargers and back down.

Buzzer pierced the Police Chief with a steely glare and allowed the man to see the anger behind his eyes. "My colleague and I have traveled long and far to come to this dismal planet and help you people put your piracy troubles to rest. The first break we've had so far on this investigation was the capture of those two prisoners who, I have just been informed, died in your custody very recently. Do you mean to tell me that two brand new prisoners were killed in this building by the food that you served them?"

"Yes, sir, Guarder," the chief said and tried to stand a little taller.

"I will tend to think that some sort of conspiracy is going on here if a decent explanation and some cooperation isn't offered up very quickly," Buzzer said. "Do I make myself clear?"

"Absolutely."

Buzzer took a deep breath to try and calm his racing heart. He couldn't believe that both prisoners were dead and he was past being certain that some crooked cops had played a part in that. "In your office, now."

Buzzer gave the man a gentle shove, light enough not to seem aggressive but strong enough to make him begin walking toward his office. Razor caught up and followed both men into the room, closing the door behind him. Inside the silence lingered for several minutes. Razor could see the chief of the CharterCity Police Department sweating profusely while Buzzer just sat there and looked at the man.

"So, why don't you tell us exactly what happened, Chief," Razor suggested and Buzzer's eyes flickered toward him for just a second before returning to rest on those of the older man.

"The name's Chief Parker, for the record," he said and cleared his throat loudly. "I know how this must look but, believe me, this kind of thing happens sometimes. Especially in this kind of environment. We deal with such scum in CharterCity, what with the raiders and pirates everywhere you turn, that our service for them isn't all that good once they land in our holding pens." Parker paused then, waiting for some type of reaction but did not receive any. "Come on," he continued. "The prisoners who come here have usually fired on and wounded if not killed one of my men. Do you expect me to treat a piece of shit like that with respect or even common decency? If most of these prisoners die while they're in my holding pens I say thank God for that. That's one less piece of scum we have to deal with at a later date. Now, I know that these two particular prisoners meant a lot to your investigation, information-wise, but it's not my fault if maybe the food they were given last night was rotten. Can you understand what I'm trying to say? I know that more care should have been taken to ensure that those two were kept in good shape but when my men checked on them this morning they were both stiff and cold. The autopsies were performed immediately thereafter and that's when we found the poisoning."

"Can I speak with the officer who found them?" Buzzer asked.

"Now, listen here, Guarder," Parker said. "I don't care who you are, no one accuses one of my men of..."

"Chief Parker!" Buzzer barked, pounding his fist down on the Police Chief's desk and shaking the entire room. "I want some Goddamn cooperation around here or else I'll have you in that holding pen for insubordination! Do you hear me?"

"Yes, sir," Parker sighed and sat back in his chair.

"Call him in then," Buzzer ordered, and Parker tried to steady his shaking hands. "Right away, Guarder."

~*~

The police cruiser eased into the underground parking garage of CharterHouse. The entire trip had been spent in almost total silence. Razor could feel the tension radiating from Buzzer in waves. It wasn't so much nervousness as frustration and rage that were eating away at his partner.

As Buzzer backed the vehicle into the nearest vacant spot and deactivated the machine, Razor couldn't help himself and let loose a small laugh.

Buzzer looked at him with all seriousness and asked, "What's so damn funny?"

"You," Razor said and laughed again. "You just took on half of the CharterCity Police Department with only me for backup. All that bullshit I'd heard about you...it's not bullshit after all, Buzzer."

"And that's funny?"

"Yeah, when you think about it," Razor managed. "You must be crazier than they say you are to pull off what you just did back at Police HQ."

"So, I'm crazy," Buzzer said. "That's no news to me."

"Well, did you even take into consideration that, if things had gone down badly in there, they would have taken me out along with you?" Razor asked, more serious now.

Buzzer's eyes seemed to widen for a brief instant as he realized what Razor was trying to tell him. He opened the driver's side door and climbed out, leaving Razor alone in the vehicle.

Razor leaned over, grabbed the key from the vehicle's activator and got out of the cruiser.

Buzzer was long gone but he guessed at his partner's most likely destination within CharterHouse. In less than a minute, the lift-car doors opened on to the upper-level lobby and he could see Buzzer and Statesman Humechy standing in a corridor, just meters away.

"Excuse me, Statesman," Buzzer said and grabbed Razor lightly by the elbow, motioning him aside. Several seconds of silence passed before Buzzer looked up. "I'm sorry, John. I don't know what got into me in that police station. I guess I'm just used to working alone these days. I never took into consideration that you were in danger—I was focused only on that idiot Parker. It was one of the more careless things I have done in my career as a Guarder. The only life that I usually place in any type of jeopardy is my own. Perhaps, taking this for what it really says about the way I operate, I may have to rethink my position in the ranks. With mistakes like the one I just made today, it might be better for all concerned if I ended my career."

"Hold on a minute, Frank," Razor said and took a deep breath. "I just wanted to point out to you exactly how ridiculous it is to take on a whole room full of armed men with nothing more than a rookie as backup...but I didn't say that Parker didn't have that coming. Those jackasses didn't know what they were getting into when they let those two prisoners die and I doubt that anyone other than a Guarder could have pulled off a stunt like you did without getting fried.

Let's make one thing clear, those two prisoners were our ticket to some useful information and because of some stiffs with badges who could care less for anything but themselves, we are back to square one. I was with you in there, my blasters were clear and ready right along with yours."

"I know, Razor, you would have followed my lead in there even knowing the odds were stacked against us and I appreciate that," Buzzer said. "But when all is said and done, I still acted prematurely back there and with little or no concern for your safety. I sometimes forget just how deadly some situations can become when I get them started in that direction. Please accept my apology and my word that I will not let it happen again during the remainder of this mission."

"Sounds good to me, Buzzer," Razor said. "As long as you stop talking about a possible retirement."

Buzzer continued to look into Razor's eyes for several seconds after that and nodded once before turning back toward Humechy. "Statesman, I have reason to believe that one or more employees currently working within this facility are acting in a traitorous manner toward Shining."

Humechy frowned and looked from Buzzer to Razor, "What exactly do you mean?" "Sometime during the night, the two prisoners that I left in the care of the Infirmary here in

CharterHouse were killed by food poisoning in the CharterCity Police Headquarters prison facility," Buzzer explained. "Now, how they managed to get transferred out of this building when I left explicit orders for them to remain here under guard is beyond me. But I will let that pass for the moment. What really bothers me is the fact that these two invaluable prisoners were apparently murdered in the care of the police forces."

"Well, I don't see how that could be, Guarder." Humechy looked genuinely surprised at this latest bit of news. "Everyone in my employ here at CharterHouse has been very keenly scrutinized by the planetary authorities, full security checks, historical profiles, the whole bit."

"Did you know that Chief Parker could care less if the prisoners he keeps in the police prison facility die while in custody there? In fact, he even said that he would prefer it," Buzzer lifted a hand to stop the interruption that he could see coming to life on Humechy's lips. "If you would like to hear it, Statesman, it was recorded by my sequencer not half-an-hour ago."

"It was recorded?" Humechy asked incredulously.

"Yes, Statesman, by this little device I use as a com-link with Aegis, the Guarder HQ and the other members of my squadron," Buzzer said. "It also serves as a message recorder and transmitter when I so desire. It is a rather sophisticated little device and its capabilities go beyond what I have explained to you thus far but I assure you that the recording is accurate. Would you like to hear Parker's exact words?"

"No, no, that's quite all right," Humechy said and glanced nervously around at the people milling about his outer offices. "Let's take this into my office where it will be somewhat more private."

"Of course, Statesman," Buzzer said and the three men crossed the lobby to Humechy's office.

Humechy slumped down in the plush chair behind his desk and the two Guarders remained standing. "What would you have me do in this case, Guarder?" Humechy asked, directing the question towards Buzzer.

"Well, for starters, I would very much like to bring Chief Parker up on charges of treason and murder."

"Murder!" Humechy stated, clearly astonished by the mention of such a harsh charge.

"Yes, sir," Buzzer said. "If this man admits to no worries whenever a prisoner in his custody should die overnight then what do you think he feels about law enforcement in general?

Obviously he despises all of the murdering and pirating that has been plaguing Shining the past several e-years but I wouldn't put it past the man to have struck some kind of deal with this filth at one time or another. He may actually be under a direct threat of blackmail or some other such pressure. If that is the case, then Chief Parker would have been nothing more than a pawn for the pirate bands all this while. That would also explain the deaths of those two prisoners last night. Prisoners who were in his custody. Prisoners who could not have been transferred from the CharterHouse Infirmary to his prison facility without his express orders."

"That most certainly does make sense, Guarder," Humechy said. "But I have known Chief Parker for a very long time and, frankly, I find it hard to believe that he could be involved in this business."

"Well, he may have been an essentially good man at one time, Statesman," Razor offered. "But pirates have a way of dealing with people that profits nobody but themselves in the long run, although the profits promised to those they seduce often look too good to be true, once offered."

"Of course, I see your point," Humechy said and stopped. "Ah, now that you bring up these filthy pirates you have reminded me. Earlier today, the Ruffian left orbit without any warning."

"Left orbit?" Buzzer snapped. "Did Captain Turner give the order?"

"As far as I can tell," Humechy said. "The CharterCity Starport received the Ruffian's transmission and cleared them for departing Shining near-space on a heading toward Sarsat-15. Their communications officer relayed that the pirate band was to be eliminated so that the Ruffian could get back to her regular mission."

Buzzer paced around the room and shook his head in amazement. "I can't believe this," he muttered. "Doesn't Turner know that the forces waiting for him on that moon may be more than his fighters can handle?"

"It seems that Captain Turner has confidence in his forces," Humechy offered in a soothing tone. "Perhaps he will be successful in doing what you two originally came here to do."

Buzzer fixed Humechy with an angry glare at that last remark and approached the desk. "Is there a ship in Spacedock or the CharterCity Starport right now that has speed capabilities greater than those of a FlightForce Carrier, Statesman?"

"None that I know of, either private or commercial. Sorry," Humechy replied.

"Dammit, you knew about this," Buzzer said, pointing at Humechy. His right hand twitched near his hip holster, wanting to feel the weight of his blaster, but now wasn't the time.

Humechy sighed with relief and leaned back in his chair. "Are we through here, Guarders?" "Not at all," Buzzer rasped and walked over to the large view window that dominated

Humechy's office. "Parker will be charged with both murder and treason. If he decides to spill what he knows and happens to implicate you in the process, we will be back, Statesman. Of that you can rest assured."

Humechy tried to press himself as far back into the cushion of the chair as his frail body would allow as he felt every nerve ending within him fire with nervous tension. He had seen the large man's right hand twitch and almost pull out the black menacing weapon strapped to his right hip. He couldn't wait for the two mysterious men to leave his office and he found himself hoping that, maybe, some horrible thing might happen to them and they would both be out of his life.

Buzzer approached Humechy and, once again, pointed an accusing finger at the man. "Hope for your sake that Parker doesn't tell me that you are involved in this, Statesman Humechy," Buzzer whispered. "Hope for your sake."

Razor watched the terror in the small Statesman's eyes slowly subside as Buzzer crossed the room and walked through the doors into the lobby. He raised one eyebrow at Humechy and allowed a smile to cross his lips as he turned to follow his partner.

Once in the lift-car, Razor turned to Buzzer and said, "All we can do now is wait, Frank. If Turner's ship gets wasted out there it won't be because of anything we did, it'll be because Turner's an idiot."

"I'll bet on the latter," Buzzer said. "How can a career military man go ahead and do something like this when he knows the stakes and the risks he's taking with his crew?"

Razor had no answer for that and quickly changed the subject. "Let's go back to the Police HQ and take Parker into custody."

"My thoughts exactly," Buzzer offered as the lift-car reached the garage-level of CharterHouse and the doors slid aside. "Maybe we can swing back by here afterwards and pick up the doctor who was on duty last night. I'm very interested in how my authority was ignored for that of Parker's when I left strict orders with the Infirmary. But Parker comes first."

~*~

"Frazier!" Thornberg called from the hallway outside Sampson's chambers. "We have readings on our long range scanner. Hurry to Control, I've got to get back."

Sampson roused himself quickly from a deep sleep and was dressed in less than a minute. He left Francesca lying there in the bed, a worried look on her face, as he stormed into the outer hallway and made his way to Control.

The Control Center was an explosion of activity when he entered the room. People were running from console to console, trying to relay as much information as they could. He located Thornberg immediately and was by his side a scant few moments later. "What in the hell is going on, Gilfred? It looks like war preparation."

"And that's exactly what it is, Frazier," Thornberg replied as he studied the scanners with intensity. "Look there," he said and pointed toward the upper half of the monitor where a series of dots littered the view. "It seems that carrier has arrived to pay us a little visit, and its fighters are already scrambled so they won't be wasting any time once the battle begins."

"There really aren't as many of them as I thought there would be," Sampson muttered and turned to look around the room. "How many pilots do we have on ready status at this very instant?"

"More than three quarters of our entire fleet," Thornberg said.

"Good! Have them off this rock and in stable orbits within ten minutes," Sampson decided. "I want them on the dark side when the carrier comes into precise scanner range. The other quarter of our strength, why isn't it ready?"

"Little problems here and there, Frazier," Thornberg said while adjusting dials and scribbling readings on a small white pad. "We've got some pilots sick, some injured from past raids, some who can't be located and also some damaged ships. There are still others who are off Sarsat-15 and on other planets arranging deals and shipping schedules. But we do have enough fighting strength and surprise in numbers to deal with this carrier...but just this one."

"Meaning?"

"Meaning that, if any back-up were to arrive while the battle was under way, we could very well be beaten and miserably at that," Thornberg said, facing his commander.

"Well, we'll just have to take our chances then, won't we?" Sampson said with a wicked grin and took a step back to gaze at the excitement running loose in his Control Center.

"Yes, Frazier," Thornberg said. "And some good chances they are."

"I agree. Let's get our battle leaders in conference, I want to get our attack strategy planned out," Sampson began as he turned from Thornberg and began heading for the exit. "We'll need what's left of our Sleeksters to ward off the first few minutes of the fighter attack. That'll give us maybe enough time to ensure that the encampment is out of danger. If we can sweep our forces around from all four sides of this rock simultaneously I think they'll be in for a rude surprise."

"My God," Thornberg said as realization swept over him. "I haven't seen that attack plan in...it might just work, Frazier."

"It just might, Gil," Sampson said with a gleam in his eye. "Ready for a little fun?" Thornberg's smile disappeared and was replaced by a look of caution.

"This is a FlightForce Carrier we are facing, Frazier, we don't really know all that it is capable of. I don't even have a schematic to work with on this type of craft. How do we go about destroying such a behemoth?"

"Your guess is as good as mine, Gil," Sampson said as he reached the doorway. "Remember, meeting in my chambers as soon as possible and I want all of our available ships in space within ten minutes. And start jamming that carrier's long and short-range scanners."

"I'm on it, Frazier," Thornberg said.

"Good, I'll be in the hangar checking out my ship."

"Frazier," Thornberg called, and Sampson stopped to look back at him. "Certainly you aren't intending to serve in this battle yourself?"

"Of course I am, Gil, and you are welcome to join me as my Helmsman while I man the battle stations."

"I would be honored, Frazier," Thornberg said. "But please keep in mind that this motley group will stand no chance in hell of regrouping and winning this fracas if your ship is destroyed during the battle."

"I am fully aware of the ramifications, Gil," Frazier said. "But I have no intentions of dying during this upcoming battle and I will take every necessary precaution to achieve that end. I hope that you will as well."

"Of course…"

"Very well, then," Sampson said and fairly ran through the doors. "In my chambers in ten minutes."

~*~

"The moon seems dormant, Captain Turner," Malone said from a console across the bridge. "But we are experiencing sporadic scanner jamming, both short and long range."

"Standard U.E.N. FlightForce procedure," Turner mumbled. "Keep our fighters on full alert status and work on bypassing their jamming methods. I want those scanners back ASAP."

"Yes, sir."

"Captain," Hansen called from the communications station. "Commander Garcia is on com- link for you, sir."

"Patch him through to my command chair."

"Yes, sir, patching." The line crackled to life and then cleared as internal sensors continually upgraded any disturbances within the link. "Captain Turner?"

"Turner here, Commander, how do things look from out there?"

"Pretty dark, sir," came the response. "I show no abnormal readings except for standard jamming tactics on our scanners."

"We get the same here," Turner said. "How are the tractor beams holding up?"

"The ride was bumpy at first but it's fine now, Captain," Garcia answered. "I have to admit, I was skeptical of a tractor for this many fighters for so long at such speeds but you were correct, sir. The ship seems able to handle it."

"Just be ready for it when we disengage you," Turner said. "Once this battle begins, the Ruffian will need all the systems power she can muster. You and your FlightCorpsmen will be on your own out there."

"Understood, sir. My men will be ready."

"Great, Avril, let's go in there and clean up for those Guarders."

"If there proves to be anything to actually clean up, sir," Garcia commented.

"Oh, don't you worry, Commander," Turner said. "They're out here somewhere, just lying in wait, trying to draw us into some kind of a disadvantage. As we get closer, they will show themselves. Of that, I have no doubt."

"Yeah, I get the feeling that they're out here as well," Garcia said. "Just like flying into a trap, Captain."

"A trap it very well may be, Commander," Turner laughed. "But does the hunter know who hunts him and what horrors he may catch?"

"Let's hope not, Captain."

"Right…stay alert out there, Commander," Turner said and broke the com-link.

~*~

Buzzer walked through the doors to the CharterCity Police HQ and was met by eerie silence. The offices were all deserted and dark, all lights had been turned off. An alarm began to ring in Buzzer's mind just as Razor walked in behind him.

"Weird," he whispered, and Buzzer nodded his agreement. "I don't like this one bit, Frank." "You and me both, partner," Buzzer said and pulled his blaster out of his right hip-holster.

"Let's be ready, the tension in here is thicker than the morning fog on Aegis."

Razor grinned at that and pulled out his weapon also. "Hello!" Buzzer called and the sound seemed to echo off the plexisteel walls. "Anyone on duty, please answer."

The two Guarders waited several seconds as silence governed the room. "There's nobody home, Buzzer."

"Don't be so sure," Buzzer said and headed for Chief Parker's office. The door was locked but a little shoulder muscle changed that. Buzzer ducked into the office and ducked back out within seconds. "Nothing."

"What do you say we leave this lion's den?" Razor suggested and started for the front doors. Buzzer took one last look around and stopped. "Wait," he whispered to Razor, and the

Guarder froze in his tracks. Buzzer motioned for the younger man to take up position behind the open door leading to the prison facility. With a show of fingers, Buzzer counted down from four to one and then dove through the door.

The hallway erupted with explosions. Blast after blast tore into the thick-layered doors, reducing them to smoking ruins. "Stay low! Stay low!" Buzzer yelled over the ear-splitting roar of blasters and chargers, hoping that his partner still possessed the ability to hear. Stashing his blaster hastily into his jacket, Buzzer unslung the half-charger strapped to his back and zeroed in on one of the two targets he had spotted as he rolled across the floor. Three bolts of return fire flew from Razor's position and Buzzer felt a wave of relief.

A lull in the barrage of enemy fire came for just one instant, a moment that Buzzer used to his advantage. Getting up on one knee, he pinpointed both of his earlier targets and popped off two shots. More fire exploded around the desk he was using for cover as he ducked back down. Both charges scored true, the faces of both attackers disappearing as their heads exploded against the wall at their backs. The sound of fresh blood smacking on the hard surface of the wall brought back bitter memories, images Buzzer would rather forget.

Razor got off a couple of quick shots from the other side of the doorway and the scream that ensued proved the shot's accuracy. "Frank!" Razor called and Buzzer answered with a grunt. "There's only two more that I can see!"

"Yeah," Buzzer answered and pulled out the blaster again. "But there isn't much left of my cover."

"I see what you mean," Razor said and delivered another barrage of fire toward the prison facility. Buzzer took the opportunity and zeroed in on the nearest remaining target. One shot was all he needed, the blast smacking into the intended chest and playing havoc with the vital organs inside. Buzzer caught a glimpse of a police uniform as the body slumped down and an already dead finger pressed the trigger on a charger. The roof overhead along with a grouping of heavy steel bars and cement blocks crashed down on the dead man just as the charger's battery ran dry.

Suddenly silence prevailed over the Police Headquarters complex. Buzzer kept both his blaster and half-charger in his hands as nothing happened for the next few minutes. "Razor," he called.

"Yeah, Buzzer," came a tired sounding reply. "I'm here."

"In one piece, I hope," Buzzer said, coughing the dust raised by so many weapons blasts out of his lungs. Razor snuck a peek around the corner of the battered door frame and sighed as the coast finally looked clear. Four men were dead at the end of the hall, lying in pools of their own gore.

"Looks clear," Razor said.

"Let's not be so quick to assume, partner," Buzzer quipped and sat up a little straighter. "I remember seeing five of them but I only count four on the floor."

"I don't think one of them was Parker," Razor said.

"Me neither, but I don't want to be waiting around here when the rest of the police force comes home."

"Good point," Razor said and stepped out from behind the doors to the prison facility.

"Wait!" Buzzer shouted and ducked back down. Razor dove for the same cover that his partner had been using and Buzzer now found his hiding spot a little crowded.

"What was it, Frank?"

"I don't know, I just heard something."

"Jesus Christ, Buzzer," Razor said and snuck a peek around the shattered desk. "You scared the living crap out of me, standing out there in the open like that."

"Didn't mean to give you a heads-up in case something was actually there," Buzzer returned sarcastically.

"Yeah, but..."

"Shhh!" Buzzer commanded, his face suddenly turning serious. "There it is again."

"I heard it this time, too,' Razor agreed. "It almost sounded like..." Razor paused and looked at Buzzer with worry.

"That's what it sounded like to me also," Buzzer said, reading the concern in his partner's face. "And if those sounds really are grenades then whoever's in there now has two of them, both armed."

"What do you say we walk on out of here?"

"I say run sounds better," Buzzer said and motioned for the door. "Once I stand up, you run hard for the front door and don't stop to open them. I'll be tight on your ass and firing all the way."

"You got it, Frank."

"And remember, Razor, be alert once you hit the street," Buzzer warned. "We won't know what's waiting for us out there until we get..."

Just then someone let out what sounded distinctly like a war cry and thundered into the hallway, a live grenade in each hand. Buzzer slapped the younger Guarder into motion just as the cop in dress blues drew back both arms to launch the explosives at the two fleeing Guarders.

Buzzer aimed his half-charger and snapped off two well-placed shots at the approaching figure. Both charges slammed home, smashing through shoulders and neck, severing the head and both arms. The legs took the body another four steps before collapsing to the floor, the head and arms falling where the body had been a brief instant earlier.

Counting off the seconds since the grenades had hit the floor, Buzzer knew that they had been activated and that three seconds had already passed since. Too close for comfort.

Razor was still a good four meters from the doors, Buzzer close behind. One more second ticked off...

Buzzer grabbed Razor by the shoulders and shoved him hard with a dive toward the blackened-out plated windows that faced the Police HQ parking area.

"Dive!" He shouted as the grenades exploded, obliterating the entire inner headquarters. The added force of the eruption propelled both Guarders through the wire-reinforced glass, taking most of the window frame and glass with them, and they flew over the outer sidewalk and halfway into the parking lot. A bone crushing collision met the two men as they slammed into the pavement and a police cruiser parked just outside.

Another series of explosions rocked the building and most of the outer wall of the police headquarters came bursting out into the parking lot. Huge chunks of plastic, metal, plexisteel and concrete sailed past them as the two bounced off the sleek side panels of the cruiser and landed harshly on the ground. Hundreds of tiny shards of glass pierced Buzzer's outer gear, some breaking through his protective clothing and digging into his back. More explosions followed as the armory was exposed to the firestorm of the first explosion and the various weapons and ammo packs contained inside went up like one combined incendiary.

Buzzer covered his face and head as best he could until the debris stopped crashing into him and the explosions ceased in their destruction.

Slowly, Buzzer shook his head trying to stop the ringing there, but he was not successful.

Faintly, he heard Razor moaning and checked him for any significant injuries. "I'm not hurt too badly, Frank," Razor muttered.

Buzzer sighed with relief at that and moaned as he tried to move one sore shoulder. He had lost his half-charger somewhere along the line but one blaster was still holstered under his left arm and the other was lying on the debris strewn pavement about a meter away. Both men tried quickly to gather their wits about them, simultaneously reaching for weapons and taking stock of their surroundings. The nearby streets were quickly filling with curious citizens.

"Jesus, Buzzer," Razor said and worked his way to his knees. Blood was all over the two men, their faces, necks and hands were covered in red. But as each inspected the other, all they could find were numerous bruises and lacerations, some of them deep but none of them very serious. "What in the hell is going on here?"

"I don't know, Razor," Buzzer said and attempted to stand up on jittery legs. "But I don't intend to stand here in the middle of a parking lot waiting to find out exactly what's next."

"This cruiser's history," Razor said as he inspected the vehicle they had just landed on and looked around. "The explosion hurt it more than it did us."

"Speak for yourself, buddy, I have a ringing in my ears that just won't quit," Buzzer said and staggered over to another cruiser parked across the lot. "What do you say we borrow this one for awhile. I don't think Chief Parker will mind all that much, not after he just tried to disintegrate us in his own HQ."

"You know what?" Razor said, stumbling along behind Buzzer. "Why don't we find the son- of-a-bitch and return the favor."

Buzzer smirked at that and used the butt of his blaster to shatter the driver's side window. As he cleared the broken glass from the seat he looked at the activator and found the key secure in place. "Thank God for small favors," he said and sat down behind the wheel. Razor climbed in once Buzzer keyed open his door and turned to face his partner. "You look like hell, Frank."

"Same to you," Buzzer said and activated the machine.

"Did you stop to think that this thing could have been booby-trapped?" Razor asked.

"Yeah, about two seconds after I turned the key," Buzzer said and maneuvered the vehicle out of the obstacle course of furniture pieces and concrete chunks that the parking lot had become.

"That's great," Razor sighed and slumped down in his seat. "It's good to know that at least one of us is on the ball."

"Still sharp as a tack despite being blown up and shot at."

"Where to now?" Razor asked.

"There's only one person on this planet who knew where we were headed besides the two of us when we left CharterHouse not too long ago," Buzzer responded.

"Humechy..." Razor said.

"He's the one," Buzzer grunted and wiped some dried blood from his face. "I checked that office for bugs when we first entered the CharterHouse Complex and it was clear. He was the only one who could have warned Parker that we were on our way."

"What have we gotten ourselves into on this cold little planet?" Razor wondered.

"A world of trouble, Razor," Buzzer said. "A world of trouble."

CHAPTER FOUR

"Captain, there are hardly any readings at all coming from the small encampment on the moon's surface," the OpsTech said from his station. "Just the regular hits we usually get from colonies. Heat radiation, microwaves, things of that nature. From what I can see in the way of space-capable vehicles, there's quite a few but most are inoperative. Other than that, the only thing that strikes me as strange is the small number of life signs I'm reading."

"How many are down there?" Turner asked.

"About three-hundred-and-fifty altogether, Captain."

Turner seemed to be weighing this in his mind as Malone watched his CO's face set deep in thought. "There's no way of discovering exactly how many of them there were when the camp was full, is there?"

"Yes, sir, I can run a scan on the camp to count the approximate number of living units which are currently operable and conduct tests to see how many of them are serving as habitats now.

That will allow me to estimate the number of people who generally live in the complex under normal circumstances."

"Good, do it and do it fast," Turner ordered and leaned forward to study the viewscreen. "I don't like this, it's so quiet down there it's almost spooky."

"Captain, visual has locked on to the location of primary activity for the life signs still on Sarsat-15," a tech said from one of the consoles on the bridge. "I can bring it up if you'd like."

"Yes, on full-view."

The view changed abruptly as the hi-mag camera lenses attached to the underside of the Ruffian's huge hull locked on to the camp below. Two hundred or so people, mostly women and children, milled about in the central square of the encampment, performing tasks and lounging around. The entire complex was completely enclosed since there was no atmosphere on the moon. But the transparent dome provided a clear image of a good-sized portion of the camp's center.

"Switch to an infra-red scan of the entire encampment," Turner ordered. "Check to see if there are any subterranean levels or hidden compartments that could hide a large number of people down there."

"Yes, sir."

"Captain," Malone interrupted. "The readings indicate that somewhere between six and seven thousand people could maintain residence inside that complex at any given time and at least that many people, if not more, were inside that complex up until perhaps an hour ago."

"That soon," Turner said and scanned the view in front of him intensely. "Get Garcia on the com-link."

"Yes, sir," Hansen said from behind Turner. "Commander Garcia is on-line, sir."

"Avril? The scans we've run so far show that there may be more than six thousand people unaccounted for on the moon's surface," Turner said and Garcia grunted with surprise over the com-link. "Where in the hell can all of those people be, do you think?"

"Good question, Captain," Garcia replied. "Did you scan for anything underground?"

"Yes, we did, sensors show some subterranean caverns and storage compartments but no life- signs," Malone said.

"Are you sure you scanned deep enough?" Garcia's voice asked through the com-link.

"As deep as our sensors can go from up here, Commander," Malone said. "It scanned to five kilometers below the moon's surface and everything I saw underground only went down to approximately three kilometers deep."

"So where did all those people get to?" Garcia wondered aloud.

"I don't know, Avril," Turner said. "But I don't like this, not one bit."

"Keep me informed if something new comes in," Garcia said and disconnected his com-link.

Turner stood and approached Malone's position hovering over the Ops station. "Did you find anything on how many ships there may have been on the surface before all these people disappeared?"

"No, sir," the OpsTech said from his console. "All my instruments show is one large mass of heat and radiation from engines that most likely boosted to orbit very recently. The best I can do is speculate and, if I had to come up with a number, I'd say six to seven-hundred ships of moderate size, perhaps more."

"Based on?" Turner questioned and looked to Malone.

"Several factors, sir," Malone answered. "The size of the ships that pirates normally utilize, the engine output for models usually fitted to those types of ships and the amount of radiation and residual heat on the sensors. I can't say if they have fighters with capabilities like ours, although that's extremely doubtful, or if they have anything in the class of a small destroyer in their fleet but the engine output readings registering on this equipment tells me that near seven-hundred ships recently left that moon."

"Very well," Turner said and once again faced the viewscreen. "So locating those missing people and their small armada of ships remains our largest concern."

"Based on speculation, Captain," came a new voice from Hansen's communications console. "Along with the slight disturbances I have been recording on the far side of this moon, I would think it's safe to say that the entire pirate fleet is hiding on the dark side."

"Jesus Christ," Turner said as realization dawned on him. It was so obvious, how could he have not seen it? "It's 'The Four-Corners-of-the-World.' I don't think it's been done since the history books."

"That's what I would guess, sir," the new voice agreed. "What's your name, FlightCorpsman?"

"Redwolf, Captain," the voice answered. "Jack Redwolf."

"Good work, Redwolf," Turner sighed and sat back down in his chair, his mind already attempting to devise a new counter-strategy. "Hansen, tell Garcia to prep his men for our disengaging the tractor beam immediately."

"Yes, sir."

"Helm, bring the engines to full stop," Turner ordered. "Once there, disengage the tractor beam and bring the Ruffian to full reverse thrust. I want to put some distance between us and that moon."

"On it, Captain."

"Sir!" One of the techs on the far side of the bridge shouted and everyone whirled toward the viewscreen.

"Good Lord..." Malone whispered as his eyes widened at the vision. The scene on the large screen now showed an enormous fleet of ships rushing from behind Sarsat-15. The small moon seemed to be leaking spaceships, both large and small, from the view before him.

"Reduce screen magnification," Turner muttered and the perspective of the scene abruptly changed. "All guns lock on targets and fire when within range, choose your targets at will."

"Aye, sir," came from Ops. "Get me Garcia," Turner said.

"Com-link established, Captain," Hansen said.

"Avril, I want your men to engage these ships as close as possible in order to evade their short-range targeting systems and confuse their WeaponsTechs. I don't want any heroics out there, just serve as a diversion so that the Ruffian can pick them off with our larger guns."

"Yes, sir."

"Incoming missiles, Captain!" A voice called. "Hundreds of them, sir!"

"Goddammit! Goddammit!" Turner blurted and pounded his fist on the arm of his command chair. "Target those missiles, get as many of them as you can. Helm, turn us around and be quick about it!"

"Retros firing!"

"Most of the incoming missiles have been destroyed, Captain," Malone said as the ship struggled with the sudden maneuvering. "Some made it through, brace for impact!"

"Keep targeting those missiles!" Turner shouted. "Punch those engines, Helm, put a fire under us!"

The ship rocked with the impact of at least twenty-five missiles. The sound of huge muffled explosions came through the confusion and Turner took a grip on his chair to keep from being tossed across the floor-plates. "Evasive maneuvers!" Turner shouted. "Collins, I want a continuous barrage of fire poured into that fleet! Let's make them think that we can keep this up all day!"

"Damage reports are coming in from all levels, Captain," Malone rasped as he strained to remain at his station.

"Captain!" Garcia's voice broke through static on Hansen's console. "We are heavily outgunned out here, sir...if you have ordered a retreat I would like permission to order my men back aboard...suffering heavy losses, Captain...won't last much longer against a force this size.."

"Call your men back, Commander!" Turner shouted as more missiles impacted against the Ruffian. Flames could be seen in one corner of the viewscreen. "I repeat, recall all of your Flight Squads! Let's get this boat out of here and rethink our attack strategy!"

"Commander Garcia's signal has faded, sir," Hansen managed as he frantically tried to reestablish contact with the leader of the Ruffian's FlightCorps.

"Damn!" Turner swore and bent to read the damage reports flashing across the small screen in the arm of his chair. The list seemed much longer than it should have been. *So much damage in so little time,* Turner thought, *this is a U.E.N. Warship for Chris' sakes, one of the largest and most powerful of its kind. The Ruffian should be able to handle a threat of this nature with hardly an effort...so why does this battle seem to be going quickly to the dogs?*

"Captain!" Collins snapped Turner's attention back to the viewscreen. "More missiles, sir! At least several hundred! Accelerating toward us at remarkable speed!"

"Guns are firing, Captain," Malone said. "Firing continuously at other targets as ordered!"

"Target those missiles!" Turner shouted.

"Trying..." a voice raged from an unseen portion of the bridge.

The Ruffian rocked again, this time from the impact of more than twice as many missiles as the initial barrage. Three consoles on the Ruffian's bridge exploded in a spray of sparks and the lights dimmed to emergency red. Men were scrambling for fire extinguishers and choking on the thick smoke as more missile impacts continued to rock the FlightForce Carrier.

"Losing power, Captain!" Malone shouted over the alarm klaxon. "In many major systems throughout the ship. The Flight decks have both been destroyed, sir, and the engine compartments are badly damaged. We are leaking fuel into space, Captain Turner, faster than we can replace it. Emergency power is fading fast and the retros are currently inoperable."

"Can we move anywhere or are we dead right here in the middle of it?" Turner asked.

"We can move, however slowly, sir," Malone said. "But not for long, the engine room says that the mains are out of commission for good. We're most likely sitting out the rest of this one right here."

"Goddammit, if that's the way it's going to be then that's the way we'll play it," Turner growled and whirled to his feet. The viewscreen showed the pirate fleet taking a beating from both the fighters and his ship's big guns. But the sheer number of ships and the missiles they were carrying were overwhelming. More missiles could be seen streaking in toward the Ruffian as Turner's eyes narrowed to slits. "Collins, I want everything we've got left rammed down the throats of all four of their formations. Start with the northeast grouping and eliminate it. Keep at least a tenth of our powerguns on other targets just to keep them guessing."

"Yes, sir!"

"Malone, status on our FlightForce Squadrons," Turner stated.

"We haven't been able to take on anymore fighters since the flight decks were destroyed, sir," Malone answered flatly.

"How many got aboard?" Turner asked as his face drained of color.

"Unknown, Captain, less than a hundred I'd say," Malone said and turned back to the console he was manning, one of the few left operational on the bridge.

"Open a com-link with Garcia, Hansen."

"I can't regain communications with the external link-ups, Captain," Hansen said. "The hull sensors and main emitter must have been destroyed both on the flight decks and underneath."

"Damn!" Turner spat and stared intently at the viewscreen. "I just hope he has enough sense to order the remainder of his men away from this battle."

"Enemy ships are closing, sir," Malone reported. "They are firing more missiles." "Reports on the Flight Squad losses, sir," Collins called. "Not good, sir."

"How about enemy losses?" Turner asked to no one in particular.

"We've eliminated at least thirty percent of their forces, Captain," Malone said.

"Brace for impact!" From some unseen crewman. The Ruffian rocked violently as several dozen missiles detonated within the hull, having sailed through breaches in the thick metal skin of the ship made by prior explosions.

"Locate those ships carrying missile stockpiles and concentrate all fire on those targets!" Turner exclaimed as the Ruffian continued to rock underneath him. "I'm tired with defense, I want some frigging aggressive offense! Everything we have left, Collins, everything!"

"Yes, sir," Collins muttered as his hands flew over the controls of his console. "Trying, sir."

"As for whatever power we have left for maneuvering," Turner said. "Aim the Ruffian back down their throats and ram as many of those ships as you can. They'll never expect that tactic."

"More missiles approaching, Captain!" "Dammit, get this ship moving!" Turner roared. "Brace for impact!"

~*~

Avril Garcia sloped around the starboard side of an enemy cruiser and fired six well-placed shots; the resulting explosion lit the interior of his small cockpit and he heard the sounds of debris pinging off the outer hull of his fighter.

The Ruffian was taking a beating and taking it hard. He had been laying back and picking off targets as they presented themselves while the bulk of his men lined up to re-enter the Ruffian's two flight decks. The sudden explosions that destroyed both flight decks ruined any chance for the rest of his fighters to get aboard the ship. Many of his pilots, brave FlightCorpsmen, died in those explosions, sitting ducks on the flight decks as missiles brought them flames and death.

After that he had ordered his men to engage at will or take up positions well out of the enemy's gun range and fire missiles to act as diversions. The initial enemy appearance had startled most of his men but they had responded with force and vigor. Their only problem was the vast number of enemy ships they had to contend with. He had watched a good many of his pilots die in that first deadly exchange of fire between sides and his feelings that the attack had been a bad idea from the start were dreadfully confirmed.

But now he had no chance to land on the Ruffian and it looked as if the carrier was in no shape to retreat. The main engines must have been hit very hard indeed to be completely shut down as they appeared to be. Some of his men had elected to stay in the thick of the fight with him, including Jack Redwolf, who had recognized the enemy's strategy before they'd had the chance to implement it. Too bad he hadn't been sooner in his recognition.

Most of the others were safely out of range and he didn't blame those guys one bit. But he felt it his duty to defend his ship until it either emerged victorious or was utterly destroyed.

He watched as more missiles hit the Ruffian; more than a few enormous holes now dotted the outer hull on the side he faced. He couldn't imagine how many crewmembers had died so far.

They were badly overpowered in this little skirmish and, as far as he was concerned, the Ruffian was doomed. But Avril Garcia had decided at the onset, as long as the Ruffian was capable of firing in her own defense, so would he from the cockpit of his fightercraft.

Pulling up suddenly, he fired a volley of missiles at two enemy targets. All exploded on impact, the ships following example very soon after. "Yeeeehaw!" Garcia called into the open com-link in an effort to rile up those remaining in his squadron. Dammit, if these dirty bastards were going to come out this strong he was determined to take as many of them with him as he could. Every single termination of an enemy target helped the Ruffian's cause, however insignificant the impact had on the battle itself.

"Commander!" Redwolf's voice reverberated throughout the cockpit. "The enemy ships are regrouping and heading toward the Ruffian en masse!"

"Shit," Garcia mumbled and stared at the onrushing mass of enemy ships. This looked like it could be the end for the Ruffian. "Pull back, FlightCorpsman, that's an order!"

"But, Commander, the Ruffian will be..."

"It will be destroyed whether we interfere right now or not, Redwolf!" Garcia said. "What we need right now is a head start on those remaining ships. Once they're done with the Ruffian they're going to come after us with a vengeance in an effort to complete the job. Open up your engines and head for Shining."

"We don't have enough fuel for that, Commander," Redwolf stated.

"I know," Garcia sighed. "But I doubt if that Guarder back on Shining will neglect the fact that we're going to need a rescue pick-up out here. Shining must be monitoring as best as they can."

"Do you think that reinforcements are on the way?" Redwolf asked.

"What reinforcements could there possibly be, Jack?" Garcia sighed. "That is a FlightForce Carrier lying wounded before us, one of the most powerful warships in the U.E.N. Fleet. What good would backup forces be against an enemy strong enough to destroy one of those?"

"I see your point..."

"Good, open up those engines, FlightCorpsman," Garcia said and turned his ship away from the Ruffian. With one last look at the once great warship, Garcia banked his fighter and headed back toward Shining. "And don't look back when the view lights up, Jack."

"Yes...sir..."

~*~

"Starboard, Gilfred!" Sampson shouted and tried to lock on to the approaching fighter. "Bank to Starboard!"

"I'm banking as hard as the controls will allow, Frazier," Thornberg rasped through gritted teeth as he struggled at the controls. "That last strafing run took out one of the engines underneath—our maneuverability has been greatly diminished!"

Sampson growled, an ugly snarl that ended up in a scream as he pressed firmly on the trigger of his weapon, the gun spewing out blast after blast of bright white energy at the FlightForce fighter soaring toward his ship. The sleek enemy craft's twin guns erupted into action and Sampson felt the effects against the hull of his small cruiser for several seconds before his aim scored true and a spectacular explosion temporarily blinded him.

"Good shooting, Frazier!" Thornberg boomed as he struggled to bring the ship back around and into the fight. A brilliant blast of white suddenly illuminated the ship's interior and Sampson turned to look at the large vessel floating in the middle of the fray. The U.E.N. FlightForce Carrier was dead in space, all engines damaged and two of the larger ones were totally inoperable. Many of the massive ship's big powerguns were still firing heavily, however, scoring mostly on the ships in his fleet that were carrying missiles.

His fleet's last barrage of missiles seemed to have damaged the carrier beyond recovery and the huge ship began to settle into a slow yet steady roll in space. The military warship had just too much mass to defend all by itself. And with what little threat remained from the fighters in the Flight Squads, the carrier was inevitably doomed to destruction.

Sampson keyed his com-link and leaned toward the microphone. "All units! Reform and await my orders. Repeat, I want all units to reform for phase-two of the attack."

Thornberg looked back at his commander and smiled wide with excitement. "We did it, Frazier," he said and grinned. "We really pulled this off."

"Yes, Gilfred, and now we will all have the pleasure of watching as the job is finished," Sampson said and released the controls of his weapon. He quickly took the empty co-pilot's seat next to Thornberg and stared in sheer delight as his fleet gathered just out of range of the big ship's guns. Smoke was billowing from several ships in his fleet but only those that were seriously damaged failed to regroup. He scowled as he watched one straggling ship in the distance try desperately to flee the guns of three enemy fighters before it was destroyed, the brief flash of the explosion lasting no more than a few seconds.

"Listen up, all units!" Sampson growled and felt his stomach twist at the losses his fleet had suffered this day. "You all know phase-two of this operation, you all know what we need to do to finish this carrier off and be done with it. We have hoped beyond hope for victory today and now that hope has been delivered. A deathblow here surely means victory for us all in the end! Now... we finish her off..."

Thornberg watched as the ships surrounding him swept into motion. As one, the wave of ships, large and small, moved forward. The carrier's guns immediately answered with continuous power blasts. Three ships were destroyed instantly but the others moved on. "Stay back, Gil," Sampson whispered.

"Yes, Frazier," Thornberg replied and watched the intensity in his friend's eyes, the hunger for victory clearly visible.

"Open fire!" Sampson yelled into the com-link, and every ship in his fleet responded before the echoes of his words died away within the small cockpit. Hundreds of missiles streaked toward the FlightForce Carrier accompanied by the blasts from hundreds of small power weapons. The huge ship took it all in, seemed to absorb impact after impact, as multiple explosions rocked the entire craft. Thousands of bits of debris scattered from the wreckage. "Fire! Fire! Fire!" Sampson repeated into the com-link, driving the members of his fleet into a killing frenzy.

More missiles and weapons fire streaked into the FlightForce Carrier. Explosions inside the enormous warship ripped larger holes through the hull as great fireballs dissipated in space. "It's all over, Gilfred..." Sampson said as his glazed eyes took in the awesome spectacle before him.

Barely two minutes into phase-two of the pirate fleet's attack, the Ruffian's already damaged reactor finally blew from the impact of so many missiles near the engine housings and power couplings. The enormous blast of painful light marked the end of Harold Turner's ship. Once the flash of blinding light passed there was nothing left but dust.

~*~

Buzzer entered the CharterHouse Lobby and walked past the desk attendant, Razor close behind. Up ahead, near the lift-banks, he could see two men dressed in police uniforms seemingly standing guard. As the two Guarders approached, the policemen began reaching for their weapons.

Some scattered screams and gasps of surprise filled the lobby as Buzzer flicked his wrists at his opponents. The knives flew with precision, hitting each wrist that held a gun, and the weapons clattered to the floor unfired. One of the men dropped to his knees in pain while the other slumped against the wall behind. Buzzer lashed out and caught the latter around the neck as Razor gathered up the fallen blasters. Razor hadn't even seen the move that had disarmed their opponents, being too busy reaching for his own blaster at the time. A quick glance toward Buzzer showed his appreciation.

Buzzer turned back to the man he had by the throat and lightly tapped the back of the guard's head against the wall. "Listen up, scum," he growled. "You don't deserve to wear a uniform or a gun so feel lucky that I'm not going to kill you outright. But, beware, if you or your buddy over there sound the alarm or flash a warning to the man upstairs I'll enjoy hunting you down and watching you drown in your own blood. Understand?"

Through a veil of obvious horror, the man found the strength to nod his understanding. "Good," Buzzer said and pulled his knife free from the man's wrist with a single vicious wrench. The policeman screamed at the pain overloading his brain and hit the floor unconscious. Razor stepped roughly on the other man's arm and jerked on the knife hilt until it came loose from the injured wrist. He wiped the blood off on the man's uniform and flicked the blade lightly to his partner as they entered the lift-car.

"Good shooting, Frank," Razor said, shaking his head in disbelief.

"Thanks," Buzzer said, pulled out two of his blasters and primed them for action. "Expecting trouble in there?" Razor asked.

"Expecting Chief Parker."

"Yeah, just what I was thinking," Razor said as a blaster filled his right hand and he checked the weapon's charge.

"We also can't account for the whereabouts of any of the police force that we didn't kill in the station," Buzzer added.

"Do you really think that Statesman Humechy is in on this?"

"No, not really in on it," Buzzer said. "But I do believe he was used as some type of unknown informant. The only other person in power in CharterCity that Humechy could trust was Parker, his Police Chief."

"Damn, you're supposed to be able to trust your own Chief of Police," Razor said.

"You are also supposed to be able to bring your law enforcement officials in on any sort of planetary problems whatsoever," Buzzer said. "Humechy's been providing valuable information all along thinking that Parker would be able to assist in coping with it when all Parker was doing was relaying that knowledge to the pirates and turning his head every single time his hand was greased."

The doors opened on to Humechy's outer office. His secretary was nowhere to be found, the entire level of the building was silent and dark. Razor flashed Buzzer a warning glance and both men melted into the interior, weapons up and ready.

Buzzer made his way forward to Humechy's office door and knocked lightly twice. No answer came but Buzzer's sixth sense tingled inside. He waved Razor down across the room and fired a quick burst through the lock. The ruined door slid halfway aside and Buzzer rolled through. Three shots rang out before Razor cleared the door.

Two policemen lay dead on the floor, a third was aiming toward Buzzer. Razor took him out with his blaster and ducked away from a volley of blasts that shattered the doorframe behind him. Buzzer was trading shots with Parker who had taken cover behind Humechy's big oak desk. Four policemen were still alive and firing, not including Parker, but Razor was surprised to see Shining Statesman Humechy sprawled atop his desk, his throat slashed from ear to ear. "Christ..." he muttered and blew away a cop who had come out from behind a pillar in the expansive office.

Buzzer fired a shot that sailed straight over his partner's left shoulder. Razor whirled around to see another dead cop, gun in fist, dead on the floor behind him. "Jesus..." Razor whispered and turned back to the firefight. "Listen up," he shouted at their opponents. "It's just the three of you now!"

"That's right, Parker!" Buzzer added and stopped firing his blasters. "I guess you thought that killing Humechy would be a good move. Actually, all it does it point the finger straight at you."

"I found him like this, Guarder," Parker barked from his hiding spot within Humechy's office. "Right, just like you found those prisoners dead of food poisoning," Buzzer said.

"Listen, I didn't kill the Statesman, I swear it," Parker said. "I admit that I was taking graft from the pirates on this dismal little planet but they're the ones who took him out, not me."

"Funny, Parker," Buzzer snarled. "But I don't believe you."

"Believe what you want, Guarder," Parker said. "If they find out that I talked to you, I'm dead anyway. Kill these bastards!"

All three policemen stood together and fired. The office erupted with the stink of blaster fire and empty charger casings, explosions filled the room with a weird illumination and several small fires started burning. The noise was deafening. Razor watched as Buzzer stood and disregarded everyone else but Parker. He caught Buzzer's eyes then, only briefly, and saw an intensity there that he had only heard about from other members of the Squadron.

Razor turned back to the immediate threat. The two remaining officers were firing steadily at his position but were allowing their aim to be affected by the pull of their weapons, amateurish at best. Two quick shots split the closer man in half at the waist, the explosion of blood and organs splashing over the other cop behind. Temporarily stunned, the last remaining officer made himself an easy target and Razor rose to a standing position to finish him off.

"Razor!" He heard Buzzer scream from across the room and he dove to the floor. Four men stood in the doorway, two of them previously encountered in the lobby downstairs and now sporting bandaged wrists. Four chargers let loose inside the cavernous room, and the entire south wall of view windows exploded outward, carrying the policeman behind Razor with them. Razor whirled as did Buzzer and fired a barrage of blasts, cutting down three men where they stood, the other ducking back behind outside the doorway. Parker had taken advantage of the situation to change his position and train his sights on Buzzer's back.

Razor caught this out of the corner of his eye and emptied his weapon in Parker's direction.

Six of his eight shots scored true, sending the CharterCity Police Chief staggering backward from the force of the impacts. Parker's mutilated corpse slammed against the window behind him causing most of the jagged remnants of the plate glass to crash out of the frame as his body slumped over and caught on the sharp edges.

Suddenly, the room was plunged into silence, only the heavy nervous breathing of the last remaining officer on the other side of the doorway remained. Buzzer scanned the room for movement but there was nothing. At last he stood up straight and walked over to give Razor a hand to his feet.

"You, out there in the hall," Buzzer called. "Lay down your weapons now or suffer the fate of your fellow police officers."

A couple of seconds later, Razor added, "It's up to you, buddy. Live or die, we could really care less."

Buzzer motioned him to silence and gave their visitor some time to think things over. In a few moments, two blasters came through the doorway and landed softly on the plush carpet inside. "I'm coming through now… please, don't shoot."

"Nice and slow," Buzzer coaxed.

"I hear you, Guarder, don't worry," came the reply as a tall man dressed in a police uniform walked through the door, his hands held high. "All that's left are some handcuffs and the billy- club strapped to my belt."

"On your knees," Buzzer said and the man complied. Razor searched him thoroughly while Buzzer covered him with a blaster. The smell of death was fast becoming overwhelming within the former Statesman's office. A brisk breeze blew in from the shattered windows. Razor discovered two small knives and a stunner during his search.

"Quite uncommon equipment for a police officer," Buzzer commented.

"Yeah, I was a cop all right," the man said. "But I worked for somebody else, not for Parker." Buzzer exchanged a glance with his younger partner and tightened his grip on his blaster.

"You were a part of the criminal organization operating out of this sector?"

The man nodded very slowly and said, "Most of us were. Parker was a pawn for the group, he hired who he was told to hire."

"Keep going," Razor said.

"Look, I'll talk," the man hesitated. "But I need some protection, a guarantee that I won't rot in a prison facility someplace where they can get to me."

"Why should we help you out?" Buzzer asked in a flat tone.

"I can tell you where our base is, who the key people are on Shining and who's running the show on some of the other nearby planets."

"How does a simple lackey," Buzzer began, "posing as a police officer on a tiny winter world know so much about the major happenings within an organization this large and well organized?"

"I'm what you would call trusted personnel," the man said. "Parker thought I was dedicated to the group enough to keep me informed of what was really happening on this ball of ice. I was just doing a job, though, you know? The money was good and the fringe benefits couldn't be beat."

"You're former military," Buzzer stated. "Yeah, Army Corps, how'd you know?"

"Because I've been coming up against scumbag mercenaries like you for a long time," Buzzer growled. "Don't think to be cutting any deals with me."

"Fine with me, asshole," the man blurted just before Buzzer cut into him with a quick series of jabs to his ribs and a kick to the face that knocked the man unconscious. Razor had to pull his partner off the battered man before the damage continued.

"Calm down, Buzzer!" Razor shouted and shoved the larger man against the wall. "Just calm the hell down!"

~*~

Sergeant Harrison Jekel tore the Hi-D Scrappy message off the printer and sat down to read in shock. A U.E.N. FlightForce Carrier had been destroyed in the Sarkennon System, all onboard personnel had been killed. Only those unaccounted of the FlightForce fighter pilots could be considered survivors. But those survivors would only be survivors if Shining sent help out to retrieve them...no fighters carried enough fuel to reach the nearest shipping lanes from that deep in the Sarkennon System, especially after fighting a battle of the magnitude that would result in the destruction of a carrier. Those pilots might very well end up drifting for eternity.

"Sarge," Cougar said and tore off another printout. "These messages didn't come from Buzzer."

Jekel looked up abruptly and stared at his communications officer. "Then where in the hell did they come from?"

"These are strictly U.E.N. Military, codes and all," Cougar answered. "I had to run them through the deciphering programs, all eight thousand of them, before I could make heads or tails of anything."

"Let me see that one," Jekel said and motioned for the message Cougar held in his hand.

Cougar handed it to his CO and turned back to his console, where still more encrypted military messages were being decoded, as Jekel read:

```
*SOURCE: SECTOR 51LK9065-V U.E.N. OUTPOST:

=REPORTING: U.E.N. RUFFIAN, FLIGHTFORCE CARRIER,
CALLED OFF NORMAL COURSE BY PRIORITY SCALE MEASURE
ISSUED BY

U.E.N. GUARDER SQUADRON SEQUENCER—DIGITIZED CODE—
OVERRULING ALL STANDARD MILITARY COMMAND CODES—RUFFIAN
FOLLOWED NEW ORDERS IMMEDIATELY—ARRIVED AT SHINING IN
SARKENNON SYSTEM, LOCAL GRID-SECTOR, UNDER ATTACK—
RUFFIAN VICTORIOUS IN FIRST BATTLE—COMMENCED
UNOFFICIAL DEPARTURE SHINING ORBIT—LAST OUTPUT FROM
TRACKING SIGNAL IDENTIFIED SIGNS OF RUFFIAN ENGINE
IMPLOSION...RESULT—TOTAL DESTRUCTION OF FLIGHTFORCE
CARRIER-CLASS VESSEL...END OF REPORTING=
```

"Buzzer, what in the devil is going on out there?" Jekel whispered to himself as he stormed out of the Control Center. "Cougar!" He called over his shoulder. "Core Meeting in the conference room in ten minutes. Get Thunder on the line, I want him en route to Shining now. Tell him he has my orders to pick a team of his choice. He is to rendezvous with me at Shining Spacedock in twenty-four hours, Aegis-standard, with three other Guarders."

"Yes, sir, I'm on it," Cougar said as he followed close behind Jekel down the hallway and into a lift-car.

"I also want a message sent express to the Statesman on Shining," Jekel said. "I want all of his military forces on call and ready for me when I get there."

"I've already tried Shining, Sarge," Cougar said. "It seems that there's been trouble in CharterHouse."

"What kind of trouble?"

"For one, Statesman Humechy was found dead, his throat slashed, after an apparent firefight in his office chambers. The Police Chief was also found dead as well as a number of other officers. The clerical staff in CharterHouse reported that two men identifying themselves as Guarders entered the building and left shortly thereafter. It was after they left that the bodies were discovered."

"Good God Almighty," Jekel sighed. "Buzzer doesn't kill police officers unless he has a very good Goddamn reason, let alone the planetary leader. Who's in charge now?"

"Well, Sarge, I did some research into that, too," Cougar said. "The only other person entitled to take over the temporary position of Statesman in a hostile situation would be the Police Chief of CharterCity. But, since both the Statesman and the Police Chief are dead, the planet is leaderless. At this moment, if Buzzer is still on the planet, that would make him the ranking official on Shining, entitling him to the interim planetary leadership position."

"Wait, I thought the next highest ranking member within the police force would assume that title," Jekel said.

"Normally, sir, that person would," Cougar explained. "But, unfortunately, all other police personnel are either dead or have abandoned their posts."

"How about the military?"

"There isn't any," Cougar continued. "The Planetary Defense Flight Squadron personnel are technically not military but a part of the police department and the combined police forces are all the military strength that Shining had to boast of. I have sent messages for the Police Chief of Shining Star Center, a quasi-resort area and the only other major metropolitan hub besides CharterCity on all of Shining, but she has yet to respond. None of the Defense Flight Squadron pilots are reporting in either."

"Dammit!" Jekel swore as the lift-doors opened and he rushed into the lower levels of the Guarder HQ. "Cougar, you're coming with me on this one. I need someone who knows something about this snowball of a planet and it seems like that's you. Begin charting all flights from Aegis over the next few hours that pass through the Sarkennon System's nearest shipping lanes. We're about to commandeer ourselves the fastest ship we can find."

CHAPTER FIVE

Thunder walked down the access ramp and into the bright sunshine of Newmantle. The little semi-resort planet was as far as the mini-cargo-liner could take him on such short notice but it was just as well. Skinner and Blitzer were waiting for him down by the riverbank.

Skinner smiled up at Thunder and said, "Bobby, imagine seeing you here."

"Yeah, surprise, surprise," Thunder cracked and lugged his gear down the ramp to the cement below. "Where's Able?"

"He's heading straight for Shining," Blitzer said and helped Thunder with his gear. "It'll be easier for him since he's coming from out that way to begin with."

"All right then, when's the next ship out of here?"

"In about five hours," Skinner offered.

"Great, let's live it up while we can," Thunder said and started walking. "So, where are you guys holed up?"

"Holed up?" Blitzer asked. "Come on, Thunder, we've been here all of half a day. We're just sorry we didn't have enough spare change to fool around with at the casinos."

"Yeah, but I need a little rest," Thunder said. "I just got pulled off a mission and I can never sleep on those minis. Even if only for a few hours, I need the rest."

"There's a hotel right here in the spaceport," Blitzer said.

"Good enough, I'll get myself some much needed sleep and meet you two back at this spot in four hours," Thunder said. "I want the captain of that ship available for a short discussion prior to boarding. Can you set that up for me, Blitzer?"

"Sure thing, Bobby," Blitzer said and watched as Thunder disappeared through the doors of the spaceport lobby.

Nobody needed a briefing on this situation. Buzzer had been sent to Shining because he was the only one Jekel trusted with handling the recent piracy problem that was quickly overwhelming the entire quadrant. Razor had been assigned because it was high time the kid got some valuable experience in the field and a chance to see the master at work. Now the situation seemed to have deteriorated drastically. If Jekel thought it important enough to call in another team, plus make the trip out to the Sarkennon System himself, things had definitely taken a turn for the worse. Thunder was especially uncomfortable with the thought that Buzzer's long streak of successful missions had finally caught up with him and...well, some things were better left unsaid and unthought.

The last time there had been a recall of Squadron personnel, the Known-Grids had been rocked by the murderous deeds of a band of renegade Guarders, something the Guarder Squadron hadn't experienced in the four centuries since its inception. Buzzer had been there to straighten things out then and a hundred other times. That was why he was the greatest single

Guarder ever to wear the badge. Every quadrant, every planet and moon, every criminal organization however small had heard the legends surrounding Frank Buzzer.

Thunder looked up to the man, considered him a mentor, especially during his early career as a Guarder. It was Buzzer who had given him the incentive to strive to be the best among the ranks. It was the man's impeccable character and deadly sense of justice that had molded Robert Thunder into the Guarder he was today. And it was Frank Buzzer's stellar performance in the ranks throughout the e-years that kept Bobby Thunder at the number-two spot within the Squadron.

That, interestingly enough, didn't bother Thunder in the least. Playing second fiddle to Frank Buzzer within the legendary Guarder Squadron was a role Bobby Thunder would be proud to play right up until the last day of his career, if that's what it came down to. He considered it an honor just being a member of such an elite group of men and women. And the opportunity to serve under Harrison Jekel was simply more icing on the cake.

Now he had been called off a mission to assemble a small team of Guarders and meet Sergeant Jekel on Shining in an effort to assist Buzzer on a mission that seemed to have gone horribly wrong. Thunder could feel the adrenaline coursing through his veins already, could feel his entire nervous system shifting into high gear. He had learned to control the excitement and the urge to explode into action over the course of his career. It was never easy but it could be done. This time, Thunder was having a hard time of it. Although he was hoping to catch some much needed rest over the next few hours, he was extremely confident that his eyes would focus on nothing but the ceiling of his room until it came time to meet Skinner and Blitzer back at the spaceport. If sleep came he would be pleasantly surprised.

Thunder instantly recognized the spaceport hotel as one of those run by Schezetti's outfit on Neo Roma. It would be good to put a scare into this hotel's security team as he checked in. They would instantly recognize him as a Guarder, had probably already done so with both Skinner and Blitzer as well. The entire hotel staff was most likely on high alert at this point, fearing the worst —a raid by the Guarder Squadron on one of the Syndicate crime lord's smaller hotel- casinos. Thunder laughed at that. How ironic, while people were running frantic throughout the hotel in anticipation of a possible battle with Guarders, Thunder would be staring at the ceiling panels of a well decorated hotel room and hoping for sleep. *The universe is a crazy place,* Thunder thought to himself as he entered the luxurious lobby and caught several quick glances by large men, in suits, placed strategically around the large room. *A wonderful yet crazy place...*

~*~

Sampson climbed down from his ship amid a hail of cheers and applause from the men and women who had already landed back on Sarsat-15. Thornberg was right behind him, his helmet in his hands and looking extremely pleased at their victory.

As usual, Sampson's features looked as though he were lost in thought, already analyzing all that had transpired during the battle and what it could mean for their future. Sure, the small hint of a smile was there to give encouragement to his people but, other than that, his computer-like brain was hard at work.

If Thornberg didn't know the man so well, he would begin to worry about his present state of mind. Sampson's subdued manner after such an unlikely victory wasn't like him, not at all. "Frazier," he whispered. "What is it that troubles you? After what we've just accomplished, this should be a time of celebration."

"I'm thinking of the U.E.N.'s response, Gilfred," Sampson said. "A response that is sure to come, swift and powerful, to this place where we now stand. I'm thinking of the possibility that every single person in this encampment may die if we do not move and move soon. Our victory was hard earned, many of these people paid the price with their blood. I am fully aware of our victory today and what it has done for the morale of this group. But that victory will be costly...unless we take matters into our own hands at this very moment, it will be costly indeed."

"Surely they won't send another carrier out here after we so easily dispatched with this one," Thornberg hoped. "It just wouldn't make sense to risk another."

"No, Gil, that is where your inexperience with the military clouds your thinking," Sampson sighed. "I know how the bastards think. They will want now, more than ever, to wipe our little band and our little moon out of existence. And if it takes two, maybe three carriers plus a small fleet of warships to accomplish that, it will happen. They will risk it. The U.E.N. Military is not so easily humiliated."

Thornberg considered this for several moments as Sampson's Utility Guardsmen continued to open a path for them through the throngs of his people crowding the hangar. "I haven't thought of it in quite that way until now. It almost makes me wish we hadn't just won this blasted battle."

"Isn't war a tricky devil?" Sampson asked and quickened his pace.

Soon Thornberg lost sight of his leader's wide back among the crowd and slowly allowed his good feelings about their victory to join those of the others around him. Still, Sampson's words continued to haunt him. No matter how hard he debated the issue within his own mind, his leader's words made sense. War was not only a tricky devil but a clever and unpredictable one as well.

~*~

Buzzer had been monitoring the situation of the fighter pilots who had survived the battle on the long-range scanners of the CharterCity Spaceport ever since he had learned of the Ruffian's destruction. Although he and Razor were trying to maintain a low profile on Shining, Buzzer had been the only official with rank enough to assume temporary command of the planetary government. As a result, he had dispatched as many cruise-capable ships as were available to help out the surviving fighter pilots.

So far there had been no word as to the fate of the rescuers. All Buzzer could do now was hope for the best. This situation had clearly been blown all out of proportion. He was still at square one in trying to understand just how the pirates were thinking, puzzling through their current erratic strategy and hoping to guess their next possible strike. After hours of contemplation on the matter, he came to a quite hopeless conclusion: figuring out their method of operation was not the easiest thing to do.

The entire population of Shining seemed to be mesmerized by the sudden turn of events in the political scheme of things on the winter world. In one fell swoop, the planetary leader, his next logical successor and the entire police force of CharterCity had been eliminated. As far as he could tell, the remnants of the corrupt police force had gone into hiding, either waiting for the right time to strike or finally fed up with the insanity of it all.

Buzzer was learning quite quickly just how messed up the infrastructure of Shining's closed society was during the reign of Humechy as Head Statesman. It seemed that the man had been blind to the illegal ways his Police Chief ran the only disciplinary force on the planet. The man had truly believed the inaccurate reports and false counsel provided by his trusted advisors and colleagues that the population of the entire planet was ultimately happy with their living conditions and the Shining way of life.

In a way, it was just as well that the old man was out of the political picture. Now, the planet just might have a chance of picking itself up off the filthy floor of the sewer it had become and begin to make some headway toward a decent existence for the people who lived there. Of course, all of that depended on the successful outcome of his mission and the elimination of the pirate presence from this quadrant.

"Guarder," a tech said from a couple of consoles away. Buzzer leaned over toward him. "I have confirmation from seven of the ten ships that were dispatched that their holds are filled to capacity with pilots from the Ruffian and they are ready to turn back for CharterCity Spaceport. All seven also indicate that their tractor beams are not strong enough to haul the fighters along at high speed."

"Tell the captains of those ships to abandon the derelict fighters and proceed back here as fast as they can possibly manage," Buzzer said.

"Yes, sir."

"What is the status of the other three ships?" Razor asked.

"They're still picking up survivors," the tech said. "It's a very slow process since they have to do it one ship at a time."

"Very good," Razor replied. "Keep us posted on the situation."

"Yes, sir."

"I want to know as soon as the last of them is picked up and all ten ships confirm that they are on their way back," Buzzer added. "Also, try to find out if Flight Commander Avril Garcia is among the survivors. If he is, let me know as soon as you locate him and have an open com-link set up immediately."

"I'm on it."

Buzzer stood and stretched out his tired muscles.

"What's the matter, partner," Razor began. "Old age getting the better of you?"

"I'm not getting any younger, Razor," Buzzer muttered and took a chair beside the younger Guarder. "Tell me, how do you think we've handled this situation so far?"

Razor looked away for a moment before turning to face Buzzer. "I think we've done a damn good job just staying alive since we first set foot on this block of ice."

Buzzer laughed for a moment and reached out to grip Razor's left shoulder. "You know something, John, I don't think I've yet taken the time to thank you for being there to save my ass so many times on this mission so far."

"Don't bother thanking me, Frank," Razor said. "We're in this together. You've saved my ass from being fried enough times, too."

"Yeah, well..." Buzzer trailed off and leaned back in his chair. "Anyway, I agree with you." "On what?" Razor asked.

"On the way we've been handling this entire situation," Buzzer said. "We've followed our only leads, tracked the trails back to where some of these problems have started, discovered the pirate's base of operations and eliminated all threats to ourselves in the process. We've also made our presence known in the best way possible."

"Yeah, by multiple visits to the hospital and what amounts to a political coup d'etat," Razor laughed. "Does this make us tyrants, I wonder?"

"Kind of funny how everything's falling together," Buzzer muttered.

"Funny, right," Razor said sarcastically and shifted in his seat. "I'm still laughing at almost getting my head blown off back there in Humechy's office."

"You know what I mean," Buzzer said. "At least we have a little time to rest for now.

Hopefully, we have some quick ships on our side."

"So, you do need to rest every now and again," Razor joked.

"Quit the bullshit, Razor," Buzzer said. "I think we're both a little fatigued on this one."

"Just a little," Razor agreed. "I mean, it's only several thousand or so of these pirate maniacs

against just us two. Piece of cake under normal circumstances."

"It certainly is one hell of a lot of people to handle for just the two of us," Buzzer added.

Razor sat up straighter as he realized just how daunting their situation had become. "Let them come, I'm more than ready."

"I highly doubt it," Buzzer said. "That type of unearned confidence will get you killed out here someday."

"Why is it unearned?" Razor asked. "We've been through so much, shot at countless times, blown out of the window of the Police HQ, ambushed at Humechy's office. And we've come through most of it with no major injuries. I'd say we've both earned a bit of confidence so far on this mission, Frank."

"It's fine to feel good about your accomplishments and learn from them, Razor," Buzzer said. "But during a mission, overconfidence can get you killed. Always expect the unexpected. Never think that the worst has passed and the rest of the way will be easy going. It often doesn't work that way. Just stay alert and take the time to revel in your victories once the mission is over and you're back on Aegis. Otherwise, you could be blind-sided at any time."

"I see what you're saying, Frank," Razor said. "But this is the very first mission I've actually seen action and played a major part in more than one firefight. I've proven something to myself since we've arrived here. I've proven that the training and hard work has paid off. That I can be an active and contributing member of the Guarder Squadron. That the skills I have learned have made me into one of the best soldiers in the Known-Grids and that I am continuing to learn from the best in the ranks. I am proud of that and with that pride comes a little confidence. While I have this little bit of down time, I'm taking the opportunity to feel good about what we've uncovered and what we've accomplished. You should do the same. Believe me, it feels good."

Buzzer nodded and smiled at his partner. They came from different times, he and Razor, or so it seemed sometimes. *The kid is good,* Buzzer thought, *better than most rookies under the same circumstances but he just needs more experience.* That's exactly what Jekel had told him when they decided to assign Razor on this mission. And that observation had proven true.

At first, Buzzer had noticed the nervousness in the kid. But as the mission had steadily grown more dangerous, Razor had become attuned to his surroundings, aware of everything that was happening around him, ready to act without hesitation. He had proven himself to Buzzer time and time again. Razor was no longer 'the Kid,' as the others back on Aegis had called him. With an enormous amount of luck, and if they survived at all, Razor would return from this mission as an equal in the Squadron. For only his third official mission as a Guarder, he was performing like the professional he was supposed to become somewhat farther down the line. He was having to learn fast, on the go, and adapting very well to all that had happened.

That made Buzzer feel very good for the young man. He felt great for John 'Razor' Brady, felt good for himself and was happy that the Squadron was gaining such a professional soldier in the ranks.

"Okay, a little confidence in this short bit of down-time couldn't hurt," Buzzer said. "That's more like it," Razor laughed and leaned back in his chair. "Let's catch some rest

while we're at it."

"No way," Buzzer said, shaking his head negatively. "I wouldn't fall asleep inside CharterHouse or this spaceport for anything at this point in time. Who knows what enemies await the weary?"

"True, very true, but I'm dead on my feet," Razor said. "I'll just be sitting here if you need me."

"Sounds good," Buzzer said and stood. "I'll wake you up once something happens. Just don't disappear on me."

"I'm staying put right here on this all too uncomfortable hard rock of a seat cushion or whatever the hell it's made out of," Razor said and shifted position.

Buzzer nodded once and turned back to the console he had been monitoring earlier. *Thank God there are still some good men to be found out there in the grids*, he thought to himself, *thank God…*

~*~

Garcia watched as Jack Redwolf's fighter was tractored toward the last remaining rescue-ship. The group of fighters that had left the point of the Ruffian's demise together had run out of fuel just hours ago. They had been pumping it at maximum speed to put some distance between themselves and any would-be followers until their fuel cells had grown dangerously close to depletion. After that, they had cruised at minimal engine power. Garcia's ship had been the first to go empty, due to the extra fuel he had consumed while continuing to defend the Ruffian after most of his men were either killed or had pulled back as ordered.

He had tried to supervise so many fighters during the brief battle that he had unknowingly used up over half of his fuel supply before the Ruffian had been destroyed. Two other fighters had tractored his ship as best as they could after that, the connection holding for no more than fifteen minutes at a time before breaking. It was soon after that most of the other fighters began to go dry as well. Since then, the entire group had been drifting endlessly toward Shining. Garcia had used his computer to make some quick calculations and found that, with no fuel, their destination was only about six years away at drifting speeds. Not good news when his oxygen supply was only enough to last thirty-six hours and his suit's ability to drain off bodily waste wouldn't last even that long on batteries.

Needless to say, the appearance of the small fleet of cruisers had been the only happy sight he had seen since this entire fiasco began. Damn Captain Turner! He had tried to talk the man out of the attack, to explain to him how futile an attempt it would be if the pirate force turned out to be more than the Ruffian could handle. But the only response he got from the man was some too- proud military bullshit about how nothing was more powerful than a FlightForce Carrier going into a battle hot and ready for action.

And now, Garcia and a small handful of fighter pilots were all that was left to show for the mighty ship captain's plan and the U.E.N. Ruffian. What an incredible waste...

A sudden jolt interrupted his thoughts and he grabbed wildly for the controls, not knowing what to expect. "Commander Garcia," a voice crackled over his com-link. "Prepare yourself for tractoring. The beam has already been implemented. You'll be inside in just a few."

"Great," Garcia sighed. "And who am I speaking to?"

"I'm Gordon Bover, sir," the man answered hesitantly. "I own this bucket of bolts off your starboard side."

"Good to meet you, Gordon Bover," Garcia said. "Looks like you not only made my entire day but that you are saving my life as well. Thank you, sir."

"No need to thank me, Commander, no need."

A sudden commotion sounded over the line and then a new voice crackled throughout his cockpit. "Avril, this is Redwolf."

"Go ahead, Jack," Garcia said, hearing the worry in his FlightCorpsman's voice.

"I just received a message here from Shining, from Buzzer, the Guarder."

"What's wrong?"

"Although this ship's long-range scanners don't show anything yet, Shining's picking up a rather large signal. It looks like what's left of the pirate fleet is heading toward Shining and we're sitting here right in their path."

"Jesus Christ," Garcia muttered. "Ask Bover how much power this bucket of bolts might possess."

"Pretty good for a cruiser class," Bover answered. "I've modified the engines myself."

"Do you think it's faster than a war fleet?" Garcia inquired.

"Good question—how fast do war fleets usually travel?"

"They usually travel at the fastest capable speed of their slowest ship in order to ensure that destination arrival times are equal for the entire fleet," Garcia said. "But, we're not dealing with a normal or usual war fleet here, Gordon. We are dealing with a rag-tag group of assorted ships. They come in all different sizes and speed capabilities. In short, these are pirates and they do not act according to any sensible plan that you would expect from an invading force. They would be more than happy to slit your throat and those of the pilots currently aboard your vessel and most likely welcome your ship into their fleet. Do you follow where I'm going?"

"Yes, sir," Bover grumbled.

"Now, how do you feel about getting me aboard your cruiser as soon as possible and getting your money's worth out of those engine modifications?"

"Don't you worry, Commander," Bover said. "I'm not giving up this ship without at least a chase and definitely not without a fight."

"Good man," Garcia said and relaxed momentarily as his ship connected with the loading dock on the small cruiser and the airlocks hissed open. He could hear the slight hum of the cruiser's main engines warming up and he thought to himself, *out of the frying pan and into the fire,* or however that old saying went.

~*~

Buzzer skulked in the shadows of the spaceport and watched as the latest arrival docked tightly against the landing platform. Fully armed and battle-ready, both Buzzer and Razor were prepared for anything. A seemingly relieving spout of steam and spent energy escaped from the small shuttle's landing gear, filling the cavernous Starport Shuttlebay with an eerie fog.

Something was about to go down, Buzzer could sense it. The combination of unusual silence at the often bustling transportation hub and an almost white electric intensity in the air made the small hairs on the back of his neck tingle and stiffen with anticipation.

Any second now...

Buzzer nodded his head toward the patch of darkness shrouding his partner across the cavernous shuttle bay and recognized an almost imperceptible nod in return. They were both anxious, willing and able to hand out whatever it took to rid the Starport of any further problems. Now he could only hope that the others would be, too.

The first shadows of debarking passengers broke through the semi-cloud as the exit doors on the small craft hissed and creaked loudly open. At most, there would be twenty of them, if they were lucky, all hopefully heading in the same direction—away from the shuttle and its deadly fuel supply.

A tiny sound, almost scrape-like, touched on Buzzer's senses off to his left. Then he heard it again, and several seconds later, again. Someone else had joined the party. That answered all of Buzzer's doubts about his initial feelings of tension regarding the Starport tonight. The pirates had at their disposal the worst kind of connections. Only government personnel, high-ranking officials, were privy to the comings and goings of Guarders. And as far as he knew, most of the

Squadron were not aware that Jekel and his select team had made the trip to Shining. Only Buzzer's sporadic monitoring of Thunder's specific sequencer frequency, and the fact that it was currently tuned into those of four other Guarders including Jekel, alerted him to their sudden arrival in Shining's near spacelanes. Guarder sequencers were only linked when they traveled in teams. Word of the Ruffian's destruction and his role in steering the carrier to Shining must have reached Aegis and been intercepted by Cougar at Guarder HQ.

The last question now remaining was how many of the attackers were waiting to spring? If only he could warn his unsuspecting fellow Guarders, although each of their respective combat reflexes should be enough to scrape them through. Now it was far too late to wonder if his low- frequency SOS transmission had either penetrated Shining's dense upper atmosphere or, for that matter, been picked up by his colleagues earlier. All he could do was stay silent and alert and hope for the best.

The first figure he recognized in the small crowd exiting the shuttle was Bobby Thunder. Tall, wild-haired and massively strong, Thunder's physical presence was a match for his admirable personality and unyielding sense of justice. The heavily laden duffel bag lying low in the mist was most definitely full of his friend's favorite weaponry.

Next, the instantly recognizable bulk of Sergeant Harrison Jekel appeared in the pale light coming from the docking bay behind. Jekel's voice was slightly overpowered by the hiss of steam accompanying the opening of several sets of cargo doors. Buzzer could barely make it out. A sudden move from Razor alerted Buzzer that it had begun. A figure swooped in fast from the exit corridor, a glint of metal and the slight click of a charger cartridge being primed was all Buzzer needed to spring into action.

"Sarge!" Buzzer yelled and leapt from behind a utility crate, blasters up and targeting. "Down! Down! Down!"

Three quick taps on both of his triggers and he had their attention. The startled attacker managed one shot before Buzzer's blasts cut him in half. Amid the screams of the innocent and unsuspecting bystanders milling about the Starport, Jekel and the others hit the deck. Thunder rolled away off the path clawing at the catch of his duffel bag. Razor appeared at the mouth of the exit corridor firing quick blasts at unseen attackers.

Shouts could be heard coming from an unknown leader among their assailants. Suddenly four more armed men appeared firing wildly, charger blasts ricocheting off of walls and smashing into various machinery and other assorted vehicles. There was no order to this attack, more men kept popping up at different spots in the shuttlebay. Obviously, Buzzer and Razor were not the only ones on Shining who were adept at silent infiltration. They were dealing with some very well trained soldiers, equipped with some of the most powerful weapons available on the military market. Mostly government issue, from the looks of them.

Jekel was up and running toward Buzzer's position in long bounding strides, enemy shots missing his large frame by mere inches. The sergeant's big guns were answering back quite effectively as two men dropped in a gory red spray, their weapons clattering away across the hard floor of the shuttlebay.

Buzzer could see almost fifteen attackers spread throughout the shuttlebay, now that most of the civilians had hightailed it out of the Starport proper, and the bodies of seven others already dead. Who knew how many more of them were being held off at the end of the exit corridor by Razor's half-charger? A close blast knocked the giant Jekel off his feet, bringing him sliding into the stack of cargo crates that Buzzer was using for cover.

A few quick shots glanced off the wall behind the two men but Buzzer's return fire soon eliminated part of that threat. "Jesus Christ, Frank, some Goddamn welcome," Jekel growled and slapped a new clip into his charger.

"Nice to see you, too, Sarge," Buzzer rasped and squeezed off a few more rounds. The entire shuttlebay was now full of sporadic light, great explosions and the faint sound of screams coming from those few innocents still unlucky enough to be caught in the melee.

Razor risked a glance at the center of the bay, trying to take it all in before a close blast forced him away. One thing had made itself clear to him from that glance, most of the attacking forces were holed up in or around the downed shuttles trying to get lost in the vague trails of steam still leaking from depressurized landing gear and winding down engines. Now, with over thirty of the mysterious aggressors crowding the shuttlebay, there was only one thing to do. No matter how long it would affect those importers and exporters who held frequent commerce on Shining.

One more look around and he was sure that all of his fellow Guarders were well under cover and away from the dangerously lethal shuttlecraft. "Guarders! Down and covered!" He shouted and whipped around to take aim on the huge gleaming fuel cells of the farthest shuttle.

"What in the hell..." Jekel started to protest but the rest of his statement was lost to Buzzer's ears when the fuel blew, taking the shuttle along with it. Something wet and bloody slammed to the floor beside the two kneeling men, something that had once belonged to the body of one of the attackers. A glance around showed Buzzer that Thunder was taking his partner's example and sighting on another of the shuttles. "Cover your head, Harrison," Buzzer said and went low again as a second shuttle erupted in a fantastic explosion. More debris hit the wall behind them and the crates in front. This time, when the smoke cleared, silence ruled the shuttlebay.

First to rise was Buzzer, guns still poised and ready just in case. Soon to follow was Jekel and Thunder as they slowly stood to take in their surroundings. Most of their attackers were dead or seriously wounded by the unexpected explosions that had occurred very near to their positions. Although they had been heavily armed and seemingly well trained, they had been foolish enough to take cover behind some very volatile material. Active fuel cells did not make for good cover.

"Good move, Razor," Jekel said in the direction of the younger Guarder. Razor nodded in return. Turning back to Buzzer, Jekel looked him up and down and frowned. "Looks like the two of you have seen some action on this rock."

"You could say that, Sarge," Buzzer replied and leaned heavily against a crate.

"Now that we have some free time on our hands, how about you explain the situation to me and the rest of us," Jekel said. "After we clear things with the head exec around here."

"You're talking to him," Buzzer said.

Jekel lifted an eyebrow at that and let a smile cross his otherwise stern looking features. "Well, now that we've taken care of that, where do we go from here?"

111

"Starport Tower Complex," Buzzer said with obvious exhaustion and turned toward the blackened and charred exit corridor. "I've got some unfinished business to attend to."

United Earthian Nations
SouthWestern Corporate Grid-Sector
Sarkennon System

Shining Mission—Day Three

In November 2079, U.E.N. President Joseph Sinclair, in the last year of his Presidential run, decided to present the Interstellar Travel Theories and Principles of Sir Walter Blemeth to the United Soviet States in an act of good will. Just three years earlier, Blemeth's remarkable feat of engineering had led to the successful venture of an unmanned U.E.N. probe to another solar system. Lesser politicians of the time blasted Sinclair for handing over what was thought to be the government's one true remaining advantage right into their enemy's waiting hands. Many thought Sinclair had made the blunder in an idiotic effort to leave his indelible mark on history. Still others thought that Sinclair had turned traitorous and demanded his execution. Before the dust could finally settle on the issue, Sinclair's adversaries gunned him down in his New York City offices in 2088, on the very same day that the United Soviet States succeeded in sending their first Cosmonaut to another solar system utilizing Blemeth's methods of interstellar travel. Some today still wonder if The New Conflict could have ever taken place if Sinclair had indeed decided against presenting his "Good Will Gift" to the Soviets...

(Excerpt:*A History of Modern Earth and Beyond—the People, the Politics andthe Insanity of Our Past*by Joseph Mullens)

CHAPTER SIX

"Garcia here, Guarder," the voice of the Ruffian's FlightForce Commander crackled through the open com-link. "Reading you kind of shaky, though."

"Commander, give me your estimated time of arrival on Shining," Buzzer requested.

"Wait a minute, let me ask the pilot," Garcia said and mumbled something to someone out of earshot then turned back to the transmitter. "Bover says maybe three more hours if we push it hard."

"By all means, push as hard as you can," Buzzer replied and glanced at Jekel in the seat next to him. "Push those engines to the limit and get here as quickly as possible, Commander. I don't know if you've heard but there's a very large fleet tight on your ass."

"Yeah, I've been informed of that," Garcia's tired voice sounded from the console. "But as far as we can see we have them outrun by little more than an hour."

"That may be so but that time frame could change at any moment," Thunder added. "They may be just cruising now but the larger ships might jump ahead and take on an early offensive."

"We're all aware of that, sir," Garcia said through the static, the signal traveling hundreds of thousands of kilometers through space. "And because of that possibility we are electing to take a more circuitous route around to Shining. That way we won't be directly in the path of one of the larger ships if and when one decides to jump."

"Good thinking, Avril," Buzzer said. "Are all of the ships in your rescue fleet keeping up with you okay?"

"Yeah, we're all doing fine with the speed," Garcia said. "But we're just hoping to get there in time for the festivities."

"Don't worry about that, Commander," Buzzer laughed. "A much larger fleet of U.E.N. warships just appeared on our long-range scanners here. Once you guys land, I want you out of the picture. You and your men have done all that your duty requires of you and far more. Please accept my condolences in the loss of your shipmates on the Ruffian. I know how hard it is to lose friends and comrades in battle."

The link remained semi-silent for quite some time then before Garcia's voice came back through the static. "Thank you, Buzzer, I really appreciate that. We all do."

"You are more than welcome, Commander," Buzzer said. "Keep in mind that it will still be dark when you arrive at the CharterCity Starport. Daylight will still be several hours away after you land. Do your best to get here quick, get here safely and find a nice little hole to disappear into once you're all offloaded."

"Will do, sir."

The link was abruptly cut, the connection lasting much longer than it should have under the circumstances. Any longer and a ship in the pirate fleet might have pinpointed the location of the transmission and zeroed one or two of their faster vessels into combat range.

Cougar came in from the next room and eyed his fellow Guarders. "Just spoke to the Admiral on the carrier that's leading the approaching U.E.N. fleet. He didn't sound too happy about taking orders from you, Sarge, but grumpy or not he knows the regulations."

"What's their ETA?" Jekel asked.

"Closer to four, maybe five hours."

"Dammit," Buzzer muttered and slammed his fist into the wall at his side. "We better come up with an attack plan fast or we're going to be overwhelmed by some very unhappy pirates."

"We'll have to hold off however many of them land here for over an hour before we can expect some support from the military," Jekel said. "Frank, where's the best place to dig in and do some surprising on our soon to be uninvited guests?"

"I couldn't say, Sarge," Buzzer said. "We haven't done much sightseeing since we've been here."

"How about the police HQ?" Razor suggested. "It's all beat to hell and looks like it should be condemned from the battle we had in there but it should provide a safe haven at least for a little while."

"Yeah, the building looks like someone chewed it up and spit it back out into the street," Buzzer added.

"It's sitting right smack in the middle of CharterCity, what better place to stage a sneak attack?" Razor continued. "We could hold up in there and if they scan from orbit all they'll be likely to pick up is the residual heat lingering around the walls and ceiling from all the blaster bolts and charger rounds that were fired and the explosion that took place inside."

"He's right, Sarge," Buzzer said. "That place is made out of good old style concrete and plexisteel. It's got a bunch of holes in it here and there but it'll still hold up to some pretty mean punishment. There's lots of walls and doorframes for cover and God knows how many offices with big bulky police furniture. Also lots of metal chairs and computer terminals to use as diversions. It is perfect for a sneak attack on targets in the street. A dead hulk on the outside but loaded with punch on the inside."

"Sounds good to me, Buzzer," Skinner said and turned to Jekel. "The only question I have is this, once we set up there, how do we get word to Able?"

"Good question," Jekel admitted. "I don't even know when he left or how fast the ship he's on can travel."

"Sarge, your sequencer has deep-coding capabilities for transmitted messages, doesn't it?" Blitzer asked.

"Yes, very limited, and I see where you're going with this," Jekel replied. "The only problem is that these pirates seem to possess some very strong intelligence. We can not take the chance that they have the ability to decipher whatever coding structure I use."

"If they do we can reserve a grave for Able right now," Thunder said and Jekel nodded.

"So, notifying Able is out of the question," Buzzer said. "Let's just hope he has sense enough to see trouble when it comes right out and leaps at him."

"I don't think we have to worry about Able, he can take care of himself," Jekel insisted. "What we have to worry about is setting up our defensive and offensive positions in the police HQ and doing it fast."

"Right, Sarge," Thunder said and stood. "We're going to need all of the armaments we can get our hands on."

"Well, then we're going to the right place," Razor said and headed for the exit. "The armory in police headquarters might be somewhat depleted but I think it'll have enough weaponry left to suit our needs."

"How's it set up for explosives?" Jekel asked as the group of Guarders headed for the doors. "Don't know, Sarge, but we'll find out soon enough," Buzzer's voice faded from the room as

the technicians stationed in the CharterCity Starport Tower Complex watched the retreating backs of the mysterious figures disappear from view.

~*~

"Did you get a fix on that last transmission, Gilfred?" Sampson asked. "Not an exact positioning, no, Frazier," Thornberg answered.

"Damn," Sampson spat and smashed his fist against the side of the terminal he was monitoring. Although they had not been able to capture much of the weak signal, it had been more than clear that some of the surviving fighter pilots from the destroyed carrier had been rescued. If they could catch up to the small fleet that had picked up the fighter pilots it would be the perfect morale booster for his troops. The target practice his fleet had performed on the empty and drifting fighter-craft actually did some good but a long and quiet journey was always the worst thing to precede a major battle. Long periods of empty time would only serve to give his people more time to think about the foolishness of their situation and might end up unnerving many of them. Right now, they were hot-blooded and war-ready but where would they stand emotionally and psychologically after say two additional hours of dead space and clear monitors?

It was all so very shaky. Their positioning, their chances for victory, their numbers, their armaments, their skill level for full-scale battle...the list seemed endless. The idea that this flight to battle may have been a hasty decision was slowly creeping into Sampson's mind.

"Frazier!" Thornberg gasped. "Look at your monitor!"

Sampson whipped around in his chair to stare at the screen in horror. The long-range scanner displayed some unimaginably large U.E.N. warships closing in on the Sarkennon System. "What's their position?"

"We'll reach Shining at least two hours before that war fleet does," Thornberg reported. "But I'd bet they'll jump some of their faster ships into Shining's orbit long ahead of the rest."

"And no doubt you would win that bet, Gil," Sampson said, his eyes studying the screen in front of him with intensity. The thoughts roiling around inside Sampson's brain were almost visible to the eye, Thornberg thought. He always wore his emotions on his face, never able to truly hide what he was thinking from those who knew him well.

"Frazier, what are we to do now?" Thornberg asked.

"We will meet them on their own terms," Sampson replied. "With ships of war in orbit around that miserable little snowball."

For the first time in his life, Gilfred Thornberg began to have serious doubts about Frazier Sampson's sanity. "You can't be serious, Frazier," he said tentatively. "We'll be slaughtered. Our forces are strong, mind you, but we are no match for a war fleet of that size."

"I hear your words, Gil, but I do not plan to meet them head-on," Sampson said with a smile. "No, that would be suicide, indeed. I am not in the mood for my own suicide, Gil, let alone watching thousands of my followers go down with me."

Thornberg frowned for a moment with confusion. "Then how shall we fight them if not fleet to fleet?"

"That I am still working on," Sampson stood and began to leave the small cockpit. "Keep on course, Gil, and call me as soon as we reach Shining orbit. Tell the captains of the other ships in the fleet that I will call a meeting at that time and they are not to fire unless fired upon until I brief each and every one of them on my plan."

"Are you sure about this, Frazier?" Thornberg asked.

Sampson's face frowned suddenly with disappointment. "I will not stand for cowardice in my ranks, Gilfred Thornberg. Least of all from you. I've never steered you wrong in all the time we've been working together and I will continue in that practice. Do you understand?"

"Yes, Frazier, I understand that very well," Thornberg said. "But what I am questioning is not your leadership qualities but your emotional state right now. Are you certain that an attack is still in our best interests after this new development or is it pure revenge driving you on? A genuine concern of mine, I would think, and one that a respected Second should feel compelled to point out." Thornberg breathed in deeply after his little speech; never before had he questioned Sampson's actions to his face and he wasn't quite sure if their strong friendship would stand up to the test.

Sampson was visibly steaming. Thornberg could see his face and neck turning red. The eyes of the man before him seemed to burn straight through his own. An all too real sense of fear washed over him and Thornberg had to fight the urge to get out of there, out of the reaches of the madman before him.

Then, just as quickly as it had arrived, the demon was gone from Sampson's face. In its place was the face of a man who looked, for the first time in a very long time, as old as he really was. "I will consider this, Gil. I will consider it long and hard. Call me when we arrive at Shining."

"Yes, Frazier," Thornberg answered, and Sampson was gone.

~*~

The body went limp and slid silently to the floor, blood streaming from the gaping slit throat.

Four down, who knew how many more were left. All he knew for sure was that someone had been expecting him here, had known when he was scheduled to arrive. The fact that the blasters and chargers had begun firing before he was even off the shuttle's ramp had proven that.

Those few passengers who had traveled with him on the shuttle had scattered at the first sounds of gunfire. Able had barely been able to make it to cover before the fire zeroed in on his position, hot and heavy. He had been made aware that there were problems on the surface just prior to landing when the shuttle pilot's voice had announced from the cockpit that the landing would be delayed due to severe damage to the Starport's shuttlebay. But he had not expected an open ambush with so many civilians in the line of fire.

There was no sign of the other members of his team in the battered Starport but he couldn't blame them for that. They didn't even know how he was getting to Shining let alone when. For all he knew, there might be another more gruesome reason why they weren't here to meet him. The battle-scarred condition of the Starport complex filled him with a sense of dread. Either way, there were still some bad apples waiting to be cored within the shuttlebay and he hadn't made it twenty meters from the shuttle.

Able moved from one shadow into the cover of another, steering toward a sound he had just heard behind some crates. The weapon's fire had ceased for the time being but he didn't know for how long or why, for that matter.

What he did know was that this mission wasn't going to be as routine as he had first thought it might be. From the looks of things, there was big trouble brewing on Shining.

~*~

Jack Redwolf looked in wonder at the state of the Shining Starport out of his port window. Although it was still somewhat dark outside, it was clear that the site was blackened and charred in several places. Huge craters marked the former positions of at least two shuttles, half of the approach lights were not functioning and the other half looked dimmer than they should have been. Most of this was evident only because of the huge holes that had been punched through the roof of the shuttlebay and the glare of the many small fires still burning within. Some major fighting had taken place down there and, by the look of it, very recently.

"Jesus Christ," Garcia muttered from behind his right shoulder. "It looks like a Goddamn battlefield down there."

Redwolf glanced over at the Commander and nodded in return. "Looks pretty bad. What do you think happened?"

"I have no idea whatsoever, Jack," Garcia said. "But whatever it was, it wasn't good."

"Hold on everyone," Bover's voice called from the cockpit. "It's going to be mighty rough going down. I don't know if I can find a level spot large enough to handle this ship."

"Well, it didn't look too bad for the other ones that have already landed," one of the

FlightCorpsmen said.

"Yeah, but my ship is the largest of our little group," Bover said with the slightest bit of pride in his voice. "One of the largest on the planet, I might add. So just hang on, it might get a little bumpy, but I'll get us down."

"Just take it down safely and we'll be happy," Garcia called to Bover and then turned to his men. "I want all of you to be ready for anything once we're down. If any of what caused all that destruction down there is still loose in the area I want us all to be ready to handle it."

The shuttle fired its retros and landing thrusters, beginning to float somewhat on the backwash of superheated air buffeting the makeshift landing deck. "There's some equipment and shuttle debris scattered around down there that I'm not going to be able to dodge," Bover shouted over the roar of the landing thrusters. "It'll be a bit choppy but we'll be okay. One more minute and we'll be down."

Garcia held on tight to a support pylon in the cargo hold of the cruiser as the ship floated down and the landing gear strained against the floor of the shuttlebay. Three hard bucks and jolts later and the engines started to wind down. The cargo hold doors slid open with a hiss of escaping vapor and Garcia studied the scene before him very carefully before motioning for his men to leave the ship.

Once all the FlightCorpsmen from the Ruffian had regrouped, Garcia thanked all of the rescuing pilots for their assistance and told them to leave their ships fastened tightly to the landing clamps and head for cover. The absence of Buzzer, the Guarder, from the Starport spelled trouble. That in addition to the burnt and blasted state of the port led him to believe that heading for cover was the best policy for his men as well. But Garcia's problem was his inquisitive nature. There were too many unanswered questions about this winter world still tickling Garcia's mind, like where all of the Starport personnel who should have been milling about the shuttlebay had disappeared to, and he wasn't about to sit and watch whatever was going to happen on his ass.

"Listen up, I want you men to spread out and try to discover what in the hell happened here," Garcia announced. "Stay under cover while you're at it. I'll need one volunteer to help me search for Buzzer. Jack, you feel up to it?"

"Sure thing, Commander," Redwolf said. "Where do you want to start?"

"I don't even know," Garcia sighed and headed for the doors of the Starport. "How about this way?"

"It's as good as any other," Redwolf said and followed the leader of the Ruffian's FlightCorps out of the desolated structure.

~*~

"Admiral," the helmsman called from his position at the front of the bridge. "I have a detailed reading on the size and strength of the war fleet approaching Shining."

"On screen."

"Yes, sir," the helmsman said, and the enormous viewscreen depicting space was replaced by multiple listings of data and statistics.

"Jesus Christ, how in the hell does a filthy band of pirates grow to numbers of that magnitude?" Admiral James Dawson wondered as the figures continued to scroll across the screen.

"Don't know, Admiral," First Officer Doug Lysak growled from his station behind the Admiral's command chair. "Looks like we have a real fight on our hands this time, people," the commander called to the crewmembers on the bridge.

"Sound battle stations on all decks," Dawson commanded. "I want everyone ready for this when things begin to get rough."

The intermittent roar of the battle stations klaxon sounded throughout the huge confines of the battleship. Wolfpack Squadron was the largest and most powerful war fleet in the U.E.N. Military Command. The Wolfpack also held the record for most consecutive victories in battle over any other fleet in its branch.

"All right, helm, back to forward viewing," Dawson said. The view of endless stars flashed brilliantly back on to the screen. That scene never failed to fill Dawson with the same sense of awe and wonder that had driven him to strive through the ranks of the U.E.N. Military forces and command the most successful fleet of warships in the Known-Grids of Space.

"Dammit, did you see the size of some of those ships?" He muttered to Lysak.

"I wonder about their armaments and overall destructive capabilities," Lysak offered. "What's there to wonder about?" Dawson shot back. "They blew the Ruffian to hell,

Commander. A full strength and battle ready carrier of the U.E.N. Military. That's not something that I am going to take lightly."

"I didn't intend it to sound that way, sir."

"I didn't think it sounded any way," Dawson countered. "I was just commenting on your questions regarding their strength."

"Yes, sir."

Dawson's gaze lingered on his First Officer for a few seconds longer before he turned and looked back at the viewscreen. "Helm, dead ahead, full engines and divert that data to the main banks down below. I want a hardcopy of that information in my hands as soon as possible."

"Yes, Admiral."

"The rest of you, listen up," Dawson said and hit the ships-com button on the com-link panel to his left. "All departmental heads, this is Admiral Dawson. There will be a briefing session in the conference hall on Deck-16 in thirty minutes. All of you are expected to attend. That is an order but does not include the medical staff if an emergency occurs. Dawson out."

Lysak sighed as he returned his gaze to the view of space crowding the main viewscreen. "Why can't any of these so-called easy missions ever turn out to be easy?"

"That would just contradict everything that the military stands for, Doug, now wouldn't it?" Dawson answered and stood from his command chair. "Lieutenant Devon, you have the con while I conduct this briefing."

"Yes, Admiral," Devon called without looking back to meet the Admiral's eyes. "Very good, carry on and inform me of any new developments immediately." "Yes, Admiral."

Dawson took one last look at his bridge crew, the best in the Wolfpack Squadron, then motioned for Lysak to follow him off the bridge.

~*~

The city was barren, the streets deserted, police headquarters a burned-out hulk, and Able was confused. Had he missed it all? Where were the Sarge and Buzzer and the others? Where were all the citizens of CharterCity? And who in the hell were the hit men who had met him at the port?

Getting rid of them had been easy enough but figuring out the rest of this puzzle was getting more difficult by the minute.

The light of a new day was just beginning to brighten the sky over the quiet capital, the wind whistled eerily as it blew steadily through the empty streets. The only thing that looked out of the ordinary was the Police Headquarters Building. From his vantage point across the expressway, the great bulk of office building looked very much like something that would result from a visit by Buzzer. Obvious pockmarks and scars on the outer walls and doorways indicated heavy weapons fire—an assault of some sort? Buzzer? No, he didn't work that way, at least not most of the time. Then who? Had some of the pirate band been here already and cleaned out the town, taken what they wanted and killed any of those who got in their way?

That would explain a lot of what he was seeing around the city. It would also explain the ambush at the port. It could very well explain the disappearance of his teammates, though he decided not to think along those lines.

A sound off to his left alerted him from his thoughts. He listened intently, staying low behind the row of parked vehicles he had chosen as a recon base. There it was again, the same sound from the same distance. Very strange. Almost too audible to be someone sneaking up on him, yet again, just low enough to be dismissed as outside noise.

Again! Only closer this time. Somewhat like a low hiss, barely audible but there nevertheless. Able pulled his blaster out without a sound and checked to see the weapon's status. Good, it was primed and ready. The sound had come from the left and was heading straight toward him.

Now something different, a flash of light. Coming from the far left window of the headquarters building. What...a code? A distraction to keep him guessing? Now, he was certain that more than one person had discovered his position. Another flash and another sound, almost rhythmic that time. And again, and again, the light flashing and the sound moving closer. Sweat broke out on his brow as Able held firm to his weapon. God! This place was giving him the creeps already and he'd just gotten here. The flashing light had a sequence to it now, coming and going in quick little snaps. Yes, almost like a code.

The sounds had quickened also, following the same sequence, just a half-second after the lights and still moving closer. Trying to psych him out? No, too elaborate. But there was an unmistakable sequence to the light, if only he could raise his head over the hood of the vehicle to decipher it. No, that would be exactly what they wanted him to do if this turned out to be a trap. He would have to figure this one out using sound alone.

It had shifted, the sound. Now off to his right, but much more distant than it had been just moments before. Wait! There it was again to his left, but closer now. Two of them outside and one in the window flashing the light, on and off, on and off, very rhythmic. Almost like ancient Morse Code, it sounded just like the letter "G" over and over again. Then stopping, then starting again. Same sequence every time.

Then it hit him, thank God, it was Buzzer. The "G" stood for Guarders and the series of G's for the members of the team. Able rapped the butt of his blaster against the side of the vehicle in answer, nice and loud, just once to see if it was really them or not.

"Able?" came a low whisper from less than three meters away. "It's Thunder."

"Jesus Christ, you really had me going, Thunder," Able whispered as he appeared at the opposite end of the vehicle, pointing his blaster at Thunder's chest.

"Let's get inside, Able," Thunder said. "Everyone's there."

"What's with all the hush, hush, anyway?" Able asked. "Why didn't you just come right out and say who you were?"

"Because we weren't sure it was really you," Thunder said. "We heard reports of fighting in the port and we didn't know if it was you who walked away or them."

"Fair enough," Able answered. "Can we stop whispering now?"

"No," Thunder rasped and turned toward the headquarters building. "So far they don't know where we are but they'll be searching. We are their number-one priority at this point. After we're all gone, they'll be free to decide on how to handle the military forces once they get here."

"Who in the hell are 'they' and what military forces are you talking about?"

Thunder sighed as he reached the side door of the damaged building and pulled it open. "It's a long story, Able, just follow me and the Sarge will brief you."

"Sergeant Jekel is inside this deathtrap, too?" Able asked. "Yeah, but don't call it that," Thunder said.

"Why not?"

"Because it's all we've got."

~*~

J.D. Satchell's shuttle was the first to land in CharterCity. All in all, fifteen vessels had landed there and Sampson had left him in charge of the entire unit of soldiers. Better than one hundred fifty men were under his command. All of them were armed with multiple weapons and outfitted with complete sets of light body armor. They were expecting the most resistance from Shining's capital city but, much to the regret of J.D. Satchell, there wasn't a trace of any opposition on the streets to meet them.

After they landed, Satchell regrouped his men and split them up into five smaller groups, spreading them out to scout the town. The incessant silence had been eerie at first and they had all expected to be ambushed at any second. This uneasiness had led to many instances of misfired rounds and that made Satchell a very angry man.

Every time one of his men fired a shot, the entire group of them would have to scamper for cover and lay perfectly still for at least ten minutes just in case the enemy had managed to get a fix on their position. After hours of this useless roaming and fidgety trigger fingers, not a sound had come from the surrounding buildings... not a one.

Sampson had ordered Satchell to take and hold three key positions in CharterCity: CharterHouse, the administrative center for the city's politicians, Main Hall, the legislative center, and Police Headquarters, the heart of CharterCity's law enforcement operation. Their first stop had been CharterHouse and the only thing waiting to greet them there was a scene right out of a gory horror flick. Blood and brains had been strewn throughout the place, mostly that of the Head Statesman who had obviously pissed off the wrong people. He had been assassinated, although for what reason, Satchell didn't know.

Their second destination had been a little more exciting. Two of the twenty-eight Heads of State who served under the Head Statesman had been sitting quietly and defiantly in the lobby of Main Hall, aiming chargers rather unskillfully at Satchell and his men as they entered. When questioned about the recent startling events in the city and the current whereabouts of any of the police personnel or anyone else for that matter, the two had utterly refused to answer. So, for their trouble, they were unceremoniously disarmed, escorted to the steps of the official building and shot in the head with their own weapons. Their bodies flopped the rest of the way down the stairs, spilling what was left of their brains as they bounced, before coming to a grisly wet stop in the street.

Satchell had ordered a small group of his men to stand and guard both of those buildings while he and the rest of his soldiers went on ahead to scout out the police HQ.

The first barrage of fire tore into his men about a half-block away from the steps to the law enforcement center, reducing his number by five before any of them were able to reach cover. Grenades immediately followed, slamming into the row of vehicles parked along this side of the expressway just outside the building. Unfortunately for many of Satchell's men, those vehicles had provided the best cover during the initial barrage of enemy fire. The explosions that destroyed the parked vehicles tore many of his men apart, their dying screams etched into Satchell's brain permanently. More charger fire and more grenades slammed into their positions and, throughout it all, none of them had been able to squeeze off a single shot in answer to the onslaught. Several interminably long minutes of deafening explosions, searing heat and falling debris followed. The screams of the dying could just be heard over the raucous noise of combat in the street... screams that were playing havoc with J.D. Satchell's tortured mind.

Then, suddenly, there was nothing but silence and he and Jimmy Ray were all that was left of the large group that had marched down this street not ten minutes ago.

The sun was not long up and the morning still had an icy chill to it. What made it worse was the fact that Satchell had worked up a mean sweat and wet his pants as he'd watched his men screaming and dying in fiery explosions and charger blasts. Now, lying here beside a thick tree with a scared kid not much younger than himself, and not moving a muscle except to breathe, the cold was ebbing its way into his bones. Satchell didn't know how the bone chilling cold was affecting Jimmy Ray but he felt like a solid block of ice. He tried to flex his trigger finger in case he had the opportunity to actually fire his weapon but found the digit extremely stiff. No gloves—he had been very ill prepared for landing on this cold little planet. A bad smell was coming from Jimmy Ray's side of the tree and Satchell laughed at the fact that the youngster had done more than just piss his pants.

"What in the hell're we gonna do, J.D.?" Jimmy Ray said with a hint of hysteria in his voice. "Shit if I know, Jimmy Ray," Satchell snapped in reply. "Where did all that firepower come from, anyhow?"

"The police building over there, I guess," Ray said between chattering teeth.

"Of course, you idiot," Satchell rasped. "I meant, where in the building did it come from? It all happened so fast that I didn't get a chance to see…"

"You mean you just ran and hid your sorry ass like I did, J.D.," Ray said.

"Now that's enough outta you, Jimmy Ray," Satchell barked and pointed his big blaster in the kid's scared face. "I'm your commanding officer out here and you will listen to me as I'm speaking, understand?"

"Yes, J.D., I understand you just fine," Ray said, eyeing the muzzle of the blaster warily. "I'm just as messed up over this as you are, that's all."

Satchell visibly relaxed and lowered the gun from the kid's face. Aiming it back in the direction of the building across the street, he said, "It's awful quiet in there, Jimmy Ray. What do you suppose they're up to?"

"I could care less as long as they're not shooting at us," the younger man sighed and sighted up the barrel of his charger toward the police HQ. "How many of them do you think there are?"

"At least fifty by the amount of firepower that came streaming down from that place," Satchell said, nodding his head with absolute certainty. "I sure hope they don't come out here searching for survivors."

"Don't even talk like that, J.D.," Jimmy Ray snapped. "Dammit, we'd be fertilizer in less time than it would…"

"Christ, Jimmy Ray," Satchell said and poked the butt of his blaster in the other man's back. "Don't make it any worse than it already is."

"Sorry, but I..."

"Shhh!" Satchell hissed. "I hear something."

They both lay quiet behind the tree, listening, straining their ears for whatever sounds they could catch. "Sounds like running, a lot of people running."

"Yeah," Jimmy Ray agreed.

"Oh no, shit, no," Satchell realized. "It's Cotton and Lacey and the rest of the men we left at those other buildings. They must've heard all the shooting and decided to come and help us out. We've got to stop them, Jimmy Ray."

"How are we going to stop all those guys sitting behind this tree without exposing ourselves to dying?" Jimmy Ray asked.

"We'll shoot at them," Satchell said as a hasty plan began to formulate in his mind. "We'll start to shoot at the buildings down the street before they round the corner and they'll have to stop to seek cover."

"No, way, J.D.," Jimmy Ray laughed. "That's bullshit. Do that and you'll make yourself a clear target for those killing bastards across the street. You're out of your mind if that's what you're planning on doing."

"It's the only way, Jimmy Ray," Satchell said. "They'll all die otherwise."

"Forget it, man," Jimmy Ray said. "Do it yourself but I'm not getting killed for them." "Dammit, don't you go turncoat on me," Satchell said. "I'll waste your little ass right here like

I did Denny when he shot at that dog a while ago."

"Go to hell, Satchell," Jimmy Ray said and pulled the muzzle of his charger around to bear on his commander's chest, finger tensing over the trigger.

Just then the world exploded again and Satchell watched more explosions tear into the men rounding the corner about a half-block away. The blood was there again, filling the gutters and splashing the walls and Jimmy Ray was watching it too. Good for him, Satchell thought, and pressed his trigger. The blaster bolt tore the kid's head clear off and sent it sailing across the snow covered grass.

J.D. Satchell smiled and gloated for about three seconds before the flying head caught Buzzer's attention and he let loose a rocket propelled grenade from his launcher. The large tree across the expressway exploded in a gigantic red and yellow fireball. The blast sprayed wood, blood and body parts all around the base of the tree. Buzzer wondered at the reason for the flying head for an instant before turning back toward the fighting at hand. He sailed three more rockets in tight succession up the street.

It was almost sickening how much blood and gore was piling up across the four-lane highway that fronted the police headquarters but there was no time to think of that now. God knew how many invaders there were out there and how many hundreds of others might be on their way to help their fellows in need.

The firing cylinder clicked up empty as Buzzer fired his last rocket and he quickly dumped the bulky weapon for a full military-style charger, the kind that reduced two story buildings into toothpicks with three shots. He hadn't seen one this big since his academy days, when weapons training took on a much broader scope. This type of weapon had been abandoned as standard police equipment many e-years ago in favor of the much lighter and more accurate yet less powerful half-charger. In recent e-years, the mini-version of its full-sized cousin had become a favorite on the military and paramilitary scene.

Suddenly, the firing stopped. Just like that. Buzzer could hear himself breathing heavily; sweat was pouring off of him in rivulets. Even though the opposition had been less than challenging this time around, the heat of battle always made its shadowy presence known to soldiers like himself and his fellow Guarders. "How's it look, Sarge?"

"All's clear up front," the big man answered. "I don't really think any of them survived to circle around back. Thunder, just in case, I want you and Able to check it out back there. Take out any of them that you see, just do it quietly and be back here in five."

Thunder nodded once before Able followed him out of the room and down the hall. Jekel leaned back against the wall and sighed in relief. "I don't even think they hit the building twice, all of them together."

"Probably not," Buzzer said. "They obviously weren't expecting us to be here when they came storming down the street. They sure made easy targets, though."

Jekel laughed at that and stared out the glass-less window frame some more.

"Don't worry, Sarge," Buzzer began. "They're not going to get up and start walking again.

Not one of them. Just relax."

"This won't work again, you realize," Jekel said.

"Yeah, I know," Buzzer sighed. "We'll have to take to the streets like guerilla soldiers and feed off the spoils of our victims."

Jekel eyed his number-one soldier with a slight grin and crept back from the window. "As soon as those two get back I want to move. We can't stay here any longer than ten more minutes. If some of those ships triangulated on the location of all that weapons fire, they could just decide to test out their main gun's accuracy through Shining's atmosphere. If they do that and they're on target, we'll be so much floatingdust."

"Good point," Buzzer said and began to head toward the door. "I'll go round up all the spare ammo I can find and all the guns we can carry. We'll need all the help we can get from this point forward."

"You got three minutes, Frank," Jekel urged. "I want to get out of here as soon as possible." Buzzer paused in the doorway and took one last look around the battered Police Headquarters.

"Too bad, I sure was hoping we'd get a lot more of them before we had to give up this spot. Good protection for the most part. It's too bad."

"Yeah, I know what you mean," Jekel said. "Hurry about your business and meet me around the side."

"Will do, Sarge," Buzzer said and disappeared from view.

Harrison Jekel felt the short hairs on the nape of his neck stiffen and rise for a moment as he looked out upon the scene of death and destruction across the street. Too much blood had been spilled on his hands during this mission for one who upheld the law to the letter. Much too much...payback could only be so far away...

CHAPTER SEVEN

"Frazier!" Thornberg came bursting into the airlock. "Satchell and most of his men are dead. They were ambushed outside the police building in CharterCity. Cotton and Lacey are dead too. From the reports, it sounds like they were torn apart. Rocket propelled grenades and other high explosives. Grant says whoever these people are, they were heavily armed, better than our men were. Even with full armor."

"How about the other squadrons?" Sampson inquired.

"All else seems to be fine, the only opposition has been in the capital city," Thornberg reported. "Shell casings and discarded weapons were found in the police HQ. But why would the police forces of CharterCity be firing on our people, Frazier?"

"Because it wasn't the police, Gil," Sampson answered with authority. "The Chief of Police down there was good at one thing and one thing only, enforcing my will. He wouldn't know how to fight a battle skillfully if the enemy came out and surrendered to him. His policemen were even less qualified to be soldiers than he was. No, men who knew what they were doing did this. I guess it's fair to say that none of the opposition were found among the dead?"

"Quite right, Frazier, not one body was found inside the building and not a hint of blood spilled," Thornberg confirmed. "As a matter of fact, Grant reported that the place was a shambles from the outside but it looked as if most of the damage had been done before this battle."

"Interesting, very interesting, Gil," Sampson said and clasped the final latch on his combat suit. "Have all of our ship's sensors scan the area of attack for movement of a medium to large size force other than our men already in place in the area. If we locate something, track it and keep it in sight. For now, I'm going to take a shuttle down there and give our troops the morale they need."

"I don't know, Frazier," Thornberg frowned. "Do you think that it is such a good decision for you to be going down there and exposing yourself to such risk? With all of the unknowns down there and the fact that a U.E.N. war fleet is about to bear down on us so soon, it may not be the best of ideas."

"I can't think of anything better to do just now, Gil," Sampson said. "Not to worry, old friend. I'll need you to make preparations for planetfall soon as well. Until then, please proceed with the scanning and do go to the cockpit and ready the hatch for shuttle-one."

"Right away, Frazier," Thornberg said. "Have a safe trip." "I certainly plan on it."

Thornberg watched his leader turn and make his way down the hall toward the shuttle bay. He silently wished him luck and made his way back to the cockpit.

~*~

Razor stared at the empty streets of CharterCity. It was as if the entire planet's population had gone underground or disappeared. There was not a single soul in sight. The shuttles had been landing for several hours, and more of the little specks in the sky were descending even now.

The pirates were in for a disappointment—there was nobody here to kill and maim and rape...their usual favorite pastimes.

Luckily enough, he and his teammates had pulled out of the police HQ within half-an-hour of the arrival of the next wave of pirate-spewing shuttlecraft. The explosion that had leveled their former hideout had shaken the ground the Guarders were standing on more than three kilometers from that location.

"How many do you think they're bringing down, Buzzer?" Razor asked the big man standing next to him.

"Good question," Buzzer answered with a whisper from his partner's side. "If they're smart, they'll send down all the manpower they have available."

"Why would they need that many men to fight an army of zero?" Razor laughed. "Just look around you—there's nobody around to provide any resistance."

"Because the Wolfpack Squadron is scheduled to arrive here pretty soon and the pirates know that they can't fight that kind of firepower with their ships' armaments with any hope of victory," Buzzer said. "Their best strategy is to run the ships on non-life support but with full-power on all systems to maintain orbit and move all their combat-worthy personnel and equipment to the ground for some good old-style trench warfare. The U.E.N.'s troops haven't seen any actual hand-to-hand combat since that little uprising on Transfacarius about a decade ago. They won't be expecting it, they won't know exactly how to handle it and they just may not realize the potential danger in fighting a ground war until it's too late."

"So what it boils down to," Razor began, "is that there is a definite possibility that these pirates, or whatever they are, could actually emerge victorious over the Wolfpack Fleet if they end up fighting them on the ground rather than in orbit fighting them ship-to-ship?"

"Exactly," Buzzer confirmed. "But, what these filthy two-bit hoods are not counting on is the Guarder Factor. The fact that we are all here, assembled together into a cohesive fighting unit, will turn the odds greatly in the favor of the Wolfpack's troops. We will be more than enough to even the odds."

"Don't get cocky on this one, Buzzer," Jekel snapped from up ahead. "If I've got the numbers right in my head, and the Wolfpack only sends down their infantry units, we may still be outnumbered down here almost two-to-one. Not good odds when you're talking hand-to-hand combat."

"No, not if you see it that way, Sarge," Thunder said. "But Buzzer's right, we eight Guarders should easily make up the difference."

"Good attitude, Bobby," Jekel whispered, and a great cloud of frost was expelled from the large man's lungs. "But this is something that you guys were not trained for. I know—I trained you myself. The tactics of army battles are very different than the tactics of striking one target at a time or taking on individual squads of opponents at once. I don't think you guys are grasping the sheer numbers of enemy troops we are going to be facing. This is going to be something totally new to each of you but if you manage to keep your heads and follow my lead, we may stand a chance in hell of walking away from this mess. To tell you the truth, with what weaponry we have strapped to our backs right now we aren't going to go far no matter how good we all are at playing the game of war. When armies are involved the entire picture is transformed. The scope becomes larger, the threat more intense."

"I see what you mean, Sarge," Buzzer agreed. "I guess we'll just have to adjust our own individual fighting skills to take into account the massive numbers we'll soon be facing in combat. I don't see any problems, though. We all can adapt to any situation and we've all seen combat before."

"That's good, Buzzer," Jekel agreed. "You're right, we do need to adjust and adapt. We have to learn to fight together as a unit and learn fast. We have all performed well in team situations before but this is the largest single war party of Guarders ever assembled off of Aegis. Eight of us in one place, fighting the same war. It won't be as easy as it sounds. We all have to watch each other's backs and be aware of each person's position so that nobody gets caught in a crossfire situation."

"We'll damn well give them the fight of their lives," Able growled. "Don't worry, Sarge, they're not going to be the ones walking away from this one."

"Let's hope not, people," Jekel rasped. "Let's hope not."

~*~

Garcia crouched low and counted the shadows approaching from the deserted avenue two blocks down. From the looks of it, over thirty men were marching straight toward them. If they tried to move now, as a group, they might give themselves away. If they stayed put and tried to hide they might be discovered. Either way, doom seemed imminent.

"What's the word, Commander?" Redwolf whispered.

"I say we move and move fast," Garcia said. "They'll be here any minute. We'll make it if we're quiet but we have to move now."

"No way, I'm not moving from this spot, Avril." Jed Taylor, one of the pilots who'd rescued the FlightCorpsmen from their derelict fighters, squirmed in horror.

"Jed, calm down, it'll be all right…" Garcia started to say when Redwolf sounded a warning signal to be quiet. The band of miscreants was almost upon them, moving along at a leisurely pace. Not having seen a soul since they landed, this particular group of pirates wasn't very worried about keeping the noise level down. The Shiningites seemed to be extremely good at hiding out, that much was evident by the deserted streets of CharterCity, and the pirates seemed to look almost bored as they marched along the blacktop.

Garcia took a deep breath and tried to squeeze a little closer to the building they were using for cover. The small stairway cut down into the ground was the best cover they could scrape up on such short notice. Their first sign of the approaching pirates had been the tremendous noise they were making from several blocks away. Not knowing where the noise was coming from, Garcia had directed the small group who elected to travel with him and Redwolf into the staircase. Now the well-armed mini-army was passing by above and he felt as if his heart were pounding loud enough for them to hear.

In a few moments, only a few stragglers remained above their position, keeping an eye out for any opposition that might appear from the rear. Soon, even they were gone from view and the noise level diminished considerably.

Garcia breathed again and tried to calm his racing heart. He gripped his blaster a little tighter as he stepped away from the building and crept closer to Redwolf. Taylor was almost comatose and wasn't making a sound at the moment although the look in the man's eyes was very troublesome.

"Jack," he grunted as he hit the cold pavement inches from the man's position at the top of the staircase. "How's it look?"

"Good and not so good," Redwolf muttered. "That particular group is gone for now but who knows if they kept several men back a ways to search for people hiding out just like us."

"I see your point," Garcia said. "Do you think they'll be coming back this way?"

"Maybe not that particular group, no," Redwolf responded. "But others most definitely, Commander. We have to keep moving."

Garcia watched the receding men as they marched farther and farther down the avenue and chills ran down his spine. "Yeah, but we're never going to make it one kilometer with guys like Jed in our group."

"I hear you."

"What can we do with some of these guys to keep them out of harm's way and out of our way?" Garcia wondered aloud.

"Shoot 'em," Redwolf offered.

"Not funny, Jack..." Garcia started as the shadow of a man ran past them up the stairs. A sudden scream and the crack of a blaster firing shattered the silence. The darkness of the night erupted in a burst of noise and spectacular light. "What the hell?" Garcia muttered as he and Redwolf got to their feet at the top of the staircase.

Jed Taylor was firing in rapid sequence toward the now distant band of invaders, actually managing to hit two or three of them before they caught on to what was happening. Once they regained their wits about them, the thirty or so men began running back toward their position, weapons blazing. Chunks of debris were flying everywhere as great explosions rocked the building above them.

"Jed! Get down!" Redwolf screamed as the first volley of charger blasts thundered into the crazed man. Taylor's body disintegrated into a fine red mist that scattered into the air like dust in the wind and Garcia nearly vomited from the sight. A slap of red sticky wetness hit Redwolf in the face and dripped on to his uniform, all that was left of a brave man who had saved many lives just hours ago. Redwolf hit the street hard and brought his blaster up, firing ten quick bolts into the onrushing attackers. Six of the pirates dropped to the ground, their blood painting the asphalt, and Redwolf kept firing.

Other FlightCorpsmen and a few cruiser pilots were following his example and began firing their pitiful blasters toward the much better armed death squad bearing quickly down on them. One, two, three of his comrades in battle went down. Redwolf could hear the thump of each of their bodies as they hit the street motionless. The enemy grew closer, their mad rush bringing them within one hundred meters.

Avril Garcia realized just how bad the situation was becoming as he rolled away from a charger blast that ricocheted off the pavement just a few meters from his position. He could see the eyes of some of the charging monsters now...crazed, sick with blood lust, they were screaming some hysterical war chant as they raced down the street. He and his men did not stand a chance...

The sky lit up then with a tremendous roar and explosion. Five of the onrushing enemy went flying into the surrounding walls as a rocket landed amidst them. In a matter of seconds their numbers were reduced by half, and more fire came pouring into the group of invaders, cutting them down in hideous displays of death and destruction. One thing was peculiar, though, Garcia thought. The firepower was not coming from the members of his group.

He glanced at Redwolf, saw the horror etched there in the man's face as he fired his blaster as fast as he could, and Avril Garcia smiled in satisfaction. Lifting his own blaster, he lent some more punch to the fight.

...six, five...four of them left. Another dropped, the barrage of weapons fire was deafening as it filled their little intersection. Garcia sighted on a figure as it was blasted from view by a small grenade exploding underfoot. The figure was swept away and there were only two...one of them left...

The last of the pirates dropped, a half-charger blast tearing into his back as he turned to flee, his body sliding to a stop in a gory pile some distance up the street. And then it was over. Garcia sighed with relief, Redwolf loosened his grip on the gun in his hand and Buzzer's voice filled the void where roaring noise had been seconds ago.

"FlightCorpsmen, this is Buzzer," the Guarder called from somewhere unseen. "As far as we can see, the opposing unit has been eliminated. Can you see any other enemy soldiers who may be in hiding?"

"Not at all, you wiped them, Guarder!" Garcia called with disbelief and laughter in his voice.

He couldn't believe he was alive, not after seeing what happened to Jed Taylor...

Eight very lethal looking men dressed in black and toting all sorts of weapons appeared from an alley halfway up the block. Although Buzzer seemed to be leading the way, another one was clearly in charge of the group. The man was the largest human being Avril Garcia had ever seen and carried himself very well for his size. A powerful looking figure who chilled the blood in Garcia's veins. The others trailed along behind, eyes searching near and far for any additional targets. The entire bunch showed no signs of the bloody battle they'd just fought and won; instead they looked calm and alert. Professional soldiers, every last one of them.

"Commander, good to see you again," Buzzer said.

"Same here and more, Guarder," Garcia said and pumped Buzzer's outstretched hand vigorously.

Buzzer glanced around and then looked down as he caught sight of the FlightCorpsmen and others who had died in the battle. "Sorry about your losses, Avril. If only we were a few seconds earlier."

Garcia looked around then for the first time since the shooting began and saw the bodies of six of the men he had been traveling with, three of them FlightCorpsmen. "Jesus, I didn't even see most of them go down."

"At least we were able to erase another group of these bastards," Jekel said and bent to shake hands with the former flight commander of the U.E.N. Ruffian. "Sergeant Harrison Jekel, Commander of the Guarder Squadron. Pleased to meet you, Commander Garcia. I hear that you and your men have been through more than your fair share of action for the day."

"To say the least, sir."

"Well, then," Jekel said. "Let's not stay around this death pit. There could be more of them lurking about in the nearby shadows."

"Have you seen any civilians around here, Avril?" Buzzer asked, scanning the area. "Not a single one," Garcia replied. "It's like the entire city is a ghost town."

Buzzer paused for a moment before answering, "Yeah, same here." He began walking ahead of the group and called for his partner. The young Guarder caught up to Buzzer and they fell in step and continued down the street. "Razor, do you remember hearing anything while we were in CharterCity that could account for the lack of people around here? This place was sprawling with crowds of people when we first arrived. They have to be somewhere."

"Nothing, Buzzer, I don't remember hearing anything that might help us."

"Me neither," Buzzer muttered. "This whole thing just keeps getting more and more mysterious."

"Spooky if you ask me, Buzz," Thunder added from several steps behind.

"Quiet," Jekel called. "Let's not give ourselves away and leave our present position open to a potential ambush. I would rather have it the other way around if you don't mind."

Cougar turned and cast a wary eye at Buzzer. Although he could shoot just as well as any Guarder, Cougar's work within the Squadron was centered more toward the technical, back on Aegis. A communications console was more of a home to him than this cold and stark battlefield. Buzzer could tell that Cougar was still in a little bit of shock at the intensity of the battle back there. Buzzer found himself wondering why Jekel would request his presence on a mission as dangerous as this.

Thoughts of Cougar's presence troubled him as he looked up and watched another small group of specks, enemy shuttles, descending to the planet's surface, surely delivering more of their deadly cargo to Shining.

~*~

Frazier Sampson looked over the scene of carnage within the Shining Starport. He was disgusted and ashamed at what he saw. All the dead, every last one of them right down to the small body parts scattered throughout the badly damaged landing pads, had been members of his band. Fighting men, at least he could take pleasure in the fact that they had died as fighting men.

"Are the explosives in place?" Sampson asked to a small man cowering at his side. "Yes, sir," Emil Grant answered. "All placed as you have ordered, sir."

"Very good, then," Sampson said to the newly appointed commander of this particular unit. "Evacuate this place and let's be done with it."

"By your word, sir," Grant said and scampered off, shouting orders of evacuation.

What a waste, Sampson thought to himself. If only the chain of events that had started this entire ordeal could have been delayed by some two to three e-years. His forces would have been much better trained and prepared. Hell, he and his followers might have even initiated a battle like this with the U.E.N. Military, just to flex a little muscle in the region.

"Achhhh! Such thoughts of suicide should not be roaming around inside my skull at times like these," Sampson muttered to himself, turned on his heel and made his way out of the Starport. *Such large ships, such power and speed! Too bad they must be lost to the cause,* he thought as he looked out over the few ships that had remained intact after the recent battles. *What welcome additions they would have made to my fleet. If only there had been more time…*

"The U.E.N. war fleet approaches quickly, Emil," Sampson said, walking past the startled man. "Blow this landing area away, disintegrate it, and they'll see just how harsh this planet can be to the landing of shuttles and battle equipment."

"Yes, sir," Grant answered to the quickly receding back. "Shall I give the order, sir?"

At that, Frazier Sampson whirled around to face the smaller man with eyes full of fury. "The order has already been given!" he growled.

"Yes, sir, of course…" Grant stammered and quickly looked away.

A slow smile crept across Sampson's face then as he realized that, in the face of almost certain doom, his forces still feared for their lives when in his presence. "Good, then," he laughed to himself, relishing the power, for there would be no mutiny on this cold, dismal little planet. No, his forces would fight bravely and, better yet, unpredictably. And for that very reason…they might just come through victorious.

~*~

The effects of the explosion were tremendous, even from several kilometers' distance. The newly darkening sky seemed to come alive with the bright light, which poured forth from the expanding cloud of flames and debris. Then, in a matter of moments, the night went black again.

Buzzer picked himself up from the filthy pavement where he had ducked for cover when he first heard the rumbling of the fireball. "Sarge?" He called in a whisper and was rewarded with a grunt from another shadow across the narrow street. Moving silently over to where his commander was huddled, Buzzer's mind went into automatic; checking every square inch of the area immediately surrounding him, identifying shapes and figures as they emerged from the darkness.

"Sarge," he said and helped the large man to his feet. Although Buzzer was a man of considerable strength, this was no small task.

Jekel brushed at his chest to remove whatever dust and dirt still lingered there and looked at Buzzer. "What in the hell do you make of that?"

"It must have been the Starport," Buzzer said.

"Yeah, I'd say the same," Jekel agreed and glanced over the rest of his men.

"It seems like these pirates aren't as stupid as we think," Thunder said as he joined the group. "What makes you say that?" Redwolf asked. "You guys just wasted about thirty of them

without taking so much as a scratch."

"Maybe those particular pirates weren't too bright," Buzzer said. "But by blowing up the Starport they just bought themselves a little more time. The U.E.N. forces that are most likely approaching orbit above this hellhole have only official maps, charts and pre-chosen landing zones on Shining to draw from in their shipboard computers. Whatever shuttles or smaller cruisers they send down to scout out CharterCity will be looking for the Starport and nothing else. When they find it destroyed, they'll probably report back before trying to make another run through and picking another landing site. In the meantime, our invaders seem to know this planet well enough and probably have hundreds of small clearings and parks pinpointed nearby in order to continue organizing their troops, equipment and supplies."

"Why would they want all of their people on the surface when they'll need as much firepower up there in orbit once the cavalry shows up?" Garcia asked.

Jekel laughed at that and slapped a hand across Garcia's back. "What you are failing to understand, Commander, is that not even pirates are stupid enough to face a military armada coming at them full force."

"Although we wish they were actually that stupid," Able added. "It would make our jobs that much easier."

"But what about all their ships?" Garcia pondered.

"It'll just add to the confusion," Buzzer said. "Think about it, Avril. The U.E.N. military blazes in, armed to the teeth and ready for anything but when they achieve orbit around Shining they find several hundred ships of various design, all fully functional with all systems running normally. Even the defensive/offensive weaponry is primed and ready. The only thing that doesn't match up is the lack of life-sign readings—not one instrument will find a thing except maybe some livestock in the bowels of one of the larger ships being stored for later slaughter.

That will cause some major confusion within the leadership structure of the Wolfpack fleet. The commanders will want to pull back to a safer distance in order to further assess the situation.

They'll want to send some men aboard a few ships at random to check it out for themselves, to make sure it's not some kind of trick, some reverse readings program, which may be affecting their instruments. Anything could be possible and they'll want to find out what's going on."

"Once they're fully satisfied that there is no threat aboard those ships," Jekel continued. "They'll waste much time and effort, not to mention energy stores and ammunition, on obliterating each and every ship out there. That could take some time. All the while, our friends down here on the surface will be digging in and devising different strategies to deal with the military once they start sending troops down to the surface."

"What's more," Thunder said. "They'll start scanning the surface of this iceball and find it writhing with life. That will start them wondering how to distinguish between ordinary citizens and enemy targets. This is when they'll try to land a ship or two in CharterCity and find the Starport blown to bits. Some time later they'll start landing shuttles in fields and clearings... that's when the fun is going to start."

"Wait a minute," Redwolf interrupted. "You mean to tell me that this ragtag bunch of bloodthirsty maniacs might actually stand a chance of winning down here?"

"No, not at all," Jekel answered in a solemn voice. "Up against the military...maybe. But, with us included in the mix, they don't stand a chance."

Buzzer smiled at that renewed show of confidence from his commanding officer and thought of how good it was to see the huge bear of a man filled with life and purpose again. It had almost seemed as if Jekel was wasting away on Aegis, never taking part in a mission, never doing more than manning his station and coordinating every Guarder in the ranks on dozens of missions taking place simultaneously. It seemed to Buzzer that the other members of the Squadron took Harrison Jekel for granted too much of the time, not ever realizing just what role he played in their everyday successes and completed missions. But it was all too good to see the man back in his element, back in his former glory, being a Guarder again—in the thick of the fight, back where he belonged...

~*~

Sharon Strassberg sat in her chair and watched one of only a precious few monitoring stations they dared allow to operate. If any sign of their presence leaked out to those monsters above...well, she shuddered just thinking about it.

"How's it going, Sharon?" asked Will McIntyre, one of the many U.E.N. Ambassadors assigned to Shining.

"Pretty quiet overall, Mac," she said with a smile and was rewarded with another in return. *He is such a sweet and caring man*, she thought to herself, the kind that would make one fantastic husband someday. *Hmmm, now there was something to think about...*

McIntyre continued walking down the long corridor. All around him faces stared back. Unseeing, frightened and nervous faces. Young faces, old faces and just everyday normal faces—there had to be thousands of them crammed in down here. Many thousands...and they were all relying on him to keep them safe, to keep them alive and to bring them out of this all in one piece. It was almost too much responsibility to handle but he had been trained as an ambassador to handle difficulties of all kinds. Too bad, though, that most of his training had leaned toward the technical side of things. After all, he wasn't the Official Planetary Ambassador to Shining, that poor guy had probably died when the invaders stormed CharterHouse. The first reports from the automated security system within the complex had been dismal at best. It looked as though every citizen the invaders could find on the surface was killed on the spot. And where in the hell were the police? McIntyre had always felt that Chief Parker was sort of off, a man to keep your eyes on, but he had never really thought anything of it.

Being the Scientific Ambassador assigned to a world where the major area of study focused on the effects of long-term winter-like conditions on human beings and human society in general left much room for research but not very much room for buttering up to the local crime fighters. The political types had always done a good enough job of that. Besides, McIntyre never stopped to think that being corrupt on this insignificant little planet would ever get a man anywhere further in life. It just didn't seem realistic.

But, then how could he explain the sudden disappearance of Parker and his entire police force just before all hell had broken loose up on the surface? The only answer he could think of to that question was an ugly one. One that involved corruption to the highest degree, probably right up to the very top. It had even been rumored that Parker was somehow involved in the events that had led to the death of Shining's Head Statesman in CharterHouse itself. However hard it was to believe that Statesman Humechy might have been on the payroll of these marauders, it was not beyond consideration at this point. The planet itself, the towns and cities that made up Shining, were in a state of utter turmoil. The reports coming in confirmed it.

The only thing that had really been nagging at him for the past few hours was the small patches of fighting the satellites were picking up in the streets. It seemed that somebody was actually fighting back up there and doing enough damage to the invading forces to make them stand up and take notice. Swift changes in troop movements and basic security had taken place within the enemy units very soon after the initial attacks were staged against them. McIntyre could only hope that such little resistance might turn the tide and drive the unwanted visitors away from here. It was the only shred of hope he could cling to for the time being. If that hope were crushed...

He couldn't bear to think about it.

Everyone down here knew that it was only a matter of time before they were discovered and subsequently eliminated by the invading army. They had been lucky enough to escape detection this long but with every step, the enemy loomed closer.

"Say, Mac," Ellie Fremont asked from a chair in front of a dormant console. "Just how deep does all this go?"

"Well, Wiley says that these tunnels and storage areas were built by the original scouting teams," McIntyre replied. "As far as I know, nobody has ever really bothered to map them out."

"The people who built this place must have kept some kind of records," Fremont said. "Engineering plans, blueprints, there could even be some sketches stored around here somewhere."

"What about these terminals?" Sharon Strassberg asked from the front of the room. "If we were able to hook them up to the infosats in orbit we just might be able to access some of the older records."

"If there are any in there," McIntyre pointed out. "Plus, we don't want to attract any undue attention to ourselves right about now. Who knows what kind of alarms the console we're using now could be giving off?"

"Come on, Mac," Fremont said. "You know that we're doomed down here anyway. If it wasn't for old Wiley spreading the word through his contacts around the city, we'd have never even known about this place. We'd all be dead right now, don't you think?"

"Ellie," McIntyre said in exasperation. "What does that have to do with us using the computer?"

"We gambled once already and that paid off in a big way," the pretty young woman answered. McIntyre felt himself staring at her and physically tore his gaze away. "And so," she continued, "what harm can it do for us to try and find out just where the best hiding spot is down here? If we find the right place to lay low, then it won't matter even if those scum up on the surface find these caverns."

"You know, Mac, the young lady has a point there." Wiley Thomas spoke from the shadows in one corner of the cavernous room. "What harm can it do just trying?"

"Plenty, Wiley, you know that," McIntyre snapped. He started to feel his control on the group slipping away. Making any unnecessary waves right now just wasn't the kind of thing that would keep them alive. "If we alert them before we can find the information we're looking for then we'll all be dead. Can't you see that?"

"I say give the girl a chance," Thomas snorted.

"Yeah, Mac, let me try," Fremont coaxed. As she began to walk over to him, McIntyre could feel his throat go dry. *God*, he thought to himself, *she's not the first pretty woman I've ever seen*. No, but she sure was the prettiest woman he'd seen since landing on Shining. He laughed to himself and a smile crept across his lips. Ellie Fremont saw it and returned one of her own. "Do I take that as a yes?"

"Now hold on there, Ellie," he stammered but she just shrugged and leaned in close. "Will," she whispered, "you and I both know that this situation is far from over. If we are to have any chance of saving ourselves from those murderous bastards we're going to have to think up some pretty original ideas, like the one that got us safely down here." She tilted her face ever so slightly in the direction of Wiley Thomas and, for just a brief moment, the dim light in the large open space caught her profile and gleamed off the curve of her neck, across her collarbones. The image sent McIntyre's mind wandering in several directions at once and he had to strain mentally to bring himself back to the conversation.

"I understand that, Ellie, but what if?" he asked. "Just what happens if those demons up there notice some telltale sign that there are people down here, defenseless people? Thousands of us. Can we truly take such a chance with those lives when, right now, we are all in relative safety from the war-zone above us? Why risk it?"

Ellie Fremont looked him square in the eye then and, for several long moments, something passed between the two of them. Something subtle...like an understanding. "You really care, don't you?"

The question caught him by surprise and he found himself answering in the same whisper as her question. "Yes, of course I care. What did you think I was down here for? Myself?"

Fremont turned away and began to head deeper into the shadows, just a few feet, where no else would hear them. McIntyre followed and stepped up close to her. "Look," she said. "I know what you're saying about alerting those crazed lunatics up there and I'm sorry for seeming like a whiny little bitch, I'm not really like that."

"I never thought you were, Ellie..." McIntyre started.

"No, let me finish," Fremont said and paused momentarily to gather her thoughts. "We have been monitoring all the blood and gore up there and the fireworks and small battles with God knows who else is defending this icerock for what seems like hours now. If they haven't caught on yet, and all readings show that they haven't, I think it best if we all start acting together on something, just to keep our spirit of togetherness alive."

"Okay, I follow," McIntyre offered.

"If we lose that cohesiveness that made us a group when we climbed down here then we'll never make it back out," Fremont said. "We have to do something that will involve everyone and if that means moving around some to find a better place to camp out or sending some of the others to look for more food, then I say we should do it. Now, you're the appointed leader so far, seeing that you have some kind of official government ties, and these people will listen to you...for a time. But, Will, when the restlessness settles in, we're going to have an uncontrollable situation on our hands."

McIntyre breathed deeply then and considered all that he had just heard. The woman was making a lot of sense, and most of it was the truth, but he still couldn't shake that eerie feeling he was having about changing things around. "You must have been doing an awful lot of thinking about this over the past few hours."

"Yeah, watching all of that unfold on the surface over Sharon's shoulder gave me a lot of food for thought," Fremont confirmed.

"Okay, I'll tell you what," McIntyre began. "You seem to be the computer whiz with this older equipment and I'm no slipshod myself when it comes to older programming. If we find something, and I mean find it fast, like in ten to fifteen minutes or so, we'll leach it for all the information we can get. But, if we're unsuccessful within that first fifteen minutes we shut the whole thing down and wait several hours before we try again. How's that sound?"

Ellie sighed and grabbed him by the arm. "It's a beginning, Ambassador, it's a beginning."

CHAPTER EIGHT

"Settling into Shining orbit, Admiral."

Dawson leaned forward and stared at the view in front of him. *All of those ships, my God, hundreds of them, maybe close to a thousand.* The sight sent shivers down his spine. They were almost like ghost ships. "Are the instruments still showing no signs of life?"

"Yes, sir," Lysak answered. "All sensors indicate no human beings on board any one of those vessels. Only a scant few of the larger ones show signs of animal life, livestock we think. It's hard to tell with all the other interference coming in from those ships, Admiral."

Dawson grunted and strained to get a better look at the viewscreen, to see something out there not immediately visible, something that would give him some leads about this damnable mission. "What in the hell are they trying to pull?" He muttered to himself.

"Hard to tell, Admiral," Lysak answered after overhearing the mumbled question. "It's kind of eerie though."

"Scan Shining itself," Dawson ordered. "Look for life signs, distress beacons, things of that nature."

"Already scanning, Admiral," the ComTech replied from his console. "Reading plenty of life signs on the surface, sir. Interestingly enough, I'm reading thousands of life signs below the surface also, sir."

Dawson leaned in close to Lysak and whispered. "Shining's not a mining colony, is it?"

"Not that I am aware of, Admiral," Lysak returned, staring hard at the screen displaying the statistics. "More of an industrial center. Just what is going on down there?"

Dawson straightened in his command chair and took a deep breath. All of the suspense and tension on the bridge was about to eat him alive. *I'm a man of action, dammit!* He scolded himself and rammed a fist down on the armrest. "That's it, I've had quite enough of this silence," he said and turned toward his ComTech. "Lieutenant Melvin, I want an all-channels broadcast, broad beam, range to include every derelict ship floating around this hunk of ice and snow. Send an official signal warning the owners of those ships about the consequences of U.E.N. General Order #2474763-J, the intentional littering of space directly orbiting a habitable planet, and the disposal methods which will be utilized unless a response is attempted within the next ten minutes."

A few clicks and buzzes later and Melvin replied, "Message sent, Admiral. Broad beam, all- channels. No immediate response."

"Continue monitoring and inform me when either a response is received or their ten minutes has expired," Dawson said.

"Monitoring, sir."

"Very good," Dawson grunted to himself.*Let's see if sacrificing every damn ship in their blessed fleet is part of their game plan*, he mused.

"Still no response, sir," Melvin said. "But I have confirmation that the message has been received by several com-links on the surface of Shining. Wait...one of them is responding, sir."

"Let's hear it, Lieutenant," Dawson said and Melvin immediately punched in the ships-com code for the bridge of the huge warship.

"Welcome to Shining, U.E.N. Wolverine," an indistinct voice sounded. "The U.E.N. Ruffian's captain and crew are sorry to have missed you, I'm sure. Please note that the ships orbiting this planet seem harmless enough but, beware, your litter disposal methods may trigger some of the dozen or so sabotaged engine fuel cells that are floating among them. Please be careful, for your own sake. Shining out."

"End of transmission, Admiral," Melvin said and turned to face the viewscreen. Dawson gritted his teeth and leaned back in his chair. "Good Lord, what do you think,

Commander? Are they bluffing?"

Lysak turned on his heels and faced Dawson from across the bridge. "No, sir."

153

"No… just like that?" Dawson queried.

"They have no reason to bluff," Lysak explained. "When you think about it, this kind of tactic makes more sense in a battle of this type."

"Yes, I see your point, Doug," Dawson said and scratched his chin. "By informing us of their sabotaged engines they are actually stalling us far longer than we would have been stalled without the warning. It also gets them more time if the threat turns out to be real and one of their reactors is rigged. When that happens, we are bound to no other course but to check each and every ship orbiting this rock until we are satisfied that there are no others or that we have found all the sabotaged power plants. That, as we all know, could take hours. Even with the help of the other ships in the fleet."

"Do we take the chance of destroying them, though?" Lysak asked. "If, say, sabotage means bombs planted on several ships, can we afford to blow up ships and risk the actual size and strength of the bomb that has been planted?"

"Another good point, Commander," Dawson sighed. "I need more of these ideas thrown at me." He pressed the com-link button on his command chair. "This is Admiral Dawson, there will be a meeting of all heads of staff in the outer-bridge conference room immediately."

Lysak glanced toward the viewscreen. "Helm, maintain this position until further orders and patch the view on this screen into the outer-bridge conference room."

"Yes, Commander," the young Helmsman said and watched over his shoulder as the Admiral and First Officer left the bridge.

~*~

Buzzer hunkered down even further in the bushes where he lay prone, about a hundred meters from Main Hall. Razor's breathing could hardly be heard from his position a couple of meters away. Blitzer and Skinner had occupied the opposite side of the street to give the entire front entrance maximum surveillance. Thunder and Able had worked their way toward the rear of the

154

large building in order to locate and stakeout any back entrances that might exist. Jekel and Cougar had left some time ago on a brief reconnaissance mission to determine the size and strength of the opposing forces occupying the legislative center.

The barely audible beep from his sequencer was what had startled Buzzer just seconds ago.

Apparently, Razor had heard it also. "What was that?"

"Sequencer," Buzzer whispered and struggled to read the fine print on the tiny screen. Razor turned his gaze back toward the well-lit structure and went back to counting targets.

"Damn," Buzzer muttered under his breath and Razor glanced at him again. "What was it?"

"A swapping of transmissions," Buzzer said. "From who to who?" Razor asked.

"It seems that the cavalry has arrived in orbit," Buzzer answered quietly. "I just read a transmission from the Wolverine. The entire Wolfpack fleet is up there. They've found the derelict ships of the pirates, tried to warn the owners of official U.E.N. litter disposal policy and the pirates responded with a warning about sabotaged engines. Right now, it's a stalemate."

Razor nodded at that and wiped sweat from his forehead. "Somehow I thought I'd be relieved when they finally got here. Now, I don't know if the situation has just gotten worse or better."

"We'll find out in due time, partner," Buzzer said and settled his gaze back on Main Hall. "But I think our faithful leader and his sidekick are on their way back." Buzzer motioned to some shadows off in the distance and within the trees. Razor squinted and tried to pick out the figures among the dark and wooded area but had no luck.

"Where do you see anything, Buzzer?"

"Right there," Buzzer pointed to the same place before and had to stifle a laugh as the younger Guarder began squinting again. Faint movements caught his eye but nothing that seemed like anything but branches swaying in the breeze was immediately perceptible.

"Look, just tell me when they get here, all right?"

"I'm already here, Razor," Jekel whispered into his left ear and nearly sent him reeling. Buzzer worked on holding back laughter some more but one stern look from Jekel and all thoughts of humor were gone.

"What's the story, Sarge?"

"We've got an average size containment force in and around the building," Jekel began. "I've already touched base with the other teams but thought it best to join you and Razor for a direct assault on the front entrance as we begin. The surprise will be just enough to send soldiers running up front to lend support. Once the other teams feel that they have their best chance to inflict the most damage, they'll start their assaults and this thing should play itself out."

"Sounds about right," Buzzer nodded and motioned for the big man to come closer. "I just intercepted a transmission from the Wolverine, Sarge. She's up there with the rest of the Wolfpack right now."

"That's Jim Dawson's fleet," Jekel said and pondered for a moment. "Damn, they didn't mess around with this one. The Wolfpack is the U.E.N.'s Flag Fleet. Dawson's got enough firepower in his arsenals to turn this planet into so much water vapor and us with it."

"The question is, will he use those methods or will he conduct a complete and thorough investigation as official protocol demands?" Buzzer asked.

Razor watched and listened as the two legendary figures before him discussed the situation. Briefly, he glanced back to where Avril Garcia's men were trying to sit as still as possible while keeping all eyes on the surrounding area. The plan was for the FlightCorpsmen and others to lend support fire from the rear to make it look like the attacking forces were much greater than they really were. All in all, a good plan to start with, but, Razor was quickly learning that nothing in combat is ever as easy as it seems.

~*~

The shock of hearing weapons fire was beginning to wear off as Emil Grant ran to the front of the building. "What was that? You there, what was that?" He shouted at another running figure.

"Someone's firing at us, or at the walls, Emil!" The figure blurted without stopping.

"At the walls?" Grant wondered and hurried to follow the man toward the front entrance of Main Hall.

He reached the ornate staircase of marble that descended from the second story to the front entrance and stopped short. The building was being hammered, huge chunks of construction material had fallen from the cathedral-style ceiling and the entire structure was vibrating from the onslaught. Several massive holes had been blasted through the thick glass that plated the front wall, spreading thousands of sharp glass shards throughout the lobby. "What in creation is going on?" Grant shouted at no one in particular as he unslung his half-charger and took the smooth railing of the staircase down to ground level.

"Emil!" A man shouted and ran toward him. "Someone is attacking us!" "Of course, but who?"

"We don't know, they're not showing themselves, they may as well be ghosts," the man said frantically. "All we know is that they are firing on us from some distance away, in the bushes."

"Get all available men up here to defend this entrance," Grant ordered. "Also send a small team out there to double back on these aggressors. The quicker we end this skirmish the better."

"Yes, Emil," the man said and took off running toward a side corridor.

Grant leaned up against a marble partition and snuck a quick glance of the outside darkness out of one of the blasted windows. "Who are these idiots?" He asked himself. A charger blast echoed off the marble staircase, taking with it most of the left leg of one of his men. The screaming drowned out all other thoughts as Grant swung his weapon through the glass-less window frame and fired several rounds in quick succession into the bushes.

He stole another fast glance outside and immediately wished he hadn't as the streak of an incoming rocket was quickly approaching the building. "Get down!" He screamed as the projectile flew into the lobby area through a window and exploded against the far wall.

The eruption that followed was enough to burst both of Emil Grant's eardrums just before a large chunk of flying marble smashed into his back, severing his spinal cord in at least three places...

~*~

Able burst through a wooden door and rolled across the rough carpeted floor, firing all the way. Two blasters were training on him, getting closer with every shot fired. He crashed to an abrupt halt at the wall and his right foot went slightly numb from the impact. In an instant he was rolling back across the carpet in the opposite direction. He wished now that he had known there was virtually no cover in this corridor before he had thrown himself against that door.

With gritted teeth, he focused his dizzying senses on one of the faces down the corridor and fired a three round burst.

Two of the three blasts found their mark, tearing away the head and shoulders of one man, while the third blast went wild, exploding into the ceiling panels above the second gunman. The startled man momentarily stopped firing to lift his arm up for protection against flying fragments. Able took the opportunity to take aim and shoot. He didn't need to watch to know the outcome of that blast.

Lying prone now, he used the next few seconds of silence to catch his breath and clear his head from the echoes reverberating through his skull. No one else seemed to be in the corridor. Just two sentries posted here meant that their forces were spread mighty thin right now, trying hard to cope with the onslaught coming at them from the front of the massive marble and stone structure.

From the sound of things, Buzzer and Jekel were hitting them hard, going all out to make it seem like a much larger force was storming the building. Main Hall was shaking violently from repeated charger blasts and rocket explosions tearing out large chunks of wall. The smoke was visible even from up here on the second floor. Hopefully, Thunder had also found such dismal opposition and had come through it all right.

Able leapt to his feet and headed for the shadows of a corner as the sound of footsteps approached. Silently, he unsheathed two slim knives from behind his back. The footsteps entered the corridor and stopped dead, probably at the sight of blood and gore and whatever else remained of two former comrades in arms.

After several seconds of silence Able could just make out the sound of boots crunching against the rough carpet fibers, coming closer to his position...closer, almost...

As the tip of a boot rounded the corner he exploded into action, lunging from his hiding spot and stabbing a knife deeply into the corpse of one of those he had just killed out in the corridor. As his mistake registered within his brain, he hit the floor hard and executed a perfect back flip that placed him up against the far wall and clutching a blaster in one fist. For one heartbeat, the two men took aim on one another and fingers tensed on blaster triggers. Once the moment passed between them, they both sighed and lowered their weapons. "I would have had you with that move," Thunder grunted and holstered his weapon.

"Yeah, don't remind me," Able muttered and inwardly seethed with anger at his amateurish mistake. Thunder was good, better than he was, and they both knew it. But, he still should not have made such an error in judgment. "Let me guess," Able said. "When you paused it wasn't because you had just been shocked by the gory scene in the hall, right? It was because you had leaned down to pick up that bastard to use his dead body against me."

Thunder nodded at him once and smiled. "I thought it would add a nice touch to the encounter if you had turned out to be one of them."

"I can't imagine the look on my face when I sunk my knife into that guy's open guts," Able said and laughed.

"It wasn't pretty," Thunder said and stepped over the corpse in the corridor. "Where do we go from here?

Able steadied himself as Main Hall shook violently and looked up and down the corridor. "Since you're up here already, I gather you didn't find anything on the first level?" he asked, and Thunder agreed. "So, I just got finished leaping in here and killing those two when you surprised me with your grand entrance. I haven't even begun searching up here yet."

"Good, let's get to it," Thunder said and began walking away from the stink of death that was beginning to overtake the small hallway. Able followed, more cautiously than before and clutching his blaster very tightly.

~*~

"What in the name of God is going on?" Frazier Sampson roared as he came out of the luscious former quarters of Shining Statesman Humechy and into the lavishly decorated outer lobby.

"A large scale attack is being pitted against Main Hall and our forces stationed there, Frazier," Gilfred Thornberg stated between gasps of air. "We don't know who or what or where they came from but they're doing quite a destructive job of it."

"Could that damnable fleet that's hovering above us have already landed a squad or two of soldiers, Gil?"

"Anything's possible at the moment, Frazier," Thornberg said. "Although the readings of all of our instruments would tend to negate that theory."

"How far is it to Main Hall from here?" Sampson asked.

"Approximately one kilometer due north, Frazier," Thornberg answered cautiously. "Whoever they are, they could cover that distance in quite a hurry."

"Yes, I can feel the shaking under my feet even now," Sampson blurted and began to pace the lobby rug. "If I send help from this position it leaves us under-protected in case we end up coming under attack from some opposing force. If I keep all personnel at this building and don't send help to Main Hall, I am dooming all of those brave men and women to death in order to save us. Based on this, my conclusion is that neither plan shall be effective. My only alternative is to move from this place and eliminate the sitting duck position I would surely be in if I stay."

Sampson continued his pacing for several moments longer, deep in thought, before stopping in front of Thornberg. "Gilfred, round up all the men except five and prepare them for immediate withdrawal from this position. We'll move out of the vicinity and head for the hills where surprise and the cover of the brush will be on ourside."

"Yes, Frazier," Thornberg said. "And what of the other five men?"

"Yes..." Sampson said and hung his head low. "They will stay here as sacrificial lambs to offer whatever resistance they can in order to give our group a better chance of survival."

Thornberg let his gaze linger on that of his leader's face for perhaps a heartbeat before responding, "Yes, Frazier, of course."

Sampson patted him on the shoulder once then turned abruptly on his heel and strode out of Humechy's outer lobby. Suddenly, there was something about all of this that Gilfred Thornberg did not like in the least. Something in the eyes of Frazier Sampson that spoke of lunacy, something that was not as it should be. Gilfred Thornberg began to seriously doubt, for the first time since he had known the man, the mental competence of the one who would lead them into battle...or, quite possibly, to slaughter...

~*~

"Oh my God!" Sharon Strassberg shouted as the center screen before her switched over to a view of Main Hall's front entrance. She quickly punched in the command to lower the volume and the deafening noise emanating from the console instantly ceased. Explosions of light were leaping from the small screen as inside the massive lobby of Main Hall men were dying.

Glancing back into the shadows, she noticed at least fifty people had gathered to watch the spectacle over her shoulder. Several times she had to turn her head away in disgust at the brutal images flashing across the monitor. The images seemed to burn directly into her mind, imprinting themselves on her memory. And yet, in all their horror, it felt very good that payback time for those invading bastards had finally arrived.

"Damn, that firepower is enormous," Wiley Thomas muttered from someplace nearby. "Those poor slobs don't stand a chance against all that."

"Well, it's about Goddamn time," an unfamiliar voice chimed in from the back of the crowd and murmurs of approval began to take over the room before Will McIntyre called for everyone to be quiet. Suddenly, the last man alive on the screen went down amid a hail of gunfire and the scene was still. Sharon raised the volume on the console and the crackling sound of small fires abruptly filled the room. Nothing moved for several minutes as the crowd gathered around her stared in awe at the devastation wrought on Main Hall.

"Huh," Sharon gasped as a dark shadow on the screen began to move forward into the dim light. "What is that?"

"Look there, another one!" came from somewhere to her right in response to the appearance of a second figure. Then a third, a fourth and finally a fifth figure became visible. Each of them were holding multiple weapons and seemed to be carrying other miscellaneous armaments. It was hard to tell in the darkness of the screen because each of the figures was dressed in black. Even their skin seemed to blend in with the shadows.

"Who are those people?" McIntyre asked in a whisper and leaned over the console to get a better look at the small screen. The figures were talking now, though their voices were nothing but faint whispers with no clear words. "Are they soldiers?"

"None that I've ever seen before," Strassberg commented. "If they are, where in the world did they come from?"

"Good question, but dammit if they didn't do their jobs," McIntyre said and began adjusting controls to bring the camera in Main Hall into sharper focus.

McIntyre immediately realized his mistake as the whizzing sound of the small motor inside the camera caught the attention of one of the...soldiers? In an instant, a weapon had been raised and fired. The intense brightness of the light contrasted sharply with the utter darkness that overtook the monitor when the camera went out. "Damn!" McIntyre swore and walked away in disgust, angry with himself for making such an obvious blunder.

Strassberg switched the view to another camera within Main Hall and was met once again with virtual silence. Two other views were tuned in with the same results. "I think that about does it for any pirates who were inside that building," she laughed.

"Let's hope that those people are on our side whoever they are," Ellie Fremont said. "The last thing we need is more killers wandering around up there on the streets."

"Cheers to that," someone called out and the laughter that followed seemed to ease the tension in the room to some degree. Will McIntyre glanced around at the smiling faces and thought that, maybe, just maybe, they all had a shred of hope left.

~*~

"Move! Move! Move!" Buzzer called and the entire team raced out of the building to melt back into the shadows of the surrounding bushes lining the street. Once they were all safely out of Main Hall, they regrouped and double-timed it back to where the FlightCorpsmen and other civilian pilots were sitting out this phase of the attack. "Don't fire, Guarders approaching," Buzzer whispered to the single posted sentry from not three meters away. The man was visibly shaken by their sudden appearance and followed them back to the group in stunned silence.

The vast expanse of snow-covered grass, trees and bushes that made up the CharterCity Downs had served them well during the attack on the legislative center. *It was too bad*, Buzzer thought, *that we have to leave the relative security that the dense growth offered so soon.*

"Sarge," Buzzer whispered into the big man's left ear. "That camera in there was being watched by someone and manually operated. That wasn't a computerized automatic response, there was someone on the other end of that thing, I'd swear to it."

"I agree," Jekel said and lapsed back into silence.

163

"What did you guys fire on back there?" Able asked from somewhere off to the right. "I didn't think we left any of them alive."

"We didn't," Jekel said and gracefully rose to his feet. "There was a security camera in there, an operational one that was probably transmitting when we came into its field of view."

"Most official buildings on these backwater planets have outmoded security systems," Cougar offered. "It was probably triggered by our movement within the room."

"No, there was plenty of movement within the room before we heard it moving toward us," Razor added. "I was pretty close to the damn thing and I didn't hear it moving around while the shooting was going on."

"There's somebody else inside that building, working security systems and quite possibly in communication with other members of this invading force," Jekel said. "We need to find out just how extensive the security system is. If it incorporates several audio/visual components throughout CharterCity, the Wolfpack's men could be walking straight into ambushes at every turn."

"If this turns out to be true, where do you think the system is being monitored from?" Blitzer asked.

"I'd say they're either inside this building or CharterHouse," Skinner offered. "The Police Headquarters Building was blown to bits. Nobody could still be operating sensitive equipment set up in that place, no matter how far underground they are."

"The camera itself is pretty straightforward in design," Cougar said, his technical expertise coming in handy. "Probably closed circuit, it may just be too simple to be operated all the way from CharterHouse. That would mean at least a kilometer of wire strung up between the two buildings. Based on everything else I've seen of this place, I'd say it would be asking a lot for such a system to still be operable. Especially after the battle we just fought in there."

"How about underground wiring?" Skinner asked.

"There could very well be some underground wiring between the two buildings," Cougar answered. "But I still don't think it would be operable after all the pressure we've been putting on Main Hall. Blaster charges have been known to crack foundations at times and we just about brought the place down to the ground."

"So, what do you think, Cougar?" From Jekel.

"Well, if there is underground wiring, I'd say it would have to go straight down for quite a ways to withstand the forces we unleashed on Main Hall."

"You mean a tunnel system?" Buzzer asked.

Cougar seemed to consider that for a few seconds and then grinned. "That would fit, Buzzer," he said and rose to his feet. "Tunnels dug under here for some kind of safety bunkers, perhaps an emergency escape route out of CharterCity or a bomb shelter."

"Jesus," Thunder rasped. "Bomb shelters haven't been built since the days of The New Conflict and that was centuries ago."

"Right around the time this planet was first settled," Jekel said. "Cougar's right, it fits. Let's look into it. Cougar, I want you to find an access panel, anything that will get us some more information about this place, any ancient subterranean construction in this vicinity or around CharterHouse."

"The best place for that would be CharterHouse itself," Buzzer said. "While Razor and I were there talking to Humechy, I noticed one hell of a computer complex."

"That's about a seven-minute hike from here. Let's move out," Jekel said as the rest stood and crept deeper into the dark shadows of the woods. "Skinner, go back and brief the FlightCorpsmen of our plans. Stay with them and tell them to remain alert and fully armed at all times. Give us enough time to get to CharterHouse and scout out the area. Then join us at the perimeter of the CharterHousegrounds."

Skinner nodded his understanding and disappeared into the growth. Jekel caught Buzzer's eye and motioned for him to lead the way. The leader of the Guarder Squadron brought up the rear as the team of Guarders moved out into the night.

~*~

"Look up there, Gilfred, do you see it?" Frazier Sampson asked his Second in Command. "The armada that will soon be pitted against us has arrived."

"Yes, Frazier," Thornberg snarled as he watched the flashes of white litter Shining's night sky. "The pigs have come for the slaughter and bloodthirsty we shall be."

Sampson smiled at that and clapped a hand down hard on his companion's shoulder. "That's the spirit, old boy," he declared with a laugh and slid farther along the shiny rock by the lake.

Amazing, Thornberg thought. *This one small body of water has managed to keep itself unfrozen on this icy world. It must be very deep, very deep indeed.*

Suddenly Thornberg winced as another flash of brilliant white against the dark backdrop of stars signaled the end of another one of their ships. The once proud fleet of vessels, all stolen or patched together with bits and pieces of other ships, had served them well. Another white flash brightened the blackness overhead momentarily and Thornberg felt his hatred for the forces above growing stronger. How long would it take? How long for one fleet of warships to destroy what took years to compile? With each tiny flash of light, their chances of ever leaving this dismal planet became slimmer.

Deep down, he knew that Sampson had gone totally insane. The man was no longer capable of making strategic decisions, he was no longer able to control himself and, so, had doomed every last one of his followers to either death or imprisonment. Thornberg laughed to himself then, for his knowledge of the true state of things did no good for anyone. The fanatics who guarded Sampson would never listen to any other human being but the leader of this Godforsaken bunch himself. Their own forces were stupid enough to believe that they just might win the upcoming battle, a war against vastly superior military forces. At least in space they had amassed enough strength and firepower to overtake one FlightForce Carrier. At least, up there in the heavens, they stood a fighting chance.

But down here, with whatever weapons they could carry on their backs, several thousand battle weary militants would trek across the barren land and wage war against countless numbers of U.E.N. soldiers, an entire fleet's worth of personnel and armaments. Sheer lunacy...

What could be done? If he spoke out now, at this seeming hour of victory, he would be killed in less time than it would take for him to apologize for running his mouth. He was doomed no matter what course of action he chose. Speak out and die most certainly, fight on and die...perhaps. At least, by following Frazier Sampson through to the end of this thing, Gilfred Thornberg might have a chance at survival. A very slim one to be sure but a chance nonetheless.

~*~

Strassberg gasped as a bank of sensors located on the surface several kilometers away began to scan several thousand people nearing the entrance to what used to be a ventilation duct but was now a small lake of unfrozen water, kept heated by the underground system's excess wasted air.

"What is it?" McIntyre asked as he rushed toward her console.

"One minute I was scanning the computer's files for any information on other deeper caverns like this one and the next thing I know an alarm indicator starts blinking," the young woman answered. McIntyre reached over and hit several switches, putting a stop to the rapidly blinking light on Strassberg's console.

"That used to be an old duct, one that was equipped with one of the few access hatches to the outside. The sensors indicate that it's covered with water now but there are several thousand people up there right next to it. If those are the invaders and they manage to find that hatch..." Strassberg allowed her thought to trail off.

"Are you sure that thing isn't malfunctioning?" Wiley Thomas said from his new position next to McIntyre. Strassberg ran her hands across the keyboard, ordering up an internal scan of the old system but everything showed fine.

"I'm afraid this console is working perfectly including the alarm indication," Strassberg said. "But the sensors do indicate that the hatch on that duct is located near the top of one of the nearer ice-capped hills.

167

"Christ, I didn't think the sensor readings could reach that far," McIntyre said, studying the data screen and the information pouring across it. "When was this thing built again?"

"It was originally built several hundred e-years ago, Mac," Thomas began. "But it sure looks like a lot more recent work was done down here. These instruments are not the originals, I can tell you that, and these consoles are very much like the ones we used to work with up in CharterCity."

"Wiley's right," Ellie Fremont said as she stepped forward. "These consoles are almost exactly like the ones I used to work with, maybe two or three models earlier. But I would guess that somebody has been doing a lot of work refurbishing this place. Just in case, maybe?"

"Maybe," Thomas agreed, "somebody was on to these tunnels and was preparing to use them someday, in case something like what's happening now actually took place. Who knows why.

It's just very strange to see this place looking as well kept as it does."

McIntyre leaned against a support pillar and thought that over for a few seconds. Wiley Thomas had a way with people, and he also had a way with figuring things out. It had been Wiley who had known about the underground tunnel complexes and it had also been Wiley's contacts who had spread the word that something had gone terribly wrong between the local police and the two Guarders who had mysteriously appeared on their small planet some days earlier. McIntytre had been truly impressed with the older man's ability to unite these people and bring them together to save themselves. He had almost single-handedly managed the entire affair. He had arranged meeting points with his contacts near CharterCity's several dozen remaining secret access ways into the underground labyrinths they now huddled in. One had been within CharterHouse itself, in a sub-basement, and another had been inside Main Hall, where Wiley's grandfather had once been an official. Obviously, the man had known about the tunnels since his youth but had never had need to use that knowledge until now. That knowledge had proven lucky for the CharterCity inhabitants who had been able to escape the horror taking place on the surface and take shelter within the underground complex. Still, thousands of others, including most of Shining's political officials, had fled away from CharterCity, to take their chances in the surrounding suburbs. A massive exodus of vehicles had taken to the streets of Shining's capital city and cleared out very soon after word of the deadly firefight in CharterHouse had spread. McIntyre could only hope that his decision to take up residence underground would prove to be the right one.

"Does it look like those people are preparing to enter the access hatch near that duct?" Thomas asked Strassberg.

"No, they're just sort of camped out along the banks of the small lake up there," she replied. "The actual duct is under several meters of water."

"What's the chances that those people, assuming they are members of the invading forces, will end up finding this place?" McIntyre asked.

Strassberg and Fremont immediately looked to Thomas, unwilling to offer any speculation on that question. The elder man scratched his chin in thought for several seconds before looking again at the information displayed on the sensor monitor. "I'd say there's a slim chance right now. They seem only to have found a place to stay for the night, right close to a water supply and a good hike up for anyone following. I think they'll pick up and leave in the morning, no harm done."

"I tend to agree with him," Fremont said and Strassberg rolled her eyes, causing a smile to play against McIntyre's face.

"All right, then," McIntyre said. "We'll announce to the others that everything is under control and we'll try our best to monitor this group of people until they're gone."

"Sounds good, Mac," Thomas said, nodding his approval.

"Yeah, sounds good to me too," McIntyre said under his breath and wiped a fine bead of sweat from his forehead. "Let's just hope that they move on come morning."

~*~

"Last target, designation #324x, Sleekster, now within range, Admiral."

169

"Lock on and fire at will," Dawson said and slapped his hands to his knees. The muffled sound of heavy weaponry brought a smile to the Admiral's lips and the bright flash of destructive power that ensued made that smile even deeper. "Well done," Dawson said with a sense of smug satisfaction. "It seems that all that can be done up here has been done. Time to move on to that nasty business below us. Commander Lysak, please see to our troops' safe departure for Shining as soon as possible."

"Yes, sir," Lysak said and moved toward the rear exit of the bridge. Dawson watched his first officer leave and then turned to face the forward viewscreen. All of the fleet's commanders had been fully briefed on the next phase of the operation to liberate the people of Shining and the Sarkennon System from the clutches of the invaders who now swarmed over the planet below.

The "war" would now become surface-based, and the soldiers of the Wolfpack Squadron were just about the best in the U.E.N. Military when it came to hand-to-hand combat tactics.

"Yes, I have you now you miserable murderous bastards..." he muttered to himself and stood from his command chair. "Lieutenant Devon, maneuver us into a position of direct support for our ground forces. I want all main weapons stations on full alert and powered up just in case we have to lend our troops a hand on the way down."

"Yes, sir," the young man answered, hands already manipulating the console in front of him. "Maneuvering into support position, all weapons stations reporting on line and operational at this time, Admiral."

"Good, very good," Dawson said and flipped the com-link on his command chair to ships- com broadcast. "Attention, crew. This is Admiral Dawson. In just a few moments the ground- phase of this war will begin. Our troops will be venturing down to the planet's surface to track down and eliminate our opponents. Please join me in wishing Godspeed and a swift victory to all of the fleet's troops. Mark my words, everyone, on this day the Ruffian and those who lost their lives aboard her will be avenged."

~*~

The knife slid easily between the man's ribs and into his beating heart. Buzzer clamped a hand down hard over the man's mouth to drown out his dying scream. Soon the tense form went limp and Buzzer gently laid the body on the floor.

If all their surveillance had been correct, this should have been the last of the sentries posted outside CharterHouse. The other four sentries should also have been dispatched by this time, so Buzzer took a chance and activated the audio on his sequencer. "Thunder, this is Buzzer," he whispered, just in case.

"Go ahead," came the whispered reply.

"I'm through with my two, how about you?"

"Same here."

"I'm finished on this end," Able's voice joined the conversation and Buzzer frowned to himself at how easy this little operation at CharterHouse had been. "Okay, let's regroup back with the Sarge and we'll go from there."

Buzzer glanced down at his fallen enemy and shook his head in disgust. "Kids, nothing but stupid young kids."

It was a short jog back to the meeting point, and the Guarders took one more, short look around before entering the darkened building together. Buzzer taxed his memory of his previous visits to this building and remembered a room off to the left near the information center that contained several computer consoles. With the others close behind, he led the way through the dark and shadowy corridor until he reached his objective.

One of the small screens blinked to life as Buzzer activated the terminal, and the sudden glow illuminated the anxious faces of his fellow Guarders. "Cougar, you'll be better at this than any of us," he said and made room at the console for the communications tech. Cougar's hands began to flash across the keyboard and within seconds he had called up a schematic of the entire facility, sub-chambers included.

"There." He pointed at a small corner of the screen and quickly tapped the keys which would enlarge the section he was indicating. "Those passageways seem to come to a dead end, but why would they suddenly stop in the middle of the complex? Why not link up with another corridor just for the sake of being useful?"

Jekel shrugged. "That's as good a place as any to start," he said and motioned to Buzzer and Thunder. "Find those corridors and see if they lead anywhere else but in a dead end. The rest of us will go back and gather up the FlightCorpsmen. I don't want to split us up any more if we can avoid it. Things are going to get pretty hairy on the surface once the troops begin unloading."

Buzzer glanced at Thunder and the two marched off into the semi-darkness of CharterHouse. Jekel watched them disappear into the gloom before motioning for the rest of his team to follow him outside.

United Earthian Nations

SouthWestern Corporate

Grid-Sector Sarkennon System

Shining Mission—Day Four

In 2147 the Phillipson Conflict, a little known and under-publicized skirmish,took place between the four Phillipson Robotics, Inc., facilities dispersed throughout the Berking System. Although history grants this incident little notice, it is of extremely significant importance—marking the first time that mankind went to war against machines. Still unknown are the specifics that led the top secret Artificial Intelligence Research Project to seize control of the entire system, ordering every available machine to attack all human targets. Despite the fact that the AI Project was quickly destroyed and order restored to the Berking System, enough damage and loss of life took place to effectively bring the entire Phillipson Robotics Operation to a screeching halt. Now, with a long-standing reputation for excellence and a grand history in the shipping industry, spearheaded by the Berking Transit System, enough still remains of the bloody legends surrounding the Phillipson Conflict to enshroud the people of the Berking System in a deep-rooted aura of spooky superstition, lasting well until this day...

(Excerpt:*A History of Modern Earth and Beyond—the People, the Politics andthe Insanity of Our Past*by Joseph Mullens)

CHAPTER NINE

The sun burned brightly in the crisp clear sky as it peeked up just over the horizon. Dawn had arrived bare minutes ago and it looked like a cold day lay in store on Shining.

"Christ, it looks like a bomb hit down there," Lieutenant Bob Moore rasped from the co- pilot's seat. The shuttle had launched less than an hour ago from the U.E.N. FlightForce Carrier Wolfbane and was now passing over the surrounding areas of CharterCity.

"Looks like the spaceport's been blown, sir," the pilot's voice crackled in his headset. "From the look of things there's been a real bloodbath down there."

"Tell me about it," Moore grumbled and looked back to the map displayed on the screen. His fingers deleted the current scan for a primary landing area and quickly entered commands for secondary choices. The computer highlighted each area, a total of three within a four-kilometer radius. "What's it look like out there, Henson?" He called to the WeaponsTech a level below them.

"As far as I can tell, sir," Henson's voice came through. "There's nothing actually moving down there. Thermals show no living people, just bodies in the immediate vicinity. That's on the surface, sir. It's a different story underground."

Moore remembered hearing about the thermal findings underneath CharterCity during the last briefing before launch. "Do you have a count from underground?"

"Not an exact total, sir," Henson said. "But it's probably somewhere in the thousands."

"I wonder if they're friendlies or hostiles," Moore mumbled and caught the pilot's eyes as they turned in his direction. "Okay, Jimenez, put us down in that clearing to the left of the main complex." Moore pointed at his choice on the screen and Jimenez nodded.

As the small shuttle banked hard toward their destination, Lieutenant Moore snapped the visor down on his helmet and checked his personal weaponry.

Satisfied, he looked back up and took in the view of Shining's capital city. "It looks like a Goddamn maze down there."

A slight chuckle came through his helmet earphones from the pilot's direction. "Just watch the road, Corporal, and get my feet on the frigging ground," Moore rasped.

"Yes, sir," Jimenez snickered. "The Lieutenant's feet will soon be on the frigging ground and in the Goddamn maze."

~*~

"Oh, no," Strassberg muttered, and Ellie Fremont rushed over to her console. "Mac! You better get over here, quick!"

McIntyre broke into a run from across the alcove that housed the computers, Wiley Thomas and several others were hot on his heels. "What's the matter?" McIntyre asked as he checked Sharon's console.

"Corridor-two, one level up, see?" Fremont pointed at a bright blinking light on the lower right hand side of the screen.

"That's a proximity sensor, Mac," Strassberg said. "Someone's down here with us." "Shit," McIntyre muttered to himself and wiped sweat from his forehead. "How close?" "Close," Fremont said. "Almost right on top of us."

"How in the hell did they get so close without any of the other sensors going off?" McIntyre wondered.

"I don't know," Strassberg said, shaking her head. "All I know is that we should have a visual of this sensor and we have nothing. Not even static."

"All right, how long before they get here?" McIntyre asked. "It could be any minute now," Fremont said.

"It depends on if they kept moving or stayed put after hearing the alarm," Strassberg said. "I know where they'll be coming in," Thomas offered. "I know those tunnels, the way that area is laid out."

"Where?" McIntyre turned to Thomas and gestured toward the tunnel schematic on a nearby screen.

Thomas took a seat in front of the console and began hitting keys. The schematic suddenly started changing, the section indicating where the alarm had gone off becoming larger until it was the only thing on the screen. The light was still blinking where the proximity sensor had been set off. "If they've been moving since the sensor was triggered they would be about here by now..."

~*~

Several shapes moved closer down the dimly lit corridor, moving toward the flashing red light of the proximity alarm.

"What set this thing off?" Wiley Thomas asked no one in particular as he walked up to the sensor and reset it to armed. The corridor was thrust into darkness and several flashlights snapped on, their small beams of light scanning the far corners of the corridor. "I don't know what's wrong with that thing, there doesn't seem to be anything down here. Maybe just a malfunction."

"Let's work our way back, Wiley," one of the men in the group suggested. "There's nothing more to see here."

Thomas peered ahead into the dark depths of the corridor. His eyes may have been playing tricks on him in the murky darkness but he could have sworn..."What was that?"

"Wiley, let's go back already," another man said.

"Yeah, fine," Thomas agreed and turned toward a com-link panel on the wall at the entrance to the corridor. "Mac, this is Wiley, we're coming back. There doesn't seem to be anything down here."

"Okay, Wiley, see you soon," came McIntyre's reply.

"Hey, Mac," Thomas called before the link was broken. "Could you turn on the lights in this section? It's pretty damn dark in here."

"Working on it," McIntyre's response crackled from the panel.

The corridor suddenly filled with a bright white light and the men covered their eyes until they could adjust. After several seconds, Wiley Thomas opened his eyes and immediately wished he hadn't.

Blocking the corridor directly ahead of him was a large group of very serious looking men and most of them were pointing some very big guns in his direction.

~*~

The U.E.N. FlightForce Destroyer Greywolf settled into a steady orbit around Sarsat-15, one of the many moons currently circling Sarkennon-8.

"I have a location on the enemy base, Captain," the Helmsmen said as he studied the readouts on the console before him.

"Stabilize position over target once we come into range," Captain Gary Tano ordered and shifted uncomfortably in his small gray command chair. "Weapons status, Lieutenant?"

"Forward guns locked on enemy target," someone said from off to his left. "Missile launchers are also locked, sir."

"Good, let's use missiles on this one," Tano said and settled back into his seat. "Two missiles, fired simultaneously."

"Yes, sir."

"I have life readings, Captain," came from somewhere to his right. "Very sporadic, I can't get a definite number but many of these readings are indicating children, sir."

"Children!" Tano snapped and stood abruptly. "Confirm those scans, Lieutenant." Silence ensued as the instruments re-scanned the small base below. "Readingsconfirmed,

Captain. There are a good amount of children within that encampment."

178

"Well...what in the hell is this?" Tano murmured and began to pace the deck of the bridge. "It could be some sort of elaborate deception, Captain," Commander Derek Hilton said from

his position beside the WeaponsTech. "Our sensors could be picking up a rigged signal."

"What are the chances that our sensors are being fooled?" Tano asked the man sitting at the

Ops station.

"Very slim, sir," the OpsTech responded. "At this range we should be able to pick up any false signals. These readings are accurate."

"Good God Almighty," Tano sighed. "They're using their own children as a shield down there."

"What a nightmare," Hilton said, knowing the inevitable outcome.

"Sensors indicate minimal readings, Captain," the man continued. "I don't have an exact number but I would guess one hundred, maybe less."

"One hundred or one," Tano snarled. "What's the difference? There's children down there!" "Captain," Hilton said, sensing his Captain's growing tension. "Need I remind you of our

orders?"

"Hell no, Derek!" The Captain snapped. "I'm damned well aware of my orders."

Silence commanded the bridge of Greywolf then as Tano continued to pace the deck in thought.

"I hate this," he muttered and turned to face his WeaponsTech. "Arm missiles."

"Missiles armed, sir."

Tano moved closer to the viewscreen and flashed a sharp glare at Hilton. Hilton met his stare and Tano saw understanding there. They both knew what must be done, however terrible. With a heavy sigh and a deep breath, Tano turned his back to the screen and stared at nothing in particular near the rear of the bridge. There was a heaviness in his heart that he knew, in time, would pass. "Fire."

~*~

"Well, Ambassador," Jekel said as he shook hands with Will McIntyre, "you have done a tremendous job getting all of these people out of danger and into these tunnels."

"Thank you...sir," McIntyre replied, not knowing the exact title to use with a Guarder. "But I owe all of that to one of the men you met earlier, Mr. Wiley Thomas."

Thomas nodded, smiling, but remained speechless. Jekel nodded in return and shook the older man's hand. "You deserve a lot of credit, Mr. Thomas. It is my understanding that not many people know of the existence of these tunnels."

"I grew up in the building that housed the entrance you used," Thomas said. "I knew of these tunnels for a very long time."

"It's a good thing for all of these people that you did," Jekel said and turned back to McIntyre. "Mr. Ambassador, there is a U.E.N. Warfleet currently in orbit around Shining. As you know, a hostile force, very well armed, has stormed CharterCity and quite possibly every other inhabited area on the planet. They are the same people who have been responsible for most of the piracy in this system recently. Ground forces have been deployed already although we have not yet made contact with them."

"You mean there's a war going on up there?" Thomas asked.

"Yes, Mr. Thomas," Jekel replied. "But it is our intention to get all of you off of this planet and into the safety of the FlightForce Carrier in orbit."

"Sarge," Buzzer spoke in a whisper from his left shoulder and motioned him to follow away from the civilians.

"Excuse me one moment, Mr. Ambassador," Jekel said and walked several paces toward Buzzer. He couldn't help but notice the awe on most of the faces

180

crowding the area. Few of these people, most likely none of them, had ever laid their eyes on a Guarder before. "What is it, Buzzer?"

"I just intercepted a message from a destroyer orbiting the moon where the enemy base was located," Jekel's eyes narrowed at that. "There were what seems to have been women and children left there. Not many but they were there. The destroyer launched two missiles at the target, both direct hits. Total destruction of the enemy base. The ship then proceeded to check out the other moons and outer planets. They found nothing else."

"So, has this turned into a suicide mission for these pirate bastards?" Jekel wondered.

"It sure looks that way, Sarge," Buzzer said. "They definitely have nowhere to go back to now. The destruction of their base just makes them that much more dangerous."

"Yes, but our knowledge of this could be very useful to us," Jekel pointed out. "Let's work on getting these people to safety, I don't want them in the line of fire."

"You got it, Sarge," Buzzer said and motioned to Thunder and Razor. "Let's move out."

~*~

"Frazier, it looks like we really stirred up the pot this time," Thornberg said with a gleam in his eye. "An entire U.E.N. Warfleet, the Wolfpack no less. Their very finest, Frazier. All of this for us, for you. You did all of this, you shook up this entire sector."

"Not just me, Gil," Sampson answered as he peered out from beneath his cover of bushes and trees. "This is for everyone, all of us. I couldn't have asked for more if we had planned all of this."

"Frankly, though, I am concerned about how thinly spread some of our forces are," Thornberg said. "Frazier, we need to link this larger group with our smaller units. Whichever are left, that is."

"I have considered that long and hard, Gil," Sampson answered as he watched the far distant military shuttles and personnel carriers looming down out of the sky above Shining's capital city. "I feel that it's time we made a move back toward CharterCity."

Thornberg's eyes widened in surprise. "CharterCity? That is where the soldiers are concentrating."

"Yes, Gil," Sampson snapped. "They will never expect it. They will not be ready for it and their sensors will not be able to distinguish between our people and their own forces."

"But we are hopelessly outnumbered and outgunned, Frazier," Thornberg argued. "For what possible purpose would we willingly return there, except to surely meet our doom?"

"Dammit, Gil!" Sampson roared. "Must you second guess my every decision? Have you forgotten who you are and who I am? I am your superior, Gilfred! You will obey my every command!"

"Yes, of course, Frazier," Thornberg stammered. "I just fail to grasp your intentions."

"My intentions are not for you to grasp, Gilfred," Sampson said sternly. "They are only for you to accept!"

"Yes, Frazier, I know," Thornberg mumbled, suddenly fearing for his life from the madness glowing in Sampson's eyes. "I…I'm sorry, Frazier. Of course I'll obey your orders, you know that."

"Very well, then," Sampson said and his eyes lost their fire as he visibly calmed. "Gatheryour best men together, it will be very important for everyone to understand my strategy."

"Yes, Frazier," Thornberg said, bowed his head and backed away from his leader. He'd been growing increasingly more frightened by Sampson's behavior and sudden outbursts of fury as this damnable mission wore on. If the speculation that Sampson might be going insane had entered his mind previously, it seemed that he had just witnessed the proof of it now.

Thornberg sighed and glanced at one of Sampson's Utility Guardsmen, standing still and brooding, one hand on the butt of the blaster at his side. The eyes of the man bore straight through him, his lips pulled tightly into a very thin line across his face. That look sent shivers up and down Thornberg's spine. Turning, he stormed off in the direction of several men he needed to talk to about the meeting with Sampson. As he walked away from the Utility Guardsman, he couldn't shake the feeling that, from this point on, there would be a target on his back. A target just waiting for a bulls-eye.

~*~

Lieutenant Moore led his team of six men down the dark and cavernous tunnel. He had seen nothing so far, at least nothing alive, and they had been down here for almost fifteen minutes.

"Henson," Moore rasped, and the WeaponsTech rushed up to his position. "You picking up anything?"

"No, nothing, Lieutenant," Henson said, checking his equipment. "I still read nothing. But these tunnels may be affecting my sensors."

"All right, take point."

Henson chuckled and moved forward. "Yes, sir, thank you, sir."

Moore leaned against the wall as the rest of the squad moved past him. *Just what in the hell is going on down here*, he wondered and fell in behind the last soldier.

What a strange situation this has turned into, he thought. First, the entire fleet had been called off of routine patrol because a FlightForce Carrier had been destroyed, amazingly enough, in a battle within the Sarkennon System, an obscure area of the SouthWestern Corporate Grid-Sector. Then, upon their arrival, they discover that a well-armed invading force has taken up defensive positions all over the surface area of a planet called Shining. Now, they find the capital city in a shambles, pockets of bodies scattered throughout and thousands of life signs showing underground. A quick call up to the Wolfbane to request the use of the warship's much more powerful sensors had revealed an entrance to an

183

underground tunnel system inside a building called CharterHouse. A building that they soon discovered had seen its share of recent battle. *Who knows what to expect next in this hellhole?* Moore surely didn't.

The group rounded a corner.

Moore hit the deck just ahead of the rest of his men as a proximity alarm went off, shattering the silence. The alarm sent a stab of pain through his senses and Moore rolled himself up against a wall. He could see that the corridor was alive with movement, although his night-vision goggles were offering little clarification.

Suddenly, he felt a weight upon his back and his blaster was being snatched from his left hand. "Jesus Christ!"

The proximity alarm abruptly cut off and the lights cut on, excruciatingly bright with his goggles on. "Damn," he rasped and tried to close his eyes tight enough to clear away the pain. "Everybody relax, calm down and no one gets hurt," a very commanding voice bellowed throughout the tunnel. "We're not going to harm anyone. Nobody is a prisoner here."

"That's right, gentlemen," Buzzer said. "We are the good guys, too. But if we had been from the other side, every single one of you would be dead."

"Let them up," Jekel ordered.

Slowly the Guarders stood and made space between themselves and the soldiers. Bob Moore got to his feet and checked out the new arrivals. His heart was pounding in his chest but, although he had been forcibly disarmed, he knew instinctively that the danger was over.

"Hand them back their weapons," Jekel motioned to the others and, one by one, each Guarder turned over the confiscated blasters and half-chargers. "Now, in case you men are wondering..." "Guarders," Moore said and holstered his weapon. "It's all right, men. Holster those weapons, we're in good company here."

~*~

"Look, Buzzer," Garcia said and grabbed the Guarder's forearm. "I won't go, I have too much at stake here."

"You mean you want revenge too much," Buzzer rasped and removed Garcia's hand.

"Well, okay, I do want revenge," Garcia said. "Listen, these bastards blew up my ship, killed my Captain and most of my best friends and damn near managed to kill me. I'm not going up to Wolfbane."

"Avril, I know what you're going through, believe me," Buzzer's eyes seemed to burn right through those of the Ruffian's Flight Commander. "I have lost many, many people who were close to me. And I have felt all that you're feeling right now. Let me tell you, it clouds your judgment."

"Don't pull this psych bullshit on me, Buzzer," Garcia snarled. "This means too much to me." "Same goes for me, Guarder," Jack Redwolf said in his low and steady voice as he

approached the two men. "I'm not going up to the Wolfbane either. I'm a part of this team of yours. Commander Garcia is as well."

Buzzer looked both men square in the eye and saw the deep sense of determination in each of them. Sighing heavily, he glanced over at Thunder, then back at the two FlightCorpsmen. Both Guarders had speculated that these two men would refuse to be taken out of the fight. Buzzer had already run this possibility past Jekel and the Sarge had agreed to accept the two military men into the team if they made the request. This confrontation had only proven how badly these two wanted to remain on the surface.

"Okay, then," Buzzer said.

Garcia and Redwolf blinked once or twice and stood in stunned silence, not daring to say another word.

"I said, okay," Buzzer repeated himself. "You both can remain. Now let's get back to Sergeant Jekel and find out where we go from here."

~*~

"Are we really getting out of here, Mac?" Fremont asked him as they hovered over the consoles, still scanning for any chance of intruders. The entire cavern seemed crowded with military men, more so by the Guarders.

"Yeah, Ellie." McIntyre smiled and lightly touched Fremont's arm. "We're getting off this hunk of ice. There's nothing left here for any of us. From what I've heard, CharterCity is in shambles, it'll take years to rebuild, and the entire planetary political structure has basically been reduced to local yokels who don't know the first thing about rebuilding a society from the ground up. These soldiers are willing to provide us safe transport off of Shining and I'm going to make damn sure that every last one of the people down here makes it off-planet."

Fremont reached for McIntyre's hand and held it warmly for several seconds. "You know, Mac, everybody here owes their lives to you. You held them all together..."

"No, no, no," McIntyre protested, shaking his head.

"Yes, Mac," Fremont cut him off. "It was you. Ambassador McIntyre. All of them looked up to you, they all expected you to lead them out of this insanity and you did. You did it, Mac. You didn't let them down. You didn't let me down." Ellie hugged him then and he could feel the warm wetness of her tears against his cheek.

"Okay, you two," Wiley Thomas said and chuckled. "Let's keep the hugging to a minimum, shall we?"

McIntyre abruptly took a step back, visibly shaken by the interruption. "What is it, Wiley?" "The Guarders would like to talk to you, Mac. Something about the evacuation."

"Thanks," McIntyre said, nodded at Ellie Fremont and made his way across the room. Thomas turned his smile on Fremont then and winked at her. "You know..."

"Not a word, Thomas," Fremont warned with a pointed finger. "Not a word."

~*~

"With all of the readings coming in from all over the planet, it's not going to be easy to pinpoint our target group, Admiral," the Helmsman said.

"Are you any closer to achieving that result now than when we first established orbit, Lieutenant?" Dawson asked.

"No, sir," Lieutenant Bill Devon answered. "Our people are easy enough to track through equipment detection but the planet was very crowded, Admiral. We have literally tens of thousands of life signs down there, all civilians. This job is better left to the ground units—we just cannot get a solid fix while in orbit."

"The last unit arrived planet-side about thirty minutes ago, Admiral," Lysak said. "It might be a good idea to secure from battle stations and let the army finish this one."

Dawson turned to his First Officer and then glanced at each bridge crewmember, studying the tired faces, the fatigued postures. Every one of these men and women had worked diligently to make the trip to Shining as smooth and quick as was humanly and mechanically possible.

Nodding, he slumped down in the command chair and gently rubbed his own tired eyes. "Secure from battle stations. I think we could all use some rest."

~*~

Gaston Pilar lay prone in the shadows of the trees. Two fully armed troop transport shuttles sat in the middle of the little square, about thirty meters in front of him. Two soldiers, full- chargers primed and ready at their sides, stood guard over the small vessels. Neither of them looked too enthused over the duty they'd pulled on this mission.

Various other military personnel were in the area but none were close enough to the shuttles to interfere. Both soldiers standing guard had their backs to his position and seemed to be fully engrossed in their conversation.

Pilar glanced over his shoulder and gave the signal for the others to move up. Jacob Dukes worked his way up to Pilar's side. "What do you think, Gaston?"

"No problem, Jacob," Pilar whispered. "The two guards won't know what hit them. The others in the area...it depends on how alert they are and how fast they can figure out what's going on."

"Don't worry about that, we're not here to take prisoners," Dukes sneered.

"I understand, Jacob," Pilar replied. "So, I'll take the ship on the left, you take the other one. I know those ships well enough, I was in the FlightForce for three tours and we used those little hoppers pretty extensively."

"Yeah," Dukes said and nodded. "I'm damn familiar with them myself."

"Good, but we need to get our teams loaded on immediately, Jacob," Pilar added. "The sooner we get off the ground the sooner we can get out of charger range. The new military versions can take out a ship that size with one charge."

"Damn," Dukes swore and glanced back to make sure the others were in position. "I'll keep that in mind. Move your team out."

"Let's do this, Jacob."

Dukes cracked half a smile in response as both teams melted into the underbrush and began moving closer to the shuttles. Just as Pilar was about to take his final position, one of his team members stumbled behind him and crashed into the undergrowth. The two soldiers guarding the shuttles immediately turned toward the commotion, bringing their weapons to bear.

Pilar screamed at the top of his lungs and broke through the bushes firing his blaster. He saw one of the soldiers go down, the body and head moving in opposite directions, before he had to dive to avoid a charger blast that snapped a tree far behind him in two.

Dukes and his team were firing heavily now but being careful not to hit either of the two vessels they were hoping to capture.

"Move it! Move it!" Pilar shouted and picked himself up from the ground. Choosing his targets very carefully, he loosed three shots from his blaster and saw two other soldiers across the square go down. Several other soldiers had responded to the firefight and more could be seen rapidly advancing.

One of Pilar's team hit the ground hard, missing an arm and screaming horribly. Pilar turned around just long enough to pump a blaster bolt into his fallen comrade, putting an end to his sudden misery, before turning back and dropping another U.E.N. soldier with his weapon.

Dukes had reached his intended shuttle, disappearing inside. Pilar could see the other two former members of Duke's team dead on the ground near the gleaming vehicle. Running as fast as he could toward his intended shuttle and firing all the way, Pilar felt the heat of the charger blasts tearing into the ground around his feet. The last member of his team screamed from somewhere behind and went down. Pilar didn't glance back this time, despite the continued screaming, but fired two more shots, hitting one soldier ahead of him before plunging headlong into the open shuttle doors.

Breathing heavily, he strapped himself into the pilot's seat and quickly engaged the engine warm-up systems. Out of the corner of his eye he could see Dukes' ship rising off the ground.

"Come on, come on," Pilar mumbled to himself, looking for the green indicator light which would tell him that all systems were GO.

Dukes' ship hovered momentarily and slowly turned toward several soldiers running toward their position. Suddenly, the tips of the forward guns glowed and let out a tremendous blast that rocked the small square.

Pilar let out a holler of victory as the green light in front of him clicked on. His shuttle rose cleanly into the air as Dukes' ship ahead of him began climbing higher.

With his heart pounding and adrenaline racing through his body, Gaston Pilar took a firm grip on the controls of the stolen troop transport and followed Jacob Dukes toward freedom.

~*~

"Lieutenant Moore," Jekel called as he walked toward the group of soldiers. "Can I have a few minutes of your time?"

"Yes, of course, sir," Moore said, inwardly cringing at his use of "sir" toward a man who was technically of lesser rank.

Jekel grinned at him; the large man had also picked up on his error. "In battle situations I find it easier to refer to my colleagues by rank, Lieutenant," the head Guarder offered. "I find it helps to make awkward conversations somewhat more comfortable."

"Yes, Sergeant, I agree."

"Good, then," Jekel said and motioned for him to follow as they walked away from the crowd and toward the wall. "As you know, your main priority right now is to guide these civilians to a position of safety. That means off of Shining, not to any safe haven here on the surface because, frankly, there is no safe spot on Shining."

"Yes, Sergeant, I accepted this mission with the full intention of landing any survivors on Wolfbane," Moore stated.

"Very good, Lieutenant. Then I leave the safety of these good people in your professional and very capable hands. The other members of my team and I will be heading deeper into the tunnels, exploring various exits."

"With all due respect, Sergeant Jekel," Moore said. "There are army units swarming all over this little ball of ice. I don't expect this pseudo-war of ours to go on much longer. It would be preferable to all involved if you and your team added your considerable talents to the rest of the armed forces on Shining and not go off by yourselves."

Jekel glanced over to his team, watching as they gathered their equipment together, preparing to leave. "Lieutenant Moore, this may sound strange but even though the Guarders are the best trained and most lethal military men in the entire U.E.N., to tell you the truth, we just aren't trained to fight the type of war you've been trained for. You see this team? There are eight of us. Eight Guarders together on a single mission—this is the largest team of Guarders ever assembled off of Aegis for one assignment. I have my hands full keeping these men out of each other's way as it is. Guarders work much better on an individual basis. As part of a large military force, we just wouldn't be as effective."

"I see," Moore said, nodding his understanding. "I've already spoken with the FlightCorpsmen you rescued from the Ruffian. All but two of them are returning to Wolfbane to resume flight duty. The other two, FlightCorpsman Redwolf and, surprisingly enough, Flight Commander Avril Garcia, requested permission from Admiral Dawson to join your group."

"I was aware of that development, Lieutenant." "And you approve, Sergeant Jekel?"

"Yes," Jekel said. "Those two are combat experienced. I have fought beside both of them and welcome them into my team."

"Very well, then, Sergeant Jekel," Moore extended his hand and Jekel accepted with an enormously strong grip. "After witnessing most of what has happened on the surface of Shining and knowing that you and your team were in the thick of it and fought your way through intact, my respect for the Guarder Squadron has grown immensely."

Jekel nodded at that and turned toward his team. "Safe travels, Lieutenant Moore. Take care of this fine group of civilians and see them safely home."

"I will do...sir," Moore called to Jekel's oversized back. "Good luck to you, Guarder."

~*~

"Admiral," the ComTech called from across the bridge. "I have a Colonel Smith on Shining with an urgent message for you, sir."

"Let's hear it."

"Admiral Dawson?" A grainy voice sounded throughout the bridge. "Yes, Colonel."

"Admiral, we've just had an incident down here that could have some serious repercussions." "Explain, Colonel."

"Several minutes ago a security detail here in CharterCity was ambushed by what we assume was a group of these pirates," Smith said.

"How many of them?" "We think six, Admiral." "Damage?"

"My unit sustained three injuries and five fatalities," Smith said, voice solemn. "We bagged four of the attackers."

"And the other two?" Dawson asked after a brief pause.

"Well, sir," Smith stammered. "The other two attackers managed to escape the area in two troop transport shuttles."

"Damn!" Doug Lysak swore.

Dawson turned toward his First Officer. "What is it?"

"Those troop transports double as light combat vehicles during missions like these, Admiral," Lysak replied. "Most of the ones operating off of Wolfbane are equipped with long-range missiles armed with tactical nuclear warheads."

Dawson's eyes widened as he realized the implications of the situation. "Is this the case with the stolen shuttles, Colonel?"

"Yes, Admiral."

"Oh, for Chris'sakes," Dawson muttered and settled back in his chair. "Colonel Smith, I want you to make every effort to search for and recapture, or destroy if need be, those two troop transports."

"Yes, sir, Admiral Dawson."

"Can we help you track them from here?" Lysak asked.

"Uh, no, sir," Smith said. "The ID codes from those shuttles were not yet logged upon landing, sir. I couldn't tell you which two shuttles to scan for at this point. We are working on it, though."

"I see..." Dawson answered, glancing at Lysak and pausing to collect his thoughts. "Colonel

Smith, am I correct in assuming that you operate off of the Wolfbane?" "Yes, Admiral."

"That would put you under the direct command of General Cartullo of the U.E.N. Army then, would it not?"

"Yes, sir."

"And you are currently in command of the ground forces on Shining?" "Yes, sir."

"Colonel Smith, I hold you personally responsible for staging the successful recapture of those two stolen vessels and the weapons they are carrying. Do I make myself absolutely clear?"

"Yes...Admiral."

"Good then," Dawson snapped. "I will be sure to make General Cartullo fully aware of your progress thus far. Dawson out."

"Smith out."

Dawson slowly turned toward Lysak with a look of sheer amazement on his face. "Dammit, Doug, what in the hell's going on down there? They're pirates for Chris'sakes!"

"If they use those missiles..."

"I know," Dawson sighed. "I know."

CHAPTER TEN

"Good work, Jacob!" Sampson shouted, rushing through the still opening shuttle doors. "You did it!"

"Yes, and Gaston Pilar should be soon to follow with another one of these birds."

"He's landing now," Sampson said and took in the view of the troop transport's interior with wide eyes. "Where is the rest of your team?"

Dukes paused for just an instant. "They didn't make it."

Sampson lowered his eyes and sighed. "I am truly sorry to hear that, Jacob, but we shall honor them with a victory here."

"Yes, sir, I should hope that we will."

Sampson let several seconds of silence linger before asking, "Any damage to this vessel?" "None that I could feel or detect as I flew here," Dukes replied.

"Good, good," Sampson said and clapped Dukes across the shoulders. "Prepare for departure, Jacob. Some of us will be leaving soon."

"Frazier!" Thornberg's voice shouted from somewhere outside. "Frazier!"

Sampson turned toward the shuttle's entrance and watched his Second in Command rush in through the shuttle doors. "You are not going to believe what we've found."

"What is it, Gilfred? More good news?"

"Most definitely, Frazier," Thornberg blurted. "We checked the armaments on the shuttle that Gaston Pilar just brought down. Fully loaded with charge-weapons and also a full complement of long-range missiles. Frazier, long-range missiles tipped with tactical nuclear warheads."

"Nuclear warheads?" Sampson rasped. "Are you sure, Gilfred?" "Absolutely."

"How about this shuttle? Does it contain missiles as well?"

"They're checking it out now," Thornberg said, shaking with excitement. "How many missiles did you find on the other shuttle?" Sampson asked.

"Gaston's shuttle carries five, Frazier," Thornberg said. "And all are fully loaded, just waiting to be armed."

Sampson stood motionless for several moments, suddenly lost in thought. Gaston Pilar rushed into the shuttle then, looking from Sampson to Thornberg. "I...I..." Pilar paused. "Is everything all right here?"

"Yes, absolutely," Thornberg replied. "What is it, Gaston?" "We've checked the missiles on this shuttle, sir..."

"And? Are they nuclear tipped as well?" Sampson asked.

"Yes, all five of them," Pilar beamed. "Just like the one I brought in."

"Very good, very good," Sampson said and began walking toward the shuttle's entrance.

"Gaston, the rest of your team?"

Pilar cast his eyes toward the floor and shook his head. "No, sir, only I escaped with the shuttle."

Sampson clasped the man's arm gently then. "You and Jacob have performed fantastically this day. Neither of you yet realize the extraordinary advantage you have just given to us. With the success of your mission we now have the ability to greatly diminish the numbers of the enemy we face. The two of you may have just provided us with the means for victory. I will not forget your courage."

"Thank you, sir," Dukes stated while Pilar remained silent.

"As for you, Gil," Sampson said, turning toward his Second. "It seems that a change in plans is now in order. With these shuttles and the weaponry they contain in our possession, I see no need for the lot of us to head back toward CharterCity. Gather everyone for a quick meeting."

"Done, Frazier," Thornberg said and exited through the shuttle doors. Sampson turned to give one last look of triumph toward the two victorious shuttle thieves and then was gone.

Jacob Dukes watched as Sampson and Thornberg disappeared from view and turned to his companion. "It was terribly close down there, Gaston," he said and slumped back down into the pilot's seat. "I still can't believe that we both made it."

"Well, I owe my life to you, Jacob," Pilar said. "You saved my butt back there and I can't ever repay you for it."

"Do the same for me when the time comes, my friend," Dukes said. "That's all I ask."

~*~

"Admiral," Cartullo called over the com-link from the FlightForce Carrier Wolfbane. "I have been briefed by my men on Shining, sir. I'm fully aware of the situation with the stolen shuttles. We are currently working on identifying those two vessels and locating them on the surface."

"That is good news, Emilio," Dawson said. "I'm sure that I don't have to remind you of the importance of your efforts in this endeavor."

"No, Admiral, not at all."

"Very well, then," Dawson paused. "Have you spoken with your Colonel Smith since the incident?"

"Yes, Admiral, I have. In fact, he gave me the briefing."

"Did he inform you of the verbal assault I hit him with?" Dawson asked. Cartullo laughed. "Yeah, he told me about most of it."

"Maybe I was somewhat harsh with him, Emilio, but dammit he deserved it. Something like this should have never happened down there."

"I agree but I'm confident that we'll get those two birds back, sir."

"Listen, don't let confidence get the best of you, General," Dawson warned. "I do not, repeat, do not want this thing to come back on us. These people now have access to sophisticated U.E.N. military vessels and weapons systems, not to mention limited tactical nuclear missiles."

"I understand that fully, Admiral."

"I am pleased that you do," Dawson said. "Are you satisfied with the leadership of our troops down on the surface?"

"Admiral Dawson," Cartullo began. "Colonel J.T. Smith is one of my best people. He will get the job done, sir."

"Yes, but this is a big operation, General," Dawson said. "A lot larger than any of us actually realized it would be, I think."

"Yes, sir, I can see where you're going with this," Cartullo said. "I'll admit that Shining has posed several problems that my troops weren't fully prepared for. But, once again, they are the best fighting men the U.E.N. has to offer. There will be no other outcome but victory, Admiral."

"Good, I like that attitude, Emilio," Dawson said. "In fact, in order to ensure our victory here on Shining let's equip our soldiers on the surface with the best possible command leadership currently available in this sector. That would put my mind somewhat at ease."

"I'll depart for the surface within the hour, Admiral," Cartullo said. "Very good, General. Good luck down there. Dawson out."

The com-link's connection filled with static for the briefest of moments before disconnecting completely and Dawson sat back in his command chair. Glancing over at Lysak, he said, "I've got a very bad feeling about this."

"Same here, Admiral," Lysak said. "I think the troops don't realize the type of competition they're up against down there."

"You mean in terms of actual military combat experience?" Dawson offered. Lysak smiled. "I see you've been doing some thinking about this situation aswell."

"Of course, Commander," Dawson said, stood and walked over to his First Officer. "It only makes sense that the scenario that has developed here is the direct result of military training."

"And quite a bit of it, I should say," Lysak added.

"I agree but how much and where from?" Dawson speculated. "That's the part I don't like one bit."

~*~

"All right! One by one, now! No rush here, people! One by one!" Sergeant Henson shouted at the mass of people flooding through the doors of Main Hall, feeling sunlight on their faces for the first time in quite some while.

Corporal Jimenez had gone on ahead to locate Colonel Smith and brief him on the evacuation procedures currently in place. Henson stood in the doorway, holding it open with his hips, waving the people through and trying to clear them out as peacefully as possible. In the courtyard, Henson could see Jimenez and Smith standing together looking up towards a descending shuttle. "Let's go! Let's go! Nice and easy, now, let's go!"

Henson saw the shock on many of the faces in the crowd as they filed out of the tunnels. This area of CharterCity was in a shambles; buildings had crumbled and toppled over during the recent combat. There was carnage in the streets and a lot of blood spilled. For most of them, this was the first time that they had seen an actual war zone, had observed first-hand an U.E.N. Military Occupation. What made it worse for these people was the fact that it was all taking place within the midst of their once great city.

Many of them were looking up at the huge troop transport as it slowly glided down to the large open courtyard. Henson wondered who it could be on this particular ship that should attract the colonel's full attention.

"Henson, how goes it up there?" Moore's voice crackled in his ear.

Reaching up to his helmet to adjust the small com-link, he replied, "All's well so far, Lieutenant. How far back are you?"

"Don't worry, Sergeant," Moore's voice rasped. "There's still a ways to go before we clear out this crowd."

Henson was about to respond with a joke when he looked back toward Jimenez and saw the corporal now standing with both Colonel Smith and a new arrival, General Cartullo himself.

"Uh, Lieutenant," he called over the com-link. "You may want to pick up the pace a little back there. It seems we have some unexpected company."

~*~

"It sure looks like an exit hatch," Skinner said as he rubbed his hands over the smooth, wet surface of the bulkhead. "But by the steady drip and the small flood, I'd say it's well under water."

"It seems we've been walking our way uphill for some time now," Jekel said. "If this is an exit hatch, it surely couldn't have been intended to be underwater."

"Couldn't we just open it up and let the water drain past us?" Razor asked.

"Absolutely not," Skinner said from atop the access ladder. "These hatches were built to survive everything from heavy weapons fire to extreme seismic activity. If water is able to drip through the seals, no matter how old, then there's a hell of a lot of it up there."

"How about ventilation?" Buzzer asked. "Yeah...you're right, Buzzer," Skinner said. "What do you mean?" Able asked.

"We're up pretty high, altitude wise," Buzzer explained. "You can tell by how thin the air has gotten."

Redwolf laughed at that. "And I thought it was just me."

Jekel shot the laughing FlightCorpsman a menacing look and turned back to Buzzer. "Continue, Frank."

"Exit hatches are usually built with high traffic in mind. When you have a lot of people moving in and out of one area, especially when it's mostly underground, you need a good ventilation system."

"Okay, I think I follow you," Jekel said. "If the vent shafts were underwater, there would be a lot more water coming into the tunnel."

"Right," Buzzer agreed. "We find the vent shaft, we find the way out."

"Good," Jekel said. He looked over his rapidly tiring team. "Let's move out then."

Wiley Thomas glanced back and saw the army lieutenant shaking hands with McIntyre and then briskly heading away. Thomas pressed back against the wall, guiding Ellie Fremont with him as Bob Moore swiftly strode by. "Looks like we just lost our military escort."

"Where do you think he's going?" Fremont asked and looked back at McIntyre. "I don't know but it sure seems important," Thomas answered.

"Hey, Mac!" Fremont called and waved the ambassador over.

McIntyre ran up from the back of the group to join his two friends and motioned for them to continue along the tunnel. "It seems like some unexpected visitors have shaken up Lieutenant Moore."

"Who are they?" Thomas asked.

"He wouldn't elaborate on that," McIntyre said. "All I heard was someone talking through his helmet com-link. Then he turned to me and told me to hold down the fort back here because he had to hightail it up front."

"I hope we're not walking into some sort of trouble up there," Wiley said. "You know, something like an ambush."

"Not very likely, Wiley," McIntyre said. "I don't think he would have been that calm had he heard that type of news. And anyway, we would be hearing shots by now, maybe some explosions."

"It was just a thought, Mac."

"Well, keep thoughts like that to yourself," Fremont said and nudged Thomas in the side playfully. "That's all he said, Mac?"

"Yeah, and then he was gone before I knew it." "I still say it sounds strange," Thomas quipped.

McIntyre laughed and shook his head. "Wiley, you'll get no argument on that from me. But, then again, this whole thing has been strange. Right from the start."

"Have any of you seen Sharon?" Fremont asked, looking around the crowded tunnel. "Yeah, she passed me by a few minutes ago," McIntyre answered. "Said she wanted to work

her way up to the front so she could catch an early shuttle. Something about wanting to take charge of the preparations for everyone on the ships in orbit."

"If I know Sharon, she'll take over the galley and set the ovens alight," Fremont said. She caught the ambassador staring at her. McIntyre quickly looked away and Fremont smiled.

"How much farther do you think?" Fremont asked.

"Not much," Thomas answered. "We're almost at the point where the tunnel meets Main Hall.

Then it's just a matter of minutes."

"Damn, it couldn't be any faster for me," Ellie Fremont said and rushed ahead to pass her two companions, skimming her fingers lightly along McIntyre's left arm as she went by.

~*~

"Welcome back, Captain Tano," the admiral's voice boomed through the destroyer's bridge. "Thank you, Admiral," Tano replied into his com-link. "Where would you like the Greywolf to take up station?"

"Work your way over to the Wolfbane's port side, Captain. Then just sit tight. It seems that our part in all of this is over for the time being. But the surface units more than have their hands full."

"Has there been any trouble since our absence?" Tano wondered.

"Let's just say we currently have a situation on our hands," Dawson offered. "Understood, Admiral," Tano said and shrugged at Hamilton's look of inquiry. "The

Greywolf will be in position within minutes, sir."

"Very good, Captain," Dawson said. "Stay sharp, we can probably expect just about anything at this point. Dawson out."

Tano fixed Hamilton with a confused expression and then turned toward the helmsman. "Helm, set us into position as the Admiral instructed," Tano ordered and glanced back at his first officer. "Now, what do you suppose that was all about?"

"Sir, I have no idea."

"A situation on our hands," Tano said. "Why wouldn't he elaborate on that?" "He did seem kind of vague, sir," Hamilton said.

"Vague? Christ, Derek, he couldn't have been more vague if he tried."

"Why don't we try to get some info out of Captain Chatty?" Hamilton asked. "Cartullo is commanding off of the Wolfbane, isn't he? Wouldn't Chatty be privy to some news?"

"Yeah, he sure would," Tano agreed. "But Captain Chatty isn't exactly the talkative type." "No, but he's got to be bored out of his wits by now with all of this waiting everyone seems to

be doing," Hamilton added.

"Unless our little situation is a lot hotter than Dawson let on," Tano said. "I guess there's only one way to find out, Captain."

~*~

"Why don't we just use a blaster for Chris'sakes?" Able muttered through clenched teeth as he and Thunder strained against the rusted metal of the vent shaft cover.

"Because that could attract some undue attention," Thunder rasped. "You know that as well as I do."

"Yeah," Able said and felt one of the corner latches give way. "Here we go now! We almost have it, Thunder."

"Buzzer," Thunder called between gasps, breathing heavily as his muscles strained against the old grate. "We could use a little more muscle."

Two hands immediately reached forward and grabbed the grating in between the two Guarders. "Let's get this over with," Buzzer said and added his considerable strength to the struggle.

Suddenly, another corner of the rusted metal gave way and Able stumbled backward a step before catching his balance.

"Pull, dammit," Thunder growled. "Pull..."

As the three Guarders reared back with all of their strength the grating suddenly gave way, sending the three men tumbling back into the shaft. Buzzer felt a sharp pain jab into his side as he collided with one wall of the shaft. One of the jagged metal edges of the newly loosened and rusty grate had caught him just under the ribs on his left side, edging up under his light armor and cutting him deeply.

Thunder landed at the bottom of the slippery shaft with a dull thud, barely getting out of Able's way as the other rolled past.

"Christ Almighty," Able grumbled and slowly stood. "You all right, Thunder?" "Yeah, just a little bruised though."

"That damn old grate is as sharp as a knife," Buzzer said and winced at the pain in his side. "Are you hurt bad, Frank?" Able asked.

"I don't know yet," Buzzer said and rolled over on the side that wasn't hurting. "But I'm bleeding an awful lot."

"Shit, Frank," Thunder said and moved closer through the crowded confines of the ventilation shaft. "You are bleeding a lot. Is it clean?"

"I can't really tell, Bobby," Buzzer said and winced again as his hand came away red and slick after feeling around the wound.

"Let me take a look, Frank," Thunder said and began to inspect the deep and jagged wound. "I'll go back and get the others," Able said. "Bring them back here."

"You go ahead, Able," Buzzer agreed, nodding to his teammate and watching as Able disappeared into the shadows of the shaft. "How bad does it look, Bobby?"

"It's pretty bad, Buzz," Thunder said and removed a small first aid kit from a pouch on his back.

"Stitches?" Buzzer asked. "Maybe a few."

"Then go ahead and start sewing me up, Thunder."

Thunder looked up, grinned at the large man lying on his side and laughed. "This won't hurt a bit."

"Sure, doc."

Thunder gave him one last smile and then bent over to begin stitching. "Hold steady now."

~*~

"You've done good work here, Lieutenant."

"Thank you, General Cartullo."

"We began the evacuation process once Corporal Jimenez briefed me on the situation," Cartullo added. "Now that you're here can I assume that this endless stream of civilians is almost at an end?"

"Yes, General," Moore replied. "I came ahead of the others once I knew of your arrival but there shouldn't be many more, sir."

"Good, once this is done we can begin working on finding our missing shuttles." "Missing shuttles, sir?"

"Yes, Lieutenant," Colonel Smith interrupted. "We had an incident out here earlier." "Yes, quite an incident, Colonel Smith," Cartullo snarled. "Please feel free to continue

briefing the lieutenant on our current situation."

"Yes, sir," Smith said and paused before continuing. "Two troop transport shuttles were stolen from an intersection near here not too long ago."

Moore remained silent and stole a quick glance at Jimenez, who was staring intently at the ground and trying not to be noticed. "Have they been tracked, General?" Moore asked, and the tension between Cartullo and Smith seemed to visibly thicken.

"No...we're still working on that, Lieutenant," Cartullo said. "In fact, with the colonel returning to Wolfbane soon along with the civilians, I'll need you to assist with the search."

"Of course, sir."

"You and your men make a good team," Cartullo said. "I'd like to keep all of you together.

Men who work well as a unit are always a plus."

"Yes, sir," Moore answered and glanced once more at Jimenez. "I have some other news to report, General."

Cartullo motioned for Moore to stop momentarily and turned toward Smith. "In a moment, Lieutenant. First, Colonel Smith, the last shuttle up to Wolfbane before the next shift will most likely be departing shortly. I'd like you on it. Dismissed, Colonel."

"Yes, sir, General Cartullo," Smith said, saluted crisply and turned on his heel to head toward the departing shuttles.

"Please, Lieutenant," Cartullo said, still watching the retreating back of the former commander of Shining's surface units. "What news do you have to report?"

"Well, General, while my team and I were in the tunnels we were met by, uh, you may not believe this, sir..."

"Lieutenant Moore, get to the point as fast as you can," Cartullo ordered.

"Yes, sir," Moore responded and looked up into the face of his new commanding officer. "We ran into another military unit down there. A group of Guarders, sir."

"Guarders?" The General barked. "Are you sure?" "Yes, sir, absolutely."

"How many?" "Approximately eight, sir."

"Just how approximate is that figure, Lieutenant?" Cartullo growled, clearly losing his patience.

"General, there were ten men in the group but only eight of them were Guarders, sir." "How so?"

"Two of them were former members of the Ruffian's FlightCorps," Moore said.

"I thought the Guarders only worked solo or in teams of two at most?" Cartullo wondered aloud.

"Yes, sir, I did as well," Moore said. "But while I was talking to Sergeant Jekel..."

"Jekel!" Cartullo snapped. "He heads that unit."

"Yes, sir, I believe he does, sir," Moore said and continued. "He explained to me that this was the largest team ever assembled for a single off-Aegis mission."

"That explains it." "Yes, sir," Moore said.

"And where are they, Lieutenant?"

"They went deeper into the tunnel system, sir." "For God's sakes, why?"

"They feel that this was their mission to start with and I don't think they are willing to stop until they complete it," Moore offered.

"Did you inform the sergeant of the vast firepower already in presence here?"

"Yes, sir. He thanked me for the information but declined to join us back to the surface."

"I see..." Cartullo said and began adjusting his helmet com-link. "Goddamn...Guarders, I can't believe it," he muttered under his breath before finding the correct channel. "General Cartullo to

U.E.N. Wolverine. I request direct communications with Admiral Dawson." Some static followed that Moore could hardly hear.

"Jesus Christ, they put me on hold."

Moore nodded at that and happened to notice Ambassador McIntyre among the last of the civilians to exit Main Hall. "General, here is someone else you may need to meet, sir."

"Who might that be?" Cartullo asked as he struggled to hear through the static in his helmet com-link.

"The Scientific Ambassador of the U.E.N. to Shining, William McIntyre," Moore said and pointed toward the approaching man.

Cartullo sighed and flashed a grin. "Just what I need, a Goddamn bureaucrat." "He's the closest thing to a government liaison that CharterCity has left, sir."

"Very well, bring him over," Cartullo said, waving Moore off while more static buzzed through his com-link. "Admiral," he called as the link finally got patched through. "General Cartullo here...yes, sir, very well, sir...yes, but, Admiral, I have a bulletin for you. In addition to pirates, Shining also seems to have Guarders...yes, sir, I said Guarders..."

~*~

"They were here. A large group, they moved deeper into the hills," Jekel stood and scanned the serene landscape. "Where are they heading?" He asked himself but Buzzer overheard.

"If I remember correctly, Sarge," Buzzer said. "There's a resort area approximately forty kilometers east of here. It's called Shining Star Center. Supposed to be some sort of metropolitan hub for the area."

"How far have we traveled from CharterCity?" Jekel asked.

"The tunnel exit was probably a good ten kilometers from CharterCity proper," Buzzer answered. "We've traveled another eight or nine since then."

"And another forty to go?"

"About that."

"Okay then," Jekel said and glanced, squinting, at the rapidly setting sun. "We move on until after nightfall. Once it's completely dark we'll catch a few hours rest then begin moving again. I don't want to lose their trail."

Buzzer turned toward the others. "Able, Skinner, take point. Blitzer, Razor, cover our asses. Let's move out."

"Hold on!" Cougar said and held up his hands for silence. "What in the hell is that?" "I hear it," Buzzer said. "Sounds like a shuttle."

"Down! Now!" Jekel ordered. "Get under deep cover."

Buzzer didn't need to hear that last part as he dove into a clump of bushes on a small decline to the left of the group. Razor appeared beside him and he could see Garcia and Redwolf following Jekel into the deep overgrowth and disappear. Two military transport shuttles shook the ground as they thundered through the sky less than a hundred meters overhead.

As quickly as they had appeared they were gone. "Which way were they headed?" Razor asked. "Toward CharterCity, I'd say," Buzzer replied. "Yeah, I thought so, too."

Buzzer listened for anything else but could hear nothing. "Anyone hear more of them?" He called out.

"No," from Jekel some distance off.

"Good," he muttered to himself and stood, brushing grass and loose soil from his clothing. "That was close," Thunder said, suddenly appearing from the bushes to his right.

"Too close," Razor added.

"If those pilots were soldiers they should have been able to detect us, even if we were under deep cover," Buzzer said. "And once we were detected they should have come back to investigate and/or destroy all targets."

"I agree," Jekel said. "Those pilots were most likely not U.E.N. Army or FlightForce." "Stolen shuttles?" Skinner asked.

"Yeah," Buzzer said.

"That means access to massive weaponry," Blitzer said. "I used to fly those birds in the army.

Some of them carry nukes when outfitted for a ground war." "I know," Jekel muttered. "That's what concerns me." "Shouldn't we alert the troops back there?" Garcia asked.

"Absolutely not," Jekel snapped. "Any attempt at communication would lead them right back to us. I cannot risk the safety of this team."

"But there are thousands of troops back there," Redwolf protested. "If there are pirates on board those shuttles..."

"I said no, FlightCorpsman," Jekel said sternly. "But, believe me, it's not something that I want to do. It's something that I have to do."

"I don't get it," Garcia said.

"Our safety takes precedence over what might happen," Buzzer explained. "If they have access to nukes there's nothing we can do about it now anyway. Somebody screwed up and that could end up in a bad way. But getting ourselves killed in the process won't help things."

"Let's move," Jekel said and moved away from the group with a scowl. "You heard him," Buzzer said. "Let's move."

~*~

"Get the word to the team leaders, Gilfred," Sampson said. "We're moving out." "Yes, Frazier."

"Also, tell my Utility Guardsmen to rally around me throughout our travels. My plans are laid thoroughly within my mind only and I do not have the time to relay them to you or to anyone else."

"I understand, Frazier," Thornberg said, breathing heavily with the effort of keeping up with Sampson's brisk pace. "Your safety is of the utmost importance."

"However often I have disagreed with that in the past, Gil, at the present time I have no choice but to agree with you."

"How soon will we know the results of our shuttles' mission?" Thornberg asked. "Quite soon, I should think, Gilfred."

"In your opinion, Frazier," Thornberg started, "will either of those shuttles be returning to us?"

"Actually, I should think not."

"Was this course of action wise, then, Frazier?" Thornberg wondered.

Sampson stopped abruptly in mid-step and turned on Thornberg, eyes blazing. "Maybe not wise my old friend but terribly necessary! I chose the pilots, I ordered the mission. I chose a course of action that may provide us with the narrow margin we will need to achieve victory on this very cold little world. I realize dreadfully the consequences of my decision. I also realize that this may all be over if our shuttles are successful. I have full control of my faculties, Gilfred." Sampson paused, took several deep breaths of the high altitude air, pure and cold, and exhaled slowly. "I know how many lives I am responsible for. I know they are depending on me to lead them through this. The truth is, Gil, many of them will not make it. I wonder at how we have all made it this far. As scavengers and petty thieves, our sizable group excelled. But against the

U.E.N. military, did you really think that we stood a chance?"

Thornberg looked from his leader to the hard frozen ground. "I would like to have thought so, Frazier."

"Then, Gil, you are a fool."

Sampson left him standing there and resumed his brisk pace up the steep slope of the hillside they were climbing.

"Remember to inform the team leaders of our destination, Gilfred," Sampson said without turning around. "And assemble my Utility Guardsmen."

"Yes, Frazier."

"And, Gilfred," Sampson said, turning to face him, "despite what you think at this very moment, I am not crazy. I assure you."

"Of course, Frazier." "Very good, Gil."

Thornberg stood and watched as Frazier Sampson marched up the hill, away from the rest of his followers. "Lord help us," he muttered to himself and turned to make his way back toward the main group.

~*~

Ellie Fremont watched from just beyond the cockpit of the troop transport shuttle that was packed with civilians. They were all so overwhelmingly crammed into the small vessel, she wondered how the engines had lifted them off the ground at all.

"What's the deal with that colonel in the back?" she asked McIntyre, who was pressed up against the wall beside her.

"Believe it or not," he whispered, "he was in charge of all the ground forces down there but two of this type of shuttle were stolen and now he's being held accountable."

"So, they're basically sending him to his room," Fremont smirked.

"That's one way of putting it," McIntyre said. "But in his circles, this is much more embarrassing than a simple banishment to the bedroom."

"Yeah, I would guess so," she muttered and tried to move a cramped leg to her left an inch.

"But if he's up here with us, who's in charge down there?" "General Cartullo."

"The man you were talking to with Lieutenant Moore?"

McIntyre nodded. "Cartullo is in charge of all the army personnel in the Wolfpack Squadron.

I'm surprised they're risking him down there."

"After what's happened in our little slice of paradise, I can see why they want only the best on the ground running things," Fremont said.

"I see your point," McIntyre said and turned slightly to look out of the small round window on his right. "Early evening or not, CharterCity looks like hell."

Fremont moved a little closer, pressing against McIntyre's chest to gain a better view out of the window. The massive city was rapidly diminishing in size as the shuttle gained altitude.

"What is that?" One of the pilots said from less than a meter in front of them as he indicated one of the tracking instruments on his control panel.

"I'm not sure," the co-pilot responded. "Looks like a couple of shuttles, though." "Where are they coming from?"

"No mission assignments were filed for that area, sir," a technician added. "Raise them on the com-link."

"Yes, sir," the ComTech responded as his hands flew across his console. "No reply, sir." "One of them is veering off," the co-pilot noticed.

"Inform Wolfbane. This is beginning to bother me." "Yes, sir."

"Sir!" A tech shouted. "The shuttle approaching CharterCity has armed weapons systems." "What in the hell is going on?" The pilot roared.

"The stolen shuttles, sir?" The co-pilot suggested. "Could they be the stolen shuttles?" "Damned if I know," the pilot snarled and began making adjustments to his controls. "Just get

me more speed and lift. We need to get away from here as soon as possible."

"The other shuttle has accelerated into orbit, sir," a voice sounded from just in front of Fremont.

"Wolfbane has acknowledged our concerns, sir," the ComTech said. "Sir, that shuttle just prepared for missile launch!"

"Get us the hell out of here," the pilot muttered as he strained at the controls.

The small vessel rocked violently as the sudden acceleration took hold. "What's going on, pilot?" McIntyre asked.

"Sorry, Ambassador, no time for small talk." "But..." McIntyre began.

"Sir! Missile launch detected, missile launch detected! There are live birds in the air!" "Hide your eyes," the pilot managed through clenched teeth as the shuttle nosed upward and gained more speed.

McIntyre barely had time to close his eyes before the insides of his eyelids burned with an intensely bright light. "Jesus Christ!"

"Brace yourselves!" A voice boomed from the open cockpit.

The troop transport began buffeting roughly through unrelenting turbulence as wave upon wave of super-heated air rocketed past into Shining's upper atmosphere.

"What's happening, Mac?" Fremont screamed.

The pilot slowly opened his eyes as the brightness diminished and said, "That, ma'am, was nuclear fucking death."

"What?" McIntyre said as he cleared tears from his eyes.

"Yes, Ambassador, those bastards just laid waste to CharterCity," the pilot explained.

McIntyre turned toward the window and saw five huge fireballs sweeping through the ruined remains of the once sprawling capital city of Shining far down below.

"Oh my God..." Fremont sobbed, over the nervous chattering of the shuttle's occupants, clinging tightly to McIntyre's arm. "Mac, all those soldiers."

"How many troops were down there, pilot?" McIntyre asked.

"Christ, thousands," the man rasped. "We literally had thousands and thousands of people in that area."

"Thousands?" Fremont whispered. "Yes, ma'am."

McIntyre tore his eyes away from the fiery spectacle below and slumped back against the wall. He barely paid attention as the pilot activated the com-link. "Colonel Smith, could you make your way to the cockpit please, sir. There's been a new...development..."

~*~

"What in the hell is happening down there?" Dawson screamed and leapt from his command chair. "That better not be what I think it is."

"Jesus Christ, Admiral," Lysak said, stunned. "That was CharterCity."

"Scans show evidence of multiple nuclear weapons detonation in and around the area of CharterCity, Admiral," a tech said from somewhere on the huge bridge.

"Target that shuttle, dammit!" Dawson roared. "Blow it away!" "Shuttle targeted, Admiral," the WeaponsTech said. "Firing now, sir."

"Die, you son of a bitch," Lysak muttered as a small flash of light appeared on the screen and rapidly faded.

"Target destroyed, Admiral." "Yes, but too Goddamn late."

"Admiral," the ComTech called out. "I have calls coming in from dozens of sources, mostly from ships in the squadron."

"Delay them all," he said and paced around the bridge. "There were two, two stolen vessels.

That was just one of them."

"No ID yet on which ships were stolen, Admiral," Lysak offered.

"Goddamn that Smith," Dawson snapped and pounded his fist down on an unattended console. "For Chris'sakes, how are we supposed to know where that other bogey is?"

"We have dozens of shuttle trackings heading directly toward us, Admiral," Lysak said. "Signal to all incoming shuttles, come to dead-stop and await further instructions."

"Sending, Admiral," the ComTech said and tried to adjust her instruments. "Communications are badly distorted, Admiral, there is intense radiation interference. Not all of the shuttles may have received those orders."

"Keep sending, infinite loop until I say otherwise." "Yes, sir."

"All but seven shuttles have stopped, Admiral," Lysak reported, leaning over a terminal and its operator. "All seven are still approaching, sir."

"How many are approaching Wolfbane?"

"Only four, Admiral," Lysak said. "The three others seem to have suffered damage to either main propulsion or directional systems."

"Keep sending that dead-stop message," Dawson said and approached Lysak's position on the bridge.

"As ordered, sir."

"Wolfbane is opening main shuttlebay doors, Admiral," Lysak said. "Comm, inform Wolfbane of the situation."

"Yes, Admiral."

"Scan all shuttles out there," Dawson said to the entire bridge crew. "Let me know if any of them have their weapons systems activated or on standby."

"On it, sir," a tech responded.

"Wolfbane says they received a warning of an approaching shuttle but were unable to confirm due to the multiple explosions on the surface, sir," the ComTech said. "And all shuttles automatically armed their weapons systems once the explosions were detected, Admiral."

"Dammit!" Dawson growled and settled back into his command chair. "Damn this whole frigging mess."

"Two other shuttles have stopped, sir," Lysak said. "Good, good, keep that message going."

"Yes, sir," the ComTech said.

Three of the shuttles formed a line waiting to enter the huge opening in the belly of Wolfbane.

Two other shuttles were drifting in no particular direction, obviously damaged and unable to control their course.

"Instruct those shuttles to disarm weapons systems, all of them, now!" Dawson said. "Instructions sent."

"Shuttle's weapons systems are disengaging, Admiral," the WeaponsTech reported then paused. "Wait, I'm detecting a preparation for missile launch!"

"Which shuttle?" Dawson demanded. "Third in line to Wolfbane, sir." "Target that shuttle!"

"Shuttle adjusting course, sir! Missile launch detected, missile launch detected!" "Fire on that shuttle, dammit!" Dawson said, his face a ghostly pale.

"Too many shuttles in the line of fire, Admiral," the WeaponsTech said. "I can't get a lock." "Target manually but shoot that bastard!"

Suddenly the main viewscreen was engulfed by a wave of intense white light. The automatic sensors in the giant screen dimmed the level of brightness and Dawson watched in horror as the Battleship Werewolf disappeared.

"Werewolf was hit, sir!" Lysak said. "Two direct hits."

"Other shuttles are scrambling, Admiral," someone shouted from across the bridge. "Lock on to that Goddamn shuttle and blow it away!" Dawson screamed. "I mean it, doit

now!"

"Firing!"

"The shuttle has launched again, sir!" Lysak rasped. "Missile launch detected!" "What's the target?"

"Wolfbane, Admiral!" Lysak said and hid his eyes.

"Goddamn it, no!" Dawson shrieked in frustration as the Wolfbane tried unsuccessfully to return fire at the attacking troop transport shuttle. Two missiles armed with tactical strike nuclear warheads entered the open hanger doors in the underside of Wolfbane just moments before Wolverine's weapons systems destroyed the tiny shuttle responsible.

"Good God..." Dawson muttered and helplessly watched as the enormous craft split into three separate pieces before disintegrating, seemingly from the inside out.

As the explosions subsided, the bridge crew of the U.E.N. Wolverine sat in stunned silence and watched the huge clouds of debris before them on the screen, all that remained of the battleship Werewolf and FlightForce Carrier Wolfbane.

"Great God Almighty," Lysak said through clenched teeth and wiped a lone tear from the corner of his eye as he suddenly realized the full impact of what had just happened. All of those soldiers, all of the civilians just off-loaded on to

Wolfbane from the planet's surface, the number of casualties had to number in the tens of thousands. "This is insane..." he managed. "Just insane..."

~*~

The orange red glow on the horizon was clearly not the setting sun. The bright flashes in the darkening sky were obviously not shooting stars or meteors.

"Shit," Thunder mumbled.

"We have troubles," Jekel said and turned toward Buzzer. "What do you think, Frank? Did they just nuke CharterCity?"

"Absolutely, Sarge," Buzzer said. "It looks like they got a couple of the Wolfpack also." "Dammit, no way, Guarder," Redwolf snapped. "The Wolfpack is the best we got, there's no

way these shit-for-brain pirates could take out a couple of those ships."

"Sorry, Jack," Buzzer said. "But how do you explain all of those bright flashes in the sky up there?"

"I don't know but..."

"Listen, FlightCorpsman," Jekel said sternly. "We've seen this type of thing before. What we just saw could be nothing else."

"And CharterCity?" Garcia asked. "The same," Able said.

"So, now what?" From Redwolf.

Jekel paused and crossed his strong arms over his massive chest. "We continue with our pursuit of this main group of pirates. When we catch up with them, we make them pay."

"For Chris'sakes," Garcia spat. "They just leveled the largest city on the planet and took out several ships in the strongest squadron in the U.E.N. fleet. Just how in the hell can the ten of us stop these guys?"

"We'll stop them," Thunder said, almost whispering. "As surely as CharterCity burns tonight, we will put a stop to these people."

"Bet on it," Skinner added.

Redwolf laughed then and said, "Your idiotic confidence is too much to take. Ten against thousands, you're all out of your minds."

"Listen to me, FlightCorpsmen," Jekel snarled. "You asked to be a part of this team and I allowed it, against my better judgment. It's too late to walk out now —you've committed yourselves. Both of you. Now take your Goddamn shitty attitudes and stuff them back where you got them. I'll have none of it from here on in. Do I make myself clear, FlightCorpsmen?"

"Yes, sir," Garcia responded immediately.

"Yes, I understand, Sergeant Jekel," Redwolf reluctantly agreed.

"Good then," Jekel said and scanned the faces of the entire group. They were tired and angry and letting their emotions get the better of them. What they needed more than anything else right now was to get some rest. He fixed the two FlightCorpsmen with a steely gaze then to make sure that they wouldn't be any more trouble and both men lowered their eyes to the ground. "Let's camp here for several hours before we move out again. But once we start up, there will be no slowing down."

United Earthian Nations
SouthWestern Corporate Grid-Sector
Sarkennon System

Shining Mission—Day Five

The Makin-Arctur Wars began in 2163 when Becker Industrial Associates and Makin Manufacturing Company fought a bitter battle for control of the Arcturan System. Becker Industrial, long known as the "Father of the Human Breathable Atmosphere Pump," a device that had first made most colonies possible throughout the Known Grid-Levels of Space, had long since passed its prime as an InterGridactic Industrial Leader and was trying desperately to find a new niche in the universal marketplace. Unfortunately, the one place that contained the necessary raw material for their newest project was already under control by Makin Manufacturing. When Makin's ambitious yet inexperienced pair of corporate attorneys failed to accept Becker's healthy proposal to share the wealth, Becker Industrial Associates attacked in force, plunging the entire system into a bloody war. Four e-years later, with nearly a million dead on both sides, the Makin-Arctur Wars ended with an even split of the Arcturan System's resources. Although small by comparison with most InterGridactic corporate wars, the Makin/Becker Conflict became known as the last major "In-House" squabble before the sheer insanity of the twelve e-year campaign of The New Conflict swept throughout the Known Grid-Levels of Space, bringing with it a virtual cosmic sea of blood and a horrific total of human casualties never before known in modern combat...

(Excerpt:*A History of Modern Earth and Beyond—the People, the Politics and the Insanity of Our Past*by Joseph Mullens)

CHAPTER ELEVEN

"Colonel," Dawson greeted Smith as he entered the briefing room. "Please, do sit down."

"Yes, sir, Admiral," Smith said solemnly and took a seat facing Dawson across the large

central table.

"Colonel, are you aware of what's transpired on the surface?"

"Yes, Admiral."

"Then you know that I am in a very rough spot at this moment," Dawson said, obviously uncomfortable in his present situation. "I relieved you of command down there because your men got careless and the results of that carelessness have been made dreadfully clear."

"Admiral, if I may..."

"Not yet, Colonel," Dawson interrupted. "Just hear me out."

"Very well, sir."

"I have a situation on the surface of Shining, Colonel," Dawson said. "I have hundreds of men still scattered all over that planet with currently no central command structure to be found.

General Cartullo was killed in the CharterCity blast along with more soldiers than I care to think about right now. This so-called easy mission has turned horribly for the worse and I blame myself for allowing my own overconfidence to get the best of me. We all should have been straight and true on this mission, spit and polish, as if we were all cadets on our very first run.

Instead, we were bothered by this measly mission. It cut into our plans, disrupted the schedule. And, now, sixty percent of all the troops who made the trip out here will not be making the trip back. That's entirely my fault, although several others are partially responsible. One of those others happens to be you."

"I understand, Admiral."

"Good, because now I'm giving you a chance to win this thing back for us, Colonel Smith." "Am I in command again?" Smith asked tentatively.

"Yes, Colonel," Dawson said. "You will be in full command of the surface forces again and I don't care what it takes. Every remaining piece of equipment we have, every able-bodied soldier will be at your disposal. Crush everything, Colonel, level every building. Hunt down everything that moves. If you meet resistance, destroy it. If you experience retaliation of any kind, terminate the source. But, do be careful. There are still civilians down there. Shining wasn't an overly populated planet but there are plenty of people living in some of the more remote areas. Try to save them if you can but destroy anyone who opposes you. And I do remind you, Colonel, anyone; man, woman or child who opposes you is to be immediately destroyed. No second- guessing. No prisoners. Do this thing and do it right."

Smith stood and stared at the leader of the Wolfpack Squadron. "Admiral Dawson, I accept some of the blame for what has happened. Believe me, it's hard to live with the consequences of what took place down there. Knowing that all of this…this death, is due to two shuttles stolen in a sneak attack during my watch…well, it hasn't been easy for me, sir."

"Let's try to put all of that behind us for now, Colonel, and focus on the task at hand." "I agree," Smith said. "Do I have full autonomy in command decisions?"

"I don't care how you do it, Colonel, just do it," Dawson sighed. "I'm sick and tired of this. I want all of them dead and done with."

"My men are the best, Admiral," Smith said. "I won't let you down this time."

Dawson looked up and locked eyes with Smith for several seconds after that last remark before finally nodding his approval. "There's one more thing," he said and stood himself. "Were you briefed on the Guarder situation?"

"Guarders, sir?" Smith asked.

"Yes, Colonel, there are Guarders down there," Dawson said with half a smile. "Eight of them altogether along with two of the Ruffian's surviving FlightCorpsmen. And listen up, Colonel Smith, they don't work for you and they don't work for me. Their law is gospel everywhere in the Known-Grids and that includes that iceball down below. If you happen to have the opportunity to see them coming before they're actually upon you, take my advice and move clear out of their way."

~*~

Ellie Fremont sat in one corner of the large dining area and cried. The main mess hall, located deep in the bowels of the U.E.N. Wolverine, was designed to seat 2,500 hungry soldiers. There were three others just like it spread throughout the enormous battleship. The sheer size of the vessel had overwhelmed her when she first boarded but thoughts of those who had been evacuated from Shining to Wolfbane had drowned out all of her emotions, turning them into sorrow.

McIntyre sat at the next table over, talking intently with Wiley Thomas. The two of them were speaking so softly that she could not hear a thing above her own sobbing.

She hated herself for crying so hard, laying herself open to the entire room crammed full of people, most of whom were crying as well. Such total losses of emotional control were the type of public exhibitions she had tried to avoid throughout her young life. This was one time, though, that she could not maintain her composure.

Lifting her head to take a deep breath, she quickly glanced around the room, taking in all of the pain and grief on the faces surrounding her. The room was so thick with sadness she felt as if it were a great weight pressing down upon her. They had overcome so much, had survived down in the tunnels, had made it to the surface protected by an army...

And now, most of the CharterCity survivors were dead. Many of them, her friends. Sharon Strassberg among them. Shuttle upon shuttle had lifted off and deposited their cargo of civilians, people she knew and had worked with, on Wolfbane. She had been on the very last shuttle to lift off and they had all watched in horror as the whole terrifying chain of events unfolded.

McIntyre had been there for her, giving her someone to hold on to while she screamed. She owed him for that and would be sure to make it up to him somehow, someday. But, for now, the only thing she could bring herself to do was curl up in the corner of this overcrowded room, hug her knees tightly to her chest and continue to cry at the shock of it all.

~*~

"How many of us made it, Mac?" Thomas whispered across the drab gray mess hall table. "Well, Wiley, there were only about eight or so shuttle loads that didn't make it into the Wolfbane before it blew," McIntyre said. "Christ, there's only about five-hundred or so of our group in this room. Who knows how many of us there actually were down in those tunnels but what we have here is only a fraction of that total."

"God, I just can't believe it…" Thomas said, shaking his head in wonder. "This entire thing is just beyond me, Mac. It's just beyond me."

"Shit, Wiley," McIntyre sighed and sat a little further back in his uncomfortable metal chair. "It's beyond you, it's beyond me, it's beyond everybody in this Goddamn room. None of these people thought they were going to die on Shining, not violently anyway. First that huge cargo- liner comes crashing down, raising all kinds of attention that most of us on Shining didn't really want."

"Yeah, but the attention was long overdue, Mac," Thomas argued. "I mean, I worked extensively in and around CharterHouse. Statesman Humechy was constantly complaining to the local U.E.N. Outpost about the criminal activity running rampant throughout the shipping lanes in the Sarkennon System. Especially around Shining itself. And let me tell you, all he got was the run around, Mac. Nothing but the run around."

"I never heard any of the other Ambassadors talking about that, Wiley," McIntyre said and paused to take a sip of water from the small cup in his left hand. "And I would certainly think that something like that would be a hot topic of discussion at the embassy. Those guys used to horde up on gossip like it was gold, I mean they couldn't get enough of it. But I've never heard of Humechy making complaints to the U.E.N. before now."

"I know what I know, Mac," Thomas said and pierced McIntyre with a steely glare. "If anything, Dabner Humechy cared for these people. He considered them*his*people, every last one of them. He cared one hell of a lot for the welfare of CharterCity. He did so much for this place. Many of those he served never even realized how much good he had done for Shining and for improving the lives of all those ungrateful people."

"You worked with his office staff pretty closely, didn't you?" McIntyre asked.

Thomas sat up against the back of his chair and crossed his arms over his chest. McIntyre could see the beginnings of a tear welling up in each eye and he suddenly felt for the older man. "Yes, I did," Thomas said quickly and ran a hand across his watery eyes. "If you weren't there, inside CharterHouse everyday, well, you just couldn't know."

"I didn't spend much time in CharterHouse," McIntyre said. "I spent most of my time with my students and experiments at the university. I bet I'd only met Dabner Humechy three or four times since I've been on planet."

Thomas fixed the Scientific Ambassador of the United Earthian Nations to Shining with a hard stare then. "And you say that none of the talk over at the embassy was about Humechy?"

"No, no," McIntyre said with a laugh. "Plenty of the talk was about our former Statesman and I'd go so far as to say that we even talked at length about the recent wave of crime in CharterCity. But I don't think we ever mixed those two components into the same conversation. You know what I mean? We talked about the local government and we talked about the rise in crime, both in detail at times, but never about any efforts by Humechy to somehow stop or at least curb the crime wave. It just never came up."

"That's very strange, now that you mention it," Thomas said. "Because whenever the ambassadors and the other Heads of State who served under Humechy got together all they could talk about was the crime wave and everything Humechy had tried to do to get some help out this way, short of secession from the U.E.N. I wonder why the embassy staff never talked about it outside of CharterHouse?"

McIntyre was thoroughly interested now, leaning forward and listening intently to the older man. "Most of the Ambassadors I spent time with were university types, you know, arts and sciences, education. Those were their specialties. I didn't meet much with the other government types. None of the others did much either, come to think of it."

"You know what I think?" Thomas asked.

"Yeah," McIntyre said. "I think some of those government-type Ambassadors who told Humechy that they would work on getting some aid out to Sarkennon were just as crooked as Chief Parker turned out to be."

"I know they were in your line of work, Mac," Thomas smiled. "But they sound awful dirty to me, too."

"I'd be willing to bet that none but a few of those requests for U.E.N. aid ever made it off- planet."

"It's starting to look like it, all right," Thomas agreed. "How about the other heads of state?" McIntyre asked.

"I don't know," Thomas replied. "But, hell, anything's possible at this point."

"I never liked Matt Tillinghast," McIntyre said. "Or Evan Birding. Never got a good feeling from those two. Even though they were fellow ambassadors they both acted more like spies.

Always turning quiet when I came within earshot and moving across the room from me as if they just didn't trust me to be in on their conversation."

"I always felt weird around Head of State Carlstadt," Thomas said. "Nothing I could ever put my finger on but there was something about that guy that always gave me the shivers. And he was the high-rolling type, you know? Always had everything around him, expensive stuff, expensive women. Always showing off."

"Yeah, Tillinghast and Birding were kind of like that, too," McIntyre said. "Now that I think about it, they were always in conference with Parker and his highest ranking officers. They were always at Police Headquarters for something or other. We used to joke about them, wonder why they didn't just put the damn badges on themselves."

Thomas laughed at that and grabbed his own cup of water, emptying it in one steady gulp. "Too bad we didn't have this talk about a week or so ago. Maybe we could have done something to prevent all of this."

McIntyre turned his gaze away as he noticed more tears in Wiley's eyes. "Well, you couldn't have done anything but get yourself killed, Wiley. As we all know now, those people do not play around. There's been killing enough down there to prove that. And with you dead, who would have led all of us to the safety of the tunnels?"

"Humph," was the only reply Tomas could muster to that.

McIntyre reached across the small table and gripped his friend's shoulder tightly. "You did good, Wiley. You couldn't have done better than you did. Saving all of us, that's what you did down there."

"Yeah, and what good did that do?" Thomas mumbled, tears rolling down his cheeks. "Most of them are dead now anyway. Most of them, innocent women and kids, mothers, wives and children! All dead anyway!"

McIntyre just kept on holding the crying man's shoulder, remaining silent and finding that he needed to wipe his own eyes, too.

~*~

"We lost most of our ground equipment when we lost Wolfbane, Admiral," Smith explained. "Our strategy was to land most of the foot soldiers on the surface to evaluate the situation before unloading the battletanks and armored personnel carriers." "How many of those did we lose?" Dawson asked.

Smith paused and breathed in deeply before answering. "We had four tanks patrolling CharterCity, six others in various other areas and ten APC's on the ground down there. We lost everything else on Wolfbane."

"Dammit!" Lysak snarled. "That's a confirmation of our suspicions in my book, those bastards must be former military."

"I agree, Commander," Smith said. "None of the other ships have anything more powerful than battle-fitted shuttles and some of the larger troop transports.

Most of our heavy surface combat weaponry was lost with the carrier. They knew exactly where to hit us."

"Poor old Chatty," Dawson said. "He didn't even see it coming. Hell, none of us did! How long has it been since we fought a Goddamn legitimate ground war? We've taken so much for granted and look where it's gotten us. Now I have to ask those brave young men and women down there to risk their necks even more than they already have! No damn armor, no heavy firepower. Just some frigging blasters and chargers."

"But plenty of grenade launchers, surface-to-air missiles and that type of ordnance as well, sir," Smith offered.

"We lost four thousand five hundred soldiers in CharterCity to some of our own nukes, Colonel," Dawson countered. "Forty-five hundred! And the total number of enemy forces we are facing in this Godforsaken fracas probably comes nowhere near that. Our opponents are well armed and have access to nukes. Our grenade launchers and missiles will only carry us so far against them. Hell, we've confirmed that their casualties have been light thus far compared to ours."

"And the majority of those casualties were most likely suffered at the hands of the Guarders, Admiral," Lysak added.

"Christ," Dawson sighed and shook his head in disbelief. "Guarders, just ten of them." "Only eight, actually," Smith corrected. "The other two with their team are Ruffian

FlightCorpsmen."

"Right, eight Guarders running amok on the surface down there," Dawson said. "And two former fighter pilots to bring up the rear. Maybe we should let them win this damn war for us. They're having a lot more luck at it than we seem to be."

"Let's hope their luck continues, Admiral," Smith said. "I think all of us could use some." "You more than us, Colonel," Dawson rasped. "Please make haste in getting down to the

planet's surface. Your men need you down there."

"Yes, sir," Smith said and turned toward the exit of the Admiral's briefing room just off of the enormous bridge of the Wolverine.

"And, Colonel," Dawson called. "Win this thing."

Smith let his eyes meet those of both Dawson and Lysak before nodding once in affirmation. "Yes, sir."

~*~

"Commander!" a young technician called from her station on the bridge of the U.E.N. Destroyer Greywolf. "Could you come here, please?"

Derek Hamilton heard that tone of voice, that tone of discovery, not necessarily good, which told him that it was probably a good idea to hustle over and listen to what the young lady had to say.

"What is it, Ensign?" He asked as he reached her station.

"Commander Hamilton, sir," she said and pointed to the monitor she had been working on. "I've been tracking a sizable group from this point in the mountains toward Shining Star Center since the early morning hours."

"Is it one of our units?" Hamilton asked.

"Well, at first I thought so by their pattern of movement, sir," she answered. "But now, I'm not so sure. They just began acting erratically."

"Explain, Ensign."

"Instead of heading into the area and proceeding toward the center of town, as one of our ground units would have done, they have broken into much smaller groups that seem to be taking up positions encircling the entire resort."

"You mean that group is now surrounding Shining Star Center?" Hamilton asked.

"Yes, sir," the ensign answered, "as far as my readings indicate, and I'm pretty confident of them. I've run this scan three times so far and each time my readings have been confirmed. I have also been in contact with our localized ground units and none of them confirm any sizable force of ours taking up strategic positions around the perimeter of the resort this morning.

Whoever they are, I don't think they're with us, sir."

"Good work, Ensign," Hamilton said and began to walk back toward where Captain Tano was sitting at the center of the bridge. "Keep on tracking that group and alert those same units you contacted that they should be expecting some unwelcome company. Keep me informed of any sudden changes."

"But, Commander," she called, and Hamilton stopped. "There's something else, sir." As he reversed direction and approached her again, he said, "Okay, let's hear it."

"Well, there's a much smaller group, approximately eight to ten, that's been following some distance behind the larger group down from the mountains," she explained. "At first I thought they might be a rear lookout but once they caught up to the main group they didn't join the others. They just seem to be sitting in the pre-dawn darkness and watching on the outskirts of the surrounding larger group. This would seem to indicate that they might be one of our units tracking the enemy. The funny thing is, when I contacted our people earlier about the larger group, none of them seemed to know anything about a small unit in pursuit of the enemy. I don't think the smaller grouping is ours either, Commander."

"Did you say approximately ten, Ensign?" Hamilton asked with a gleam in his eye. "Yes, sir, approximately."

"Thank you, Ensign, good work," Hamilton said and smiled. "You may have just helped our efforts up here quite a bit. Keep tracking and I'll brief Captain Tano on your findings."

"Yes, Commander."

Hamilton turned briskly and walked across the bridge to the Captain's command chair. "Captain," he said, and Tano turned to face him. "I think Ensign Fulcher just found our main group of hostiles."

"Where?" Tano asked.

"Surrounding a small resort called Shining Star Center." "Fantastic news," Tano said. "Let's contact..."

"Wait, there's more," Hamilton interrupted. "What else?"

"I think she's found our Guarders, as well," he said and smiled again. "And they're almost upon their prey."

"Good Lord," Tano whispered. "And imagine us with a bird's eye view."

Hamilton nodded in agreement. "I believe it's showtime, Captain."

"ComTech," Tano called. "Contact the Wolverine. Admiral Dawson has got to hear this."

~*~

Gaston Pilar felt an eerie sense of dèjá vu as he crouched in the early morning darkness behind some bushes not far from an U.E.N. Army unit providing security for the Starport's western entrance.

"Just like last time, Gaston," Dukes grunted under his breath. "What do you say?" "Let's ram it right down their fucking throats, Jacob," Pilar snarled and scanned the area ahead.

Fourteen soldiers were in position just ahead, all looking much more intent and alert than those Pilar had encountered earlier guarding the shuttles he had helped steal. These were also fully armed: full-chargers, portable missile launchers and an assortment of other heavy weapons.

"But not so easy this time, Gaston," Dukes rasped.

"I was just noticing that very same thing," Pilar replied. "At least we have more than two men each for back-up this time."

Dukes nodded in agreement. "I wonder how many soldiers are in place within this area?" "I think I heard Thornberg say there were nearly a thousand," Pilar said. "All well armed." "One thousand soldiers?" Dukes asked.

"According to Gilfred."

Dukes gulped and checked his weaponry in the darkness. Pilar glanced at him and laughed. "Don't worry, Jacob. These men won't know what hit them."

"I hope you're right, Pilar," Dukes said. "And remember, it's your turn to get me through this one."

~*~

Frazier Sampson watched Gilfred Thornberg's retreating back. His Second in Command was on his way to dispatch several urgent orders to various group commanders at their posts.

Sampson motioned to the head of his Utility Guardsman. The large, stony-faced individual moved gracefully through the dense overgrowth until he was at Frazier's side. "Keep your eye on Thornberg," Sampson ordered.

"Gilfred Thornberg, sir?" the man uttered in disbelief. "Isn't that what I just said, Ronald?" Sampson demanded.

"Yes, sir," Ronald Leon answered. "Of course, I'll post sentries on him from this point on." "Very good," Sampson said and smiled.

"Anything in particular that I should have them watching out for, sir," Leon asked. "Do you suspect him of treachery?"

Sampson remained silent as he continued to watch the dark shadow of Gilfred Thornberg quickly disappearing into the inky darkness. "Yes, I do," Sampson whispered. "Watch out for signs of treason or betrayal, Ronald. Gilfred has been acting very shifty of late. I fear that he no longer believes in our cause and may just turn tail for the other side in order to save his own skin."

Leon's eyes turned to slits at the mention of treason and betrayal. "I'll take care of it, sir." "Yes, see that you do," Sampson muttered and turned to look up at the cold, hard face before

him. "Also, at the slightest suspicion of foul play by my good friend, Gilfred Thornberg ...feel free to kill him."

"With pleasure, sir."

232

"And if it does come to that, Ronald," Sampson started and paused for just a beat, "don't make it quick."

~*~

"What are we waiting for?" Redwolf asked too loudly from their position of cover. "We could take out half of them before they knew what was going on."

"Calm down, Jack," Buzzer spat. "If you don't lower your Goddamn voice, I'm going to lower it for you. Do you understand?"

"But he's right, Buzzer," Garcia whispered. "What in the hell are we waiting for?"

"Listen, both of you," Buzzer rasped. "If we take any action before the actual battle begins we risk discovery. Sure, we'll kill maybe a hundred or so of them but, due to their greater numbers, they'll quickly regroup and wipe us out in the long run. Do you understand? If we allow them to get a fix on our position, we're all dead. Every one of us."

"But their first volley will kill hundreds of troops, Buzzer!" Garcia pleaded. "How can we stand by and watch that happen? Haven't enough of us died already? I don't see any of you lying dead, pouring your life's blood into the snow and ice of this miserable planet."

Several seconds of awkward silence ensued before it was broken by Sergeant Jekel's voice. "That's a valid point, Flight Commander, and unfortunately you are absolutely correct. There's been enough dead soldiers on this iceball. Let's take a step in the right direction. What do you say, Guarders?"

"Sarge?" Buzzer asked suspiciously, "are you suggesting that the ten of us hit these bastards full on? A quick hit and get?"

"What else, Frank?" Jekel replied. "Although that may not be the strategically correct decision, it's the right one. For Chris'sakes, what's happened to us? Are we all that damn important? Why should we sacrifice those fine young men and women for our own safety? That's not what the Guarders are all about! You know that better than anyone else. Now, what do you say?"

233

Buzzer blinked several times and began to laugh. "Dammit, Harrison," he said. "I say, let's do it. I've only been playing it by the Goddamn book so far because you're here."

"He's not kidding," Razor's voice intoned. "You should have seen the shit he pulled before you got here, Sarge. I couldn't believe it."

"What in the hell's going on here?" Garcia asked.

"Well," Jekel snarled and shook his head in disappointment. "It looks like I've been holding this team of mine back some, doesn't it? But, not anymore, though, Avril. Now that it's clear exactly what my presence here has done, how it's held back my people from doing this job the way it should have been done from the start, I say that all previous imaginary protocols are off. Let's start this little party, shall we?"

"It's about Goddamn time," Thunder mumbled. "Code twenty-one on three?" Buzzer asked.

"Code twenty-one, on three," Jekel confirmed. "On my mark..."

"What does that mean?" Redwolf asked as the team of eight Guarders began priming their weapons.

"One..." Jekel said.

"Get ready for a show, FlightCorpsmen," Buzzer whispered into the dark and readied several half-charger cartridges for quick reloads. "It's about to get hairy. Avril, stick close to me."

"Two..."

"What should I do?" Redwolf asked hurriedly.

"Just follow my lead, Jack," Thunder said. "Three!"

"AMBUSH!" All eight Guarders screamed at once into the thick blackness surrounding their position, then began firing multiple charges into the darkened sky just outside of Shining Star Center. "U.E.N. soldiers, down!"

Buzzer dove to the ground, taking Avril Garcia with him. As the two hit and rolled, Buzzer glanced at the former flight commander and smiled. "Now, Avril, all hell breaks loose."

Jacob Dukes saw the black sky overhead light up, heard screams piercing the darkness and did not understand what was happening. "What's that?"

"Let's move!" Pilar shouted and headed off towards the U.E.N. troops just ahead of their position, firing his half-charger all the way.

The military units began firing almost immediately into the woods and bushes surrounding Shining Star Center. Jacobs watched in horror as Gaston Pilar was cut to shreds and his body hit the ground in several bloody pieces. Firing his weapons wildly toward the soldiers, Dukes crouched and ran in the opposite direction. His heart pounded in his chest as he stumbled his way through the darkened woods.

Free, almost free! He thought to himself as he came closer to the clearing and ultimate safety. Glancing back at the firefight one last time, he grinned to himself and began thinking of ways to escape this miserable planet. Not far now, he knew, as he crested a small hill. The stand of trees up ahead represented his last remaining obstacle before smooth ground would lead the way away from this death-trap. Looking ahead, he grinned in satisfaction and just had time to notice the dark shadow blocking his path.

Jacob Dukes' eyes went wide with shock and pain as the smile fell from his face and his body landed hard on the cold ground.

Blitzer wasted no more time than was absolutely necessary. He quickly pulled the dagger from the man's abdomen and plunged it deep into his chest. Convinced that the man was dead, he wiped the bloody blade on the corpse's shirt and continued to make his way toward the battle.

~*~

Gilfred Thornberg ran through the snow and trees back the way he had just come from, firing quick precise blasts from his half-charger into the throngs of

U.E.N. soldiers all around him. The lights of Shining Star Center cast an eerie backdrop to the battle at hand. His breathing was fast but controlled, the adrenaline rush coursing through his body making every step sharp, painful and glorious.

He was in his element, now. Using all of the skills taught to him by Frazier Sampson, through those long, hungry years. Another blast and he saw a soldier go down, minus some vital organs and most of his ribs. It felt good, damn good, to finally put all of that close-quarters combat training to good use. He felt close to invincible as he sprinted through the dense foliage, taking out enemy targets every twenty meters or so.

Up ahead he could hear the tremendous crash and thunder of a much larger battle raging.

Sampson was there, he knew, in the thick of it. He had to be; the thunderous noise was emanating from the direction Thornberg had just come from right before the sky started raining down on top of them.

"Hold on, Frazier," he grunted to himself and let loose another volley of half-charger blasts. "I'm almost there, old friend. I'm almost there…"

~*~

Sergeant Kevin Green popped up over the front end of his armored assault vehicle and let loose several rounds from his blaster. Great geysers of snow and dirt sprang into the air in the darkened woods but he heard no screams of pain, usually associated with a hit.

"Shit!" he grumbled and frantically searched his combat gear for his grenades as the enemy's return fire pounded against the far side of the tank, shaking the entire machine like a quake. "Goddammit! I just had those frigging grenades this morning!"

"We left them inside, Sergeant Green, sir," one of his many young faceless and nameless crewmen said through gritted teeth. "All the explosives are inside this hunk of shit."

"Yeah, well this hunk of shit is the only thing keeping you from an appointment with the worms!" Green snarled. "Now just keep firing your weapon in that direction and shut the hell up!" Green motioned toward the woods just meters away.

Several other soldiers must've heard him because the thunder of five full-chargers firing all at once bounced off the thick metal skin of the tank and rang in his ears. Snapping tree trunks like twigs, the charger blasts lit up the area like mid-day and Green snapped off several shots with his blaster into the surprised faces of opponents.

"Pull back! Pull back!" Green shouted and watched as his men hot-footed it out from behind the tank to deeper cover.

"All right, you bastards," Green muttered and climbed up the side of the immense vehicle to the open side hatch. "Now you'll see how we really like to fight our wars."

The hatch slipped closed with the hiss of escaping oxygen. Flipping switches at random, Green activated just about every system in the tank. While the tank rose slowly on a powerful cushion of air, Green maneuvered the three forward main guns of his iron beast around to face the woods and the advancing enemy. The targeting system clicked green on all three screens, locked on multiple heat sources.

"Fry, mother fuckers!" Green screamed and hit the auto-fire mechanism. The thirty-five ton vehicle rocked with the blasts as each forward gun fired simultaneously, releasing massive amounts of explosive energy into the surrounding trees and bushes.

Glancing at the longer range scanning terminal, he could see the heat source indicators disappearing off the monitor. "Yeah! Yeah, that's right!" Green screamed above the roar of the heavy weaponry and began maneuvering the tank towards the other enemy positions showing on his scanners. With the absence of both his OpsTech and his WeaponsTech, the tank moved all too slowly under his limited control. With both eyes glued to the weapons console, Green never saw the incoming missile indicators blinking red behind him at the operations console. Three shoulder launched missiles streaked through the trees and smashed into the massive fuel cells lining the back half of the tank.

Despite the fuel cell's extensive shielding, the combined force of all three missiles tore directly into the tank's main source of power. The ensuing explosion incinerated everything within one hundred meters. Green and his crewmen never felt a thing.

~*~

"I don't give a shit, Peterson," Colonel Smith roared at his Second-in-Command. "I know the Goddamn stars are falling down around us but we need to get these last two shuttles full of civilians up to the Wolfpack! Do youunderstand?"

"Yes, sir, Colonel."

"Good, now do it before these bastards get any closer to the city center. Move!"

Peterson saluted hurriedly and ran across the commons toward the last two shuttles. Wide- eyed and terrified men, women and children stared back at him as he motioned to other soldiers to begin loading the civilians on.

"J.T.," Smith heard his name called from behind. Turning around, he recognized one of the shuttle's pilots who was advancing toward him. "J.T., you can't expect us to take these people up through all the fireworks."

"I expect it and you'll do it," Smith said. "Case closed, Teddy. Now go rev those engines." "I'll override you, J.T.," the pilot countered. "I'll call Dawson."

"You do whatever the hell you want to, Teddy, including calling the Admiral," Smith snarled. "But any more delay out of you and I'll personally see to your court-martial and dishonorable discharge. We're trying to win a war out here in case you haven't noticed and I don't have the time to stand here and argue this bullshit with you. Understand?"

"Excuse my bluntness, Colonel, but fuck you!" The pilot spat at Smith's shoes and turned back towards the shuttles.

"Goddammit," Smith swore and entered his shuttle. Accessing the com-link, he began calling his field commanders. Just then, Peterson appeared in the doorway.

"Colonel, the last two birds are up. I've ordered extra covering fire until they punch up through the atmosphere."

"Now, that's more like it, David," Smith said and motioned for the major to join him in the small vehicle.

"How goes it so far?" Peterson asked.

"I was just finding out when you came in," Smith said and once again gave his attention to the com-link.

"From the sound of it, they're all around us, Colonel," Peterson said. "I realize that."

"Most of the heavy stuff sounds like ours but we can't really be sure," Peterson continued. "I know."

"At least we haven't lost anything..."

Just then the intense explosion of Sergeant Green's tank disintegrating shook the ground, lit up the night and caused a ringing in Smith's ears.

"What in the hell was that?" Peterson asked, still holding his head.

"I think we just lost something," Smith answered and keyed the com-link for the unit who was covering the area where the blast came from. Peterson looked on inquiringly and Smith shook his head in disgust. "No response."

"It sounded big, like a tank or personnel carrier," Peterson offered. "If we lose a couple more of those it's going to get sticky around here."

"Jesus Christ," Smith grunted and looked up as another explosion rocked the other side of Shining Star Center. "Of all my potential campsites, I choose the one about to be attacked.

Goddammit!"

"Luck hasn't exactly been with us too much since we got here, Colonel," Peterson said.

Smith looked up into the younger man's eyes with fire burning in his own. "Don't talk to me about luck, Major, talk to me about tactics. I'm not depending on any frigging luck to pull my ass out of this one! I'm depending on our combined experience and training. This is our job, David. Let's finally get to doing it right. Maybe we'll both get a raise."

Peterson cracked a smile at that last reference, wondering if money would really be all that important once this was finally over. "Yes, sir, Colonel. A raise would be nice right about now," he decided.

~*~

The five men hustled by in the darkness, obviously trying to keep quiet but failing miserably. Their targets more than likely were the three shuttlecraft sitting under the subdued lighting of a small clearing about fifty meters ahead.

Redwolf and Thunder popped out from the cover of some thick bushes and quickly dispatched the potential attackers. Return fire came surprisingly from behind and Thunder knocked the FlightCorpsman to the hard crunching snow.

"Watch yourself, Jack," Thunder called over the roar of charger blasts. "Let's move!"

Redwolf was still trying to catch his breath as the Guarder sprang up and sprinted across the snow, disappearing into the dark.

"Goddamn," he muttered and remained low on the cold unyielding ground as more enemy fire rained down near him. Redwolf began to shift position in order to fire his blaster in return before remembering that his opponents would see his weapon's discharge and zero in on him, probably killing him in the process. In short, he had almost attempted sure suicide.

"Dammit!" He cursed himself for not following the Guarder immediately when he saw Thunder break for it. Another charger round exploded in front of him, the remnants of the blast slightly charring his right shoulder. Screaming with pain, he rolled several times through the snow to try and quell the burning in his shoulder. "Damn, damn, damn..."

From his new position some four meters from where he had been hit, Redwolf decided it was indeed time to move out. He half-crouched, holding the bloody shoulder, and sprinted across the snow. Immediately, the enemy fire began tracking him as he ran, one blast knocking into the snow at his feet sending him sprawling.

Redwolf screamed again at the excruciating pain in his shoulder and scrambled behind the trunk of a large tree for some cover. A barrage of blaster fire and charger blasts slammed into the surrounding snow and overgrowth.

A tremendous explosion rocked the tree he was nestled up against, the bright flash temporarily blinding him as the trunk snapped in two way up high in a showering spray of bark and sap.

Must've been a full-charger, that one, he thought to himself as he struggled to squeeze as close to the base of the tree as possible. Somewhere up above him, he wasn't sure exactly where, the top half of this tree was coming down and coming down hard. He could only hope that it wouldn't land directly on top of him.

The sound was intense, causing pain in his ears, as the top half of the twisted blackness of wood that passed for a tree here on Shining slammed to the ground very close beside him.

Redwolf's ears rang for several seconds before clearing and, then, suddenly all was quiet.

The eerie silence filled the void of his immediate area and Redwolf tried desperately to figure out what his opponents had planned for him now. He could still hear the wicked sounds of various battles raging in the distance but he couldn't hear anything nearby. He gasped raggedly and noticed that he was holding his injured shoulder with his left hand while maintaining a solid grip on his blaster with his right.

A far off explosion startled him and he laughed nervously at his anxiousness.*Good Lord, let'sget this over with,*he thought to himself and took a deep breath to clear his lungs and head.

The hand came out of nowhere and grabbed his uninjured left shoulder. Redwolf's shout of surprise and terror was cut off by another hand, now clasped tightly across his mouth. That horrible and interminable moment where death loomed large over him passed quite rapidly as he recognized the face of Thunder in the darkness just inches from his eyes.

"I thought I told you to move, FlightCorpsman," he said sternly. "When I say move out, I mean it. Please remember that."

"Go to hell, Thunder," Redwolf rasped as the larger man helped him to his feet. His heart felt like it would burst from his chest but sudden relief washed over him, warm and welcoming. "I thought I was a dead man there for a moment."

"What a coincidence," Thunder said. "So did I. Now move out."

~*~

Buzzer swung his fist viciously, connecting with the butt of his blaster against the smaller man's temple. His opponent went down hard, stirred briefly, then slumped face down into the snow.

Wasting no time, he cleared a dagger from his boot sheath and neatly cut the unconscious man's throat. He just as quickly cleaned the weapon free of blood on his victim's pants leg and resheathed the blade, all the while watching intently for signs of other company. The wound in his ribs hurt like hell and he could feel a good amount of blood trickling down his side.

Somehow, he had lost Avril Garcia in the woods surrounding Shining Star Center. One moment the former flight commander was running along behind him and, in the next moment, he was gone. After that, Buzzer had run head on into three separate members of the invading force and hadn't really had the time to think about where Garcia could be. Now that the last of his opponents was dead, he could concentrate on his present situation.

Crouching in the dark and cold, Buzzer quickly keyed in his sequencer to contact Jekel. After several seconds with no response, he came to the conclusion that either Jekel was far too busy to respond or something much worse was happening. Hopefully it was the former and not the latter. Actually, it would be a good idea to locate the other members of the team before too long. They had all been separated almost since the initial fighting broke out.

Several large and noisy explosions lit up the sky near the center of town, in the general direction of where the headquarters of the army's CO would most likely be set up.

Buzzer took another quick look around but saw no one. At an intensely brisk pace he set off toward the heart of Shining Star Center. If the others acted as he pretty much thought they would, they should all be heading in that very same direction.

CHAPTER TWELVE

"We've loaded the last of the passengers off of those two shuttles, Colonel," Dawson said into the com-link. "Should we send both shuttlecraft back down?"

"Hell, yes, Admiral!" Smith's raised voice answered through a cacophony of explosions and what sounded like heavy weapons fire from the surface of Shining. "And with as many heavily armed troops as they can carry, sir! We're getting our asses handed to us down here!"

"They're on the way, Colonel," Dawson answered. "Good, just make it quick, sir."

Dawson paused at that, then replied simply, "Dawson out."

"Good Lord, Admiral," Lysak said as he turned back to the console he was monitoring. "There's an awful lot of weapons fire registering down there, sir."

"This is outrageous..." Dawson muttered. "Who in the hell are these people?" "They're monsters, Admiral," Lysak snarled. "Nothing but fucking monsters."

"Admiral," Lieutenant Cummings called from across the bridge, "both shuttles have departed, sir. Full of troops, as Colonel Smith requested."

"Very good, Lieutenant," Lysak answered. "Let me know when they land and begin to engage the enemy forces."

"Yes, sir," Cummings said crisply and turned back to her Ops Station.

"Admiral," Lysak whispered, just several inches from Dawson's left ear. "Do you think we should call for back-up, sir?"

Dawson turned sharply and stared at his first officer. Never before had such a question been posed in his presence. "Absolutely not, Commander," he growled.

Lysak backed up several inches and nodded affirmatively. "Of course, sir."

~*~

"Commander of U.E.N. Army forces, please return communications," Jekel called into his sequencer as Cougar looked nervously on, his half-charger gripped tightly and primed for action. "Commander of U.E.N. Army forces currently under siege within Shining Star Center, this is a communication from additional military personnel in your area. Please respond to this transmission."

Static filled the tiny speaker on Jekel's wrist unit before a response began to crackle through. "Who is this?"

"I might ask you that very same question, soldier," Jekel returned.

"This is Colonel Smith of the U.E.N. Army, currently acting commander of Shining ground forces," the voice replied.

Jekel raised an eyebrow at that and glanced at Cougar. Turning off the audio on his sequencer momentarily, he leaned over to the other Guarder and said, "A colonel, in charge of *all* ground forces?"

"What's he doing down here on the ground, in the thick of it?" Cougar wondered aloud. "Good question," Jekel said and re-keyed the audio on his tiny transmitter. "Colonel Smith,

this is Sergeant Harrison Jekel of the U.E.N. Guarder Squadron. A team of Guarders are currently engaged in combat with the forces attacking this city and working steadily toward your command center."

"How far away are you, Sergeant, and how much support can you offer?" Smith's voice could barely be heard over the sounds of explosions and nearby weapons fire coming across Jekel's sequencer.

"This is an open line, Colonel," Jekel said. "I've said far too much already. We'll let you know when we reach your position."

"Sergeant, we are coming under heavy fire..." Smith responded, once again, over the din of the battle taking place. "You and your men may not like it here."

Cougar suddenly sprang from cover, fired at a group of attackers stumbling through the brush near their position and watched two of them go down in a spray of gore.

"Move! Move!" Jekel shouted and had to grab Cougar by the arm to get the man moving for deeper cover.

Answering fire from what seemed to be full-chargers blasted into the thickness of trees and dense vegetation behind the two men as they rushed closer to the edge of the city.

Jekel spied a small depression in the shadows some ten meters away to the left and steered Cougar toward it. As they both lay low in the small hole, Jekel keyed his sequencer again for transmission. "Colonel Smith, we're moving closer to your position and should be there to assist you shortly. And don't worry about us, Colonel," Jekel said while grinning wickedly at Cougar. "We love it here."

~*~

Avril Garcia tripped on something in the dark and fell painfully down the small incline, coming to rest suddenly against the trunk of a black and twisted tree.

"Jesus Christ!" He muttered and shook his head to clear the blurriness in his vision. Suddenly, his eyes widened as his ears registered the soft snap of a twig cracking under pressure nearby.

His right hand immediately began searching for his holstered blaster but found nothing.

Remembering that he had been holding his weapon before falling head first down the hill, he faced the fact that he was now unarmed.

Damn, he thought to himself, realizing instantly that the lack of hand-to-hand combat experience he'd gained as a FlightCorpsman could very well get him killed right now.

Straining his ears to listen for another telltale sign of his stalker, Garcia's eyes also worked hard to penetrate the inky darkness of these woods.

Silence...

He could neither see nor hear anything moving nearby. The sounds of battle within Shining Star Center rocked the entire area but somehow he was able to filter out all that.

There it was again...

A twig cracking, somewhere off to his right. Garcia caught himself holding his breath as his heart pounded rapidly in his chest. He had to steel himself to fight the urge to get up and run, making himself an easy target to whomever was out there hunting him.

He had lost his original blaster when he had been separated from Buzzer, after the explosion of a particularly close charger round had sent him tumbling. Buzzer had been out of sight well before Garcia had stopped rolling. Since then, he had been relying on his back-up blaster, a smaller and less powerful weapon that he had kept in a leg holster.

Now, even that was gone.

Garcia raised his head several inches and searched the area surrounding his position. He kept his eyes open as wide as possible so they could adjust to what little light was penetrating into the darkness from the outskirts of Shining Star Center.

"I can see you, sir," a voice called from nowhere and nearly made Garcia jump out of his skin. "Shit..." he muttered and began to crawl away from the tree.

"Now, now, stay put, right where you are," the voice called again. "Moving around like that will get you killed much quicker than I currently plan."

"Go to hell, you son of a bitch!" Garcia shouted and was met by an eerie laughter.

A loud thump sounded in the grass beside him and was followed quickly by another. Garcia's nerves were suddenly at odds with him as every last one of them seemed to search frantically for the quickest way out of his body. What light there was for his eyes to pick up gleamed off of the small metal objects on the ground and Garcia quickly thought, *BOMB!* Another moment revealed the objects to be the two blasters he had lost earlier.

"Don't worry, friend," the voice almost whispered. "Both of the charge packs are missing. I just thought you might want to see them again, before..."

"Who are you?" Garcia shouted.

"That won't really be a matter of importance in just a few moments, I assure you."

Garcia stood up then and came out from behind the tree, anger more than anything else now controlling his tortured mind. "Show yourself, coward!"

"I've been following you for quite some time," he heard. "Did you happen to notice?" "Fuck you!" Garcia screamed, all his anger, fear and frustration suddenly boiling over and bursting forth. "Show yourself, you bastard! Come out, let me see you! Face me!"

"Calm down, soldier!" the voice barked, and Gilfred Thornberg stepped forward, appearing seemingly out of nowhere. The half-charger he held looked huge to Avril Garcia in the pre-dawn darkness, especially since the round maw of the barrel was pointed directly at his chest.

"You would kill an unarmed man?" Garcia asked.

Thornberg snickered once and fired twice. As the blasts bore into Avril Garcia's mid-section his thoughts fleetingly turned to his three-year-old daughter, so very far away. Garcia's body exploded as it was torn into pieces and death followed quickly. What remained of his corpse slapped wetly to the ground. Thornberg could see lifeless eyes looking in his direction. "Hell, yes, soldier," he sneered and disappeared into the darkness.

~*~

Sampson had quickly studied the small battlefield when he and his Utility Guard had first begun to attack the U.E.N. Army command post. His small group had started out much larger but had sustained numerous casualties throughout their push into Shining Star Center.

He had specifically ordered his people not to fire at the two command shuttles sitting in a small courtyard just ahead of them. Right now, what they needed

248

most were as many operational shuttles and personnel carriers as possible. Otherwise, there really wasn't any other way off of this cold and dismal planet.

His Utility Guard had done a fine job of protecting him from danger thus far but they had more than paid for doing so with their own blood. Their number had been halved since storming the resort town. Frazier Sampson could only hope that the rest of his people were faring better, although the possibilities of that were quite small against the well-organized U.E.N. Army forces they were facing.

Now he and his small band also had to contend with two large shuttles, most likely personnel carriers, making strafing runs at everything that moved, keeping all of them deep behind cover while the soldiers in front of them slowly picked them off.

"This is ridiculous, Ronald!" Sampson snarled under his breath and turned to face the head of his Utility Guard. "We've got to move, Ronald, they're killing us here."

"If we move from here they'll surely pick us off, every last one of us," Ronald Leon replied. "They have us covered much too well. Especially with those two attack craft firing at us every other second."

"Well, let's knock them out of the sky then!" Sampson roared.

"Our small weapons are ineffective against those shuttles at this range," Leon said. "But we're working on a solution at this very moment."

"What kind of a solution?" Sampson demanded.

"Just watch the next strafing run," Leon said and smiled as he raised his blaster. "We've gotten our hands on some heavier artillery. Once the real fireworks start we'll lay into the soldiers positioned ahead of us with our smaller weapons. The confusion ought to be just enough for us to capture the two shuttles in the courtyard."

"Yes, capture being the key word, Ronald," Sampson warned. "I want absolutely no damage done to those shuttles. Right now, they are our only way off of Shining."

"We all realize that, sir," Leon said. "But what of the others?" "What others, Ronald?" Sampson rasped.

"We began this thing with thousands of people, sir," Leon sighed. "Obviously we have suffered tremendous losses. But, there are still many hundreds of your loyal followers left doing battle out there, in this city. Hundreds, sir. What becomes of all of those who are left here and in the surrounding woods once we leave?"

"This venture is truly over, Ronald," Sampson said sternly. "You know that as well as I do. Any fool could see the truth of our dismal situation. We are extremely overmatched here. My one remaining mission is to flee Shining with as many of my people as I possibly can while also destroying as much U.E.N. military property in the process. That includes killing off these Godforsaken, pain-in-the-ass soldiers. Do you understand me?"

Ronald Leon stared intently into the eyes of his crazed leader, the loathing and contempt for his opponents clearly apparent in their depths. "Yes, sir, I understand all too well."

"Good then," Sampson snapped. "Here come those shuttles on their next strafing run. This show of yours better be worthwhile."

"Don't worry, sir," Leon muttered. "If it's death and destruction you want, you won't be disappointed."

~*~

"The shuttles are coming in again, Colonel," a young soldier called from behind the cargo bins they were all using for cover.

"Peterson!" Smith called. "Get a link going hot with those shuttles! They're still not clear to land. We need more supporting fire so the troops they're carrying can get down here on the frigging ground!"

"Yes, sir," Peterson answered and began keying in commands on the mini com-link strapped to his back.

"Everyone down!" Smith shouted, hoping everyone within earshot had heard him.

The shuttles thundered by overhead, forward guns blazing toward the surrounding woods.

Great explosions of sound and light shattered the darkness. The agonizing screams of many men could be heard coming from the shredded remnants of trees near the edge of the woods.

"Die, you bastards..." Smith muttered under his breath and pounded his fist to the cold hard ground.

"Second pass coming, Colonel!" Peterson's voice gasped from his side. "How much more of this can those people take?"

"As much as it takes to kill every last one of them," Smith answered. "Every last one."

The shuttles had turned around from their last pass and were now approaching low over the trees back towards the encampment. The big guns opened fire on the woods again, producing the same fireworks as before.

Smith's eyes opened in amazement as he watched a series of rockets, probably shoulder launched, streak up out of the trees. "Jesus Christ..." he swore as both shuttles exploded upon impact. Throwing himself to the ground and rolling as close to the crates as possible, Smith covered his head as best he could to protect against the torrent of debris raining down from above.

Two smaller explosions sounded from several blocks away as the remaining bulk of both shuttles crashed into the towers of three large buildings.

Small weapons fire swept the area, barely missing the two command shuttles sitting in the courtyard to his left.

"They're advancing, David," Smith called to Peterson. "We need to pull back, ASAP!"

"Let's go, people!" Peterson shouted. "Pull back, phase two! Repeat, phase two! Move, move, move!"

Smith rose to a crouch and snapped off two quick blaster bolts before breaking into a run for better cover in the streets of Shining Star Center. A quick glance

251

over his shoulder proved that the enemy troops were indeed advancing. "Goddamn," he mumbled to himself and fired off several more blasts. "Where in the hell are those Guarders?"

~*~

Able yelled at the top of his lungs from his perch six meters high in the tree as he pumped round after round of half-charger fire into the remaining targets below.

Blitzer was some twenty meters across the small clearing using his blasters to create a deadly crossfire. The deafening combination of rapid weapons fire and Able's screams were enough to make their victims think that a small army was attacking them.

The initial attack had taken out almost half of the opponents they were facing, before others had broken for cover and began returning fire. The two Guarders were firing rapidly with alternating, precisely timed bursts, keeping their quarry off guard and confused. That initial lapse in concentration by the unsuspecting pirates had allowed Able to take out seven targets in a matter of seconds while Blitzer's handguns were able to nullify four more.

After that, several shots rocked the tree very near Able's position, prompting him to step up the fire from his half-charger and spread the blasts over a wider area to keep his opponents down.

Blitzer was forced to change his position several times as a result of answering fire but their crossfire had been effective in cutting down the enemy forces. With blasters in both hands, Blitzer focused on two crouching shadows seeming to move slowly through the brush and snapped off two quick shots with each of his weapons. The brief flash of light created by the blasts confirmed the Guarder's suspicions a moment before both targets went down and stayed down.

Abruptly, all was quiet. Blitzer signaled toward the tree where Able was perched and saw a quick flash of movement in reply. Only the slight moans of the injured and the crackle of burning leaves ignited by the hailstorm of weapons fire could be heard in the area.

The signal had instructed Able to begin a slow descent from the tree while Blitzer provided a cover watch. Blitzer scanned the darkness trying to discover any still hidden assailants and noticed Able as he neared the base of the tree. Able hit the ground and began to search the area for wounded. Blitzer joined him in the undesirable task, working toward his partner's position. Able had shouldered his half-charger and now held a blaster outstretched and pointing downward.

One blast shattered the silence and the moans of the wounded grew louder with fear and dread. Blitzer came upon a pair of legs trying frantically to move their owner deeper into the brush. With barely a glance, Blitzer aimed and fired. The legs stopped moving. Another blast from Able rang out, and another. Blitzer dispatched one more wounded opponent before he met up with Able and the two confirmed that all targets were dead.

Able bent down and picked up a small but deadly looking knife lying by the side of a corpse.

Blitzer raised an eyebrow and shook his head. "Robbing the dead, Able?"

"Hell, yeah," Able laughed. "This thing's no use to him anymore," he said, motioning to the body at his feet.

"Well, let's try to get some replacement ammo off these guys," Blitzer offered. "I don't think many of them had a chance to use much of it."

Able chuckled at that, pocketed the knife and moved off toward another body. "Able," Blitzer called, and the other Guarder turned around. "Let's make this quick. I'm getting a bad feeling all of a sudden."

"You, too?" Able asked and briefly glanced around the makeshift battlefield. "Yeah, a bad feeling."

~*~

Razor watched as the small U.E.N. Army contingent pulled back from the two shuttles in the square amid a barrage of weapons fire coming from the edge of the woods just behind them.

Skinner dropped to one knee, aimed his half-charger into the woods and fired four rapid rounds toward the quickly advancing enemy. Razor added blaster fire to the mix. The small wall providing them cover had also acted as a good area for their stakeout of the city proper before the other shuttles had been blown out of the sky, crashing into buildings across the street.

The ensuing explosions had sent the two Guarders diving for cover as a steady rain of debris had pelted them for several seconds. Once clear, they had crept along the wall and looked over the top to see retreating soldiers heading straight for them.

Skinner ducked back behind cover as several soldiers began to fire at their position. "Shit!" Razor muttered, then he yelled out, "U.E.N. Guarders! Hold your fire!"

"Hold your fire!" A strong voice bellowed in the distance. "Hold your fire!"

Razor took a chance and raised himself over the wall with his blasters held high. "U.E.N. Guarder!"

"Guarders! Hold your fire, boys," a man wearing colonel's stripes yelled and motioned his men forward. Razor waved them on and, one by one, the soldiers dove over the small wall.

Colonel Smith was the last one to join the group.

"Good to meet you, Colonel," Razor said and signaled to Skinner. Simultaneously, the two Guarders rose and began firing rapid blasts past the two grounded shuttles and into the woods where a large number of heavily armed men were emerging. Answering fire drove them both back down.

"Christ Almighty," Smith muttered and tried to catch his breath back. "Good to see you, too, Guarder. Where are the others?"

"Just the two of us for now, Colonel," Skinner answered. "The others will be here soon." "But, for now, I suggest we find another hiding place," Razor said. "We're seriously overmatched and outgunned here."

Smith laughed at that and sneered. "I thought the Guarder Squadron never ran."

"Well, that's what you get for thinking, Colonel," Razor replied sharply. "Dead soldiers can't eliminate enemy targets. Repositioned ones can. Now, let's move out."

"Don't get smart with me, kid," Smith began, and Razor held up a hand for silence. "Remember, Colonel, I am a U.E.N. Guarder and so is my partner. Either one of us currently outrank you in the strictest of military terms. Now, I agree that your men answer to you. I'd like that to continue but it will not unless I get some cooperation. Do you understand, Colonel?"

Smith bit his lower lip in resentment but knew that the man facing him was correct. "Yes, Guarder, I understand you perfectly."

Razor's eyes burned intently into Smith's for several lingering seconds before he said, "Very good then, let's move out."

"Move out!" Smith barked, snapping his fingers, and the soldiers began their journey down the block and deeper into Shining Star Center.

"Colonel," Razor said and motioned toward the two vessels sitting in the courtyard behind them. "Are those shuttles equipped with nukes?"

"Yes, Guarder, they are."

"Then we better not venture too far from this position," Razor suggested.

"You've got that right," Smith agreed.

"Are those two shuttles our only option for escape from this city?"

"No, there's several ships of various sizes docked at the port," Smith replied. "About two kilometers to the east.

"Okay," Razor said. "There may be hope for us yet."

~*~

"Admiral!" Doug Lysak called across the bridge. "We've lost contact with our two personnel carriers."

"What?" Dawson snapped.

"There's nothing there, sir," Lysak said and glanced down at a monitor from his position right beside the ComTech. "No response."

"Ops," Dawson called to the OpsTech. "Are we tracking those shuttles?"

"Not at the moment, sir," Lt. Cummings answered. "Both vessels were in the vicinity of Shining Star Center aiding Colonel Smith's forces in combat until several moments ago."

Dawson fixed Lysak with a frustrated glare. "Track for blown fuel cells over Shining Star Center, Ops."

"Yes, Admiral."

"Communications," Dawson sighed, already knowing what the OpsTech would find after running her scan, "raise the colonel, please."

"Admiral," the OpsTech interrupted, "I have confirmation of blown fuel cells matching those outfitted to our personnel carriers in the vicinity of Shining Star Center. I'm detecting enough leakage to account for both vessels, sir."

"Goddammit!" Dawson roared. "Communications, where's Colonel Smith?"

"There's no response, Admiral," the ComTech said. "He hasn't responded to any of my hails, sir."

Lysak slammed his fist down on the edge of the communications console. "One-hundred-and- fifty men, Admiral! Those bastards just blew away over one-hundred-and-fifty men!"

"Recall all soldiers, recall them now," Dawson said. "I've had enough of this."

Lysak glanced nervously toward his commanding officer and then let his gaze fall on the incredulous stares of everyone else on the bridge.

"Recall them all, sir?" The ComTech asked. "What in the hell did I just say?" Dawson barked.

"Yes, sir, Admiral," the young woman replied and flashed another look toward Lysak before turning back to her console. "Issuing the recall order now, Admiral."

"Admiral Dawson," Lysak said softly as he approached the large command chair in the middle of the bridge. "What exactly do you intend to do, sir?"

"I intend to clear all of our personnel off that little icy hellhole and really give that planet the abrasive cleansing it deserves, Commander," Dawson stated.

Lysak remained silent for several moments then, collecting his thoughts before he uttered his next words. "There could still be civilian survivors on the surface after we evacuate our people, Admiral. We must think of their safety under these..."

"I'm fully aware of that, Commander," Dawson said very calmly. "But at this point, Doug, we can't continue our current strategy. It's not working and we're losing. Losing badly. I shouldn't have to point that out to you. We've already lost a FlightForce Carrier on top of the one lost before we ever got here. And a battleship for Chris' sakes. This has to stop."

"I understand that, sir," Lysak offered. "But I feel our first priority is to protect however many citizens may still be alive on the surface, as well as the property of those citizens. I do not agree with a formal cleansing at this time."

"I appreciate your candor, Commander Lysak," Dawson said, his voice soft yet menacing. "And under normal circumstances, I would be agreeing with you. But considering the situation at hand and the tremendous losses we have suffered, these are not normal circumstances. I see no other course of action but to proceed with a..."

"Admiral, I protest this decision," Lysak said in a tone loud enough for everyone on the bridge to hear him clearly.

"Understood, Commander!" Dawson snapped. "Your protest will be duly noted in both of our logs, no doubt. Nevertheless, my decision stands."

Lysak stared levelly into Dawson's angry eyes, trying to understand the insanity of the desperate act he was planning to commit. "Understood, Admiral."

"Very good..." Dawson muttered and turned his gaze forward. "Very good."

~*~

Buzzer knelt down and grimaced over the remains of Avril Garcia. "Poor bastard," he said to himself and closed the man's unseeing eyes. The body was

257

so badly torn apart, he could only hope that death had come quickly for his former comrade in arms.

He had been working his way toward the center of the large city at a frantic pace when he heard what had sounded like charger blasts somewhere behind him in the woods. Although the sounds of combat were exploding all around him and he couldn't be exactly sure of just what he'd heard, the urge to turn around and backtrack had been irresistible.

Now, after a brisk run back into the woods, Buzzer had found exactly what he had hoped not to find. A member of their team dead. He remained bent over the body of his fallen comrade for many moments, trying to gain his breath back over the stench of Avril Garcia's misfortune. When Buzzer finally began to stand, the intense pain in his ribs drove him back down to one knee. "Son of a bitch," he growled through gritted teeth and looked down to see that the bleeding had intensified after his trek over the hard terrain. He could feel the stickiness of his black uniform and lifted his shirt to inspect the wound.

Even in the diminished lighting from Shining Star Center filtering in through the branches and bushes, Buzzer could tell that the wound didn't look good. Most of Thunder's stitches had ripped free, and the wound was none too clean. The jagged edges looked sickly black in the dim light and the bruised area seemed to be growing larger. "Goddamn," he swore to himself. "I'll probably need medical leave after all of this is over."

This time he slowly got back to his feet. The pain was there but he was more than used to pain. Very briefly, his head swam, as though in a fog, before he shook it clear. He could vaguely make out the prints of military issue boots in the snow, leading away from Garcia's corpse and into the woods.

Buzzer broke into a run and winced as each step drove the pain deeper into his ribs.

Gradually, his breathing settled into a steady rhythm and he began to mentally block out the pain. Many of the mental self-control techniques he'd learned since becoming a Guarder had helped him tremendously throughout his career. He veered slightly to the left as he caught a glimpse of another boot print similar to the one he'd seen earlier.

There's another, he thought, *and another.* Although he hadn't intended to track down Garcia's killer, the man was making it all too easy. Actually, much too easy. Garcia had been a good soldier and had shown efficient combat skills while with the Guarder team. He wouldn't have been that easy to take out. The person good enough to eliminate Avril's threat should not have been this easy to track.

Buzzer slowed down and tried to extend the range of his hearing for any telltale sign of an ambush. He quickly peered around, taking in as many details of the scenery rushing by as possible. He could feel his grip on both blasters getting tighter and could feel the weight of the half-charger strapped across his back.

Up ahead he could see asphalt and buildings through the edge of the woods. The street looked deserted except for the bodies of three U.E.N. Army soldiers strewn about the blacktop, bloody and unmoving. The wall of the long building facing the woods was pockmarked in several places from obvious weapons fire. Up the street a bit he could see the hulk of a blown out battle tank, the flames still burning bright within the now dead vehicle.

Buzzer burst through the woods and on to the hard unyielding asphalt, almost missing a step as he left the snow and dirt. His boots thumped loudly against a street covered only slightly with snow. He ran low and fast as close to the long building as possible. The ground underneath his feet shook slightly as several explosions sounded off in the distance. Buzzer crossed the street quickly and took cover behind the burning battle tank.

The immense metal vehicle was hot against his back and his breath came in short gasps. The crackling of the flames within the tank blocked his hearing. He could just make out a battle raging toward the center of the city and he cursed himself for not being in there with his teammates.

Once on the street he had lost track of Avril Garcia's killer but something in the back of his head told him that he was very close to his intended victim. Deep down, he knew he had been tracking the killer out of a sense of responsibility for Garcia's death. But, equally deep down, he knew that such cravings for revenge could be his ultimate undoing. Losing focus on this mission would be his worst mistake and, he knew, dispatching Garcia's killer was most definitely not his mission at this time.

Buzzer performed a quick check of his weaponry, finding both of his blasters were low on juice. He took two deep breaths and broke into a run back down the street toward the nearest intersection. He hadn't gone more than ten meters before weapons fire rang out from around the corner ahead of him.

He dove hard against the ground, crashing heavily into the base of the long building. Buzzer growled at the pain in his ribs but forced his body to roll as additional blasts tracked toward him. His movement was stopped forcibly by a thick metal lamppost whose light was not working.

Snapping off three quick shots with his blasters in the general direction of the fire coming toward him, Buzzer lunged up from his position and hurled himself into a small entrance of a building. More weapons fire pounded against the elaborate stonework of the structure, sending razor sharp shards of cement raining into the doorway.

Buzzer slumped to his knees and held back the scream of agony threatening to burst forth from deep within him. He glanced down and saw the sticky spot of blood on his black shirt growing with each passing second. Dumping both blasters to the cold cement floor of the doorway, he pulled his half-charger across his chest from his back, stepped around the edge of the doorway and fired five quick rounds into the woods across the street. Answering fire immediately followed, driving him back into the small enclosure of the doorway.

Abruptly, the fire stopped and an eerie sort of silence filled the night.

Buzzer could hear his rapid breathing, his heart pounded in his chest and for the first time in longer than he could remember, he felt actual fear. He dove to his stomach and belly-crawled to the edge of the doorway, retrieving both blasters along the way. Peeking around the edge, he caught a faint glimpse of movement, the form of a man moving across the street from the woods.

In a heartbeat, he was up and running after the man, leveling his half-charger and firing blast after blast into the night. Pure adrenaline drove him on, making him forget about the intense pain in his side and, more importantly, making him forget his fear.

The man rounded a corner and disappeared. Buzzer ran ever harder, jumping over debris and the bodies of more dead U.E.N. soldiers. Pulling one of his blasters from its holster, he stopped near the edge of the building on the corner and whipped the weapon around with his left hand.

An arm lashed out and struck the blaster free. Before he could react, his left arm was clasped tightly and twisted backwards and behind him. Buzzer was caught unawares, something that genuinely surprised him, and he allowed himself to be tossed backwards to the ground. As he rolled he could see the man trying to take aim on him with a small weapon, most likely a mini- blaster stolen off of one of the dead soldiers he had passed.

Buzzer came to an abrupt stop lying flat on the cold street and snapped off a blast with his half-charger. His adversary dove to the side to avoid the blast, his own shot veering wildly into the woods.

Up and running toward the man, Buzzer covered the short distance in less than two seconds. He crashed into the smaller man with everything he had just as the other was gaining his footing. Buzzer heard a loud grunt escape from his opponent and the sound of a weapon clattering to the asphalt. They both hit the street hard and bounced away from each other.

Buzzer was up first and began to bring his half-charger to bear but the man dove at his knees, sending him sprawling to the street once more. The Guarder saw the glint of what seemed to be a blade rising above him and hit the man hard in the abdomen with the butt of his half-charger.

The man's breath exploded out of him and he rolled frantically away. Buzzer rose to one knee and, leaving the larger weapon slung from his shoulder, grabbed his second blaster and fired at the rolling figure. A large chunk of asphalt popped out of the street inches from the man's face but missed the target entirely. Buzzer fired again but heard nothing but a click. The blaster was fully drained.

His opponent, realizing that Buzzer's weapon was dry, scrambled to swing the same mini- blaster he'd tried to use earlier. Buzzer ran straight at his enemy, bowling him over again and both men crashed to the street. Rising to his knees, Buzzer slapped at the little weapon in his opponent's grasp and knocked it free but had to lunge off his prey as a swipe of the blade he'd seen earlier nearly reached his throat.

The smaller man gained his feet and kicked savagely at Buzzer's abdomen, connecting with the wound in his side. Buzzer shrieked in agony at the excruciating pain and rolled away, shaking his head from the blackout he felt approaching.

He looked up and saw the man swinging the blade down toward his head. Buzzer lashed out with a kick and knocked the blade away. He got to his feet just in time to feel the crunch of knuckles against his jaw. The blow sent him staggering against the wall of a building. He saw and blocked another punch but was hit with a knee in the stomach again.

Several seconds of hazy gray followed and consciousness crept back slowly. Buzzer could feel his half-charger being yanked from his shoulder strap. He struck upwards with both hands, connecting with the man's chin and knocking him flat on his back, but the man's grip on his half-charger was strong and the weapon came free into his enemy's hands.

Buzzer staggered over and began directing vicious kicks at his opponent's head before he'd had time to regain his footing. Two of the kicks connected and the half-charger skittered across the street, landing several meters out of the man's reach.

The Guarder shook his head to clear it and was able to stumble over to the half-charger while his dazed opponent tried warily to make it to his knees. He bent down to retrieve the large weapon and checked its charge to see how much ammo was left. He smiled and turned toward his attacker just as the man gained his feet and stood facing him, unarmed.

"You've been tracking me," the man said, and Buzzer nodded."Why?"

"If I make my guess correctly, you killed a member of my team back there a ways," Buzzer replied.

"I don't know, sir," the man said. "I've killed many men tonight."

"I bet you have," Buzzer growled.

"I almost had you, too," the man laughed and opened his arms to show he was weaponless. "Yes, you did," Buzzer said but no smile touched his lips.

"Well, I am your prisoner," the other said. "I will offer no resistance."

"I wish you would," Buzzer muttered. "Did you kill a man back there, in the woods? Nearly split him in two?"

The man's face twitched and his eyes widened with recognition. "No," he stated flatly. "No?" Buzzer questioned. "Then I have no need of you as a prisoner," he said and lifted the

half-charger into firing position.

"Wait!" The man pleaded. "Yes, yes, I did kill that man. Two blasts with a half-charger, he never felt a thing, I swear to you. Death came quick and painless for him."

"I see," Buzzer nodded, his eyes never leaving those of his new prisoner. "I guess that would feel something like this," he said and fired twice with his half-charger.

Gilfred Thornberg was very dead before what was left of his body hit the snow-covered asphalt several meters from where he'd been standing.

CHAPTER THIRTEEN

Jekel popped around the corner, firing rapid bursts down the long avenue. Cougar was doing the same from his position across the intersection. The small group of U.E.N. soldiers charging around the corner were retreating from a much larger force, whose heavy weaponry seemed to be making the ground around them shake and tremble.

Large chunks of the surrounding buildings were exploding onto the street as multiple blasts rocked the intersection. Razor followed behind the soldiers along with Skinner, firing at their pursuers as much as they could while they tried to reach the cover of the large buildings crowding the corner.

"Clear, Sarge! Clear!" Skinner shouted as he passed Jekel's position.

The invading force was approximately one hundred meters behind but still firing heavily. Several U.E.N. Army soldiers lay unmoving on the cold hard surface of the street as a result.

Razor and Skinner joined Jekel at the corner to help slow the group down with covering fire as Colonel Smith and his men made their way deeper into the city.

The first blast from Razor's weapon tore into two men, sending them sprawling into several others. Jekel selected his targets carefully now that he had some help on his side and dropped one man after another before the large group began to break up and take cover along the wide street.

Jekel quickly signaled to Cougar to make his move across the intersection in order to re-join his teammates and watched as the Guarder nodded his understanding.

"Pour it on, Guarders!" Jekel shouted and all three of his men stepped from cover, weapons blazing.

Cougar rolled into the intersection and fired three times with his half-charger before gaining his feet. Jekel, Razor and Skinner were filling the entire area with a multitude of high-energy blasts, driving many of their opponents deeper behind cover.

Taking advantage of this opportunity, Cougar sprinted across the intersection with blinding speed. One man broke from his cover down the avenue and fired what seemed to be a military- style full-charger toward the running Guarder. Two blasts tore into the aggressor simultaneously, one each from Razor and Skinner, but not before one blast from the full-charger slammed into Cougar's left leg, taking the lower portion off at the knee.

Jekel cried out in anguish and frustration as Cougar's lower-leg exploded and the Guarder was sent sprawling across the slick, icy asphalt leaving a shiny red streak of blood behind him.

"Cougar!" Skinner screamed. "Stay down low and crawl toward us!"

"Do it now, Guarder!" Jekel barked. His booming voice seemed to register within Cougar's pain-clouded brain. The wounded man began crawling very slowly across the street amid gasps of breath as the Guarders sent round after round hurtling toward their enemies.

An awful lot of blood is squirting from the ragged stump at Cougar's knee, Razor thought to himself as he fired at an unfortunate opponent who took the brunt of the blast full in the chest. Razor's eye immediately tracked on to another target and he took the man out with a well-aimed blast.

Members of the opposing force were breaking cover up and down the street, apparently driven by bloodlust at seeing one of their quarry writhing on the cold blacktop. The three Guarders were dropping them with ease but the enemy's numbers were just too many. Cougar's weapon had lent more to the battle than any of them had realized, and Razor had to fight the urge to turn and run. His intense fear was nearly paralyzing.

Jekel's face was set firm in a tight grimace and his eyes blazed with fury as his weapon swept the street from side to side. Skinner was snapping off quick but devastating bursts with his blasters. The two men worked together in perfect synch, trying to win this battle even though the odds were stacked heavily against them. It was a sign of men who had worked long and hard together, men who trusted each other implicitly and who would die for each other willingly.

Razor was filled with a surge of adrenaline and intense hatred towards the oncoming swarm.

His grip tightened on his half-charger as his heart pounded. He glanced toward his fallen comrade crawling in pain toward their position amidst an unbelievable shower of weapon's fire and explosions.

Slapping a hand across his commander's shoulders, he called, "Cover me," and bolted into the intersection followed by angry cries from both Jekel and Skinner.

Razor dove toward Cougar, landing heavily on his stomach in the street. "Hold on, Cougar," he rasped and brought his half-charger to bear on the advancing group. Cougar's eyes were glassy and it looked as though he were fading fast but he managed to nod his head and wink at his fellow Guarder. Razor fired three quick bursts at the onrushing mob, bringing several of them down hard, then grabbed Cougar by the neck and hauled him to his remaining foot.

"This is suicide, Razor," Cougar managed through gritted teeth. Razor was hot-footing it as fast as he could across the intersection, dragging the wounded man along with him. Jekel and Skinner broke from cover and entered the intersection, firing wildly and trying to draw away some of the enemy fire.

"Go down!" Jekel shouted and Razor dove, taking Cougar with him, just as several major blasts burst through the air over their heads. Razor rolled himself until he was behind cover once again. He looked up to see Jekel reach down with one huge hand, pick Cougar up from the street and throw him to cover. Jekel poured more fire into the intersection as Cougar landed hard and screamed in pain.

Razor joined Skinner around the corner of the now battered building they were using for cover and let his half-charger add to the massive firepower of the battle.

Jekel quickly made his way over to the injured Guarder, tore several loose strips from what was left of Cougar's tattered pants leg and tied them hurriedly around the stump just above his left knee. Dark red blood was everywhere, mostly on Cougar. Jekel fumbled for the small first aid pack strapped to his side and brought out a syringe filled with an amber-colored liquid. "Prepare yourself, Kenneth," he said to Cougar and plunged the needle deeply into the man's left thigh. Cougar seemed to stiffen momentarily, eyes wide with the shock of the chemicals coursing through his bloodstream, before he collapsed mercifully in to unconsciousness.

Razor continued firing, watching target after target fall to the bloody street. Skinner's luck was just as good and together the two Guarders had managed to drive their remaining opponents back under cover.

Jekel leaned down and hauled the unmoving Cougar up over one massive shoulder. "Let's move, Guarders! Now!"

Razor and Skinner stopped firing immediately and were up and running down the connecting street, Jekel and his cargo right behind them. The Guarders quickly rounded another corner and disappeared from the view of their relentless pursuers.

~*~

"Frazier!" Ronald Leon called. "These personnel carriers are fully loaded. We have more missiles!"

"Amazing," Sampson said to himself as he leaned on the shiny port engine of one of the stolen shuttles. "Are they operational?"

"Yes, Frazier," Leon answered anxiously. "The missiles are fully operational and they're ready to fly."

"Then load everyone on, Ronald," Sampson said as he keyed the outside controls and the entry-hatch slid open. "All who will fit."

The expression of pure victory on Ronald Leon's face was replaced almost instantly with one of confusion. "But we must wait for the rest of the group, Frazier."

"NO!" Sampson boomed from his position at the hatch. "I have my chance at this very moment to escape this insanity with my life! I will take advantage of this opportunity immediately! Any fortunate enough to board the shuttles before liftoff will follow me to victory. All others must be considered casualties, as nothing other than lost in battle." Sampson fixed Leon with an icy stare; his eyes reflected the white glare of the surrounding snow with a sinister quality. "Now board the other shuttle and follow my lead."

Leon watched his leader disappear into the large U.E.N. Army personnel carrier, followed by most of his Utility Guard, men who had once recognized Leon as their leader but who now clearly pledged their undying loyalty to no one but Frazier Sampson. The ship immediately fired up its engines, wasting no time on a normal pre-flight checklist or warm-up.

Several of his men came rushing around a corner several blocks down, dragging seriously wounded men along with them. Leon frowned as he realized that these few were all that remained of the much larger force that had rushed after the previous protectors of the two shuttles they now occupied. Waving the stragglers forward, he ducked into the hatch of the second shuttle, made his way quickly to the cockpit and fired up the engines. Using his experience as a former U.E.N. FlightCorpsman, he quickly checked the weapons console and saw that all five missiles on board were live but not armed.

He was fine-tuning the targeting systems when the small group of running men finally reached his shuttle and scampered aboard. Surprisingly, the engines were still relatively warm and the pre-flight checklist was complete within seconds.

Leon noticed Sampson's shuttle lifting slowly off the ground and he made a brief long-range scan of the surrounding area for any other surviving members of their original group. Sadly, neither his eyes nor the sensors could find anything farther out, and anyone nearby would be lost in the sensor-wash of his engines. Looking over his shoulder at the sixty some-odd filthy, exhausted and mostly wounded men crowding the passenger area, Ronald Leon shook his head in disgust. The force that had traveled from Sarsat-15 had numbered in the thousands. Now, after what seemed like an eternity, all that remained of their once-proud band were inside the confines of two stolen shuttles—two U.E.N. Army Personnel Carriers that had recently carried many of the soldiers who now lay dead on the surrounding streets into battle.

"Where are we headed, Commander Leon?" A battle-weary youngster in tattered fatigues asked from one row back.

"I don't know, son," he replied and slowly lifted his shuttle to follow Sampson's. "Wherever our great leader takes us, I guess."

The young warrior grunted and lapsed into silence. Taking one last look around, Leon realized that he hadn't seen any sign of Gilfred Thornberg. "I wonder what sort of demise met you in those bloody woods, you slithering old..." Leon's muttering trailed off as he noticed some movement downbelow.

He craned his neck to gain a better view of the square. A glance down at the sensors confirmed his suspicions. There were men down there hiding in the thermals of his small ship's engine output. Leon's eyes went wide with horror and he slammed the personnel carrier into an evasive maneuver. "Brace yourselves!" he screamed as he strained against the controls. All he saw, before his world went black, were several bright flashes from below...

~*~

Blitzer and Able had raced from their position at the edge of the woods at the first sound of the engines igniting on the two shuttles in the square.

By the time they reached the large clearing both vehicles were in the air and rising rapidly. "Fuel cells!" Able called, and both Guarders raised their weapons. "Aim for the fuel cells,

Blitzer!"

Blitzer answered by letting loose a brutal series of blasts toward the closest shuttle, Able close behind with his half-charger. The powerful combination slammed into the aft fuel cells and starboard side engine housing. The nearer shuttle shuddered in flight and began losing power very quickly. The pilot then obviously tried to kick in his boosters for extra climbing power but the smaller engines must have been damaged by the initial blast. A bright white flash signaled the end of both boosters and primary engines, and the closest shuttle plummeted like a rock, exploding upon contact with several buildings down the block.

Able immediately switched targets to the first shuttle, firing blast after blast with his half- charger. Blitzer looked on, realizing that the vehicle was too far out of range for his blasters. The first three half-charger blasts scored true on the craft's lower engine, and several others struck glancing blows over the fuel cells. The vessel began to rock violently, the pilot attempting to fight the controls and compensate for the swinging, but Able's other shots were falling short as the shuttle smoked its way deeper into Shining Star Center.

"Shit!" Able snapped. Blitzer slapped him on the back.

"Not to worry, Able," Blitzer said and pointed to the steadily sinking shuttle. "You got that bird, she's going down."

"I hope you're right," Able answered.

"I know I am," Blitzer called over his shoulder as he broke into a run down the long deserted avenue. "Let's go, we have a shuttle to catch."

~*~

"Reading you, Wolverine, over," crackled through the now quiet bridge of the battleship. "Colonel," the ComTech said as she adjusted her headset, "Admiral Dawson has ordered a

complete withdrawal, do you read?" "Affirmative, Wolverine."

"Roger that," the ComTech replied. "Your instructions are to comply immediately with withdrawal procedures. Are you currently in a position to do so?"

"Negative."

"Explain," the ComTech ordered.

"No operable shuttles are currently within reach, Wolverine," Smith's voice was more garbled than clear. "We'll have to head toward the local starport and commandeer vessels in order to depart Shining."

The ComTech glanced over her shoulder toward Dawson for further instructions. Lysak punched in the communications access code on Dawson's com-link. "Colonel," Admiral Dawson called. "Do whatever is necessary to remove yourself and your troops from the planetary surface. Make it fast, Colonel."

"Admiral," Smith's voice said, "there's still work to do down here, sir. After we clean up we'll be returning shortly."

"My orders are for immediate evacuation, Colonel," Dawson replied. "All unfinished business will be dealt with upon the return of all ground forces still operating on the planet's surface."

"Cleansing?" Smith asked, his voice sounding surprised.

Dawson paused, clearly angered by having to explain himself. "Affirmative, Colonel."

"Begging the Admiral's pardon, sir," Smith snarled. "But you must be out of your frigging

mind!"

"Colonel Smith!" Commander Lysak snapped, but Smith continued.

"There are countless civilians still on this planet. God knows where they all are, for Chris'sakes. I still have enemy targets running loose within the vicinity of my current position and my men need to cover several kilometers before we reach any type of escape vessels. You can forget evacuation, Dawson. I'm seeing this thing through."

"Listen here, Smith!" Dawson growled. "Unless you want to see your ass on the wrong end of a court-martial you will follow my orders! Do you understand?"

"Kiss off, you son of a bitch!" Smith shouted into his com-link.

Lysak stood back and watched fury engulf his Commanding Officer. Dawson's face was a red mask, the veins in his neck pulsing with each rapid beat of his heart. No one had ever stood up to Dawson in quite this way, at least not while Lysak had been serving under the man. The Wolverine's First Officer quickly turned his head to hide the grin on his face.

"Consider yourself stripped of command, Colonel!" Dawson screamed, spittle flying from his lips. "I will not stand for insubordination..."

"Calm down, Admiral," a new voice interrupted. "Just calm the hell down." "Who is speaking?" Dawson demanded.

"This is Sergeant Harrison Jekel, U.E.N. Guarder Squadron, Admiral Dawson." The cool, deep voice reverberated throughout the bridge. "And, sir, although you may still retain command of your orbiting fleet you may consider yourself

271

relieved of command of the ground forces. As you are well aware, as a member of the Guarder Squadron, I am fully justified in assuming command of the ground operation. I currently outrank you under these circumstances and will make an official note of this with the Judiciary Board upon my return to Aegis. Please feel free to check current U.E.N. Military regulations for confirmation."

"Without the proper authorization, I'm afraid I do not recognize this procedure, Sergeant," Dawson said, drawing out the last word. "Unless you can confirm your identity and..."

"Admiral," the ComTech interrupted. "I have a Priority-One Command Sequence coming in from the planet's surface, sir. It lists the rank and Squadron Number of Sergeant Harrison Jekel, Commander of the U.E.N. Guarder Squadron. His identity is confirmed. The serial number and sequence codes are correct."

Lysak took special notice as Dawson visibly deflated in his command chair.

"Admiral," Jekel called. "Please continue to monitor the planet's surface for signs of combat, especially within the area we occupy. If you detect large troop movements, other than our own of course, contact me immediately. Otherwise, stand by until the ground operation is complete."

Dawson stared at the com-link incredulously and remained silent. "Do you understand these orders, Admiral?" Jekel asked, his voice crackling throughout the silent bridge.

Upon realizing that the Admiral was not going to respond to the Guarder's question, Lysak leaned over the com-link and keyed the transmit button. "Understood, Sergeant Jekel. Wolverine out."

~*~

Thunder and Redwolf rushed toward the area where the shuttles had gone down. With weapons drawn, they proceeded through the eerily deserted streets making very little noise as they went.

Hunkered down low, Thunder allowed the FlightCorpsman to lead the way by several steps. As they approached an intersection, the two completely stopped to scan the area visually before continuing. Redwolf saw nothing as he inspected the intersection and rose to proceed but Thunder immediately grabbed him by the arm to pull him back down.

"What is it?" Redwolf whispered and Thunder quickly motioned him to silence.

After several moments, Thunder shook his head and said. "I thought I heard something, I could have sworn..."

"Hold it! Both of you!" A voice sounded from not very far behind. "Hold those weapons high and do not move."

Thunder slowly lifted both arms over his head and turned slowly to face his new captor. The sun was just about to clear the horizon but he could make out the dark shadow of a man obscured by predawn light.

"Do as he says, Jack," Thunder said, a quick flicker of recognition gleaming in his eyes. "And don't make any hasty moves."

"Are you crazy? What are you saying?" Redwolf gasped. "This guy's going to kill us both!" "No, he won't," Thunder said and smiled.

Jack Redwolf looked at the man beside him in amazement. "Don't be so sure, Guarder." "Don't worry, Jack," Thunder mumbled as he holstered his weapons. "While this man

definitely poses a very serious threat to both of us, he's not going to kill us."

"Your friend's right, you know," the man said and stepped from the shadows, his tired features clearly visible now. "I might have before I knew who you were but I won't now."

"Goddammit, Buzzer," Thunder sighed. "You look like shit." "Yeah, I feel like it, too."

Redwolf glanced past the big man to the deserted street behind. "Are you alone?" Buzzer glanced back at him and cast his eyes away quickly. "Unfortunately, yes."

Thunder put a sympathetic hand on Jack Redwolf's shoulder, immediately recognizing the meaning of Buzzer's words, and said, "I'm sorry, Jack."

"Redwolf," Buzzer said, meeting the FlightCorpsman's eyes with a steely glare, "I want you to know that I killed the man who did it. I made him wait for it, made him look me in the eye as I ended his life. Believe me when I say that he paid for what he did. He paid for Garcia."

Redwolf remained silent for several seconds as he looked into the intense eyes of Frank Buzzer. "Jesus," he rasped through suddenly dry lips as he realized just how dangerous a human being Frank Buzzer really was. "It sure sounds like he did."

Thunder leaned down by Buzzer's side and lifted the man's torn shirt to reveal his jagged bloody wound oozing new blood, thick and black. He looked up quickly into Buzzer's eyes.

"This is bad, Frank."

Buzzer laughed and coughed, wincing at the pain in his side. "No shit, Bobby."

Thunder touched his friend's forehead and felt the warmth immediately. "Frank, it's a wonder you're even standing and not in shock. We've got to get you some medical attention."

"Not yet..."

"No, listen," Thunder interrupted. "This will kill you, Buzz. It's badly infected and your fever has settled in to stay."

"This is almost over, Bobby," Buzzer said very slowly. "Let's finish it and then we'll work on making me healthy again. All right?"

"You'll never make it, Frank."

"I'll bet you on that, Thunder," Buzzer said.

"At least let me clean out that nasty wound and sew you up again before we start gambling," Thunder said and began threading a needle with sutures from his first aid kit.

~*~

"Hurry!" Sampson roared over his remaining men. "Quickly now! They'll be upon us shortly!"

Several Utility Guardsmen were working frantically on the underside of the smashed shuttle. The Personnel Carrier had been hit badly by ground forces and he had quickly lost maneuvering control of the craft.

He had seen the bright flash signaling the destruction of Ronald Leon's shuttle just before his vessel had been damaged. Then it was just a matter of fighting the controls until he could find a place to land the thing. The city's starport had abruptly come into view and before he knew what was happening, the small ship had lurched down to the Northeast Tower's landing pad, skipping twice with harsh metallic screeches of protest before skidding to a stop partially on its side and very close to the tower platform's edge.

Eighteen of his passengers had been killed in the crash and ensuing explosion. Once the flames had cleared and the remaining survivors had escaped from what was left of the shuttle, he had regrouped his men and began issuing new orders.

Now, all five of the nuclear tipped missiles were almost unloaded from the underside compartment of the large vessel. The blinking lights of the landing tower were still on although the sun was now up over the horizon. Across the newly scarred tarmac of the landing pad, Sampson saw what appeared to be a very large pleasure cruiser gleaming in the brand new dawn.

"Marcus!" he called. One of the remaining men quickly ran over. "Yes, sir?"

"Is it possible, Marcus," Sampson began, "to arm these missiles and attach them somehow to that cruiser across the platform?" Sampson pointed to the sleek vessel.

"It depends on the model, sir," the young man answered. "I'd have to get a lot closer look before I could tell you anything else."

"If it's not possible to attach them outside will we be able to arm them and get them inside that cruiser?" Sampson asked.

"Yes, sir," Marcus agreed. "That should be no problem with that particular cruiser. The missiles themselves are relatively easy to arm."

275

"Very good, very good," Sampson stammered and paused to wipe sweat from his brow. "Once you have the missiles removed, move them directly to that cruiser and load them inside. Do not waste time, we have barely any to spare."

"Yes, sir."

"I'll be warming up the engines on that cruiser in the meantime," Sampson said. "Yes, sir."

Frazier Sampson turned and walked away from the young former U.E.N. Army WeaponsTech and motioned for two of his Utility Guardsmen to accompany him across the landing pad. The three of them broke into a brisk run, weapons raised and ready.

"Our Father who art in heaven..." Marcus whispered under his breath before turning back to his work on the missile clamps. "Hallowed be thy name..."

~*~

"Razor's returning, Sarge," Skinner said. "And he's got company."

Jekel grabbed the viewers from Skinner and grinned at what he saw. "Good, I was beginning to worry about those two."

Skinner glanced back at Colonel Smith and said, "Don't worry, those guys are with us." Smith nodded and noticed most of his soldiers visibly relax. "Sergeant," he mumbled and

Jekel turned to look at him. "Pardon me for asking, sir, but what possible reason do we have for waiting like this? They only have four men posted at each corner of the Northeast Tower. The other three towers are empty. All of the other men are up top. What exactly are we waiting for?"

Jekel looked away from the army man just long enough to nod a greeting to Razor, Able and Blitzer. "Report, Razor," he said.

Razor knelt down beside his commander and peered around the corner of the building they were using for cover across the street from the Starport Complex. "In addition to the four landing pad sentries above they have one man positioned

276

at each ground floor entrance, all four sides, and several men positioned one floor above each entrance."

"How many of them would you say are left?" Jekel asked.

"Judging from what I could see…" Razor paused in thought before continuing, "probably anywhere between thirty and fifty."

"How do you arrive at that figure, Guarder?" Smith asked.

"Those shuttles only hold somewhere around fifty or sixty men, seventy if you cram them in real tight," Razor said. "There are sixteen of them posting sentry duty. There are several more up there on the landing platform, probably outfitting a docked cruiser for escape. And then there are the dead from the explosion when the shuttle crashed. Altogether, my best guess is between thirty and fifty survivors."

"I agree, Sarge," Able said. "Blitzer and I did some recon of our own before we met up with Razor. We both came up with approximately the same number, between thirty and fifty."

"I like the odds," Skinner said.

"In case you've forgotten, Guarder," Smith sneered. "There are only twenty-two of us combined, several of whom are injured and incapacitated. Our enemy probably outnumbers us by more than two to one right now. I personally do not like the odds."

"Well, good enough, Colonel," Able said. "The six of us are better off without you and your bunch of rookie recruits. You'll just slow us down."

"Enough," Jekel snapped. "Colonel Smith, I will offer this to you just one more time. If you do not wish to participate in this mission any longer then, by all means, please take your troops and leave. If your intentions are otherwise then, from this point on, you will take your orders from me."

"I'm sorry, Sergeant Jekel," Smith interrupted. "But the Admiral left the completion of this mission under my command and I intend to keep it that way."

"The Admiral no longer commands down here, Colonel, and neither do you," Jekel said sternly. "I do. Take it or leave it."

Smith turned away in frustration and stole a glance at his rag-tag bunch of battle-weary soldiers. As he examined their faces he saw each of them meeting his stare with raw fear and hopelessness in their eyes. They were too young, much too young, to be laid waste on the cold hard surface of this planet. And deep down he knew that only the appearance of the Guarders had kept them alive up to this point. He also realized that without the mysterious men of the Guarder Squadron, he and his men did not stand much of a chance of getting off this iceball alive.

"All right, Sergeant Jekel," Smith sighed. "We're with you. You'll have no more arguments from either myself or any of my men."

"Don't make any promises you can't keep, Colonel," Jekel warned.

"You have my word, Sergeant," Smith said as he craned his neck to meet the enormous man's eyes with his own.

"That's more like it, Colonel," Jekel extended his hand and Smith accepted the gesture with his own. "Now, why don't we get down to ending this little game. I want off this shithole planet and I'm sure you feel the same."

~*~

Young Jerome Reasons squinted into the shadows of the new dawn and tried to believe what his eyes were showing him. The dark figure of a lone man approached down the long deserted avenue.

The Utility Guardsman crept closer to the edge of the western entrance to the Starport Complex Northeast Tower, and primed his charger as the man got closer. He fumbled for his com-link and clicked it twice to signal to his counterpart on the roof. "Henry! This is Jerome! Do you see that guy?"

"Yeah, I see the fucker, Jerome," Henry Appleton answered, his voice sounding raspy coming through the miniature speaker contained within the small communications device. "But just who in the hell is he?"

"I don't know," Jerome responded while trying to improve the reception on the battered and outdated com-link. "Is he one of ours?"

"Hell if I know, Jerome..."

"Jesus Christ," Reasons muttered and flexed his fingers along the synthetic grip of the cumbersome weapon. "Look at him, Henry, he's waving to us."

"I see it," Appleton's distorted voice replied. "I'll cover you, Jerome. Go out and see who this guy is."

"Screw that, Henry!"

"Listen up, Jerome!" Appleton ordered. "I will cover you and I'll also inform Phil and Taylor about what's going on. They're only one flight above you. You'll be just fine."

"For Chris'sakes, Henry..."

"Just do it, Reasons, Goddammit, or I'll come down there and fry you myself! Is that clear?"

Reasons silently flipped Appleton his middle finger from approximately a hundred meters below. Slowly he got to his feet and took a deep breath. The approaching man carried only a half-charger and was dressed in a black sort of uniform, not too different from what most of the other guys in his group were wearing. With the man's arm still waving, Jerome suddenly felt somewhat at ease and took the first step to the street, his weapon only half raised as he began to wave back at the approaching figure.

He never felt the blaster bolt that tore his head off, sending scattered remnants of thick gray brain matter splattering against the sidewalk alongside the building. Able sidestepped the still twitching body and entered the tower.

Henry Appleton saw a flash below, near the building but did not realize what it was. He took his eyes off of the man approaching along the avenue for one brief instant as he tried to identify the source of the flash.

Out on the avenue, Blitzer took the opportunity to drop to one knee, switch his half-charger for his blaster and squeeze off two rapid shots. Appleton took the force of both blasts full in the chest. His body toppled over the railing on top of the landing tower and, with a wet smack, landed heavily on the cold concrete sidewalk.

"Let's move!" Jekel shouted and was up and running with the injured Cougar still draped over his shoulder. Razor and Skinner followed their commander across the wide avenue along with Smith and his men. As a unit, they quickly entered the Starport's Northeast Tower.

In the entrance they found more results of Able and Blitzer's handiwork. Two dead Utility Guards lay sprawled across the steps leading up to the first landing and the immense lobby above.

Shining Star Center's Starport Complex was truly massive. Made up of four full-sized landing towers surrounding an immense central hub, the starport was slightly larger than its rival in CharterCity. Situated some sixty kilometers east of Shining's capital city, Shining Star Center was a major metropolitan quasi-resort area, frequented by many of the SouthWestern Corporate Grid-Sector's financial giants. Unlike other resort areas, where hot weather and water served to attract tourists, Shining Star Center relied almost entirely on gambling and entertainment to combat Shining's usual freezing temperatures. The Starport Complex provided much of the access to tourists for these vices, containing seven extravagant gambling casinos and at least thirty nightclub hot spots, each catering to the various tastes and preferences of its particular clientele.

The rest of the city contained more of the same, including one of the most highly respected and professional live-theater programs in the entire sector. A multitude of lush restaurants and sporting facilities capped off the city's major attractions.

In stark contrast, CharterCity was built from a strictly business viewpoint. Existing almost entirely to support the small planet's government, the capital city had been agleam with tall skyscrapers housing thousands of offices serving an unfathomable variety of business organizations before this little war had begun.

Although bulky and situated much lower to the ground, the CharterCity Starport was very popular among tourists and business travelers. Made up mostly of elaborate conference halls and majestic meeting rooms, the starport was nearly equal in size to the one in Shining Star Center.

As the Guarders and soldiers entered the huge lobby area of the Northeast Tower, they could see the remains of several bodies scattered across the carpeted floor. The strong stench of death lingering throughout the oversized room told

Jekel that these men had been dead long before Able and Blitzer had stormed through here. The corpses seemed to be an equal mix of U.E.N. Army soldiers and the invading forces.

Smith paused to survey the carnage and leaned down to inspect one dead soldier's wounds.

He looked up at Jekel and began to explain, "These soldiers were part of General Cartullo's original landing parties. This particular unit was to isolate the Starport Complex and secure the outer-perimeter of Shining Star Center. I think they also had orders to try and evacuate most of the civilian personnel."

Jekel gently removed Cougar from his shoulder and placed his limp form on one of the lobby sofas. The seriously injured Guarder was not faring very well. His fever was high, and he was still in shock, both from the incident itself and from extreme blood loss.

"It doesn't look good for him, Sergeant Jekel," Smith spoke softly. "When or even if he does regain consciousness, he'll be in sheer agony."

"All of which I realize, Colonel," Jekel answered.

Smith stared into the larger man's brooding gaze and had to look away. The fierce loyalty to his men was more than evident in Jekel's eyes. His fierce loyalty to the legendary Guarder Squadron burned just as intensely if not brighter. Jekel was already mourning the loss of the man code-named "Cougar", a man not yet dead but swiftly working toward that end.

"If we do not get him some serious medical attention at the earliest possible opportunity..."

"Once again, Colonel," Jekel whispered. "I realize this."

After a brief pause, Smith said, "He's going to die, Jekel. Probably within the next few minutes. Why not make it easier on him?"

"You take care of your men, Colonel," Jekel rasped. "And I'll take care of mine."

"Understood."

"Very good," Jekel said and examined the room. "We need to locate the emergency stairwells.

The elevators will not be safe."

"That's thirty stories..." Smith began to protest.

"I'm well aware, Colonel Smith," Jekel said, raising his voice slightly, "of the architecture of this landing tower."

Smith bit his tongue, swearing inwardly for having pledged his soldiers and himself to the Head Guarder's leadership. "They are too busy at whatever they're doing up there to be monitoring the elevators. Why increase our fatigue factor?"

"Because of our attack, we have alerted those above us to our presence," Jekel said. "They will be waiting for us and searching for us. Perhaps even going out of their busy way to do so. We must take every precaution against being captured or defeated. Need I remind you that the shuttle that crashed up there was outfitted with several missiles tipped with nuclear warheads. The people we are dealing with are acting both desperately and irrationally. From what I've seen thus far they will be more than willing to use those nuclear weapons to their greatest advantage. At all costs, we must survive long enough to stop them from whatever it is they plan to do." Jekel abruptly stopped talking and walked swiftly across the lobby, pausing only to call over his shoulder, "If I am through explaining myself to you, Colonel Smith, may we continue?"

"Absolutely," Smith snapped and signaled for his men to follow the leader of the Guarder Squadron.

Razor brought up the rear and looked back to see Skinner slip a small blaster into Cougar's limp right hand and cross his right arm over his chest. Skinner looked up and saw Razor watching him. "You never know," he said and sprinted across the lobby to catch up with Razor. "It just might come in handy."

"Yeah..." Razor said and glanced back at Cougar's unmoving form. "It just might."

CHAPTER FOURTEEN

Marcus Vinoen worked quickly amidst the insanity that erupted on the landing platform when Appleton pitched over the side of the tower. The other sentries had immediately begun yelling out warnings of attack and talking of an opposing force within the building working their way upwards. All of this was serving to make Marcus more nervous than he had already been.

His hands were slick with sweat as he tried desperately to figure out how to load the damn missiles onto the customized cruiser parked on the platform. Perspiration dripped steadily from his nose despite the sub-zero degree weather.

"For God's sakes, what's the meaning of this delay?" Sampson roared. Vinoen nearly jumped out of his skin.

"The owner of this vessel has slightly customized the original design, sir," he explained. "He did away with the normal cargo doors that should have been located on this side of the fuselage and replaced it with a standard access hatch."

"You told me this would work, Marcus," Frazier Sampson growled. "And I will hold you to your word."

"I am trying, sir."

"Trying is not good enough!" Sampson's fury was more than evident in the insane expression on his face. "The enemy is almost upon us, you imbecile! We need to leave this place and leave it now. Do what you said you could do, Marcus. Do it."

"I understand, sir," Vinoen stammered. "I need only to pry off the hatchway door, unlock the missiles from their expanded mooring clamps which will not fit into the hatch of this cruiser and then several of us will simply have to load the missiles on board."

"Then, as I said, do it."

"I will, sir," Vinoen said. "But...I think I have to arm the missiles before detaching them from their mooring clamps."

Sampson's eyes narrowed down to slits as a slight tremor of anger wracked his entire body. "You mean to tell me that those weapons are not yet armed?"

"No, sir, not yet," Vinoen replied, his voice barely a whisper.

"Then hear me when I say this, Marcus Vinoen," Sampson said. "I will personally oversee the removal of the hatch door on this cruiser. If by the time I have accomplished this you do not have those missiles armed and loose from their mooring clamps, I will shoot you in the face while you are watching and kill you dead. Is that understood?"

Vinoen gulped once and felt as if his heart was about to explode. "Yes, sir."

"Very well, then," Sampson said and visibly relaxed. "Get to it and let's leave this rock."

Vinoen didn't answer as Sampson snapped his fingers at two Utility Guardsmen and they immediately raced to his side to assist him with the cruiser's modified hatch.

"Marcus," one of the men who had been helping him work on the missiles whispered at his side. "Snap out of it! We can do this! You want to get off of this planet alive, don't you?"

"You bet, George," Vinoen said and sucked in a deep breath. "Then you best get to it," the smaller man said.

Right, Vinoen thought and bent down over one of the missiles. With a flick of his wrist, he opened the missile's access panel and began to program in the arming sequence.

George Preston worked diligently on the mooring clamps. *Together,* Vinoen thought, *we just might do it.* Vinoen laughed at himself then as he suddenly realized that Sampson might just kill them both for having made him angry earlier. None of this made any sense at all as far as he could see. But for now, at least, he was still among the living and breathing. And that was about all that mattered.

~*~

"Admiral," Lysak spoke softly from his commanding officer's elbow. "The evacuation of all available ground units is complete except for Colonel Smith and his men."

"And the Guarders," Dawson stated. "That is correct, sir."

"What's it look like down there, Commander?"

"Our readings indicate that the main body of the opponents' forces originally set down near CharterCity and worked their way slowly eastbound toward Shining Star Center, where all who have survived thus far are holed up in the Starport Complex," Lysak explained. "There were several smaller enemy groups that landed in more remote areas of the planet during their initial invasion. Our forces were quickly able to pinpoint their locations and destroy them. Other than the few remaining pirates in Shining Star Center, our scanners aren't picking up any additional enemy positions on the entire planet."

"How many of Colonel Smith's men are still on the planet's surface?" Dawson asked.

"Assuming that all of the Guarders are still alive, sir, there should be sixteen of our men down

there," Lysak answered.

"How many Guarders again?"

"Eight in the original party, that number expanded to ten with the addition of the two FlightCorpsmen formerly of the U.E.N. Ruffian, Admiral."

"So twenty-six friendlies on the surface right now, only sixteen of which are my direct responsibility," Dawson muttered. "How many enemy targets are we showing down there?"

"Approximately forty or so, Admiral," Lysak said. "Perhaps, forty-five."

"Let's see then, Commander," Dawson said. "Sixteen men sacrificed to eliminate an enemy force of forty-five, who are laying siege to an operational starport. If the enemy force happens to gain access to a ship, they could make good their escape. If they are able to escape this system with any sort of weapons of mass destruction, there's no telling what they could do, what other systems they could terrorize."

"Admiral," Lysak interrupted, "no ship, regardless of how fast, could escape this system, or this planet's atmosphere for that matter, with the sheer amount of firepower currently possessed by our warships in orbit."

"As things have been going lately, Commander, I do not fully agree with that sentiment." "Admiral Dawson," Lysak said. "Do you still intend to perform a cleansing, sir?"

Dawson raised an eyebrow at that and chuckled openly. "I have no need to explain myself or my chosen course of action to you, Commander. But, if you are so interested, I will announce my plans."

All eyes on the bridge turned to the man in the command chair. "I feel that I have given this Sergeant Jekel of the Guarder Squadron sufficient time to crush the remaining enemy forces," Dawson began. "He has not. I ordered Colonel Smith of the U.E.N. Army to evacuate Shining with due haste and he denied that order. The good colonel has also elected to follow the orders of the Head Guarder over those of my own. Under these circumstances, I would label our men down there a group of inept renegades who have already wasted too much of our precious time and resources. I intend to commence with the cleansing of planet Shining, Commander Lysak.

Would you care to dispute this decision?"

"I sure as hell do, Admiral!" Lysak shouted. "Need I remind you that we are still reading hundreds of civilian life signs scattered throughout that planet below?"

"No, Commander, you do not need to remind me..."

"Then, what is your reasoning behind the utter annihilation of hundreds of innocent people?" Lysak wondered aloud.

"The fact that those remaining enemy targets still pose a major threat to not only the safety of these ships in orbit around us but to the rest of this entire sector should they somehow escape, Commander."

"That is so much bullshit!" Lysak roared and slammed his right fist down on an arm of Dawson's command chair.

"You are out of control, Commander," Dawson barked.

"I think cleansing a planet whose only threat posed to us is forty-five men out of what began as thousands is out of control," Lysak argued. "I think it's pretty damn crazy as a matter of fact."

"You are out of line, Commander!" Dawson stood to face his First Officer. "Consider yourself relieved of duty."

"For what possible reason?" Lysak demanded. "Gross insubordination, for one."

"Once again, bullshit, Admiral," Lysak said. "I am relieving you of command for lack of mental stability."

"Oh, that's a good one," Dawson laughed. "I'm sure the Judiciary Board will take that charge very seriously."

"I'll see that they do."

"No more of this," Dawson said and sat again in his command chair, waving Lysak away. "Confine yourself to quarters, Commander Lysak. Sit the rest of this one out."

"ComTech," Lysak called across the bridge, shifting his attention to the communications console. "Send a Priority-One Command Sequence to the local U.E.N. Outpost en route to Aegis informing the Judiciary Board of the Admiral's intentions and requesting their express permission to proceed."

"Belay that order, Comm," Dawson said.

"This is standard procedure, Admiral," Lysak stated. "Why deviate from the standard procedure?"

"I'll not have you on this bridge another moment," Dawson rasped, seething in rage. "Now remove yourself or I will have you removed by force. Do I make myself clear?"

"You can go to hell!" Lysak swore and leaned in close to the Admiral's face. "And rot there, Dawson. 'Cause that's where you'll go after doing this."

"Enough!"

Lysak turned on his heel and exited the bridge, shoving his way through two tense crewmen. Dawson watched the man leave and tried hard to steady his nerves. "ComTech, inform the ships of the Wolfpack Squadron to commence with cleansing warm-up procedures and await further orders."

"Yes, sir," the ComTech stammered and quietly set about her task.

~*~

"What was that?" Captain Tano asked.

"Cleansing, Captain," Derek Hamilton repeated himself. "The crazy bastard wants to do a cleansing."

"That doesn't make sense," Tano said. "We need to have those orders confirmed."

"Already done, Captain," the ComTech of Greywolf said from his console. "I've asked for and received the same orders four consecutive times. The cleansing order has been confirmed."

"Patch me into Wolverine," Tano ordered.

"They're not accepting transmissions, Captain."

"Now just what in the hell is going on here?" Tano asked no one in particular. Hamilton just shook his head in wonder. "I agree with you, Captain. This is crazy."

"I won't be a part of this," Tano decided. "Our sensors show hundreds of life signs still down there. It would be murder, no other name for it."

"Does he have the legal right to order such action?" Hamilton wondered.

"Good point, Commander," Tano answered and turned again toward his ComTech. "One last transmission to Wolverine."

"Go ahead, sir."

"Captain Tano desires proof of official Judiciary Board approval of the plan to cleanse Shining before participating in such action."

"Sending, sir," the ComTech replied and paused for several seconds before continuing. "Still not accepting transmissions on Wolverine, sir. No response."

"Damn!" Tano muttered and began to pace the deck of Greywolf's Bridge. "Patch me through to Moreyev on Canis Lupus."

"Done, sir," came the reply. "Andre?" Tano called.

"Yes, Gary," the heavy missile cruiser's captain answered. "Are you okay with all of this, Captain?"

"Hell, no," Moreyev bellowed. "I think Dawson's finally lost his mind. He won't send you any proof of Judiciary Board approval, you know."

"Yeah, we tried that, too," Tano said.

"I sent one of those messages myself," Moreyev sneered. "He doesn't have any damn proof to send us, Gary. I bet he hasn't even cleared this with Aegis yet."

"What's he trying to prove?"

"I have no idea..." Moreyev said and sighed. "But I think he'll go through with this himself, whether we help him or not."

"No way, Andre," Tano said. "I won't let the bastard get away with it."

"I don't see how you have much choice," Moreyev countered. "Nothing short of firing on him is going to stop him this time. I know him too well—he means to do this dreadful thing, and if you open up on a warship of the U.E.N. FlightForce, any warship in the fleet, you may as well forget about going home. No matter how crazy you say Dawson was, they'll ruin you in seconds. It's not worth it, Gary."

"It's worth it to me," Tano said. "Those men he plans to kill don't deserve to get fried by their own damn side. Neither do the civilians."

"But what can you do?" Moreyev asked. The question hung heavy in the bridge of the Greywolf.

"Don't you worry, Andre," Tano finally answered. "I won't fire on him but I'll damn well slow him down."

~*~

289

"He's going to do what?" McIntyre demanded.

"You heard me, Mr. Ambassador," Lysak said. "He is going to cleanse your planet Shining, and all of the civilians and U.E.N. soldiers still down there will die."

"He's obviously out of his mind, Commander."

"I agree with you but he will not listen to reason," Lysak said. "He has relieved me of duty and banished me from the bridge. He is enraged. Nobody will stand against him while he is in this state."

"Well, what can I do about it?" McIntyre asked.

"You are the closest thing to an official U.E.N. Government representative that Shining has left, Mr. Ambassador," Lysak offered. "If you demand that he seek Judiciary Board approval, as is standard U.E.N. FlightForce procedure in such matters, it may convince him to comply."

McIntyre began shaking his head in disagreement and looked into the shocked faces of Ellie Fremont and Wiley Thomas.

"You've got to do this, Mac," Thomas urged. "At least give it a try."

"I'm just a scientific Ambassador," McIntyre argued. "I hold no official political power in this situation."

"Mr. Ambassador," Lysak urged, "in his current state of rage the Admiral may only recognize your title and not your profession. Whether you want to believe it or not, you are government. In fact, you're the only government Shining has left. Those are your people down there, sir. Do something to save them."

"Shit..." McIntyre mumbled.

"Mac," Fremont said as she reached out her hands and cradled McIntyre's face. "Give this a shot. You owe those Guarders and all of those soldiers down there something for getting our asses out of CharterCity. I won't even mention all of those innocent civilians..."

"All right, all right," McIntyre sighed and stood. "I'll give it a try, but I can't promise anything."

"I'm not looking for promises, Mr. Ambassador," Lysak said. "Only a miracle will do."

~*~

Jack Redwolf followed Thunder and Buzzer into the eerily empty lobby of Shining Star Center's Starport Complex. Distant weapons fire could be heard from above and the structure itself seemingly vibrated at the sound of each discharge.

"It sounds like the Sarge is keeping himself busy," Thunder rasped as his attentive gaze took in every portion of his surroundings.

"Looks like there's been a war in here," Redwolf muttered as he scanned the bodies of the dead lying scattered throughout the lobby area.

Thunder moved closer to Buzzer who was leaning over the body of a fallen soldier. Once he was close enough to see the dead man's face, Thunder gasped in surprise and fell to his knees beside Buzzer.

"He's dead, Bobby," Buzzer merely whispered and removed the small blaster from Cougar's limp grasp.

"Are you sure, Frank?" Thunder asked and looked into his friend's face. The answer was clear in Buzzer's eyes; the stony glare seemed to bore straight through him, and Thunder felt a chill creep up along his spine.

"Let's get to the top," Buzzer said, rose and sprinted across the lobby to disappear into a stairwell.

"Sorry, Ken," Thunder said and took one long last look at the fallen Guarder. Cougar was completely covered in blood, most likely his own, which explained the pale look of his skin against the black combat suit and light armor he wore. The lower half of his left leg was gone and Thunder could see the makeshift tourniquets that had been tied around the stump below his knee in an effort to staunch the flow of blood.

"Dammit, he's still frigging warm," Redwolf said in disgust and put a hand on Thunder's shoulder. "Let's go, Thunder," he said to the mourning Guarder. "I've got some paying back to do to these bastards."

"You and me both, Jack," Thunder answered and the two men simultaneously broke for the stairs.

~*~

"And just who in the hell are you?" Dawson asked as he looked over the nervous form of William McIntyre standing before him. "Get off of my bridge you..."

"I am William McIntyre, U.E.N. Ambassador to Shining, Admiral Dawson, and you will hear me out."

"I don't give a damn who you are, Ambassador," Dawson said. "Just get your ass off of my bridge and be quick about it."

"I am the last semblance of authority representing the planet Shining, Admiral, and..."

"Shut up, Goddammit!" Dawson said, lunged out of his command chair and grabbed McIntyre by the arm. Motioning toward one of the bridge crewmen, Dawson shoved McIntyre in the man's direction. "Ensign, kindly escort the Ambassador off of my frigging bridge and take former Commander Lysak into custody."

"Uh, Admiral?" the young man stammered.

"Just do it!" Dawson's scream reverberated throughout the expansive bridge of Wolverine. "Admiral Dawson!" McIntyre barked. "I demand that you perform your duty as pledged to the

U.E.N. FlightForce and obtain official Judiciary Board approval for cleansing the planet below before commencing with such drastic measures!"

"You are nobody here, Ambassador," Dawson snarled.

"If you do not comply, Admiral," McIntyre continued with a renewed fire in his eyes in the presence of this mad man. "I will see to it that you are prosecuted to the fullest extent of existing military law. In cases of multiple homicide of both innocent civilians and other military personnel, I should think that the penalty would be quite harsh. Think this through completely before you act, Admiral Dawson. I implore you."

"Ensign, remove these gentlemen from my bridge," Dawson said and waved them away. "In fact, contact a security detail and have them taken down to the brig."

"Yes...sir," the young man answered and hit the com-link on a nearby console before starting toward where McIntyre and Lysak were standing. "Security Patrol, to the bridge."

"Admiral," the helmsman called. "Greywolf is taking up position straight ahead of us, sir. She is blocking our path to Shining."

"What in the hell is this now?" Dawson questioned. "Way to go, Tano!" Lysak cheered.

"Remove those men!" Dawson shouted. "I won't issue those orders again!"

"Greywolf's weapons systems are activated, Admiral," the OpsTech said. "But no weapon locks are being detected."

"Patch me through to Greywolf," Dawson said. "Done, sir," came the ComTech's reply.

"Captain Tano," Dawson said dryly, his voice cool and calm. "Are you experiencing navigational trouble?"

"Not at all, Admiral Dawson," Tano's voice replied over the bridge's com-link. "Then may I ask what your ship is doing in its present location?"

"This seems to be the only way I could get your attention, Admiral," Tano said. "Wolverine isn't answering any of my calls or any calls from the Canis Lupus."

"This is serious business, Tano," Dawson said. "What exactly are you trying to do here?" "Cut the shit, Admiral Dawson," Tano replied. "I'm not letting you carry through with this until I see some proof of official Judiciary Board..."

"Cut communications," Dawson said, and Tano's voice abruptly ceased. "Helm, take up position away from Greywolf. Adjust our position if she continues to chase."

"Yes, sir, Admiral," Lieutenant Devon replied. "But Canis Lupus has taken up position to Starboard. Captain Moreyev seems to be utilizing the same tactics to block our path to Shining." "Jesus Christ!" Dawson roared and turned to find both McIntyre and Lysak still standing in the same spot. Dawson's face visibly reddened but his voice remained calm. "For the very last time, remove these two men from my sight and escort them to the brig."

"Yes, sir," answered one of the Patrol Officers who had just arrived on the bridge as he grabbed each man by the arm. Lysak nodded at McIntyre and both men let themselves be led off of the bridge.

"Quite a show, Ambassador," Lysak laughed. "Quite a show indeed."

McIntyre just rolled his eyes and sighed with relief as the lift doors closed behind them.

~*~

"He's cut communications, Captain," the ComTech said and Tano swore to himself. "Captain," Hamilton called. "Canis Lupus is cutting him off from the other side."

"All right, then," Tano muttered. "Now we have something going here. Dawson knows that he can't take both of us on."

"Canis Lupus has activated missile launch systems, Captain," the OpsTech called from the front of the bridge. "They have not yet locked on to Wolverine."

"Thank God for that," Hamilton added.

"Captain," the WeaponsTech said nervously from his console. "Wolverine has just activated weapons systems and I am confirming weapon locks on both the Canis Lupus and Greywolf, sir."

Tano exchanged worried glances with Hamilton and imagined Moreyev doing the same with his First Officer. "This is where it gets hairy, people."

"Should I lock weapons on to Wolverine, Captain?" The WeaponsTech asked. "Absolutely not," came Tano's terse reply. "Just keep Wolverine loosely in our sights." Hamilton looked carefully at his Captain and posed a question. "Is he bluffing?"

"Shit if I know, Commander," Tano said and once again left his command chair. "Patch me through to Wolverine, Comm."

"Wolverine is not accepting transmissions, Captain," the ComTech answered.

"Damn," Tano whispered under his breath. "If he really means to do this, Derek...then he's not bluffing."

Hamilton let out a long deep breath and laughed. "Somehow I knew you were going to say that."

"Yeah," Tano said. "But somehow, I don't find it all that funny."

~*~

Buzzer's ears were ringing with the explosive sounds of the battle raging above. The Guarder climbed rapidly up the small duralloy maintenance ladder leading to the Northeast Tower's landing platform. Shining Star Center was in a sorry state down below. Several fires burned intensely throughout the large metropolis.

As he neared the top of the ladder Buzzer checked his weapons. The wind hurtled past him, threatening to rip him from the ladder's rungs, but his grip on the cold metal was firm.

Buzzer stole a quick glance at the landing platform as he reached for the ladder's top rung.

Nearby, what was left of one shuttle was still burning bright against the new morning sky. Another vessel, a much larger cruiser, was sitting off in the distance across the tarmac.

The other members of his team were pinned down within the two entrances that opened on to the Northeast Tower of the Starport Complex and were coming under extremely heavy fire.

Buzzer took one final deep breath and launched himself onto the landing pad. He immediately dropped flat and rolled closer to the burning hull of what he now recognized as one of the stolen military shuttles. A quick check revealed that all five of the nuclear missiles that should have been nestled in the underside compartment were missing.

"Damn," he mumbled under his breath and primed his half-charger. He could see frantic activity taking place near the larger cruiser across the platform but several members of the opposing force were laying down a heavy covering fire while also drawing fire away from the vessel.

Buzzer could hear the cruiser's engines humming steadily, indicating that they were already past the pre-warming stage prior to launch. His mind raced with the implications of that cruiser safely launching with five nuclear missiles on board.

Pulling three explosive marble grenades from a small pocket on his side, he quickly armed them and threw them toward his left. Less than three heartbeats later the mini-bombs blew, shaking the entire structure and sending fireballs soaring above the landing tower.

The firing abruptly stopped as both sides paused to assess this new threat. Buzzer took the opportunity while all eyes were on the fading flames to spring from cover and train his half- charger on some unsuspecting targets.

~*~

"Bobby!" Jekel's voice carried over the deafening roar of charger blasts tearing into the outer walls of the landing platform access ramp. "Where in the hell is Frank?"

Thunder yelled back from his position at the second access ramp. "He came up here ahead of us, Sarge."

"Son of a bitch," Jekel rasped and let loose three blasts from his charger. The entire mixed group of Guarders and soldiers were very badly pinned down at this location. The only other alternative to gaining access to the landing platform itself was to leave their current position and try to find some other way to the top.

The only problem with that alternative was giving the opposition the upper hand for a few precious moments, just long enough to let the cruiser they were protecting so ferociously take off. And, at all costs, that could not be allowed to happen.

A charger blast rocked through the open doors of Jekel's entrance and burst against the far wall with a tremendous explosion. Jekel covered his head with his left arm as another blast crashed through. One of Smith's soldiers screamed briefly and crumpled to the tiled floor to join two others.

"Goddammit, Jekel!" Smith shouted over the din of explosions and weapons fire. "They're picking us off in here, we're dying for Chris'sakes!"

"Restrain yourself, Colonel," Jekel responded.

Smith snarled and fired twice through the open doors. "Screw this, Guarder! Soldiers, pull back!"

"Colonel!" Jekel barked. "You and your men are more important to this mission now than at any other time. Rescind that order."

"I said screw this, Jekel," Smith's voice was drowned out by the sounds of combat. "There's got to be a better way."

"I agree," Jekel began. "But for now..."

Three massive explosions rocked the landing tower then, sending Guarders and soldiers alike diving to the floor. A moment of eerie silence followed and Jekel could see the fiery remnants of the explosions fading away.

"What in the hell was that?" Smith muttered and his question was immediately followed by a series of charger blasts and screams coming from the landing platform.

Jekel rose from the floor and aimed his weapon toward the enemy positions on top of the tower. With a knowing smile on his face he turned to Smith and said, "That's Buzzer."

~*~

The blasts came out of nowhere immediately following the mysterious explosions, cutting into his men and tearing them to shreds. Sampson swore as three of them went down with the first volley and two more with the second.

The black tarmac of the landing platform was smeared with blood and littered with bodies. Sampson watched from the big cruiser's cockpit as his remaining men turned to face the new arrival to the battle.

"Marcus!" Sampson called and the young technician looked up from the missile he and George Preston were working on inside the cruiser.

"Yes, sir?"

"Are all of the missiles now armed?" Sampson asked, the deadly tone of his voice making the consequences more than clear if they were not.

"Yes, sir," Vinoen managed. "They are armed and ready."

"Quickly! Tell me how to activate them."

Marcus turned back to the missile he had been working on and pointed at the control panel. "The lights are green on the inside of these panels," he explained. "This means that they are active and armed. This switch on the left is for manual detonation. Flip it upright and the light should turn red. Once they've been tripped there's no turning back."

"How long before detonation once activated?" Sampson asked. "Not very long, sir," Vinoen replied.

"Exactly how long, Marcus?"

"Approximately thirty seconds, sir," Vinoen said hurriedly. "But each missile varies due to individual design, construction and the tampering I had to do in order to override the command codes."

"One-half minute..." Sampson said.

"Approximately, yes."

"Very good, Marcus," Sampson nodded and turned back to the bloody scene outside the cockpit window. "We'll be leaving very soon. You and George need to round up the others and get them on board."

"Yes, sir."

"Go now, Marcus," Sampson barely whispered.

Marcus Vinoen paused. He had recognized something in his crazed leader's voice. "It means death for us out there, sir."

"Go now!"

Preston grabbed his companion's arm and led him toward the aft access way. "Come on, Marcus."

"But he means to leave us to our deaths!" Vinoen protested. "You don't know that, Marcus."

"Yes, George, I do."

"I don't care!" Preston pleaded. "He'll kill us both if we don't leave and leave now!"

"Well, let's at least grab some weapons before we head into that firestorm," Vinoen offered. "I'm one step ahead of you, Marcus," Preston said and handed him a blaster from his jacket

pocket. "Now, let's go."

CHAPTER FIFTEEN

Buzzer had succeeded in his plan to catch their adversaries in crossfire. The returning fire was heavy and he could not get a clear shot of the cruiser. Only a very few of his first shots had scored on the vessel so far.

One by one, the enemy targets were dropping. From across the landing platform he saw several figures leave the relative safety of the two landing platform entrances and dash across the tarmac with weapons blazing toward the cruiser. One was the unmistakable form of Harrison Jekel and Buzzer had to laugh to himself. "Okay, Harrison, it looks like a good idea to me, too."

Buzzer filled his empty hand with a blaster and headed out from cover with both weapons firing. He did his best to ignore the fever and fatigue that were threatening to shut his body down; the lust for vengeance against those responsible for the deaths of his teammates drove him on.

He could feel the pain in his side with every excruciating step but the pain was only fueling his anger. Several of the opposition had turned toward the other onrushing Guarders but a few were still concentrating fire on him. One charger blast came a bit too close and Buzzer stumbled to the ground, falling hard on his shoulder and wounded side. His charger went skittering away out of reach. Gasping for breath, he fought against the blackness of unconsciousness that so wanted to overwhelm him. Looking up he could see the cruiser lifting off of the landing platform, its ascent made slower by some damage apparently done by Buzzer's previous few charger blasts.

Jekel and another Guarder, most likely Thunder but Buzzer couldn't be sure, raced toward the cruiser amidst the blasts being discharged throughout the landing platform. A smaller group whom Buzzer couldn't recognize followed not far behind. Two new opponents had appeared from inside the cruiser just moments earlier with weapons firing but both now lay dead on the hard, cold tarmac, the results of Sergeant Jekel's unwavering aim.

As their opposition watched the cruiser lifting off, seemingly intent on leaving them all behind, they were momentarily distracted and the Guarders were relentless in making them realize their grave mistake.

Buzzer watched, still flat on the landing platform, as Jekel reached the cruiser first and made a great leap for the still open access hatch. Thunder made a similar attempt but was unsuccessful as the large vessel moved just out of reach. The Guarder hit the ground hard, rolling to a stop several meters away, but quickly regained his footing to continue his chase of the fleeing cruiser.

Jekel's grip had been firm when he hit the still open portal and he was able to quickly pull his giant form up onto the rapidly closing hatch. Buzzer saw his commanding officer's enraged face as he disappeared inside the cruiser.

The weapons fire abruptly ceased as all combatants watched the sleek ship sail upwards into the morning sky. The few remaining members of the opposition rapidly dropped their weapons and raised their hands in the universal sign of surrender. Buzzer knew what was coming. The other Guarders unmercifully eliminated these men with quick charger blasts. No prisoners on this mission. They had all agreed on that from the beginning. The brutality and viciousness displayed by the pirates throughout their invasion of Shining warranted no mercy whatsoever to be shown on them in return.

Slowly, Buzzer got to his feet and waved over at Bobby Thunder. He grabbed his side and felt the warm blood flowing freely now from his wound. He noticed that his heart was pounding and he was breathing in gasps. All he could think to himself was, *thank God all of this is finally over,* as he dropped to his knees on the landing platform.

But then he remembered that it wasn't over, not yet. Sergeant Harrison Jekel was somewhere above and still fighting on. Those thoughts lingered in Frank Buzzer's mind as his vision faded to black…

~*~

"Power up the main forward batteries," Dawson commanded, and the young WeaponsTech gulped but obeyed. "Lock forward mains on target."

301

"That target being, Admiral?" the WeaponsTech asked.

Dawson fixed the ensign manning the combat console with an icy glare. "You know damn well what target I am referring to, Mister," he rasped. "Now aim your weapons as I've instructed."

The WeaponsTech turned away from his console to lock eyes with Admiral Dawson. "If the target you are referring to, sir, is either U.E.N. Greywolf or U.E.N. Canis Lupus, then I am unable to do so, sir."

"This is mutiny, son," Dawson cautioned. "This will ruin your already bright but young career. Consider this..."

"I have already considered it, sir, and I have rendered my decision," the ensign countered. "Listen, listen to me everyone," Dawson said with panic in his voice, realizing that he was

about to lose control of his own bridge crew. "What we are doing here may seem monstrous to some of you but let me assure you that our victory here will only bring security to many other worlds in this sector. We are sending a clear and brutal message to any and all who might try to fight against the superior forces of the U.E.N. Military. That message is, rise against us and die. It's that simple. Cruel to those people left below but necessary. If we can deter a situation similar to this at any time in the future by our actions here today, then we have served the U.E.N. well. I am not a madman. No, in fact, I am merely following standard FlightForce policy in such situations."

"Then, sir, may I ask why the other ships in this fleet are currently opposing you in this decision?" Devon, the helmsman, asked.

"They don't want to stand up to the horror that their sworn duty sometimes becomes, Lieutenant Devon," Dawson said.

"How about Commander Lysak, Admiral?" the ComTech asked. "And that Ambassador from Shining? Why did they confront you on this decision earlier?"

"As I said before," Dawson said, rising from his command chair, "they are afraid of this. They dread what they know must be done in order to be victorious in this mission. They seek to place blame on me so that they don't have to face up to this in the future."

"You don't really believe that, do you, Admiral?" from the WeaponsTech. "Yes, Ensign," Dawson answered. "I do."

"Then you are as crazy as they've been saying, sir," the young man said and stood. "Nothing you say will convince me to fire upon either of those two ships."

"You are relieved of duty, Ensign," Dawson said and approached the combat console. "Don't try to get past me, Admiral Dawson, sir," the young man said, standing his ground. "Out of my way, boy!" Dawson shrieked.

"Not today, Admiral!"

"Security Patrol!" Dawson called, and a large man near the bridge's access door approached. "Please escort Ensign Biggs to the brig."

"Yes, sir," the security man said with uncertainty and leveled his blaster at the frightened young man's chest. "Let's move, soldier."

"I don't think so," Biggs said, his voice cracking in fear. "Now!" The big man barked.

"I said no, I'm not leaving my post," Biggs countered.

"Jesus Christ, kid," the Security Patrol Officer said. "Is this really worth it?"

"Yes, sir, I think so, sir," Biggs replied in a shaky voice.

"Don't negotiate with him, idiot," Dawson raged, losing all that was left of his composure. "Arrest him."

"You'll have to shoot me," Biggs said, still blocking Dawson's path to the combat console.

The entire bridge crew watched, mesmerized by the events playing out before them. "Move it, Biggs," the security man pleaded. "Do it now before this gets ugly."

"No..."

"Mutiny!" Dawson screamed and made a grab for the Patrol Officer's blaster. He managed to partially aim it at Biggs before the larger man was able to gain control. As he tried to wrestle the weapon away from the crazed grasp of his commanding officer, the blaster discharged.

The round slammed into the forward viewscreen, which exploded in an enormous shower of sparks and debris. Chaos erupted on the bridge of the U.E.N. Wolverine as crew members dove away from the spray of red-hot shrapnel. Several larger chunks tore into the communications console, instantly shorting it out and sending more sparks flying into the bridge's interior.

Biggs dove to the floor and Dawson staggered over to the combat console. The Admiral's fingers found the small controls that activated the forward guns just before the security man tackled him to the ground. With a surge of brilliant white energy, the enormous main weapons systems erupted. A tremendous force of destructive power hurtled from Wolverine out into space.

~*~

"Evasive! Evasive!" Hamilton swore. "They're firing on us!"

Tano strengthened his grip on the command chair as his ship surged to life, avoiding the massive energy weapons of the Wolverine by scarcely a few meters.

Still, the effects of the near miss could be felt throughout his ship as the deck plates underneath him trembled and shook.

"Return fire!" Tano ordered. "Goddamn that lunatic, return fire!"

"Firing, Captain," the WeaponsTech replied, frantically working the controls on his console. "Several hits on Wolverine, Captain. Their mains are damaged, sir, but still operable."

"Helm, get us behind her," Tano said. "Yes, sir!"

"How's Canus Lupis?" Hamilton wondered.

"Free and clear, sir," came the response from somewhere across the bridge.

"Are we damaged?" Tano asked.

"No, sir," someone shouted. "Other than some burn marks across the outer hull."

"Good," Tano said through gritted teeth. "Lock on to secondary targets on Wolverineand fire."

"Yes, sir," the WeaponsTech said and another series of short blasts burst forth from Greywolf, hitting strategic targets along Wolverine's hull.

"Pull back out of range, helm," Tano ordered, satisfied with the results.

"Pulling back, sir."

Hamilton let out the breath he'd been holding in and turned toward his Captain. "Dawson's lost it this time, lost it for good."

"There'll be a court-martial for this, I'll see to it," Tano snarled. "Firing on his own damn ships, what was he thinking?"

"Who in hell knows, Captain," Hamilton answered.

"I'm beginning to think that someone in hell knows very well," Tano said. "Good point," Hamilton agreed.

Tano felt the sudden tension on the bridge give way as his ship reached safety in its distance from Wolverine. The only problem was Dawson now had a clear path to Shining. If his weapons were still on line, the cleansing could still take place.

~*~

Frazier Sampson was trying to figure out exactly how to phrase his threat to the remaining ships above. He had narrowly escaped the landing platform in Shining Star Center. He alone had made it. Out of thousands of his followers, he was the sole survivor. Sampson was glad to be alive but slowly contemplated what sort of life lay ahead of him now. His future looked bleak at best. He was now a wanted man, seriously wanted. Probably the most wanted man in the Known Grid-Levels of Space. A title he did not value holding in the least.

He was surprised to find the ships above suddenly begin to fire on themselves. His cruiser was still too far away to watch the exchange with his naked eye but his instruments were picking up the short battle very clearly.

"Well, what's this now?" he muttered to himself as he increased speed and closed the distance to the Wolfpack Squadron. "Now, now, boys, stay calm."

No sooner had the fighting started than it stopped. *Too strange,* he thought, *much too strange...*

Sampson activated his com-link, keyed it for communications with the ships above and cleared his throat. This would be the best time to deliver his demands, while they were confused and disoriented, fighting amongst themselves.

Confirming that the link was active and open to all of the ships in orbit, he began. "Attention

U.E.N. FlightForce vessels. This cruiser contains five nuclear missiles that are armed and ready. From my current position any action taken against this vessel will result in the destruction of your fleet as well."

"Approaching cruiser, identify yourself," a static-filled voice came from his com-link.

"Idiots!" Sampson screamed. "Did you hear my last statement? I have five missiles bearing armed and ready nuclear warheads aboard this vessel. At my command, I can render all of you dead and your ships destroyed."

"You would die as well," a new voice sounded from his com-link "I am prepared for that," Sampson countered. "Are you?"

Several seconds of silence followed. Sampson waited for the telltale signs of weapons batteries glowing to life on the gigantic behemoths floating before him. None did.

Finally, a response from the fleet came through. "State your intentions?"

"I plan on gliding safely past your fleet and to never return to this Godawful place," Sampson said.

"That is unacceptable," crackled through his com-link.

"Perhaps to you, sir," Sampson laughed. "But what choice do you have? I am now close enough to destroy every ship in your fleet if I detonate my cargo. Your ships would not have the time to get out of range of the resulting explosion."

"What proof of your weapons can you show us?" came from the com-link.

"I don't think you want a demonstration, sir," Sampson replied.

His remark was followed by several more seconds of silence before the voice returned. "Approaching cruiser, our sensors show that the threat as you have explained it is real. I am Captain Andre Moreyev of the U.E.N. Canis Lupus. This is a heavy missile cruiser. Once you are safely out of range and past us, sir, I warn you that I will personally blow you out of space."

Sampson quickly cut his engines and drifted toward the enormous ships ahead. He tried to think quickly but his senses were reeling. "Then shut down your power! Now! All of you! Or I will detonate these missiles!"

~*~

"Yes, Captain," the WeaponsTech of Canis Lupus replied. "Those five missiles are as close to detonation as possible. He could blow himself and all of us to bits at this range."

"Dammit," Moreyev muttered. "Patch me in to Wolverine."

"Still no answer, sir," the ComTech replied.

"Damn!"

"Do you hear me?" the voice of the unknown pilot on board the approaching cruiser rasped through the bridge's communications system. "Do it now! Power down!"

"If we do that, Captain..."

"I know, Sam," Moreyev said to his First Officer. "He'll be well out of range before we can power up again."

"All of your ships!" the voice yelled again through his bridge. "Power down now!"

"Patch me through to Greywolf, Comm," Moreyev said.

"Patching, sir," the ComTech said. "Ready."

"Captain Tano, do you hear this madman?"

307

"Loud and clear," came Tano's hurried reply. "What do you suggest?"

"Well, even if the two of us power down, there's no way of knowing if Wolverine will or not," Tano said.

"That's true, Gary," Moreyev said. "They haven't responded to any of my messages since that little stunt they pulled."

"Same here," Tano agreed.

"Let's pull back some," Moreyev offered. "What do you mean?" Tano asked.

"Pull back, very quickly, out of the range of those missiles," Moreyev explained. "Then we can pick him off."

"That's an awfully risky proposition, Andre," his colleague on the Greywolf warned. "If Wolverine doesn't back off, she could be destroyed. I don't doubt that crackpot's willingness to end his own life just to screw us out here."

"What else can we do?"

"Anything but pull back," Tano said. "We can't be responsible for the deaths of the Wolverine's crew. You know as well as I do how much crew she holds."

"Gary, hear me out," Moreyev insisted. "Wolverine fired on the both us and now does not answer any of our calls. For all we know, they've all killed each other over there. We can not risk the lives of our own crew to protect Dawson and his ship."

"I don't agree," Tano said.

"All right, all right," Moreyev sighed. "Then let's just pull back out of range, quickly.

Hopefully, the Wolverine will follow our example. Our ships are fast enough to make it before those missiles blow."

"It just sounds too risky," Tano said. "That lunatic could activate those missiles at any second.

Anything we do, any action we take, could trigger his breaking point. From the sound of his voice, he's already pretty close to it."

"Well, I'm not powering down this ship," Moreyev said. "Canis Lupus will not be defenseless at any point within this madman's presence."

"I agree with you," Tano said. "I won't power down Greywolf either."

Moreyev clapped his hands together, at last he had established some common ground with the Greywolf's Captain. "Then, let's pull back together. Very quickly. The cruiser's pilot will not be able to react fast enough."

"But what about Wolverine?" Tano countered again.

"To hell with them, Gary!" Moreyev snapped. "I will not risk my people for Dawson's mental lapses. Just let them go to hell!"

~*~

The door to the brig slid aside to show an armed Security Patrol Officer standing in the hall. "Commander Lysak," the large man said. "Admiral Dawson has been brought to sickbay, sir. Your presence is required on the bridge immediately."

"What has happened to the Admiral?" Lysakasked.

"He was injured while being restrained on the bridge, sir," the man blocking the doorway answered.

Lysak flashed McIntyre a worried glance. "That explains all the firing and impacts we felt earlier."

"Yes, sir," the Patrol Officer replied.

"I see," Lysak said and turned toward the doorway. "The Ambassador will accompany me." "That was not included in my orders, Commander," the security man said.

Lysak fixed a commanding stare on the young officer and asked. "I presume I am now the acting Captain of Wolverine?"

"Yes, sir, but the Admiral..."

"I could care less about anything that Admiral Dawson said or did," Lysak said and took Will McIntyre by the elbow. "The Ambassador's stay in the brig is now over as well."

The Patrol Officer smiled and nodded in agreement. "As you wish, Captain Lysak, sir."

Lysak smiled at that and left the bland white confines of the Wolverine's brig. "Now that has a nice ring to it."

"We should hurry, sir," the man standing at the door to the cell suggested. "Are there still problems up there?" Lysak asked.

"Yes, sir," the officer replied. "To say the very least, sir." Lysak picked it up a step and all three of them entered the lift.

~*~

Jekel had hurriedly yet stealthily made his way through the moderate sized cruiser's cargo area and living quarters until he reached the cockpit area. Once there, a closed access hatch halted his progress. Behind it he could hear the lone occupant screaming at the top of his lungs, the words barely discernible.

But those that reached Jekel's ears spelled nothing but trouble. The lunatic, just meters away, was threatening to blow all of the ships in the Wolfpack Squadron to dust if they didn't power down immediately.

Jekel could tell by the crazed tone of the voice that the stranger on the other side of that door meant what he said. The missiles weren't in the cargo area nor in this corridor leading to the cockpit. That meant that they were on the other side of the door as well, most likely sitting in the recreational area that was a part of the larger cockpits in this type of luxury cruiser.

"Jesus Christ," Jekel muttered and checked his weapons. "How did I get myself into this one?"

"Bring those ships back!" The man in the cockpit shrieked. "Do you hear me? I will detonate these missiles! Do it now or I will kill us all! Stop, stop your movements!"

Jekel heard the heated exchange that followed between his one remaining adversary and whoever it was that he was linked to with the Wolfpack. It sounded as if the man had been pushed that one last step over the edge, the hysteria mounting in that voice was proof enough of that. And, that being the case, all of the continued shouting most likely meant imminent disaster.

His body responded immediately to what his mind had deduced and, in a surge of adrenaline, the leader of the Guarder Squadron raised his weapon to the cockpit access door's control panel.

~*~

Bobby Thunder carried Buzzer's unconscious form over his shoulder as the surviving soldiers and Guarders rode the northeast landing tower's lift down to the main lobby of the Starport Complex.

They had noticed several vehicles of various types and classes on the other three landing platforms and had decided to make their way to one of them as soon as possible. Thunder believed that the feeling was mutual among every single one of them that all of this would somehow not be over until they actually left the surface of Shining.

Although the actual battle conditions had now tentatively ended, the group still needed a commanding officer to lead them off of Shining. With Jekel off-planet and Buzzer indisposed, Thunder had assumed the leadership role. Surprisingly enough, Colonel Smith had not complained.

"Skinner," Thunder said. "Have you had any luck raising the Sarge?"

"No response, Bobby," Skinner said. "I've sent him two messages on his sequencer but he's probably a little too busy to answer right now."

"That cruiser's just about the last place I'd want to be," Smith said. "That thing's probably loaded with nukes."

"Sergeant Jekel knows how to handle himself, Colonel," Able said. "It's just a matter of time now before this mission is finally over."

"That's exactly what I'm afraid of, Guarder," Smith gibed. "And time is a wasting, buddy.

"Tick, tick, tick."

"That's enough, settle down," Thunder barked and fixed Smith with an angry glare. "Let's just concentrate on getting off of this little nightmare of a planet."

Other than a few moans and grumbles, the others remained silent until the lift reached the bottom level and the doors slid open. As the men filed out of the large cargo lift-car, Razor sidled up against Thunder. "I can take him from you now, Bobby," he said, referring to Buzzer's still unconscious form.

Thunder patted his teammate on the back but kindly declined. "Not just yet, John. It's my responsibility to deliver this package intact. But I'll call you if I need to."

Razor nodded and ran ahead to catch up with Able, Skinner and Blitzer. Thunder suddenly felt very proud of just how seasoned the youngest member of their team had become.

~*~

"Goddammit, Commander Lysak," Tano said. "Pull the Wolverine back out of range. What are you waiting for?"

"Listen, Captain Tano," Lysak said into the com-link on the Wolverine's command chair. "We can not allow this lone lunatic to escape with those missiles intact. You know that as well as I do."

"He's threatening to kill all of you, Commander," Tano reminded him.

"I understand that, Captain, but I still think he's bluffing, sir," Lysak said.

"Lysak," Tano's voice came through clearly over the bridge's sound system although there was no visual due to the forward viewscreen's earlier destruction. "The man we're facing is not bluffing. Check your sensors, they'll tell you. Those missiles are red hot and armed. One flick of his finger and you'll have less than half-a-minute to clear the detonation sphere."

"Then why hasn't he blown them yet, sir?" Lysak asked.

"Because he's desperate, Commander," Tano explained. "He's fighting for his life right now, but if he's cornered with no way out, you better believe that he'll try to take as many of us with him as he can. You know what his people did down there on Shining, what they did to the Ruffian and the other two ships that won't be coming home with us. It's a clear textbook example of insanity, Lysak. He'll blow those missiles right outside of your hull, I'm telling you. Please don't make him prove my theory."

Lysak considered that for a moment. "When I pull back, what happens then?"

"Then we wait for him to start moving," Tano replied. "Once he's out of range the Canis Lupus can pick him off with their long range missiles."

"Why don't we just pick him off from here?" Lysak offered. "Blow him away and the missiles with him?"

"Because the way he has them rigged, they'll detonate upon any weapon's impact with his ship."

"I see," Lysak said and took a deep breath. The lunatic's rambling and hysterical shouts were still coming through the bridge on a secondary com-link with the audio level turned down. There was no doubt about the man's current mental state. "If I back away slow, he could also detonate before I clear range."

"It's better to die trying than to die a sitting duck, Commander," Tano urged. "Look, Dawson lost it earlier and nearly killed everyone aboard Wolverine because of his crazed actions. Now that you're in command, do the right thing and bring those people with you to safety."

Lysak weighed his options and then made his decision. "All right, Captain," he said. "I'll pull Wolverine back just as soon as I try to talk to this man one last time."

"What?" Tano asked incredulously but Lysak motioned for the ComTech to cut the link with Greywolf.

"Patch me through to that cruiser, Comm," Lysak ordered. "And patch it through to the smaller screen on the command chair."

"Yes, sir," the ComTech said, and the cockpit of the small cruiser abruptly appeared on the tiny screen set into the arm of his chair.

313

"Power down your ships! Do it, now!" the man shrieked. "Or I will vaporize all of us!" "Calm down, sir, just calm down," Lysak began but was cut off immediately by the mad ravings of the man before him.

~*~

"I assure you, young man, that I mean what I say and your apparent lack of cooperation will only mean a quicker death for every last one of us!" Frazier Sampson screamed and pounded his fist into an instrument panel.

"Sir, we can resolve this situation to everyone's satisfaction," Lysak urged. "Believe me, we can work this out. This can end peacefully for you if you only let me work with you."

"You are a liar," Sampson said and laughed. "You and I both know that I probably won't live or breathe for very much longer. The other two ships out there plan on making my life as short as possible right now, of that I assure you."

"Listen, you can trust me..."

"If I can trust you then how come you haven't yet powered down that behemoth?" Sampson raged.

"To be perfectly honest with you, if I power down this warship and you decide to detonate, I would not be able to regain power fast enough to avert disaster," Lysak responded. "I can not be responsible for the deaths of my crew nor for the loss of this ship. You can surely understand my situation."

"I am quickly tiring of this game you're playing," Sampson spat. "This is no game, sir."

"Then why did the other two ships pull out of range?" Sampson countered.

"They were acting on my orders," Lysak said, the lie rolling off of his tongue just a little too quickly.

"Your orders?" Sampson asked. "My boy, your insignia indicates you are but a lowly Commander. A battleship of that size surely rates a Captain, no? In fact, if your ships are indeed the almost holy Wolfpack Squadron, I would hazard a guess that the flagship rates at least an Admiral. Wouldn't this be correct?"

Lysak listened to the low growl of the words and felt a chill move slowly down his spine. "Who are you?" He asked and waited patiently for the reply.

The wait was almost the better part of a minute before the answer came. "I venture to say that it really doesn't matter much anymore to keep my identity a secret from you, does it?"

"No, it doesn't," Lysak offered.

"Well, then, just for the record," Sampson stated. "I am Frazier Sampson, formerly of the U.E.N. Marines, dishonorably discharged, and the fearless leader of the several thousands who fought you and yours to the death and nearly won at that! I have shamed the mighty Wolfpack Squadron, supposedly the best in the fleet, the crème de la crème! Nearly beaten, forces more than halved by my lowly minions. I can laugh at your less than heroic efforts, Commander."

"All this talk and yet you float there before me in defeat aboard a tiny cruiser," Lysak argued against his better judgment.

"Yes, yes, I am defeated," Sampson said sternly. "But not by the likes of you, sir! No, there were devils down there on that cold and cruel planet. Relentless devils, all in black! It was them who drove me to my present position. Only a few but, nevertheless, their unwavering pursuit whittled away at our strengths, cut down our numbers! And now I am only one! It is they who are responsible for this, sir, not you and your Wolfpack Squadron."

Lysak smiled then as realization dawned on him. "You're talking about Guarders, Sampson.

There were Guarders down there on Shining. They're the ones who hunted your men." "Guarders?" Sampson blubbered, awestruck by this news. "They were Guarders...I should

have known! What made you send Guarders against me this far out from Aegis?" "That information has not been made available to me, Mr. Sampson," Lysak said.

"You lie!" Sampson roared, briefly startling everyone on the bridge as his voice came over the tiny speaker in the command chair's viewscreen.

"No, sir, I do not lie," Lysak said. "I sincerely have no knowledge of the circumstances that led to the appearance of the..."

"Quiet, fool!" Sampson screamed, the rage threatening to overwhelm him. "I am sick and tired of sitting here and not achieving any results! I will once and for all avenge my brothers' lives! I may be only one, Commander, but I will take all of you with me!"

"But..." Lysak started, then heard only the static of a broken connection as Sampson's face disappeared from the tiny screen.

~*~

"He's powered up his engines, sir," Helm reported. "He's moving away from us, now at top speed, headed for Greywolf and Canis Lupus,"

"Restore that com-link," Lysak ordered.

"Unable to, Commander," the ComTech replied. "Dammit!"

"Greywolf and Canis Lupus are attempting evasive maneuvers, sir," the voice came from Ops.

"Goddamn," the WeaponsTech swore. "He's activated those missiles! That boat's gonna blow!"

~*~

The small cargo shuttle lifted off nicely from the southeast landing tower and glided upward toward the orbiting ships. Thunder piloted with Able in the co-pilot's seat. The others were trying to sit still in the empty cargo hold. They were packed in there pretty tightly but all were anxious to see this thing through.

Buzzer lay prone off to one corner of the hold. His fever was high and his breathing was shallow. He was pale as a ghost and, by all rights, should probably already be dead. But, staying true to form, the tough bastard was holding on to what little life he still held inside.

The team was beyond fatigue, especially Smith's men, who were not used to the type of intense combat they had just experienced. Needless to say, any conversation at all being made on the shuttle was kept to a bare minimum. Thunder glanced over at Buzzer and saw Razor sitting close by, holding vigil over the still form. He had been Buzzer's original partner on this mission, before it had become an all out war, and he would remain by his partner's side until the mission was over. Thunder liked that about Razor. In fact, he liked everything he had seen in the young Guarder so far.

"We're breaking through the atmosphere, Bobby," Able said. "Everyone hold on."

The ship rattled and shook somewhat before finally settling down. The sensors immediately came to life, seeing everything much clearer in the vacuum of space.

"There they are," Able pointed at a certain point on the viewscreen. Thunder looked up to see several of the large ships in the Wolfpack Squadron scrambling away from the much smaller cruiser class vessel being piloted by their one remaining opponent.

Able checked the scanners and punched in a code to monitor all com-link frequencies. Several worried voices exploded into the shuttle's cockpit simultaneously. Frantically they were trying to coordinate evasive maneuvers. And yet, Thunder noticed, none of them were firing on the smallership.

"Send a message, broad band, that one of our own is on that ship," Thunder demanded and Able immediately sent off a message from the comm panel.

"Guarders," came the terse reply, "sorry to tell you but your man on board that cruiser won't be around much longer."

"What?" Blitzer's voice came from the cargo hold.

"Those nukes are now live and activated," the voice returned over the com-link. "Turn back, there's less than fifteen seconds until detonation!"

"Son of a bitch," Able muttered but Thunder reacted in the only way he knew how. In order to save the remaining members of his team and Colonel Smith and his men, he gripped the controls and turned the small ship around, squeezing the engines for all they were worth.

"But what about the Sarge?" Skinner called from in back.

"There's nothing we can do for him now," Thunder said with tears in his eyes.

"Dammit! There's nothing we can do..."

~*~

Jekel burst into the cockpit through the still flaming debris of the access hatch and rolled to a stop against the opposite wall. His opponent looked at him in terror from his position standing over the missiles. "It's too late, devil!" He shrieked. "You will not keep me from my final victory!"

Jekel's eyes moved to the missiles and he saw that they were all now live and activated. The red glow from their activation lights beat steadily in the interior of the small recreation area. *How much time?* His mind raced to find that information. *Was it thirty seconds or sixty? Perhaps only fifteen!*

He could see the ships of the Wolfpack Squadron scrambling out of the way on the forward viewscreen as the cruiser accelerated through space toward them. "You fool," he said to the lunatic still standing over the missiles.

"You'll die too."

"I'm already dead...Guarder," Sampson growled.

Jekel's anger at the hopeless situation took over then and he snarled, "Not just yet," before letting loose with his blaster.

Without waiting for the pilot's remains to hit the floor, Jekel stood and ran to the cockpit. The viewscreen showed the ships still frantically trying to flee from the doom on board his cruiser.

He tried to figure out how large the detonation sphere would be when these five missiles blew. There weren't any numbers counting down on the missiles themselves so he had no idea how much time he had left.

He grabbed the controls of the cruiser and quickly found out that they were rigged in their current position. He tried cutting the engines but it didn't work. All of the controls were frozen in place; the lunatic had been successful in locking the controls of the craft straight on a path to the ships ahead before Jekel had been able to make it through the door.

He took one last look back at the red glow coming from the missile panels and heaved a great sigh. *It's over now,* he thought and came to grips with his present situation. Turning back toward the cruiser's controls he saw the readout showing the current distance to the ships ahead. *I might still be far enough away...*

Hitting the com-link in the small cockpit, Jekel spoke rapidly. "Wolfpack Squadron WeaponsTechs, destroy this vessel now! I repeat, open fire and destroy this vessel now!"

~*~

"What in the hell?" Gary Tano said. "That's not the same damn voice."

"There's someone else on that ship, Captain!" Hamilton said. "Someone else is now piloting that cruiser!"

"But who?"

"My guess would be one of the Guarders," Hamilton offered.

"Well, I'll be damned," Tano laughed. "They're going to save our asses up here too!"

"Helm," Hamilton called. "Are we out of range yet?"

"Barely, sir, just barely but that cruiser keeps coming!" the Helmsman answered. "Canis Lupus is now out of range too, but just barely. Wolverine is still in range but almost out. Only seconds now before detonation."

"Captain," the WeaponsTech said. "Should I comply with the fire order, sir?"

"Goddamn," Tano swore, sick of all the death and dying. "And kill that man in the process?"

"The cruiser is gaining speed, Captain," Ops called. "We are now back in the fringes of the

detonation sphere's range, sir!"

"Shit!" Tano snapped. "Is Wolverine out of range yet?"

"Not yet, almost," from Helm.

"Wait, one second more," Tano said.

"Then should I fire, sir?" The WeaponsTech asked.

"Yes, Goddammit, yes!" Tano rasped.

"We're out of range again, Captain," Ops called and Tano made a mental note to give his engineer a raise for his work on pulling more speed out of the engines. "And so is Wolverine!"

In the background of the chaos on the bridge, Tano could still hear the new voice begging to be destroyed from the com-link on his command chair. The man was asking for certain death, willing to sacrifice himself for the thousands of other lives at stake.

Moreyev must have been monitoring the distances involved in their mad scramble away from the cruiser, too, because just as Tano's WeaponsTech fired their rear guns, a faint glow could be seen emanating from the weapons aboard Canis Lupus as well.

Tano slammed down on the SEND button of the com-link on his command chair, the one still spewing out the order to fire coming from the man on board the cruiser. The voice of a man about to meet his creator.

"I salute you, Guarder!" He called into the com-link just as the cruiser disappeared in a small flash of white.

"Fucking Guarders," Hamilton swore from somewhere off to Tano's left. "I just can't believe this..."

"That man is a hero," Tano mumbled and then ordered, "Viewscreen dark!"

A blaze of white just made it into the bridge before the OpsTech complied with the order for darkness. In that one split second, Tano knew that the nukes had detonated. "Everyone hold on, this is going to get a little bumpy!" he said and braced for impact. Although he knew his ship was just barely out of danger, he had never been this close to five nuclear missile detonations in a ship as large as Greywolf. He could only hope that they would make it through.

As the ship began rocking and trembling with the shockwaves of the detonation, Captain Gary Tano noticed that the com-link on his command chair had fallen eerily silent.

~*~

Thunder closed his eyes as the blast of white-hot brilliance washed over the shuttle from the rear. Even from behind, the glaring brightness of five nuclear missiles detonating simultaneously filled the small cockpit with painful light.

Shockwaves cascaded past the small vessel, which bucked and strained against the violence of the exterior forces now battering its hull.

Finally the light ceased and the flight returned to a smooth glide through space. Sensors all over the control panels were blinking red, indicating damage of one sort or another throughout the shuttle. Able leaned toward Bobby Thunder and tried to loosen his white-knuckled grip on the ship's controls. As quietly as possible, he said to his friend and teammate, "It's over, Bobby."

Thunder took in a deep breath and opened his eyes again. He glanced at Able and nodded his understanding. "Take over for awhile."

"Sure," Able said and grabbed the copilot's controls in front of him.

Thunder rose from the pilot's chair and walked through the small crowd of Guarders and soldiers crammed into the cargo hold until he reached the unmoving form of Frank Buzzer.

"How are you, buddy?" Thunder asked his friend, not really expecting a reply. "He's not doing so well, Bobby," Razor said. "He needs a medic and quick."

Thunder looked up at the young Guarder and said, "You really proved yourself here, Razor.

You performed extremely well. I'll include that in my report to the Sarge...I mean, to the Judiciary Board." Thunder realized his error but not fast enough to stop the words.

"So, what now?" Razor asked, and Thunder looked back down towardBuzzer.

"Now," he said, dragging a filthy sleeve across his eyes to wipe away at the wetness forming there, "we plot a course for one of those ships out there and hope that this man survives. We've already lost two of our own on this mission. There's no way we're losing three..."

EPILOGUE

Frank Buzzer stood somewhat painfully over the empty coffin that would represent Sergeant Harrison Jekel's final resting place once buried in the Guarder Graveyard, here on Aegis. The room was crowded with thousands of people. Dignitaries, politicians. And there were Guarders as well. He couldn't remember the last time he had seen so many Guarders present in one place at the same time.

He sensed that he was now the center of attention at the front of the enormous room. All eyes in the Grand Hall were on his back. As the soon-to-be appointed leader of the Guarder Squadron, it was his privilege to be the last mourner to pay his respects to his former commanding officer. A man who had been his mentor for so very many years of his life.

"Well, what can I say, Harrison," Buzzer spoke to the cold, hard surface of the closed and empty coffin. He instantly realized just how completely quiet the entire room had become. With hands clasped behind his back, he looked up to the ceiling of Grand Hall and tried to will his teary eyes dry. "You always told me that I'd take over for you someday, Sarge," he whispered. "But I always thought that it wouldn't happen until you were ready to retire." Buzzer took several moments then to inspect the cold steel plaque, bearing Harrison Jekel's name and rank, attached to the top of the coffin. A flag showing the Guarder Falcon Symbol was folded neatly atop the front end of the casket, waiting to be draped across the smooth brown wood when it came time to be put into the ground.

"When I first learned that you were on the way to Shining, I couldn't help but wonder if you weren't making a mistake," Buzzer continued. "If you weren't rushing headlong into something that might be bigger than all of us. As it turns out, you were the one person who needed to be out there, Harrison. You were the only one out of all of us who was able to finally finish it, who was ultimately responsible for bringing the remainder of the Wolfpack Squadron back home safely."

Buzzer hesitated then and noticed Robert Thunder standing a few meters behind him. Thunder had taken over on Shining when Buzzer's body had succumbed to the deep and infected wound in his ribs, a wound that would still take some time to fully heal. Thunder had saved the lives of his team and the soldiers with him on the shuttle instead of rushing to Jekel's aid, an act that would have gotten them all killed. He had done the right thing out there in the Sarkennon System but, Buzzer knew, Thunder would have to live with himself for turning away from Jekel for the rest of his life. Jekel would have ordered him away if he had tried to get closer but, nonetheless, it was a scar that would remain with Thunder for a long time to come. Buzzer knew that he bore some of that responsibility as well. After all, he had actually started the events in motion that resulted in the invasion of Shining by the pirate band. He more than anyone else bore the ultimate responsibility for the death of the Squadron Commander. It was another wound that would take some time to heal. For both him and Thunder. A long time indeed.

He nodded to his friend and fellow Guarder once and turned back to the coffin. "Anyway, Harrison, it's probably better this way," he began. "Retirement wouldn't have suited you well at all. You wouldn't have been able to sit still for two minutes let alone the rest of your life..."

Buzzer paused again and tried to deal with his grief. "If only we had something to put in the damn ground besides this empty box, Sarge. We all miss you already."

Glancing over at Judiciary Board Chairman Mozart Livingston, his new boss, Buzzer realized for the first time the political arena he would soon enter. "I swear to you, Sergeant Jekel, I won't let the Squadron down. I won't let you down..."

He tapped the lid of the coffin twice with his right hand, nodded to Chairman Livingston who nodded solemnly in return, and walked off the small platform where Jekel's coffin was perched. He caught John Brady's eye and gave him a slight nod of acknowledgment as he walked past the young Guarder. Jack Redwolf was also there, in the next row over, but wasn't looking in his direction as Buzzer headed for the exit. The bodies of both Cougar and Avril Garcia had been retrieved during the clean-up phase of the mission and rushed back to Aegis and the Guarder HQ. Garcia had been allowed a Guarder funeral and burial for the active role he had played with the Guarder team during the battle with the pirates. The funerals for both men had taken place the day before Jekel's.

Buzzer walked alone with his thoughts for several seconds before Bobby Thunder caught up to him as he approached a rear exit in Grand Hall. The two men walked silently beside each other until they had left the building and were out in the sun and fresh air of Aegis.

"Where are you going, Frank?" Thunder asked.

Buzzer loosened the tight collar of the U.E.N. Guarder Squadron formal uniform he was wearing and squinted off into the sun. "I don't know yet, Bobby...anywhere but here, at least for awhile. First Garcia, then Cougar, and Jekel. So many funerals...I just need to get away."

"I know how you feel, Frank," Thunder said and extended his right hand. Buzzer returned the handshake and the two friends embraced briefly to console each other's grief. "Wherever you go, Frank, just go knowing that when you come back, we'll all be waiting for you."

Buzzer smiled at that and said, "Thanks, Bobby."

Thunder watched his new boss as he walked off toward Shepherd Lake just beyond the

U.E.N. Governmental Complex, on his way to anywhere but here, and smiled in return. "You're welcome," he said and then paused before adding, "Sarge."

~THE END~

Table of Contents

About the Author of THE GUARDER FACTOR

Shawn P. Madison, creator of the Guarder/U.E.N. Universe, currently lives in the beautiful Garden State of New Jersey with his wife and a veritable cornucopia of kids. Although he has written in many different genres, he tends to write mostly science fiction and horror. He has published more than eighty short stories in thirty different magazines and anthologies, both electronic and print, so far this century. Other than his Guarder novels, his collection of short Horror Fiction, THE ROAD TO DARKNESS, was released by Double Dragon Publishing (www.double-dragon-ebooks.com) in April of 2003 and his novella, THE EMPIRE OF THE IRON CROSS, was released by Cyberwit Publishing (www.cyberwit.net) in March of 2019. You can reach Shawn via e-mail at: asm89@aol.com

www.ingramcontent.com/pod-product-compliance
Lightning Source LLC
Chambersburg PA
CBHW082010170626
46817CB00009B/3045